COME AWAY, DEATH

Gladys Maude Winifred Mitchell – or 'The Great Gladys' as Philip Larkin described her – was born in 1901, in Cowley in Oxfordshire. She graduated in history from University College London and in 1921 began her long career as a teacher. She studied the works of Sigmund Freud and attributed her interest in witchcraft to the influence of her friend, the detective novelist Helen Simpson.

Her first novel, *Speedy Death*, was published in 1929 and introduced readers to Beatrice Adela Lestrange Bradley, the heroine of a further sixty-six crime novels. She wrote at least one novel a year throughout her career and was an early member of the Detection Club along with G. K. Chesterton, Agatha Christie and Dorothy Sayers. In 1961 she retired from teaching and, from her home in Dorset, continued to write, receiving the Crime Writers' Association Silver Dagger Award in 1976. Gladys Mitchell died in 1983.

ALSO BY GLADYS MITCHELL

Speedy Death
The Mystery of a Butcher's Shop
The Longer Bodies
The Saltmarsh Murders
Death at the Opera
The Devil at Saxon Wall
Dead Men's Morris
St Peter's Finger
Printer's Error
Brazen Tongue
Hangman's Curfew
When Last I Died
Laurels Are Poison
The Worsted Viper
Sunset Over Soho
My Father Sleeps
The Rising of the Moon
Here Comes a Chopper
Death and the Maiden
The Dancing Druids
Tom Brown's Body
Groaning Spinney
The Devil's Elbow
The Echoing Strangers
Merlin's Furlong
Watson's Choice
Faintley Speaking
Twelve Horses and the Hangman's Noose
The Twenty-Third Man
Spotted Hemlock
The Man Who Grew Tomatoes
Say It With Flowers
The Nodding Canaries
My Bones Will Keep
Adders on the Heath
Death of the Delft Blue
Pageant of Murder
The Croaking Raven
Skeleton Island
Three Quick and Five Dead
Dance to Your Daddy
Gory Dew
Lament for Leto
A Hearse on May-Day
The Murder of Busy Lizzie
Winking at the Brim
A Javelin for Jonah
Convent on Styx
Late, Late in the Evening
Noonday and Night
Fault in the Structure
Wraiths and Changelings
Mingled with Venom
The Mudflats of the Dead
Nest of Vipers
Uncoffin'd Clay
The Whispering Knights
Lovers, Make Moan
The Death-Cap Dancers
The Death of a Burrowing Mole
Here Lies Gloria Mundy
Cold, Lone and Still
The Greenstone Griffins
The Crozier Pharaohs
No Winding-Sheet

GLADYS MITCHELL

Come Away, Death

VINTAGE BOOKS
London

Published by Vintage 2011

2 4 6 8 10 9 7 5 3 1

First published in Great Britain in 1937 by
Michael Joseph

Vintage
Random House, 20 Vauxhall Bridge Road,
London SW1V 2SA

www.vintage-books.co.uk

Addresses for companies within The Random House Group Limited can be found at: www.randomhouse.co.uk/offices.htm

The Random House Group Limited Reg. No. 954009

A CIP catalogue record for this book
is available from the British Library

ISBN 9780099563280

The Random House Group Limited supports The Forest Stewardship Council (FSC®), the leading international forest certification organisation. Our books carrying the FSC label are printed on FSC® certified paper. FSC is the only forest certification scheme endorsed by the leading environmental organisations, including Greenpeace. Our paper procurement policy can be found at www.randomhouse.co.uk/environment

Printed and bound by
CPI Group (UK) Ltd, Croydon, CR0 4YY

AUTHOR'S NOTE

All the chapter headings in this book are quotations from *The Frogs* of Aristophanes, translated by D. W. Lucas, M.A., and F. J. A. Cruso, M.A., 1936

'Just as when a man from its dark spring leads forth a stream of water along a channel amid his crops and garden, and, a mattock in his hand, clears all hindrances from its path; and, as it flows, it sweeps the pebbles before it, and, murmuring, swiftly on it slides, down a sloping place, and outstrips even him who leads it; so did the river-flood overtake Achilles, make what speed he could; for the gods are mightier than men.'

HOMER, *The Iliad.* BOOK 21

Translated by Peter Quennell

CHAPTER ONE

'Phoebus Apollo! Give me your hand, let's kiss and kiss, and in the name of Zeus, the patron of our knavery, tell me, what is all this hubbub of shouting and cursing within?'

I

SEATED in the launch, waiting to be conveyed from the side of s.s. *Medusa* to the shore, Mrs Bradley found herself chiefly aware of the smell of sewage, which seemed, like a siren-song, to emanate from everywhere, subtle as the colours of the bay, and yet all-pervading as the sea-mist through which the ship had sailed upon leaving England.

The launch, collecting flotsam about its bows, was almost as still as any of the buildings which could be seen on the edge of the bay. South of it was the island of Salamis; to the north the rock of the Acropolis stood up hard and square, framed against dark Lycabettos, with bare mountain slopes beyond it, and the ruins of pillared temples crowning its head.

A Cypriot of dark and pitted complexion who had been making persistent efforts to interest the passengers in sheets of used postage stamps, views of Athens, and small dolls dressed in the peasant costume of Greece, now leaned confidentially towards Mrs Bradley and pointed over the rail.

'Acropolis,' he said; then, with the air of a conjurer who produces the rabbit, he whipped out a sheet of stamps. Mrs Bradley grinned. The vendor, letting go the sheet of stamps, muttered anxiously in prayer and crossed himself. He then retrieved the stamps and gave them a vigorous shake before spreading them out in front of the next passenger.

Mrs Bradley, still inhaling, perforce, the smell of the bay, watched two sailors putting her luggage on to the launch.

She got up and gave them some money. Two little boys, who had been restlessly touring the launch, came up, stared at the baggage, and then went off to their people.

'Somebody else is staying off, as well,' said one.

'The bearings are getting red-hot,' declared the other. As though the captain of the launch had also observed this idiosyncrasy on the part of the bearings, the launch gave a sudden, defiant toot on her whistle which echoed round the harbour, and, with all the bustle and excitement lacking which, in a foreign port (Mrs Bradley had often noticed), it seemed impossible to persuade any vehicle, whether mechanically propelled or otherwise, to start on its way, the ship began to grow smaller, the houses on the shore more distinct, the smell of the sewage more intense, the air, if possible, hotter, and the Cypriot more cajoling, fluent, and inspired.

Greece approached them in the form of a long iron jetty. The launch drew up; was moored; the passengers climbed iron steps and then walked ashore. The smell of the sewage (even more difficult to ignore than were the persistent vendors of wooden serpents, photographs, dolls, and small white statuettes of Milo's Venus who thronged the quay and solicited every traveller), caused Mrs Bradley to walk briskly towards the cab-rank. Hired men followed with her luggage. The broad walk, yellow and sanded, stretched before her. Little boys bathed in the sewage-haunted water. Taxi-drivers leapt on her and her porters. She produced quantities of drachmas and disbursed them. The taxi-drivers grew frenzied. She pointed at one and observed :

'Sir Rudri Hopkinson's house.'

'Yes, yes,' said the taxi-driver. He wrenched open the door of his vehicle. Other taxi-drivers, deprived of the main source of revenue, fell upon the luggage. Amid pantings, scufflings, and rapid modern Greek, it was got on to the taxi. There was a slight jerk or two as the taxi reared and bucked over half a dozen pot-holes and a piece of paving-stone which appeared to have been left in the way by accident or because those responsible for it had grown suddenly weary of their responsibility, and soon Mrs Bradley found herself careering madly from Phaleron into Athens at the risk of her own life and the lives of some dozens of intrepid pedestrians who democratically refused to recognize any point of view but their own, and crossed the road almost under the bonnet of the car, most of them reading newspapers.

In an incredibly short time the taxi drew up outside the Hotel Grande Bretagne, the door was wrenched open again, the driver handed Mrs Bradley out, the commissionaire held open the hotel door, a page swiftly cleaned her shoes, and a desk-clerk advanced to meet her.

'I don't want the hotel; I want Sir Rudri Hopkinson's house,' said Mrs Bradley firmly. So they handed her into the taxi, two pieces of luggage which had been dumped on to the ground were put back, the driver was addressed by the commissionaire who had been addressed by the desk-clerk, and the taxi leapt to life once more. In less than five minutes Mrs Bradley was being greeted by her hostess.

'But Megan and Ivor went to meet the ship,' said Marie Hopkinson. She was a large, slightly untidy woman, friendly and pleasant. 'I can't think why they didn't bring you back in the car. I described you to them, and everything.'

Mrs Bradley removed a mauve motor veil with yellow spots and took off a small, dark crimson hat. Then she smoothed her black hair with a claw-like hand, and grinned.

'I expect your description erred on the side of tactfulness, dear child. How old is Ivor?'

'Twelve, and Megan is nineteen, and my poor dear Olwen twenty-four.'

'Then Gelert, I suppose, is twenty-seven.'

'Awful, isn't it?'

'But what a satisfactory family, dear Marie.'

'I don't know so much. Are you tired? Do you want to be shown your room? Not that you'll be in it long, poor dear. I do think,' she continued, without troubling to get her questions answered, 'that it really is rather a fortunate thing, Beatrice, that you *did* miss the rest of the party and come on ahead. You see, I'm terribly worried.'

'My dear Marie!'

'Yes, indeed I am. Olwen is going to have a baby – her first – you know she married the headmaster of that ridiculous school – and I feel I ought to be with her. It is due at the end of this month – absurd in all this heat.'

'There's no need to worry, even about a first baby, with Olwen, my dear. She's a splendid girl.'

'It isn't Olwen. She's in excellent form. I just feel I'd like to be there, that's all. It's Rudri.'

'Sunstroke?'

'Heavens, no! It's only in England that English people get sunstroke. They take precautions when they are abroad. But my poor Rudri! – Now, Beatrice, you're to pretend you know nothing of this when Rudri tells you. I wouldn't for the world have him think that I'd gone behind his back, but I do wish you'd agree to go with them. It would be such a weight off my mind. I hate to ask you, but if only you would go!'

'But where, dear child?'

'Where? Where *not* would be a simple thing to answer.

He's got one of his crack-brained ideas.' She went over to the door and closed it.

'Not like the one when he went to the British Museum and tried to raise the ghosts of the Egyptian kings with the intention of getting them to verify the information given in the Book of the Dead?' said Mrs Bradley, with interest and considerable relish. 'I often think it was short-sighted of the trustees that he couldn't get permission. I thought it a splendid notion, and really, for Rudri, almost practical.'

'Exactly like that one, only a great deal worse.'

'I am afraid you've been discouraging him, Marie. What do you mean by worse?'

'Virgins,' said Marie Hopkinson, in tragic tones.

'Virgins?' Mrs Bradley gazed with benign inquiry at her hostess. Marie Hopkinson nodded.

'You'll hear all about it soon enough. Of course, I had no idea when I invited you. I mean, I wouldn't have let you in for it for anything!'

'Tell me from the beginning. I am all ears and interest.'

'Well, it all began with the Eleusinian Mysteries You see, Eleusis is only thirteen miles from here, and the road follows the old Sacred Way. Rudri walked it as a kind of pilgrimage – of course we'd both been several times in the car – but I think the walk went to his head, and anyway, he came home very tired, and slept in his chair the whole evening, and in the very middle of the night he suddenly said, "I wonder what the Mysteries really were?" I made some snarling reply, because, after all, if *he* had slept all the evening, *I* hadn't, and the subject dropped for the time, but was revived and made energetic in the morning.'

'And what *were* the Mysteries?'

'Nobody really knows. But Rudri thinks – or *says* he

thinks – that if one could reproduce all the conditions, one would find out.'

'Doubtful, don't you think, dear child?'

'Quite mad. In fact, most unlikely! But you know what he is. So now nothing will satisfy him but to make this ridiculous tour. All the children are to go, and he's sent for Alexander Currie and *his* two children – and that Cathleen Currie – twenty, my dear – at school with Megan until two years ago – *far* too beautiful to be allowed to roam about Greece with a lot of young men – not to mention the Greeks, who, my dear, have to be *experienced* to be believed!'

'How curiously unnerving, dear child.'

'Most forward and immoral, and so *feline*, Beatrice.'

'Delicious,' said Mrs Bradley with a cackle. 'Are we now referring to Cathleen Currie or to the Greeks?'

'So I wish you'd go, because he's not going to stop at Eleusis if I know anything about him,' went on Marie Hopkinson, disregarding the pertinent query.

'I am to go to chaperone Cathleen and Megan. Is that it?' asked Mrs Bradley, after spending a moment's thought upon the ambiguity of her hostess' last sentence.

'Good gracious, no. They will have fathers and brothers for that. No. It's the boys who worry me most – after poor Rudri, of course.'

'The boys?'

'Ivor, Kenneth Currie, and a little fellow the Curries are bringing with them – you used to know his mother, Beatrice, surely? – Paterson their name is. She married again after that dreadful accident. You remember? A self-contained and rather clever girl.'

'I remember. I didn't know there was a child.'

'Oh yes. Posthumously born. Nobody imagined for an instant that he would live – a most intelligent little boy. Eleven years old last month. Freckled and rather solemn. Quite a dear. I think I hear Rudri. Now, Beatrice, please know *nothing*. He'll want to tell you all about it, and then you can offer to go – as though you are interested, you know.'

'But why are the boys to go with him?'

'I don't see very well how to leave them behind. Of course, they'll run completely wild, but I don't see how it can be helped. Of course – I don't mind for Ivor, but I feel responsible for Kenneth and little Stewart – you know how it is with other people's children. Anyhow, Rudri – oh, hush, now! Here he comes. Now, lead him up to it – oh well, he won't need that – he's more than full of the subject.'

Sir Rudri Hopkinson was a tall, fair, greying man with the eyes of a visionary, the hands and shoulders of a blacksmith, and a luxuriant Viking moustache. He greeted Mrs Bradley, and plunged immediately into what were evidently some of the details of the proposed expedition.

'I've got young Armstrong to come and take the photographs,' he announced to his wife, 'and Dmitri Mycalos is coming as well.'

'I don't like either of those young men,' said Marie Hopkinson, but the remark was waved aside by her husband, who continued, turning to Mrs Bradley:

'We are going first to Eleusis, Beatrice; from there to Epidaurus, to see what we can do with the Aesculapius cult – the god of healing – thence to Mycenae for the Homeric offerings, then back here again before we cross to Ephesus, unless it seems better to return to Nauplia and take a boat from there. At Ephesus, of course, we revive the Artemis worship.'

'I think it would be far better to take the train from here

to Corinth, and to approach Mycenae from the north,' said Marie Hopkinson. She went to the window and peered out between the slats of the blind. 'Those children seem to be taking their time for Phaleron.'

'Hanging about for Beatrice. Where's Gelert?' asked Sir Rudri.

'He is at the museum, I expect.'

'What, again? I shall be glad to have him come on this expedition. The fellow's gone mopy. Wants some fresh air and sunshine,' said his father.

Gelert came in as he said it. He was a tall young man, not much like either of his parents in appearance, for where Sir Rudri was somewhat leonine, and Marie was pleasantly large with dark hair and a wide friendly smile, Gelert was like a greyhound. His fair hair was long, but was brushed severely from his brow. He wore pince-nez, chiefly, Mrs Bradley decided, as an affectation, for, when his father had gone, he sat at the side of the room and read a book of which the print was small and close whilst the pince-nez dangled at the end of their moiré ribbon.

'And how do you like the thought of the excursion, dear child?' said Mrs Bradley, when he laid the book aside as his mother went out of the room and he was left for a minute or two to entertain the guest.

'Oh, I don't know. Are you coming, Aunt Beatrice?'

'I haven't been invited.'

'You will be. We've all been dragged in. The idea is ridiculous, but the actual walking should be good fun. Greece is easily the most uncomfortable of all the countries of Europe. No inns, many bugs, high mountains, no roads, a difficult language, uneatable food – I quite adore it.'

'So do I, dear child. I once walked from the Vale of Tempe to Sparta.'

'Did you? I say, that's rather nice! Do tell me about it. What do you think of Delphi? And how did you get on with the dogs?'

'I sat down, like Schliemann, and prayed to Olympian Zeus.'

'That's marvellous. Are you serious? But, yes,' added the young man, replacing his pince-nez, 'I can see you are.'

They talked on, Mrs Bradley noting that Gelert seemed tired and under nervous strain. Their conversation was interrupted by the entrance of Marie Hopkinson.

'Go and wash, dear, if you're going to. Lunch is in five minutes,' she said to her son. 'Beatrice — By the way, Gelert,' she added, 'you might just see whether – oh well, never mind! Here they are.'

The party which now invaded the house consisted of the two little boys Mrs Bradley had seen on the launch and one other, whom she recognized as her hostess' younger son. Following them came two girls and a bald-headed man of about fifty. There were introductions – although Mrs Bradley had already met the Curries, father, daughter, and son, and little Stewart Paterson, on the ship. Explanations, exclamations, interjections, and conversation followed. This was continued during lunch, and Sir Rudri's project was not mentioned.

After lunch Sir Rudri carried off Alexander Currie, Gelert went off with his sister and Cathleen Currie, the little boys – their hats placed firmly upon their heads by Marie Hopkinson – went out in the broiling sunshine to explore the city under Ivor's guidance, and the two women were left together.

'I'm worried about Gelert,' said his mother. 'He'll be in

love with Cathleen Currie before he's known her twenty-four hours. It is always the same. I quite dread his meeting any fresh girls. His heart has been broken six or seven times already in the twenty-one months we've been here. It's really too unnerving. I've had to tell him that I won't have any more of them in the house.'

'Girls?'

'No. Broken hearts. He's such a nuisance with them. Mopes and moons, and finds fault with his meals, and absolutely refuses to go *near* the museum, and quarrels with Greeks – very insular of him, I think. And the only way I can possibly run this house, Beatrice, so that Christians can occasionally come and stay in it, is to keep him and Rudri fully occupied, and out of one another's way. Of course, they can't bear the sight of each other! Too terribly Freudian and Oedipus. You'll understand all that. I don't know why Rudri wants Gelert to go with him; and I'm sure I can't understand why Gelert has consented to go. He's supposed to be so busy.'

'But if he is interested in archaeology, dear child —'

'Yes, but this isn't archaeology. It's just sheer idiocy. If they were going to do a bit of honest digging, I shouldn't worry so much. But it's all this classical philandering that I find so tiresome and upsetting. Oh, and Beatrice, you *will* be careful of Rudri and Alexander Currie, won't you? They always quarrel so bitterly. That's the worst of having been friends for forty years. And that boy Armstrong. I don't like him. He's half-Greek and looks like Apollo or someone. Perfectly tiresome. Besides, I caught him ill-treating the cat. I expect he'll interest you. I believe he's sadistic. I don't really think he has any morals at all. He has the most unpleasant table manners I think I ever saw.'

2

During the next few days Mrs Bradley had ample opportunity for becoming acquainted with the members of the expedition and of acquiring first-hand information from its promoter as to its object.

'The worship of the gods of Greece,' said Sir Rudri, vaguely, but with magnificence, waving his hand.

'Rubbish!' said Alexander Currie, his bald head sweating and shining in the heat, and his blue eyes bright and fierce.

'Horribly unscientific,' said Gelert.

'A fearful rag, though,' said Megan. She was in a way like her mother – large, but far more muscular and not nearly as pleasant and friendly. Cathleen Currie, aloof, secret, and beautiful, said nothing, and the little boys, Ivor, dark-haired and thin, Kenneth Currie, with his father's bright blue eyes and beefy redness of complexion, and Stewart Paterson, serious-faced, red-haired, and heavily freckled, kicked one another, joyously wordless, but full of intelligent plans for making the most of their time.

'Whipping-boys,' said Marie Hopkinson to Mrs Bradley, under cover of an argument about the sixth city of Troy which had now broken out among her husband, her son Gelert, and Alexander Currie. 'That's what he wants them for. That's what he told me at one o'clock this morning. Although *why*, I can't see. I don't believe in all this flogging. It just makes boys irresponsible. It covers such a multitude of sins that they end up by not caring *what* they do or how much annoyance it is!'

Mrs Bradley, with black eyes as bright as a bird's, absorbed this startling contribution to one of the questions of the day, and glanced from the whipping-boys to the virgins, and from them to her host, his friend, and his elder son. The argument had grown acrimonious except on the part of Gelert, who, pince-nez dangling, had merely assumed an expression of bored amusement which was driving his father frantic.

'But what do we *do* at Eleusis?' asked Cathleen Currie. Gelert suddenly hitched himself out of the sphere of the older men, looked at her with the air of brooding protection which his mother had been expecting since Cathleen came into the house, and, leaving his father and Alexander Currie in the middle of the sixth city, went over and sat beside her.

'Oh heavens,' said Marie Hopkinson, with great exasperation to Mrs Bradley. 'It's happened! I knew it would. He's fallen in love again.'

Gelert, who overheard her, shot at her a glance of mingled pleading and fury, but, ignoring this appeal to her finer feelings, she went on calmly:

'And then there's that poor boy Ronald Dick! Heaven knows why, but he's *madly* in love with Megan. I only found *that* out yesterday, but I must say, Beatrice, I think it so unsuitable that they should both be going. He's such a temperamental boy – most boys with spectacles are! – and dear Megan, although I say it, is entirely crude and heartless. And little Stewart Paterson' – Mrs Bradley looked across at him – 'I've realized, since he's been here, that he'll lead the others into mischief. He has twice the character of Ivor, and, of course, little Kenneth is like his father – entirely volatile and ridiculous.'

Mrs Bradley nodded and sighed. She would be sorry, she reflected, to give up the comfort of this modern Athenian house and her hostess' refreshing adjectives, for the dangers and discomforts of the tour.

'It will be pleasant to have the boys with us,' she remarked.

'I'm glad you think so,' said Ivor's mother, without irony, but pensively. 'And that Dmitri! I wouldn't trust him an inch. All Greeks are pick-pockets and extremely lustful. But he will be invaluable for the language. Rudri and Gelert make themselves understood very well here in Athens, where the people, on the whole, are courteous and intelligent, but I shall never forget the day at Tiryns, when Rudri addressed a girl who was harvesting tobacco. My dear, she positively fled, and that with the shrillest cries! You might have thought that Rudri was a Mormon elder – although I believe the reports about them have always been exaggerated. But what can one expect in a country like this? I don't wonder it has such a bad effect on Gelert. He's a very impressionable boy. Dear Dish is going with the expedition, by the way, just in case.'

In case of what, Mrs Bradley did not discover. Sir Rudri, escaped from the toils of the Trojan argument, which had gone heavily against him, spoke to the little boys, and at that moment Kenneth came over to her and said:

'I say, excuse me, but would you come with us to bathe? We've all got to bathe to-day. It's to do with the doings, you know.'

'Ah yes,' Mrs Bradley remarked, recalling Sir Rudri's instructions to mind. 'We are to go for purification to the sea.'

'You mustn't rot about in the water. It's like being christened, you know,' said Ivor, going to Kenneth and leaning affectionately on his neck. To Marie Hopkinson's relief, all three of the little boys had accepted the fact of Mrs Bradley's presence on the pilgrimage as a matter of course.

'She will be in my place,' she had informed her son Ivor, who had replied:

'O.K., big baby.'

As soon as the bathing party – more correctly, the lustration party – augmented by Cathleen, Megan, and Gelert, had gone, another acrimonious argument broke out between Alexander Currie and his host.

'The purification ought to take place at Eleusis, not here,' said Alexander.

'What gave you that ridiculous idea?' said Sir Rudri.

Marie Hopkinson sewed placidly, and then, as soon as she could get a word in, said:

'Whatever does it matter? Where would you all like tea? I don't really think it will be too hot in the portico.'

This well-meant red-herring did nothing to deflect the flood of argument, quotation, counter-quotation, instance, and (last magnificent effort by Alexander Currie, whose face was so red and bright blue eye so fierce that Marie switched the electric fan to a faster rotation to cool him) appeals to common sense. Even when the young people and Mrs Bradley had returned to the house, the discussion was still at its height, and scarcely died down before the protagonists had tea.

'Oh well, we can bathe again at Eleusis if the bathing's good there,' Megan observed, in the manner of her mother. Sir Rudri snorted; Alexander Currie ate sandwiches with savage intensity; the little boys swung their feet and stodged; Gelert held a *sotto voce* conversation with Cathleen; Megan and her mother talked with Mrs Bradley; the paint on the portico blistered in the sun.

'It is not the little boys who need to be managed and kept

in order,' Mrs Bradley said later, to her hostess. 'I think Rudri and Alexander ought to be searched for knives before the party sets out.'

'They used to write horrid letters to each other in learned journals,' Marie Hopkinson replied. 'But even that outlet is denied them here in Athens. I can't think *why* Rudri asked Alexander to come. They've annoyed each other since boyhood. I can't think why they're still friends.'

'You think they are friends?' said Mrs Bradley. 'You don't think that Sir Rudri has brought Alexander here to score off him in some way or another?'

'He may have done. I don't know. One comfort, the feud doesn't seem to have been taken on by Ivor and Kenneth Currie. Sometimes I think that Ivor makes friends too easily. He has no discrimination. Gelert has discrimination, but it leads him astray.'

3

A day or two later, very early, Sir Rudri marshalled the company in the shadow of the house and addressed them. The party was at full strength, and included, besides the families of Hopkinson and Currie, Mrs Bradley, little Stewart Paterson, and a couple of young men whom Mrs Bradley identified as Mr Dick and Mr Armstrong. Ronald Dick was short, intelligent, nervous, and spectacled. Armstrong was tall, arrogantly handsome, straight-nosed, and golden-haired; but, in spite of his god-like good looks, his face gave an impression of brutality. He carried a camera and took no notice of Dick, although he had nodded offhandedly to Gelert when they met. At the left side of the party stood Dish, the English manservant, an ex-sailor, and

Dmitri, the sleek-haired, half-smiling Greek interpreter.

Mrs Bradley surveyed her fellow-adventurers with interest and amusement. The young people – Ronald Dick excepted – were obviously looking upon the sacred quest as an informal holiday; Cathleen and Megan, in fact – leaning against the pillars of the portico – were exchanging low-voiced views on the care of the complexion in Greece. A change had come over Cathleen, Mrs Bradley had noticed. From the dreary, lethargic person whose beauty had been her only recommendation, she had become, by turns, lively, jumpy, shy, laughter-loving, solitary, sociable, and nervous. Mrs Bradley suspected at first that Gelert had been responsible for this mercurial behaviour, but it was soon obvious that this was not the case.

Of the three young men, only Dick, the archaeologist, small and pale, appeared to be listening to the leader of the expedition. Armstrong was fastening the strap of his smaller camera-case, and Gelert was seated cross-legged upon the ground on his shantung jacket, absorbed in a book. Dish stood to attention, for having been in the Navy, he was accustomed to unnecessary dissertations from his superiors. Dmitri, still smiling faintly – his habitual expression, it seemed – was rolling cigarettes which he placed with neat despatch in a tin box. Alexander Currie was nowhere to be seen.

'Yesterday,' concluded Sir Rudri, 'we prepared ourselves by fasting until the evening. The day before that, we went for purification to the sea. Now we go to Eleusis along the Sacred Way, to penetrate the meaning of the Mysteries. . . . We are only waiting for the wagon,' he added, with an incongruous lapse into the practical, and Mrs Bradley was startled to see, coming round the bend of the road, a quartette of magnificent oxen. The young men raised a cheer at their approach. The boys followed suit. The girls drew back. Dish stepped forward and saluted, for Sir Rudri, who had his back towards the road, had not seen the oxen coming.

'Sir, the draught animals,' said Dish.

Sir Rudri turned round.

'Ah, here we are,' he said. 'The wagon is at the Dipylon Gate then. Come. Women, pick up your caskets.'

Feeling not a little foolish, except for Mrs Bradley, who was enjoying herself, and Dick, who apparently took the expedition seriously, the little procession moved off, the oxen and Dish in the van, followed by Sir Rudri and the politely smiling Dmitri, the three boys next, the girls and Mrs Bradley close behind them, and the young men bringing up the rear. Marie Hopkinson waved from the house. The little street turned into a larger street. From this they came out into the Place de la Constitution and turned into Hermes Street. Down it they were accompanied by a policeman and two soldiers, and some of the Athenian citizens, who, being early astir, were sufficiently at leisure, apparently, in spite of the hour at which business commences in the city, to follow the procession to the Dipylon.

'I wish,' said Sir Rudri, turning and speaking over his shoulder to his son, 'that we could have prevailed upon some of them to undergo the purification rites and follow the wagon to Eleusis.'

Gelert snorted. Armstrong hitched his camera up; Dick put on his sun-glasses over his spectacles. Traffic rushed by and motor-horns hooted continuously. The boys, taking turns with a catapult belonging to Ivor, potted the policeman and the soldiers. Gelert, quickening, cuffed his younger brother's ear. Armstrong laughed. The soldiers looked round, and the policeman scowled. Mrs Bradley glanced about her with basilisk eyes which took in everything. She cared nothing for heat, flies, or dust, for she had the constitution of a lizard. Perceiving, however, that the catapult was going to be a nuisance, she twitched it from Ivor's hand and put it into her casket. From the north-west side of the Acropolis they came to the Street of Tombs. Here the party halted. The wagon, drawn up at the right-hand side of the street, and bearing a wattled crate of pomegranates and poppy seeds, was made fast to the oxen, and the Hera-eyed creatures were prodded forward by Sir Rudri, who elected to walk at their head.

'Women in the rear, bearing their caskets; men and boys grouped about the wagon,' he said, in tones of dignified leadership. 'To-morrow we bring the statue of Iacchus.'

'The next day, surely,' said Alexander Currie, who had been waiting beside the wagon at the Dipylon Gate.

'I meant the next day,' snapped Sir Rudri, the Viking moustache appearing to stiffen at the ends.

'That's well,' said Alexander Currie, soothingly. 'I should be sorry to have everything miscarry because of an error in the very beginning. Detail was never your strong point, my dear fellow.'

CHAPTER TWO

'I want you to tell me whose houses you stayed in that time when you went to fetch Cerberus. Tell me whose, and then tell me all the ports, the bakeries, the brothels, the resting-places, the cross-roads, the wells, the roads, the cities, and the apartments and landladies where there are fewest bed-bugs.'

I

THE walk was long and tiring. After the first few miles, along a dull and dusty road which led them westwards from the Dipylon gate with its slums, the party, becoming for the most part a little sullen because of the dust and flies, showed a tendency to straggle and loiter, and had to be whipped up by Sir Rudri, who seemed, like Mrs Bradley, impervious to dust and heat.

Three and a half miles out from Athens the road began its ascent of the pass over Mount Skaramanga, and it seemed a long, steep climb. The heat became more intense, and there was general grumbling, from the bitter invective of Alexander Currie to the 'Golly! It's hot' of the little boys, until at five miles out the road descended to Daphni and its convent.

Here they halted and rested, and inspected the eleventh-century mosaics on the walls of the little church. Here Armstrong took the opportunity to remark upon the character of the last inmates of the convent. He was silenced by Gelert, who displayed a sudden fierceness which his appearance would not have led one to suspect he could summon up to deal with such a situation. The girls were regretful, and encouraged Armstrong to continue, but, meeting Gelert's eye, the tall youth laughed somewhat awkwardly, got up, and strolled away.

A narrow descent to the sea was the next stage of the journey. The little boys, prevented from bathing, looked longingly at the water. The pass ended. The road followed the line of the bay, and great hills descended to the shore. The road was at sea-level, but, turning northward again at about the nine-mile mark, it crossed pasture land, the hills first receded from and then re-approached the sea, and about a mile farther on, olive-groves and vineyards took the place of the pasture. The party had reached the fertile plain of Eleusis with its artesian wells.

Lunch had been eaten on the sea-shore in the full glare of the sun, and the pilgrims, coming at last within sight of the cement and soap factories of Eleusis, were hot, weary, footsore, and very dirty.

'I'm dead,' said Megan. Cathleen also looked tired. Even the little boys sat down, and were silent for nearly ten minutes. The sun beat down on the Bay of Salamis and on the mountains of the island. The stones on which the travellers had seated themselves were hot.

Mrs Bradley looked benignly towards her charges, and then observed, as she stroked the patient oxen with a claw-like yellow hand, 'I trust that we are not proposing to sacrifice the draught animals to Demeter?'

'No, no,' said Sir Rudri, who had halted the wagon some distance from the ruins of the hall. We shall now go to the inn for food. There, too, the women had better sleep.'

'And the boys,' said Mrs Bradley firmly.

'And I,' said Alexander Currie, wiping off sweat with a handkerchief which soon turned khaki with the mingled dust and perspiration it was removing from his cheeks, his ears, and his neck.

'Then,' Sir Rudri continued, ignoring him, 'my son, myself, Dick, and Armstrong – oh, and I suppose Dmitri – will return to Athens by bus and return to-morrow night bearing torches. We shall represent the Mystae. The Statue of Iacchus we shall bring here on the day following. Then the heralds – the boys – I have coached them in their speeches – will bid the profane depart. Then —' His eyes seemed to grow larger. They were filled with mystic light. In spite of the long walk in the heat and dust, his energy and enthusiasm were unimpaired, and he stretched his arms dramatically towards the ruined Hall of the Mysteries. Mrs Bradley studied him with interest.

'And then?' she said, in her deep, mellifluous tones. Sir Rudri looked at her sharply, his eyes suspicious, the light in them suddenly gone.

'Then the experiment begins. If all goes well, we ought to be able to unravel the Mysteries, and learn the secrets that are believed to have died with the Initiates.'

'Rubbish,' said Alexander Currie, crudely. Mrs Bradley's opinion coincided with his, but she was careful not to give voice to it. She rested for a bit, and then went off with the two girls and the young boys to have a look at the inn which Sir Rudri had chosen.

'I think,' she said quietly to Megan when they had all inspected it, 'that, in spite of the kindly demeanour of the innkeeper and his wife, we should be better accommodated in Athens.'

'I know,' said Megan. 'I've already killed two bugs, and the two of us have to sleep in the same bed. What's your room like?'

'Embarrassingly over-populated, dear child.'

'Still,' said Megan, brightening, 'the whole thing's rather a rag, and I'm jolly glad father thought of it. He's had much worse ideas. Oh, Lord, though, how my feet ache! And I wish we could have a bath!'

'You don't think, dear child,' said Mrs Bradley, pressing the point a little anxiously, 'that we might sneak back by bus to Athens, and return here early in the morning?'

'Father would have a fit. It would upset the sequence of the doings. You know what he's like when he gets a bee in his bonnet! They've got to go back, so that they can come again with torches. Then there's Iacchus to bring, but our job is to stay put until we're told to depart.'

The little boys had found lizards, and were chivvying them with bits of dry stick.

'The beggars won't come out again,' complained Kenneth. 'Most unsporting animals.'

'So are you,' Mrs Bradley pointed out. 'It's the close season for lizards. Have you seen your bedrooms yet?'

'Oh, we haven't got bedrooms,' said Ivor. 'We've all got to sleep on the fodder.'

'On the what?'

'On the fodder. I don't know what it is; it's not hay – at least, I don't think so – but it's pretty nifty, and it looked to me that it crawled.'

'I should say we shall catch the plague,' observed Kenneth brightly. 'I say,' he said, turning on Ivor, 'if we catch the plague, my bloke will sue your bloke for compensation, and so will this man's bloke,' he added, indicating the innocent, green-eyed Stewart.

'Oh, rot. You can't be sued for compensation unless you've given the party of the other part a contract. I read it about film stars.'

'That's all right about film stars! But all the same, if *your* family gets *our* family some fearful pestilence or skin disease or something, you can claim compensation. I mean, we can. I read it in the papers about some woman who went to some hairdresser's and they brushed her hair with some brush that had somebody else's skin disease on it – so you jolly well can't get round that!'

'Yes, I can. I bet you anything you like —'

'Stewart,' said Mrs Bradley, turning from the debaters to their audience, 'take me and show me this fodder.'

'This way, then.' He stood by, silent and observant, whilst she mounted six wooden steps and peered into the sleeping-quarters which had been assigned to the boys.

'Impossible,' she said firmly to Sir Rudri, whom she found measuring the ruins and muttering.

'Eh? Why? Add thirty-one and allow seven,' he added to Dick, who was jotting down notes and digits. "Farther to the left a couple of feet,' he added to Armstrong, who was setting up his camera on a tripod. Mrs Bradley, gazing with a benign expression at the island of Salamis just across the water, said with great firmness:

'Because it is.' She then described to him – not mincing her words – the condition of the bedding at the inn. Sir Rudri was scornful and annoyed.

'Good heavens, Beatrice! Suppose a boy does get a flea-bite? Does it signify anything?'

'Only that he'll probably die of it,' said Mrs Bradley mildly, still gazing out across the water. She turned on the experimentalist decisively, like a suddenly swooping bird. 'I'm not asking your permission, my dear man! I'm telling you that those children *cannot* stay at that inn! We're going to catch the next bus back to Athens!'

'Oh well, if you are, you are,' said Sir Rudri, secretly relieved at having the decision made so uncompromisingly.

'You had better get something to eat first. We are going to have some goat and a cheese and some fruit when we've done this bit of measuring. I do wish,' he added peevishly, 'that we could manage to get a photograph without these wretched little sheds coming into it.'

'I could easily take them out, Sir Rudri,' said Armstrong.

'No, no! We can't have anything faked! I must have exactly what's there.'

'Let's wait until morning, then, sir. The light is a bit peculiar,' said Dick.

'Nonsense!' said Alexander Currie, lighting a cigar in the vain hope of keeping the flies from his bald head. 'Rudri, this whole place is a hotbed of mosquitoes.'

'That is as nature intends it,' Sir Rudri replied. 'Beatrice, oblige me by walking westward to that farthest pillar, holding the end of this measuring-tape. Alexander, go due north, please, with this one. The orientation of this place is of the first importance. Wait. Let me take the compass off its chain.'

The ruins, in the full light of the sun, had little glamour or attractiveness. Of the great Hall of the Mysteries below the ancient acropolis, only some of the stone seats, cut out of the solid rock, and the scattered bases of slender pillars, once the roof-supports, were still to be seen. A rough path led from the road among the ruins, and beyond them the Bay of Salamis glowed against the dark mountains of the island's northern coast.

'Queer place,' said Armstrong. 'Queer old bird, the old man, to come here, too,' he added.

Mrs Bradley said nothing. She did not like Armstrong, a fact which interested her.

'Still,' Armstrong continued, in no wise abashed by her silence, 'I suppose we can't grumble. He's paying me well.

That's all I care about. But photograph it! What is there here to photograph? That's what I'd like to know.'

Mrs Bradley could not enlighten him, and continued to say nothing. After a short pause Armstrong picked up his traps and followed Sir Rudri to the inn. Mrs Bradley did not feel the slightest desire for goat or cheese, and intended to dine in Athens, so she walked up the rough path to the Hall of the Mysteries, and then climbed the seats of stone for the view. Suddenly she caught sight of Kenneth and Stewart. They were making an obviously stealthy progress towards the sea. Divining their intention, which was to bathe, she shouted after them. Unwillingly they turned and waved to her.

'Come back!' cried Mrs Bradley. They were too tired, she thought, to bathe, and she did not know how safe the bathing would be.

'We're so dirty,' said Stewart.

'Absolutely filthy dirty,' said Kenneth.

'We're going back to Athens,' said Mrs Bradley. 'Please go and find the girls and tell them so.'

'And Ivor?'

'Yes, child. Where is Ivor, by the way?'

'The heat makes him sick. He was sick over there. He's gone to try and get a drink of water.'

'He ought not to drink the water here unless it's in a bottle,' Stewart remarked. 'I bet this water's all germs.'

'All water's all germs, you ass,' said Kenneth. 'Old Potty Percy showed us, last term, under a microscope.'

'I don't mean those kind of germs. I mean the other kind, you ass.'

'There are all kinds, man.'

'Oh, dry up, man.'

They were met on their return to the inn by Ivor, now obviously restored to his usual health.

'I was sick,' he said. 'I'm hungry now. I bet I catted up every single thing I had for lunch. I say, I do feel empty. I say, I bet—'

To save further revelations or reminiscences, Mrs Bradley gave him a couple of biscuits which she had in a small round tin in the capacious pocket of her skirt, and the party made its way towards the road.

2

After having made the return journey in the evening, they dined, as is usual in Athens, at ten o'clock, and the three boys went to bed. Mrs Bradley, who was not tired, went for a short walk to see the acropolis by moonlight. There were plenty of people about; the roadside cafés were full; a wireless loud-speaker broadcast an American crooner, and the Greeks talked politics with passion. At the end of about an hour she returned to the hotel. Megan had gone to bed.

'I suppose I might as well go, too,' said Cathleen, glancing indifferently round the lounge. Mrs Bradley was reading a Greek newspaper. Most of the English and American guests were playing bridge. What Greeks there were, again were talking politics, except for one, a slim, black-haired young man who came up, and after glancing uncertainly at Mrs Bradley in the most frank, disarming, courteous way, invited Cathleen to spend the night with him.

'I have the most beautiful type of love for you,' he said softly, with ingenuous earnestness. His lisping English was pretty. Cathleen smiled without looking at him, and, with a polite bow, and a regretful gesture, he went away. Mrs

Bradley gazed after him and gave a sudden, alarming cackle of amusement. Cathleen looked at her in some slight surprise, and then remarked :

'I think, if you don't mind, I'll go to bed.' At Megan's door she paused, reflected for a moment, and then knocked.

'I wonder how the others are getting on?' said Megan, bouncing up in bed and beckoning her in. She giggled. 'Poor father ! He gets so worked up about his ideas; and he'll hate this one before the trip is over.'

'Yes, I know,' said Cathleen. She spoke soberly, and sat on the end of the bed.

'You can't know. You don't know father. But he's just like a child – crazy about a thing one minute, and sick to death and finished with it the next. Still, he can't very well throw this up now that he has asked your father to come all the way over here to go with him, and all these other people.'

'I know,' said Cathleen again. She hesitated. Then she said : 'There's something I ought to tell you.'

Moonlight streamed through the window and on to the narrow bed. It lighted Megan's head, but Cathleen turned away from it and her beautiful face was in shadow.

'Go on,' said Megan. 'I suppose you mean Gelert's proposed. I'm sorry. But he will do it. Of course, it's a nuisance —'

'It isn't that,' said Cathleen, gazing into the darkest corner of the room. 'At least, I mean, he has, of course, but I shouldn't take any notice.' She paused again. 'On my mother's side we have the Gift,' she added.

'That's prophecy, isn't it?'

'No. Well, we don't think of it like that. It just means that we can see into the future sometimes. Sometimes we can foretell things.' She stopped again. 'We can foretell death,' she added.

The Welsh blood in Megan stirred uneasily. She looked at the coverlet instead of at Cathleen.

'Are you certain, Cathleen?'

'Yes.'

'Who?'

'I don't know that. If I did know, I would warn him not to go, although I don't know whether that is of any use. But it isn't strong enough in me; it isn't clear. I think perhaps that I don't know the person very well.'

'It isn't one of your own family, then?'

'It is not. Nor, I think, is it Stewart, whom we have known since he was a baby. It is not yourself, Megan. I would know, I think, if it were you.'

'Oh well, that's something!' Megan felt a surprising amount of relief, and immediately exclaimed: 'But, look here, Cathleen, I shouldn't think about it any more. Don't you think, perhaps, you're only tired – and in all this heat?'

'But I knew this morning, before we got to Daphni. And I never mind the heat. Do you think it's any good saying anything to your father?'

'Look here,' said Megan, inspired, 'tell Mrs Bradley. She's sensible. She'll know what you ought to do.'

'I will, then, to-morrow morning. Good night, Megan.' She got up off the bed and went to the door.

'Leave it open a minute,' said Megan suddenly. 'Good night. Sleep well.' She waited to hear Cathleen lock her door, and then got out of bed and locked her own. No longer sleepy, she went to the window to look at the clustered houses under the moon.

On the floor above, angelic in their nakedness (for Mrs

Bradley's forethought for their comfort had stopped short after providing them with respectable beds and had taken no account of their summer-weight pyjamas which were still – so far as they knew – neatly packed in the ox-wagon with the crates of pomegranates and poppy heads) Kenneth, Stewart, and the miraculously re-conditioned Ivor were congregated upon Kenneth's bed deep in nefarious plotting.

'The thing is,' said Ivor, 'that we really ought to have Megan.'

'One can't have *her* without letting Cath know,' said Kenneth, 'and Cath's an ass.'

'She looks it, rather,' said Ivor. 'But Megan could wangle the doings far better than we could, I bet you.'

'The Greeks,' said Stewart, who spoke seldom, 'were not like that about girls.'

'What about Clytemnestra, you ass?'

'She wasn't a girl. The Trojan War lasted ten years.'

'Well, what about the Amazons, anyway?'

'They weren't much. It was merely so that Theseus could conquer them.'

'What was?'

'Oh, shut up, man! Why dig up all that rot? The thing we have to decide is, do we have Megan or not? Personally, and knowing her, and allowing that women are mostly warts, I'm in favour.'

'She'd give it away.'

'Oh no, she wouldn't.'

'It's too risky, I say. We ought to do it ourselves, or not at all.'

'Yes, but can you *see* those Greeks letting us have it?'

'Yes, if we pay them.'

'Yes, but we haven't any money, you ass!'

'Then we'll have to borrow off Megan. And if we borrow we'll have to let her come in.'

'Perhaps she won't want to.'

'Well, it's Stewart's idea.'

'I think,' said Stewart placidly, 'we ought to ask Mrs Bradley.'

'For the money?'

'Well, no – but we could tell her our idea and she'd probably sub up, I should think.'

Mrs Bradley was awake and not in bed. As she looked up from her book an owl flew across the moon. Impressed by this signal sign of favour from the goddess of the city, she went to bed and almost immediately slept.

Next morning she rose at five and went for a walk. On the top of Lycabettos she met the three little boys.

'Good morning, Aunt Adela,' said Ivor. 'We thought it might be a good idea to get some fresh air before breakfast. It gives you an appetite to get some fresh air before breakfast.'

'So it does,' said Mrs Bradley, regarding him with benevolent interest. 'And how goes the deep-laid plot?'

'Plot?' said Ivor, trying his hardest to look puzzled.

'We'd better co-opt her,' said Kenneth.

'You have to co-opt them or kill them,' agreed Mrs Bradley. She turned to Stewart. 'Yours is the casting vote.' He nodded. 'We want to startle Sir Rudri into a fit,' he said concisely.

'A worthy aim,' replied Mrs Bradley, nodding slowly and continuously. 'And at what point in your deliberations —'

'It's a bit of a mess,' said Kenneth. Mrs Bradley sat down encouragingly. 'You see, Ivor wants to have Megan in it, and we don't, much. What do you think? It's the hire of the boat, you see.'

'Boat, child?'

'We thought we could sneak round the coast by boat, and land at Eleusis without anybody knowing, and more or less leap on the rest of them and startle father into a fit. Into ten fits,' he added, an innocent, ruminating expression upon his thin face.

'The chief trouble, if we don't let Megan in, and make her pay, is the hire of the boat,' he added, underlining the chief trouble in what he hoped was a sufficiently ingenuous way. There was an awkward but illuminating pause.

'Two pounds will buy my life and secure me from complicity, perhaps?' said Mrs Bradley.

'O.K.,' said Ivor, smiling.

'O.K.,' said Kenneth, dancing about.

'O.K.,' said Stewart, nodding.

'Are you proposing to disguise yourselves, or do you adventure in your own persons?' Mrs Bradley inquired, glancing at her watch.

'You know Iacchus? You know – that statue father had copied in wood so that it can be carried?'

'Aha!' said Mrs. Bradley, gazing at them in admiration.

'We thought we'd steal it and – and get it there by sea – Stewart says that's how they used to, you know, before old What's-it bucked them up into taking it along by road again —'

'It ought to be a jolly good rag,' said Ivor. 'Father *will* be sick when they come for it and it's gone.'

'A *jolly* good rag,' said Kenneth. 'Stewart thought of it. He mugs these things up. It comes in useful sometimes.'

'It will put Sir Rudri's back up,' said Stewart, thoughtfully. 'We don't want to queer our own pitch. That's the only thing. I didn't realize, when I suggested it, that he was quite so apt to lose his wool so easily.'

'You can't back out,' said Ivor. 'After all, he's *my* father. I shall be the worst off if he goes rabies.'

'I'm not backing out. He can't leave us behind, whatever we do, because there's nobody in Athens to leave us with. I merely said, it will put his back up, and it will.'

'We must chance that,' said Sir Rudri's heroic son.

'Here is the money,' said Mrs Bradley. 'But where is Iacchus, my dears?'

'We don't know, but we're going to pump Dish.'

'We thought we'd pump him now, before breakfast. They've all come back to the house, the others, ready to walk to Eleusis again to-day. It's the Torch Procession to-day.'

'Let's go,' said Kenneth. He led the way down the hill-side, skipping goat-like. Ivor followed him. Stewart walked sedately beside Mrs Bradley.

'Do *you* know where Iacchus is?' he asked.

'No, child.'

'You couldn't very well have told me, anyway, could you? You know, to do it properly, we ought to have our own Iacchus, and let Sir Rudri keep his.'

'Mr Armstrong could look like Iacchus if he chose.'

'He wouldn't do it, though. He's a clouter of heads. Very vicious. I'm quite as used to a ciné-camera as he is.' He brooded a moment, then added: 'Personally, I'm in favour of raiding the Athens museum for something authentic – a real statue – we could easily get one. They've got dozens. But the others won't entertain the idea.'

'I think it might lead to unforeseen complications, child.

Besides, a stone statue would be very heavy to carry. That is why Sir Rudri had his copied in wood.'

'Do you know what struck me this morning?' Stewart asked. 'We shall be a party of thirteen. Do you think that's altogether wise?'

'Thirteen?' Mrs Bradley made a calculation, envisaging, as she did so, the several members of the party. 'Hopkinsons, four; Curries, three; yourself, myself, Mr Armstrong, Mr Dick, Dmitri, and our good Dish. To be sure; thirteen.' She nodded. 'I'm not superstitious,' she added.

'Cathleen and Kenneth are. Ivor is, too, I think. I'm not. We're Maclarens, you know. We merely say: "The Boar's Rock", and annihilate people like the Buchanans of Leny.'

With mutual interest they then discussed the history of the Maclarens, the Macphersons, and the MacDonalds of Clan Ranald until they reached the hotel.

'We've got all day,' said Ivor, who, with Kenneth, was already seated at table when they arrived. 'To-day father and the other three go back to Eleusis with the torches and then, to-morrow, they're supposed to take Iacchus.'

'But if they can't find Iacchus – I mean – if we've pinched him – they merely won't go. We hadn't allowed for that,' said Stewart soberly.

At this point the girls joined them.

'There must be two statues – ours and his,' Stewart continued.

'Why?' asked Megan. 'Oh, Kenneth, haven't you caught the sun!'

The waiter came up.

'He's wearing an amulet,' said Kenneth, to change the subject.

'I *bet* you he's wearing an amulet,' said Ivor. Stewart turned to Mrs Bradley.

'I have a theory that when the Greek Church finally declines, these Greeks will go back to the worship of Dionysus,' he said. The waiter flicked imaginary crumbs off the cloth to draw attention to his presence, scratched himself irritably, and said, with some suddenness, directing the words at Mrs Bradley as though they were an ancient curse :

'The bacon and egg.'

'No, no,' replied Mrs Bradley. She gave her order painstakingly, in Greek, and, having listened perfunctorily, the waiter bowed and expostulated. He brought fried pig and over-fried eggs for the rest of the party, went away, and returned shortly with a newspaper which he spread temperamentally in front of Mrs Bradley, jabbing his finger upon one of its columns and speaking rapidly and with obvious feeling.

'Oh dear,' said Mrs Bradley regretfully, 'I seem to have been misunderstood.' She tried again. This time the waiter emitted an exclamation of satisfaction, snatched away the newspaper, and, after he had served her with bread, honey, and fruit, stood perusing it himself with every evidence of close and sustained interest.

'Two *what*?' asked Megan suddenly. The boys eyed one another.

'Canoes,' replied Kenneth, the rapid thinker. 'We're going to bathe and canoe.'

'I expect you two will want to show Aunt Adela the shops,' added Ivor, achieving what he believed to be a charming and sympathetic smile.

'Look here, what are you infants up to?' demanded his sister, immediately and justifiably suspicious of brotherly kindness. Three blank faces looked at her, stupid with bovine innocence. 'You can't start anything daft to-day! You'll wreck all father's plans if you aren't in your places to do that herald stuff.'

'Herald stuff? Oh, *gosh*!' said Kenneth bitterly. 'I'd forgotten all that rot! Oh, I say, dash it, Oh, look here, dash it!'

'But we don't have to be heralds until the sixth day,' said Ivor. 'There's no need to sweat over there until to-morrow. And, even then, we don't do that bit until dusk.'

'Please yourself, then. You know what father is. I'm sure he'll expect us to-day,' said Megan, giving it up.

Sir Rudri, in fact, came round to the hotel at half past nine to make certain that all of them were in readiness for the Ceremonies. But, to the concealed delight of the boys, he intimated, with a sour glance at Mrs Bradley, that he should not expect them at Eleusis until the morrow, since it was impossible, apparently, for them to sleep at the inn. He drew her aside, however, when the boys and the two girls had gone, and lowered his voice.

'Beatrice, I don't care for young Armstrong,' he said. 'He's going to be rather a nuisance, I'm afraid.'

'Stewart doesn't care for him, either,' said Mrs Bradley composedly.

'He's really a bit of a responsibility,' went on Sir Rudri. 'He got drunk last night, and had to return from Eleusis on a motor lorry. We couldn't possibly have him on a public omnibus. Gelert accompanied him. He didn't know how to behave, and Gelert very kindly assumed the responsibility. Dmitri and Dish we left at the inn. Of course, Armstrong seems very sorry for himself this morning, but I don't know, I'm sure. I've been rather sharp with him. If he weren't such a clever photographer I believe I'd try for somebody else, even at this eleventh hour. I suppose he won't attempt to misbehave with the girls?'

'Hardly. The girls are sensible,' Mrs Bradley replied. 'Stewart says he's a clouter of heads. That's not a desirable trait. I don't like heads to be clouted.'

'He'd better keep his hands to himself,' said Sir Rudri, scowling. 'I don't approve of young men clouting little boys. It is not the spirit. Not the spirit at all. Besides,' he added firmly, 'I can do any clouting that seems necessary. My children are not accustomed to be clouted. Nor Stewart. A delightful little chap. Really very intelligent. No, no. I won't have it. Something will have to be done. He must mend his ways.' Sir Rudri's Viking moustache, always the most obvious index to his emotions, began to lift at the end.

'Quite so,' said Mrs Bradley. 'How fares Iacchus?'

'The men who take the money for admission to the Acropolis have the statue in their charge. They have strict orders to deliver him up to no one but myself,' replied Sir Rudri. He smiled. 'I have been the victim of practical jokes before now.'

3

'The thing is,' said Kenneth,, 'that the idea was a wash-out from the first. Let's admit it, and give it up. We can have plenty of jolly good rags which aren't half the fag. Give Mrs Bradley her money back, and let's go and annoy that old chap at the gate of the Stadion. You know, the one dressed in national costume. You've only got to call him Kora!'

Mrs Bradley, informed, not of the pious object of the morning's outing, but that they were prepared to give up all thought of attempting to obtain possession of Iacchus, went off by herself to spend a couple of hours in the museum. The day was even hotter than the previous day had been, and she was glad to think that the long walk to Eleusis would not take place until the evening. This time there would be torches and mystic songs. . . . She stood before the Stele of Aristion, contemplating, not only the greaved and kilted warrior with his curled locks and long, straight feet, but the imaginary spectacle of Sir Rudri walking with torches in the dusk of the Greek evening, chanting strange hymns and sorrowful litanies to the Eleusinian gods Iacchus and Dionysus, and to the goddesses Persephone and Demeter, and to the god-king Triptolemus. She could see him, dogged idealist and romancer, proceeding ploddingly the while along the petrol-haunted, dusty Sacred Way which now led, in the age of progress, the world no longer young, from one Greek slum to another. Absently, still gazing at the tombstone, she quoted Aristophanes, and regretfully clicked her tongue.

CHAPTER THREE

'Iacchus, O Iacchus.'

I

THE boys did not appear at lunch. The waiter explained that at ten o'clock they had asked for food and had gone to bathe. Sir Rudri, Alexander Currie, and the nervous, spectacled Dick joined Mrs Bradley at the table. The two girls came late to the meal, but of the erring Armstrong and of Gelert Hopkinson there was still no sign.

'And what,' asked Alexander Currie, peering at the wine in his glass as though he suspected that his host might have poisoned it before it had been brought to table, 'do you expect to gain from all this Iacchus tomfoolery?'

'I don't know,' Sir Rudri replied. 'I wish you could be a little more open-minded, Alexander. It does not help matters when you are so determinedly and obstinately prejudiced.'

'I'm not prejudiced at all. I merely say what I think. If I think the whole thing is a lot of tomfoolery, I presume that nothing is lost by my saying so,' retorted Alexander, who had suffered greatly already from the heat, the dust, and the flies, and was beginning to regret that he had ever consented to come.

'You should keep an open mind,' Sir Rudri responded. He turned to his daughter.

'Where's Ivor?'

'Picnicking, father.'

'Are those other little scoundrels with him?'

'My son is not a scoundrel,' observed Alexander Currie, 'and neither is Stewart Paterson.'

'Where are Gelert and Mr Armstrong, father?' inquired

Megan, adroitly entering the lists between the combatants.

'Gelert is getting Armstrong into some sort of shape for tomorrow night, I presume. That young man has broken purification. I shall not attempt to let him take part in the Torchlight Procession to-night, and even to-morrow he had better not touch the Iacchus.'

'Tight as an owl,' said Alexander Currie, regarding his portion of ice-cream with exaggerated aversion, and pushing it to the side of his plate. As though it were hemlock, he raised and drained his glass. 'Can't think how he managed it on this stuff.' He wrestled with a slender flask of whisky which had stuck fast in a long, narrow pocket of his shantung jacket. It emerged at last and he filled his glass. 'Have some of this, Rudri,' he said. Sir Rudri waved it aside, then suddenly changed his mind. 'Yes, thank you, yes. Just half a glass, if I may. Thank you, plenty, plenty.'

The party were to be provided with sleeping-bags for the night, which they must inevitably spend at Eleusis.

Mrs Bradley had hired a car, and she, the three boys, the two girls, and the baggage were all packed into it.

The car caught up Sir Rudri's procession about seven miles out from Athens. The statue of Iacchus, Mrs Bradley was relieved to notice, appeared to be in its normal state – she had wondered whether the little boys' sense of fun would have led them into giving it a red nose or some other crudely humorous embellishment – for in spite of Sir Rudri's precautions, there had been just time for some such trick to be played when the statue had been surrendered by its guards – but all appeared to be well. Just after eight o'clock in the evening the car drew up at the ruins, and its occupants got out and waited for the little procession of walkers.

Mrs Bradley looked at her watch and then glanced towards the ruined Hall of the Mysteries. The evening was darkening in. The stepped seats of the roofless Hall were almost indistinguishable. The little path which ran between the bits of ruined masonry, the stumps of slender pillars, and the treacherous floorings of stone, led upwards and then disappeared towards the sea. A faint gleam of water betrayed the Bay of Salamis, and looming mountain-tops, black-purple against the sky, showed where the rocky island lay across the water.

'It's really rather eerie,' Megan said. 'Oh look! What a queer-shaped boat!'

It had no oars and one square sail, and it was coming up before the evening breeze, slowly and rather clumsily, nearer to the mainland than to the island, but even so, at some considerable distance from the watchers.

Sir Rudri and his little party were nowhere to be seen, for Mrs Bradley glanced round to find out whether they had arrived. The three little boys gave a sudden, almost synchronized, squealing shout, and began to run towards the sea. Cathleen clutched Mrs Bradley's arm, but it was Megan who said, in tones of excitement, and almost, Mrs Bradley thought, of relief:

'It's like the ship on the vase!'

Mrs Bradley, who had field-glasses, directed them towards the ship. The ship sailed on. It was, in some ways, not unlike the usual sailing ship to be seen in Mediterranean waters, but the square instead of the usual lateen sail, a curious, high balustrading along part of the deck, and the ship's deep waist and high three-ended prow, gave it a breath-takingly romantic, impressively archaic appearance which no modern ship unaided could achieve.

'Well,' said Ivor, coming back to Mrs Bradley when the

ship had sailed past the ruins and appeared to be rounding towards Megara. 'What do you think about that?'

'What do *you* think, child?'

'I don't know.' He glanced over his shoulder as though he had begun to feel nervous. 'It strikes me as being a bit queer. I mean, that's what *we'd* thought of, only not the camouflage, which really was absolutely right. Is somebody ragging, do you think?'

'What do *you* think, child?' Mrs Bradley asked, turning to Cathleen.

'I suppose we all saw the same thing?' was Cathleen's quiet reply. Ivor stared. Mrs Bradley cackled, a weird sound at which Cathleen jumped and a bird flew up with a startling whirr of wings from the back of a hut near the ruins. Megan, stumbling on the rough, uneven path, came running back to them. She had followed the boys towards the ship.

'I don't like it,' she said. 'You don't think father's doings have started up something supernatural, do you?'

'What?' asked Ivor.

'The men. They were dressed like Greeks.'

'Well, we're *in* Greece.'

'Yes, but you know what I mean.'

'Yes.' He hesitated. 'We saw them, too,' he blurted out. 'But I think it must be someone ragging.'

'So we did all see the same thing?' said Cathleen, as quietly as before.

'The whole idea is obviously intended for a joke. It has missed fire, though, because Sir Rudri wasn't here. They misjudged the speed of their craft, I should imagine,' said Mrs Bradley, who was interested to see the obvious alarm of Cathleen and the feigned discomfort of Megan, who was pretending an alarm she did not feel. Kenneth and Stewart just then came up, and the party walked back through the dusk to the gate which led from the road. It was now quite dark. Large stars came out, but that night there would be no round moon to shed its watery light on the quiet bay.

It was Ivor who described the ship to his father, when, footsore, tired, and, it was soon apparent, not on the best of terms with one another, the Iacchus party, sick of the walk and of carrying the heavy wooden statue (a little larger than life-size) of the god, finally arrived at the ruins. Sir Rudri, not at all the man to be sceptical or incredulous, was immediately and immensely excited about the ship.

"Who knows! Who knows! Oh, what a pity I wasn't here! Who knows what it may mean? We may have set things moving already! This is wonderful! Oh, why was I not here to see it?'

'Because you were helping to bring the statue of Iacchus by road,' remarked Mrs Bradley. 'If the ship was a sign, then other signs must follow. But if it was a joke, or a fishing boat, or something belonging to a carnival, a pageant of the Greek navy, then, my dear Rudri, you have nothing to grieve about. Nothing to grieve about either way," she added, driving the point home.

Sir Rudri accepted this opinion with a grunt. The scene was now a picturesque one. The torches of the Mystae, as Sir Rudri had begun to call his followers and himself, lighted the rather squalid yet not unimpressive landscape with a ruddy glow which deepened the colour on the faces and bare arms of the pilgrims to a dark tan, and made of their eye-sockets shadowy pools of blood. Shadows were flung on the bare ground – bizarre, unusual shadows, at the sight of which the imaginative Cathleen glanced round fearfully, as though to ascertain by what strange and fiendish agency they were occasioned. Even the little boys drew close to their elders, and Megan said, in a cheerful though rather high voice:

'I say! It does get rather convincing, doesn't it?'

Sir Rudri concurred in this view.

'I think we've done very well so far,' he said. Little showers of sparks from his torch kept blowing over the heads of those on his left, for the breeze which had carried the mystic ship on its wings had not died down. 'And now,' he added, 'all those who desire to celebrate the Mysteries with us, onward to the Hall.'

This was the cue for the little boys. First Ivor and then Kenneth lifted a treble voice, which quavered slightly – whether from nervousness or by reason of suppressed amusement it was difficult to determine – and, in what is now accepted in England as the language of ancient Greece, bade the profane depart. Armstrong, who had received previously his orders from Sir Rudri, walked off towards the road, where, on a level patch of ground inside the gates which gave admittance to the ruins, the sleeping-bags had been laid out for those who were to occupy them.

The statue of Iacchus, representing a young man garlanded and holding a torch in his hand (which hand had been closed by the wood-carver to the shape of a candle-socket), had been placed in position to face the worshippers as they occupied the galleried seats of the Hall. Sir Rudri, in the presence of his son, of Ronald Dick, and of Alexander Currie, solemnly lighted the torch held out by the god, and chanted a kind of litany as he did so.

Cathleen, Megan, and Mrs Bradley went off with the boys towards the sleeping-bags. The children, intrigued by the camp-like atmosphere, were soon in their bags, except for

Stewart, who waited until Mrs Bradley had placed her bag near the wall so that she could sit down on it and rest her back against the stones, and then came over quietly and seated himself beside her. Megan and Cathleen, thoroughly distrusting the sleeping apparatus, had placed their bags side by side, and lay not in but on them, their arms round one another for warmth and reassurance.

Stewart, hugging his knees, suddenly spoke:

'The wind's veered. Do you notice?'

'I hadn't noticed, child.'

'We should see that ship come back, if it weren't so beastly dark.'

'She may not come back, child.'

'I rather think she will.'

'I wonder why you say that?'

'Well, you know the rag we planned. Don't you think some ass may have overheard it and taken up the idea? Somebody older, with money.'

'What are you telling me, child?'

'Nothing, really. I just thought that the ship turning up like that seemed queer, after what we'd planned.'

'Tell me all,' said Mrs Bradley firmly.

'I don't know. But Cathleen's scared stiff of something. That's obvious, isn't it?'

'I know. And I know the reason.'

'Yes,' said Stewart, lowering his voice, 'I know what you mean, and it's going to wreck the whole holiday. She *is* a silly ass. When we were in Edinburgh there was a chap, but old Currie couldn't stick him.'

'I see. You're telling me that Cathleen's young man has followed her to Greece?'

'Came on the same ship. I spotted him at once. I spent

most of the time in the engine-room, and I saw him the third day out. I didn't let on, though. He's at the University, and his people have a bit of a farm. They came from Barra, but they don't live there any more. He works most vacs. to get his keep and a bit towards his fees – they're frightfully poor, but he's an awfully good chap, and he's got an uncle in Canada who's going to leave him some money.'

'Where are you leading me, Stewart?'

'Well, I think this chap follows us about, and I know that Cathleen met him once in Athens in that rather slummy market where the fruit is sold.'

'Does Megan know?'

'Sure to. Girls always tell each other everything.'

'I'm sure you're right. But I doubt whether Cathleen is alarmed because of the young man. I think there is something else.'

'You don't mean about us being thirteen, or anything?'

'It is difficult to say. Go to bed, child.' Stewart got up.

'Good night,' he said. But before he left Mrs Bradley, Megan came up and said:

'I say, there's something funny going on. Look! Can you see! Up high against the rock! That's got no business there! The beasts! They'll ruin father's experiment, messing about like that!'

Stewart gave Mrs Bradley his hand to help her up, so she got to her feet, and began to walk towards the Hall. The Mystae, obeying Sir Rudri's instructions, were wandering all over the ruins with their torches, and in the Hall the only light left burning was the torch in the hand of Iacchus. Keeping to the right throughout the secret scramble, and dodging the Mystae every time they came near, Stewart led Mrs Bradley up on to the ruins and along behind the seats which later on would be occupied by the Mystae. Above the Hall of the Mysteries had stood the acropolis of Eleusis in the days before the small city was dominated by Athens, and the natural rock stood unchanged, although the Temple of Demeter below it was almost gone.

'Look!' he whispered. But their progress had not gone unnoticed. Sir Rudri, behind them, said sharply:

'What on earth are you doing? You'll spoil my experiment, Beatrice.'

'I don't think so,' Mrs Bradley answered. She had seen what Megan had sent them to see. 'Look what the ship carried, Rudri.'

'What? Where?'

Against the dark background was a suspicion of dim whiteness. Mrs Bradley, who usually carried a small electric torch, brought it out and switched it on and held it in front of her, pointing at the whiteness with a claw-like yellow hand.

'I thought you placed the statue of Iacchus in the Hall of Mysteries,' she said. Sir Rudri, with an exclamation, held up the torch he carried. The white dim form on the acropolis, shut in on three sides because of a natural fissure of the rock in which it stood, was revealed as a second statue. It was dead-white, like wood that had been plastered, and was that of a young man, crowned and garlanded. In his hand was an unlighted torch. The torch of the other Iacchus burned, plainly to be seen, below them in the roofless Hall of the Mysteries.

Sir Rudri stretched out his arms, then kissed his hand to the god, and with his own torch lighted the torch in his hand. Then he leapt, at risk of his neck, down the rock-hewn steps, and cried to the others to come up.

The Mystae, consisting of Alexander Currie, Gelert, Dick, and Dmitri, tired of their aimless wanderings with the torches, swarmed up the seats towards him, pleased to have a diversion. At the sight of the second Iacchus, a buzz of excited conversation filled the air.

'At the gate, something's happened,' said Megan to Cathleen. 'You don't think they've spotted Ian, by any chance?'

'I say, something's broken loose,' said Kenneth to Ivor. 'I thought there was something up when Mrs Bradley and Stewart hopped it like that.'

Boys and maidens stood up and ran towards the ruins. Just after they arrived upon the scene to hear Sir Rudri frantically appealing for silence, there was a sudden gasping cry from Alexander Currie, and a tinkling sound on the stones. Mrs Bradley stooped quickly – she was standing next to him – and handed him back what had fallen from his hand.

'But what was he doing?' asked Stewart in a loud, excited whisper, of his neighbour Ivor.

'Sticking his penknife into the statue's bum,' Ivor accurately answered.

'There's something fishy going on,' said Kenneth in a slightly louder whisper.

'People shouldn't carve names on statues,' said Stewart in clear, severe tones.

'The whole thing's weird,' said Ronald Dick, who had his own reasons for suspecting a practical joke, but did not like to put his suspicion into words.

'Get along, get along, get along, all those who have no business here! You'll spoil the whole thing,' said Sir Rudri, at last making his voice effective. 'We shall all know more about it in the morning.'

Shepherded by Mrs Bradley, and accompanied by Megan and Cathleen, the little boys, still talking, returned to their base near the gate. When they had all been put into their sleeping-bags, and were happily engaged in spirited argument, Mrs Bradley went across to bid the girls good night. But Megan was there alone, and Cathleen was nowhere to be found, nor could Megan answer questions about her.

'She was scared when Mr Currie dropped his penknife,' Megan said. 'I shouldn't wonder if she's sneaked back to the Hall to stay with him.'

It seemed a possible but not a likely explanation. The Mystae they had left in front of the second statue of Iacchus in hot discussion and far-reaching argument. Even from where she stood beside Sir Rudri's daughter, Mrs Bradley could hear his excited tones, whilst Alexander Currie's machine-gun rattle of 'Rubbish! Rubbish!' could be plainly heard at every interval in Sir Rudri's long harangue.

'Nevertheless, Alexander, I defy you to deny that the more one thinks about it, the more odd it becomes,' Sir Rudri could be heard to say at last.

'Rubbish,' said Alexander Currie, his loud voice coming clearly down the slope from the ruins to the gate.

'I think it is some youth who is in love with one of the girls,' ventured the nervous, spectacled Dick, blurting out his thought with a sudden completeness which startled Mrs Bradley, fresh from hearing Stewart's revelations. Thinking of Stewart, she became aware again of all three of the little boys, who, with their heads protruding comically from their sleeping-bags in a way which reminded her of people who had fallen over in a sack-race, were still in excited conversation. She had switched on her torch again to flash it about for Cathleen.

'But it says so in *Wisden*,' said Ivor.

'I bet the Australians don't read *Wisden*, you ass.'

'I bet the Australians *can't* read.'

'Of course they can read! I bet you Bradman can read.'

'Well, reading's not cricket, is it?'

'Well, who said it was?'

'Well, you just said —'

'No, I didn't, you liar.'

'Don't be a liar, you ass.'

At this moment Cathleen walked into the circle of light cast on the ground by Mrs Bradley's torch. Without a word to any of them she walked to her sack – Mrs Bradley lighting her steps – lay down on it and suddenly began to cry.

'Cath!' said Megan. 'Stop that!' She lay on her own sack beside her. Mrs Bradley gazed at their humped forms benevolently, went across to her own place, sat down on her sack, and rested her back against the wall. Suddenly there loomed up before her the chunky body of Dish, on self-appointed sentry-go for the camp.

'All well, mam?'

'All well, Dish.'

The sentry marched away. The darkness closed down save where the torches of the Mystae, and the torches of the gods, still kept the night awake and consumed themselves, smoking and flaring.

2

Ivor had turned his sleeping-bag so that he was facing towards the Hall of the Mysteries. Long after everyone else was still, he wriggled and fidgeted, watching the glow of the torches held by the two statues of Iacchus and wondering whether anything was happening. He was an imaginative boy, and although in public he affected to despise his father's theories – taking his cue in this from his elder brother and his sister – in private he half-hoped, half-dreaded, that something would come of all the preparations.

The second statue of Iacchus had promised well, but the high spot had been, he considered, the curious behaviour of Alexander Currie, and the even more curious behaviour of Mrs Bradley. Why, he wondered, had she taken upon herself so instantly the responsibility of jerking the penknife from Mr Currie's hand to protect the statue from injury?

Now, as he lay sleepless and uncomfortable in his sack, with the dark night around him and the murmuring wind in the dark trees near at hand, and, not far distant to the southward, the ever-murmuring sea, he feared the second Iacchus, which in some mysterious way had got itself on to the acropolis of Eleusis. He felt that it had demanded, as it were, a share of the worship of the Mystae.

Then the obvious solution occurred to him; he perceived why Alexander Currie had wanted to test the statue with his penknife. The second Iacchus was no statue, but a man! Ivor stared, enthralled, at the sky, and then looked, resentfully, to where he could see his sleeping companions darkly huddled on the ground. Quietly he reared himself up and counted the sacks. As he did so one of them stirred. From it crawled Cathleen Currie. Without a sound she began to creep away on all fours, up towards the sacred Hall of the Mysteries.

Although intrigued, Ivor was still nervous. He longed to follow her, for he supposed that she was on her way to some vantage point from which she would be able to see the Mystae and know all that was going on – if anything *was* going on. From the silence it seemed unlikely that anything, so far, had happened, but then, he reminded himself, even the second Iacchus had come to Eleusis in silence. Suddenly an owl hooted.

He lay for a while and pondered. At last he could bear his curiosity no longer. He crawled out of his bag, put on his sandals, and began to move off in the direction which Cathleen had taken.

He could not see where he was going. The night was now pitch-dark, although the dawn was less than two hours off. From somewhere near at hand – from the cypresses which so oddly mixed themselves up with the factory chimneys of the town – again he could hear the hooting of an owl. The cry was answered. Ivor, thrilled, immediately recognized that no owl was calling, but that the cries were from human beings.

Just then he reached a vantage point from which he could look down upon the Mystae, who, still faintly lighted – this time by a small lantern placed before them in the ground, for the torch of Iacchus and their own torches were burnt down to the sockets and had had to be stamped out – were seated patiently or irritably (according to their natures and the degree of their enthusiasm for the business in hand) in a wide semi-circle opposite the first statue. With his hair pricking on his neck, Ivor waited and listened, but the human owls called no more, and nothing appeared to be happening in the Hall, so he crawled upwards and onwards towards the niche where the second statue had been discovered.

Believing what he now believed, he was not at all surprised to find it gone. Cautiously and bravely, he felt carefully all round the four-foot niche, but his hand encountered nothing but bare rock. On the ground his fingers came in contact with the stump of the burnt-out torch. Suddenly, from the seashore, he heard a faint cry of alarm.

Below him in the Hall, the Mystae suddenly broke into chanting, Sir Rudri's deep bass and Alexander Currie's baritone forming a not disagreeable background to Ronald Dick's beautiful tenor voice and clearly enunciated words – the dirge-like tones came upwards to the ears of the boy like the mystic smell of incense. This, too, was soon wafted towards him. Sir Rudri was playing his last card.

Ivor listened a moment, sniffed the air, and then, feeling suddenly protected by the proximity of the worshippers, crawled on, beyond the point where they were sitting, and made his stealthy way towards the sea. Suddenly he stumbled. A stone slid from beneath his sandalled foot. A startled voice – a man's voice – said, 'What's that?' A girl's voice stifled a gasped exclamation of fear. As though determined to surprise and startle them thoroughly, Ivor completely lost his footing, and half-sliding, half-rolling, he began to descend the slope.

At the noise he made the circle of the Mystae broke up as though at a signal, Sir Rudri crying, 'A manifestation! Be careful! Don't crowd! Don't crowd!' Alexander Currie more sceptically saying, 'Damn kids! Mistake to have brought them!'

As it happened both had justification for what they said. Having picked up Ivor and cursed him, they heard, still farther down the slope, the sound of scurrying feet.

'Who's there? Is that another of you young devils?' Alexander Currie bellowed. Suddenly up flared a torch, and by its light they could see a figure in white in the middle of the roofless Hall. 'Stand still,' said Sir Rudri to his party. 'Are we all here? Dick? Alexander, Gelert, Dmitri?'

All were there. Sir Rudri flung wide his arms. The running figure came to a halt. It seemed to be looking towards them. Then it lifted a bare arm, red in the torchlight, beckoning them to follow. Scrambling, sliding, risking their limbs and their necks, the Mystae descended towards him, but as soon as Gelert, the first of them, was within ten yards, the second Iacchus – there was no doubt in any of their minds that such the stranger was – doubled back on his tracks, and, leaping and prancing as he ran, so that he seemed to be treading the pagan measure of some erotic dance, he disappeared in the direction of the sea.

Ivor, who had kept as close as he could to his strangely athletic elders, stood still beside his brother. The night, without the guiding will o' the wisp of the flaring torch of Iacchus, seemed suddenly dreadfully dark. Ivor crept close to Gelert and felt for his brother's sleeve. He remembered, however, the original purpose of his journey.

'Gelert,' he said, 'Cathleen's somewhere about. Did you know?'

Gelert was immediately attentive.

'What's that? Cathleen? Where?'

'She crawled away from the base, and I meant to follow her. But I didn't catch up with her. She's somewhere about. I believe she was one of the owls.'

At this point Sir Rudri, whose momentary inaction had been for the purpose of deciding what next course to pursue, now ordered the Mystae back to their seats in the Hall.

'If further manifestations occur —' he began. Before he could complete his sentence they saw a dancing torch far out on the water. Iacchus, who had been brought from Athens by sea, appeared to be returning to the city.

3

Although they themselves were not aware of the cause, the stealthy departures of Cathleen and Ivor had wakened Kenneth and Stewart.

'I say,' said Kenneth, snuggling into his bag, 'it's rather beastly here.'

'It is, rather,' Stewart agreed. He shivered, and wriggled a little lower in his sack. 'I say, where's Ivor? Ivor!' he softly called. There was no response. He crept from his sack and went over to inspect Ivor's. 'I say!' he said. 'He's gone, and so has Cathleen. I say, do you think – I say, where have they gone?'

At this point Megan woke up and told them crossly to go to sleep again. This advice she herself immediately followed.

'We ought to tell someone!' said Stewart.

'Yes, but who, you ass? Anyway, I expect it's quite all right. It's sure to be, I should think.'

'Yes, but why has he moved?'

'Crawled up to see the fun,' said Kenneth, suddenly inspired. 'I say, I vote we go too! If there *is* anything to see, bags I to see it.'

'Yes, but what about the profane departing? We're not *supposed* to see the fun!'

'Well, we're not the profane, you ass! We're heralds, aren't we? If we've *been* there once, we can jolly well *go* there again. Anyway, I'm going to put my sandals on.'

'All right, then, man. So will I.'

They were soon creeping quietly up the path towards the Hall, unaware that Ivor was near them.

'You go first. You snake better than I do," said Kenneth.

'No, let's both. It's quite all right if we don't kick stones about or stumble. Don't get too near, that's all.'

'Come on, then.'

They crawled deviously up through the great Hall of the Mysteries and lay almost at the feet of Sir Rudri. But, although they lay there, motionless as Red Indians, nothing happened, and after about four minutes Kenneth touched Stewart's leg and they glided away. Even Ivor, waiting and listening above them, neither saw nor heard their progress. Thus, before any of the excitement had begun, the two boys had returned to the base. They found Mrs Bradley awake, and armed with her small electric torch. She switched it on them as they approached.

'What is happening, children?' she asked.

'Nothing in the Hall,' Stewart answered.

'Cathleen and Ivor have gone,' Kenneth blurted out.

Mrs Bradley betrayed some interest in these tidings.

She produced from her pocket – for she was fully dressed – the catapult which she had impounded before the party first left Athens for the celebration of the Mysteries, and put it into Stewart's hand.

'Have you any slugs?' she asked.

'Little round stones,' said Stewart, feeling in the pocket of his shorts. He checked the tally. 'Seven.'

'Ample,' said Mrs Bradley. 'If at any moment I say 'Now!' I want you to empty this weapon against the person upon whom I flash my torch.'

'O.K.,' said Stewart, pleased.

'You, Kenneth, are to be prepared to run in any direction I say. Are you familiar with the lie of the land here? Do you know east from west?'

Kenneth, a Scotsman, grunted scornfully.

'Come, then.' She led the way briskly and boldly towards the Hall of the Mysteries. She did not stop, however, but, keeping far out to the left and picking her way carefully between the scattered ruins, she walked still onwards towards the sea.

Beyond the steps whereon the Mystae sat, the path wound serpent-wise between some unoccupied huts and some ruined walls. The little boys followed her closely. Suddenly she flashed her torch. 'Now!' she said clearly and sharply. There was a glare of white as the ring of light from the small torch picked out a fluttering garment. With commendable speed and accuracy Stewart slugged the gleam with a round stone from his catapult. At almost the same instant there was a slight sound on the slope to their right, a stone came bouncing down, a man's voice said, 'What's that?' and a girl's voice stifled a gasped exclamation of fear; to conclude the display, somebody could be heard descending the slope in a manner which suggested that he had completely lost his footing. This person, of course, was Ivor.

As the circle of the Mystae broke up to investigate the noise and rescue Ivor, Mrs Bradley hissed at Kenneth, 'South!'

Kenneth ran on towards the sea. She herself ran eastward. The quarry, however, quickly doubled back, and tore along the middle of the now deserted Hall towards the gate which led to the road. This time they saw him clearly, for his torch flared up triumphantly, and revealed him, white-clad and be-wreathed, the god Iacchus. Above them slithered, stamped, and pounded the Mystae, like a brood of satyrs disturbed at a midnight tryst. Iacchus stood still and beckoned. Then he turned in his tracks and doubled southwards, passing Kenneth less than four yards away. Kenneth pluckily made for him, but the flaring torch was suddenly extinguished. The darkness was black and seemed thick. Kenneth was suddenly frightened at finding himself alone among the ruins. He heard the voice of Stewart :

'Kenneth ! Are you there ?'

'Yes,' replied Kenneth, bold again directly. 'I've lost him ! Where did he go ?'

'We don't know. Mrs Bradley says we'd better go back to the base.'

'But —'

'It's no good. There he goes !'

The great torch was alight again, it seemed. They saw it, far out on the water.

'He must have gone on to the ship again,' said Kenneth.

'Then he must have flown,' said Stewart.

Mrs Bradley saw the torch, too. She was walking southwards again, towards the sea, flashing her torch, and calling softly, 'Cathleen !' But nobody answered, although she searched the ground and entered the huts. It was Megan, following her, who said at last :

'I expect she's gone back to the gate by now, Aunt Adela.'

They returned to the base. Sir Rudri, Alexander Currie, Ivor, Gelert, and Dick came running along with the lantern.

'Roll-call !' said Sir Rudri. 'Now, are we all here ? Oh, Beatrice, was that you in the Hall just now ? Did you see or hear anything there ? What's happening ? What's been happening ?'

The little boys, Mrs Bradley, Megan, and the party of the Mystae were soon accounted for. Dish, having done his sentry duty, had gone to sleep at the inn. Gelert was sent to picket the inn until daylight, and then to make sure that Dish had not left the place during the night. Cathleen they found, as Megan had prophesied, in her sleeping-sack; Armstrong was virtuously in his, which he had carried some way up the slope in order, as he had already explained somewhat sulkily, to be near at hand in case they wanted any flashlight photographs taken during the night. He blinked at them all in the beam from Sir Rudri's lantern, and said he had heard a noise.

Sir Rudri could scarcely contain his excitement at having discovered a listener to whom he could pour out afresh all his theories and hopes.

'It was wonderful! Wonderful, my dear fellow,' he asserted. 'I should have liked a photograph above all things, but don't distress yourself. There really wasn't time.' He was no longer angry with Armstrong, Mrs Bradley observed.

'There was time all the while the second statue was standing up at the top of the steps,' said Kenneth. Alexander Currie patted his son on the head as Sir Rudri scowled.

'Profanity, Kenneth,' said Sir Rudri. 'It would have been profanity to have photographed the statue.' He turned to the reclining Armstrong. 'I am more than satisfied,' he said. 'After all, we were all witnesses. We can testify to what we saw.'

'Ship and all,' said Mrs Bradley heartily. She followed this promising remark with a deep chuckle which wiped the look of self-congratulation from Sir Rudri's face and made him frown instead.

'It isn't a laughing matter,' he said heavily. 'Not a laughing matter at all. Mystae, return with me to the Hall. There is one more ceremony.'

'Yes, one more. We have had the ritual marriage,' said Mrs Bradley under her breath. Sir Rudri was the only person who heard her.

'What do you say, my dear Beatrice? Surely not! You don't mean you saw? – One has always supposed, of course, that that was the culmination of the revelation to the Mystae —'

Mrs Bradley nodded solemnly.

'One has always understood so,' she observed, 'I, for one, shall now have no further doubts.'

Torn between the gentlemanly knowledge that he ought to respect her wishes if she did not want to carry the subject further, and an almost rabid desire to know exactly what she had seen, Sir Rudri said :

'You are fortunate. I wish I had had the happy experience. But there! You probably have psychic qualities.'

'I have never thought that,' said Mrs Bradley mildly.

Almost sadly, Sir Rudri, followed by the Mystae, returned to his own statue of Iacchus and poured the libation of water east and west. He prayed to the sky for rain, to the earth for increase. Mrs Bradley went back to Cathleen Currie, who was now sobbing exhaustedly, her head on Megan's breast.

4

'So it *was* that fellow? I saw him following us. He was in the little church at Daphni looking at the mosaics, the first day we came here from Athens,' said Ronald Dick next day.

'I wonder that Mr Currie did not recognize him,' Mrs Bradley suggested.

'Mr Currie did not go into the church. He sat in the bit of shade and took off his boots, you remember.'

Mrs Bradley did remember; she also remembered every one of Alexander's blasphemous comments on the state of his feet, and the way the khaki-coloured sweat had poured down his angry red face. She remembered all his comments on convents in general and on the one at Daphni in particular. She sighed and quickened her pace a little, mindful of Marie Hopkinson's injunction that she was to see that Sir Rudri and Alexander Çurrie did not quarrel. They were already in heated argument, although the day was young. She had no compunction in leaving Dick, for she knew he wanted to walk alongside Megan.

'But I see no point – no point at all,' Alexander was saying peevishly, 'in going from Athens by sea to Nauplia and approaching Mycenae from the south. The best way, by far, is to take the train from Athens to Corinth, and go south to Mycenae from there.'

'The only possible way to approach Mycenae,' said Mrs Bradley, 'is by way of Argos and Tiryns.'

'Not only that,' said Sir Rudri, who, all the morning, had been rendering himself an object of amusement or irritation to the party – according to their various temperaments – by a display of lightheartedness and kindly tolerance, the result of what he regarded as the peculiarly auspicious beginning to their researches. 'Not only that, my dear Ronald, and my dear Alexander; remember, we go to Epidaurus before we visit Mycenae. Therefore we go by sea to Nauplia.'

'You didn't make it clear that we were to go to Epidaurus first,' grumbled Alexander Currie.

The pilgrims were walking back, in the heat and dust, from Eleusis to Athens, except for the boys, who had been left in charge of Dish to return by the first bus they could board. Dmitri was retained – much against his own wishes – to lead and minister to the oxen. These, decked with garlands – as indeed, were the whole company – in honour of Demeter, Persephone, and Iacchus, were being brought back along the Sacred Way with, on Sir Rudri's part, rejoicing, and on the part of everyone else with a profound sense of thankfulness that most of the remainder of the pilgrimage was going to be made by car.

'My feet!' said Megan to Mrs Bradley, as they walked beside the empty ox-wain. Cathleen, pale and preoccupied, was walking beside the adoring Gelert, and little Dick trotted on the other side of Megan, and once he seized her hand, but she gave an exclamation of pain and dragged it away. Dick blushed, and stammered an apology.

'Don't apologize,' said Megan. 'I don't mind having it held if you want to, Ronald, my sweet. But I bruised it on a mutual friend of ours last night whilst all the jollity was in progress, and it's jolly tender this morning.' She nodded towards Armstrong, who was of the party, but was stalking along beside Dmitri. Both looked stern and aloof – Dmitri because he hated to walk and had made a date with his girl which he would be unable to keep, and Armstrong because he had a painful bruise on the right buttock and another on the left shin. The flies bit all of them except Sir Rudri and Mrs Bradley. Alexander Currie they particularly teased and exasperated, and their onslaughts gave his argument an even more peevish and ill-tempered tone than usual.

Nevertheless, he was glad to see the last of the bare cliffs of Salamis, of the cypress trees and the factory chimneys of Eleusis, and the ruined Hall of the Mysteries. When the argument dropped he did not attempt to revive it, but fell back unostentatiously until he was in step beside his daughter. He began to talk of family affairs, and Gelert, who detested such domestic conversation, and sensed that, in any case, Alexander did not want to include him in the talk, stepped up beside his father in Alexander's place, and they were soon engrossed in an argument – ill-informed on the one side, and contemptuous on the other, respecting the merits of sixth- and eleventh-century mosaics.

When Alexander Currie was sure that the young man had relieved them permanently of his company, his tone altered. He suddenly dropped the subject of letters from home, illnesses and marriages in the family, and such other trivialities of existence, and asked suddenly and fiercely:

'What were you doing last night?'

'Poking about,' replied Cathleen, her eyes on the road.

'Poking about, were you? And what was the result of your poking?'

'I found out that the second Iacchus was a joke.'

'Did you so?' said Alexander, his eyes gleaming as he looked at Sir Rudri's back. 'Tell me more about that.'

'I can't tell you much more, father. When I went up to see the statue it wasn't there. The lighted torch was stuck on the rock with – with clay or something, I think, to look as though the statue was still in place, but the statue itself was gone.'

'Are you sure of this?'

'Yes, father, of course I am.'

'And where was the statue?'

'I can't tell you that. I don't know.'

Alexander looked at her serious, beautiful profile.

'Will not, you mean? Do you take me for a fool?'

'Not always,' said Cathleen, her obvious truthfulness managing to rob the observation of offence. Alexander Currie snorted.

'That MacNeill has not followed you here?'

'I don't see how he could afford it, father. He's got all he can do to pay his fees at College.'

'You'll not see a penny of my money if you marry him, Cathleen, mind that!'

The tiring journey came to an end at last, and, later, Megan said, when both girls were doing their hair in Cathleen's room:

'It was MacNeill, then, at Eleusis, Cathleen?'

'Who else?' said Cathleen, reasonably. 'I told him he was a fool to have come all that way.'

'Was he Iacchus?'

'No, of course he wasn't. Megan, by Scots law, Ian and I are married.'

'Married!' Megan sat down on the bed, overcome by the tidings. She rallied, however, in characteristic fashion.

'Well, I do think you're a fool!'

'You're welcome to your opinion,' Cathleen replied, with spirit.

'But what did you do it for, silly?'

'I wanted to, and so I persuaded him. I didn't know he would come out here, though, the gawp!'

Megan began to giggle.

'I'd like to see your father's face when he knows!'

'He won't know. We shan't live together until Ian has finished his course and got a job.'

'If I were you, I should tell him and brave it out. And, Cath, why didn't you yell the place down last night? I'd have found you much quicker if you had.'

'I couldn't. Everybody would have known. He didn't mean anything, Megan.'

'He's a beast, that's what he is!'

'I lost Ian's call. The darkness is very deceptive.'

'But how —'

'I expect he followed me. Twice I went to meet Ian. He must have followed me each time.'

'But, Cathleen, that's awful! You'll have to tell my father. He'll soon put a stop to that.'

'I'll be with Ian after this. He's going to drive one of the cars. It will be all right after this.'

'Well, I bet I left my mark on him, anyway, the nasty beast!'

CHAPTER FOUR

'Xanthias!
What is it?
Didn't you notice?
What?
He was scared stiff of me.
Lord, yes, he was afraid you might be barmy.'

I

At Athens Mrs Bradley had a letter from Marie Hopkinson. After news about her daughter Olwen, Sir Rudri's wife went on to talk about him.

'I do hope,' the letter ran, 'that Rudri and Alexander are getting on together. I forgot to tell you about the Archaic Apollos. You know there are several – at least, I didn't, until this awful quarrel began – but there are the Strangford Apollo, and the marble Statue of a Youth and the Sunion Apollo (I think) – anyway, Alexander played a horrid trick on Rudri and got a sculptor he knows to make a new one and fake it to look old. Then he pretended that a friend of his had found it somewhere in Sicily. My poor Rudri fell for this beastly thing and wrote an article on it for *The Archaeologist* and then right at the last Alexander wrote to the editor and questioned the authenticity of the statue. Of course Rudri was laughed at for being taken in. It really was too bad. He thinks he'll never live down that article, it was so *very* scholarly, poor darling. He would do anything to get even with Alexander. It was all very malicious and upsetting. I still can't think why he asked Alexander to go on the expedition. He must think he's going to show off . . .'

Mrs Bradley read to the end of the letter, which concluded with vague, gossiping generalities, sighed, and, lighting a match, burned the letter in the hearth.

The whole of the next day was spent quietly by the whole party. Sir Rudri wrote up his diary and versed them all in the arrangements for visiting Epidaurus and Mycenae, but otherwise he rested, a disquieting sign, Mrs Bradley thought, in one of his temperament and character. Alexander Currie, brick-red and short-tempered, chartered the ship in which the pilgrims were to cross the sea to Nauplia. Whatever his shortcomings, he was not the man to be beaten over a bargain, and although Sir Rudri criticized adversely the terms upon which Alexander had obtained the use of the vessel, the price was remarkably low.

The ship was lying in Phaleron Bay and the company went out to her in rowing-boats. She was named the *Argos* and was a coasting vessel possessed of great breadth, shallow draught, noisy machinery, and a peculiar bucketing motion all her own which gave her decisive although unpopular individuality. She struck boldly across to Aegina and on to Hydra, the pilgrims crowding her stout and clumsy rail – repaired at Sir Rudri's expense before they set out from Phaleron – and so to Spezzia and up the gulf to little, friendly Nauplia, with its dusty harbour, its dirty litter of wind-blown paper, its pot-holes, cliff, surrounding mountains, and out-thrust, rocky neck below the walls of the Palamidi.

With shouts of delight from the sailors, who appeared to think that they should be warmly congratulated upon having brought the ship to the port specified by Sir Rudri, the anchorage was made, and landing was effected by means of little boats. The port of Argos was not, at first sight, impressive, except for the scowling citadel on the high cliff which the little boys immediately clamoured to be allowed to climb, but as it had taken the ship the best part of two days to make the journey, and the sun was already setting, Sir

Rudri announced that the party would remain in Nauplia for the night, and proceed to Epidaurus on the morrow. The whole party thereupon elected to climb the Palamidi. They mounted the steps opposite the Venetian lion, plump and apparently smiling, which was built into the wall, and were soon at the top amid the deserted, doorless cells which had once housed convicts. They toured the fortress, its courtyards loop-holed for muskets, its ramparts battered and broken.

From the top the landscape was spread beneath them in all its breadth and beauty of sea and mountain, cape and triangular plain. The older members of the party pointed out to one another how the plain of 'horse-rearing Argos' narrowed to enclose the pass to Corinth; the younger either exclaimed at the beauty of the view, or threw little stones down on to the lower citadel, scoring hits on the cactus plants which grew on the rocky walls.

'There,' said Mrs Bradley to the stone-throwers, indicating a small island to the south, 'is the island of Bourtsi. The Greek executioner lives there.'

The little boys gazed (with an interest which Mount Euboea with the Heraeum, the mound of Tiryns, or the snow-capped mountain which rose from the coast of the gulf had not awakened in them) at the home of the ex-convict who only saves his own life by depriving other criminals of theirs. They questioned her closely regarding the executioner's tasks and inclinations, mode of life, and chances of flight and escape; she replied with picturesque but mainly truthful detail, and the discussion was still going on when the party went back to the level ground and made their way to the inn.

Nauplia, almost unique among smaller Greek towns in

having a habitable inn, housed them respectably, and Mrs Bradley was on the point of putting down her book of modern poetry and getting into bed when there came a tap at the door. She put the book down, but, instead of getting into bed, she said, in her most dulcet tones, 'Come in.'

To Cathleen, who accepted the invitation, was presented the spectacle of a yellow-faced little old lady in a magenta dressing-gown – the little ship had been able to accommodate such tributes to civilization as dressing-gowns and bathing-costumes – who grinned amiably but fearsomely at her, and for whom she felt a sudden, trusting affection.

'It's only me,' she said. 'I wanted – could I speak to you? Are you tired?'

'Not in the least, child.'

'Well, look here, then, I think there's something I ought to tell you. At least, I want to tell somebody, and Megan thought you'd be the best person – know what to do —'

'Yes, child?'

'I don't like this business. Somebody is going to die before we get home.'

'Oh, you think that, do you?' said Mrs Bradley, interested. 'Who?'

'That's what Megan asked me – I don't know. It's a feeling I've got – my people – second sight. It's not very strong in me, but I've got it a bit. What can be done?'

'Why, nothing.'

'Don't you believe me?'

'Yes,' said Mrs Bradley, nodding slowly and rhythmically, 'yes, I believe you. Tell me, what were you doing at Eleusis?'

Cathleen flushed painfully. It did not seem as though she were going to speak. She managed to smile, however, and finally answered:

'Kissing Ian.'

Mrs Bradley, accepting this reply, mentally registered it as less than half the truth.

'Ah yes, of course,' she added.

'We're married,' Cathleen continued.

'Have you broadcast the fact?'

'Everybody knows now, except father and Sir Rudri, and, of course, the people who aren't in either family.'

'Gelert, then?'

'Yes. It's —' She lost her anxious expression, and suddenly chuckled. 'It's broken his heart.'

'His mother was afraid of that,' said Mrs Bradley. 'I'm glad you've made everything clear to him, all the same. And where is Ian now?'

'Still in Athens, poor man.'

'Man!' said Mrs Bradley.

'You haven't relieved my mind. Megan said you'd tell me what to do.'

'I have told you what to do, child.'

'Nothing?'

'I see nothing else to be done.'

But she sat thoughtfully for some time after the girl had left her. Next morning, however, in spite of the late hour at which she had gone to bed, she was up as early as the little boys, whom she watched bathing from the rocks. A little later the girls and the young men came down from the inn to join them, and by about nine o'clock, with the day already hot, the party was proceeding, in three cars, eastwards to Epidaurus.

Sir Rudri's plan at Epidaurus was simple. He proposed to make sacrifice to Aesculapius, bed out the party among the ruins, and see what happened. He had also explained, as soothingly as he could, that Aesculapius, god of healing, sometimes manifested himself to his worshippers in the form of a snake, and that, should snakes be discovered at Epidaurus, they must be used with reverence.

'Snakes!' said Alexander Currie, with nervous irascibility. 'Snakes! Beastly things. I've always hated them! Rudri, I shall sleep at the inn.'

'There isn't one,' Sir Rudri replied with triumph. 'There's nothing but the museum. You can sleep there, if you want to. The keeper allows it, I believe.'

'There won't be any snakes, father,' said Cathleen. She and Megan were sharing a car with Alexander Currie, Sir Rudri, and Kenneth. Quickness and craftiness had enabled Alexander Currie to obtain the seat beside the driver; the two girls had already established themselves in the back seat, and that left the tip-up seats for Sir Rudri and the boy. Dick, who was in the second car with Mrs Bradley, Gelert, Stewart, and Ivor, had offered to change places, but Sir Rudri refused to give up his uncomfortable seat, even to his daughter; in consequence, the constant jolting and jerking to which he was subjected as the car bucketed along a narrow, pot-holed road between poorish olive-yards and indifferent pasturage, through dust and always within sight of mountains, should have been making him more and more irritable as the journey proceeded. That this was not the case made Alexander Currie suspicious and watchful.

Fortunately the ride was not a long one. The car swung off to the right, bumped a bit more than before, and came to rest by some trees. The parties of people bundled out, and, walking up a slope to their right, began to look about them. The magnificent theatre with its fifty-five tiers of seats was in almost perfect preservation. The little boys immediately proposed a race to the top; Gelert sat half-way up and read Greek tragedy conscientiously for nearly twenty minutes. Even Sir Rudri, to whom the theatre was of no importance, commanded Megan, Cathleen, and Dick to ascend into the auditorium, whilst he himself stood in the circle at the bottom and declaimed in trumpet tones a Pindaric ode in order to test the truth of what he had heard about the acoustics of the theatre.

'Now you, Dick!' he called out, when he himself had finished.

Dick, sun-glasses covering his spectacles, turned nervously to Megan.

'I say, do you mind if I do? They say the acoustics here are remarkable – they're good in all Greek theatres, of course, but here —'

'Go right ahead, big boy,' said Megan, leaning back against the seats behind and stretching out her feet. Beyond the theatre were trees on gently undulating ground. Blocks of grey stone showed clean-cut against the brownish turf. The bright sky, broken by the branches, was blue and deep, and the sun shone on porous stone and gleamed on Dick's white hat as he walked down the shallow, broken steps to the stone-edged circle below.

'That poor boy,' said Cathleen, shading her eyes to look after him as his slight figure retreated. 'Why don't you put him out of pain?'

'One reason, he hasn't said anything that one could call definite; also, because I'm not sure what I'm going to say when he does get to the point.'

'Oh?' said Cathleen. The admission appeared to cause her some slight surprise, and the courtesy of her Highland ancestry asserted itself in consequence by making her appear confused. 'I thought – I'm sorry. I see.'

'Not sure that you do,' said Megan in cheerful tones. 'Not sure that I do myself. I suppose it's my motherly instinct that draws me towards him, poor little beast. He's brainy, though, you know. Even Gelert admits it.'

'Admits what?' said her brother, from a section nearly twenty yards away. 'Why the deuce can't you stop babbling in a place like this? Who do you think wants to overhear your idiotic remarks?'

'Listeners never hear any good of themselves,' said Megan, the schoolgirl retort being the only one which rose immediately to her tongue. 'Anyhow, you can put your old book down. Ronnie's going to mouth out, "Gunga Din".'

Dick had reached the bottom, and now, his figure foreshortened, but not extraordinarily so, by the height and the distance, was waiting whilst Sir Rudri, who seemed to think that he had done his duty by the theatre and for the entertainment of the two young ladies, ambled briskly towards the rough track by which they had reached the theatre. He crossed it, and was lost to sight. He had gone to inspect the Hieron of Aesculapius, which lay in the valley below.

Ronald Dick waited until he had gone; then, his feet apart, his hands slack at his sides, and his chin raised, he began to speak, from Book Twenty-two of the *Iliad*, of the death and shameful treatment of goodly Hector, and the lament and grief of Andromache.

'And about Hector, as they dragged him along, rose the dust, his dark locks streaming loose on either side; and soon in the dust lay that head once so fair, for Zeus had given him over to his enemies, to suffer shameful treatment in his own native land. . . .

'. . . and, standing still, she looked and saw him . . . ruthlessly were the swift horses dragging him away towards the hollow ship of the Achaeans.' [1]

Gelert, who had been listening closely, put his book into his pocket, and sighed. He got up and came towards the gangway.

'Fancy Ronnie being able to recite like that,' said Megan, as she and Cathleen went out to the same line of steps. Gelert snorted, a contemptuous sound, and made way for them to go down in front of him. His broken heart was now dissolving in a flood of healthy ill-temper.

'Poor Gelert has taken Ian very badly, Cathleen, you know,' said Megan, when they reached ground level and were strolling away towards a little group of pine trees in order to benefit, if only for a moment, from the shade. Mrs Bradley, who had been an appreciative listener to the efforts of both orators, now descended also, and joined them by the trees.

'I've some bottles of water in the car if anybody wants a drink,' she said, looking up at the top of the theatre for the little boys, whom she appeared to have taken under her guidance and care. They were not visible, however, having pushed through the fringe of dark bushes which topped the auditorium in order to explore beyond them. Supposing that they would descend when they were ready, and having faith in the uncanny ability of the young to preserve their lives and their limbs in the most dangerous surroundings (among which she did not particularly include the theatre at Epidaurus) she led the way back to the cars and produced for her thirsty satellites two bottles of mineral water and a tin mug.

1. Translation by Peter Quennell.

2

'And now,' said Sir Rudri, when, their thirst assuaged, the three young people (now made into four, having been joined by Dick, who had also been given to drink) joined him outside the museum, 'you would probably be well advised to go inside this place and make a careful study of all that is here. After that I may require some assistance with the serpents.'

'Serpents!' said Alexander Currie, who had also appeared, apparently from the dip in the land which they had just crossed. 'I shall go nowhere near them!'

'I was not asking for your assistance, my dear fellow,' replied Sir Rudri, soothingly. 'You are probably quite right to sleep in the museum, and I have already made arrangements with the good person who looks after it to give you a bed.'

Alexander snorted, a speech of thanks which Sir Rudri, who seemed inordinately pleased with himself, received with a sweet smile. His Viking moustache, Mrs Bradley noticed, already seemed less grey than it had done in Athens; a golden tinge appeared to illumine it in the bright clear light of the sun-filled upland valley, as though the god Apollo, come from Delphi, had laid his fingers on it.

'Serpents?' said Mrs Bradley, mildly, but in a tone of faint surprise and very faint reproach. 'Surely you are not persuaded that this is the Garden of Eden?'

'It is, at any rate, no place for facetiousness,' Sir Rudri answered, still good-naturedly. 'Let me persuade you that the serpent is the symbol of the god Aesculapius, the son of Apollo. With serpents he healed the sick and bestowed families upon the childless, and in the form of a serpent he would come upon his worshippers, infesting – I should perhaps rather say, insinuating himself into – their dreams, and thus he healed them.'

'Serpents?' said Cathleen. 'I think, father, I would prefer to spend the night here, in an unzoological building, as you are going to do.'

'I am not so sure about its being unzoological,' said Megan. 'Judging by other buildings in Greece we have stayed at, I should say that the serpents might be the lesser of two evils. Where are they, father?'

'Yes, where are they, father?' asked Gelert; whilst Dick, who did not care for them, and would have been sick if he had been obliged to lay his hand on one – legacy of a visit to Regent's Park when somebody, probably meaning well, had put one round his neck when he was seven – recoiled completely, and began to walk with brisk furtiveness in the direction of the theatre.

So Gelert and Megan went off with their father to the third car, which, having had the most room in it, had been chosen as the repository for the serpents. The reptiles were in a long tin box with air-holes. It had been placed across the two tip-up seats and, being weighted with dry sand to accustom the reptiles to the arid nature of the sphere in which their activities would be required, it had been strapped firmly into place and padlocked. Sir Rudri had the key and, so far as he was aware, there was no duplicate.

Gelert and Megan unfastened the straps, and then Sir Rudri and his son lifted the tin box from the car and placed it gently on the ground.

'Hi! Dish! Dmitri!" yelled Sir Rudri. The servants, English and Greek, came up to him. They had been standing, smoking cigarettes, a short distance from the cars, with the three drivers. 'Unload the food and water,' ordered Sir

Rudri. 'You men had better help.' Having watched them for a minute or two to make sure that they were going to work methodically to unload the stores, he decided that the work, supervised by Dish, was going to be carried out satisfactorily. He pointed out the museum to Dish, for the provisions were to be stored there, and then, assisted again by Gelert, he lifted the box of snakes and bore it tenderly towards the Hieron of Aesculapius. 'There! They won't hurt for a bit. They are quite accommodating creatures,' he observed, when the box had been placed in what had been one of the hostelries for visitors in the days when Epidaurus attracted its patients from all the country round and had housed them as near as possible to the sanctuary of the god of healing. 'Later on we can come and let them out for a bit. The man assured me they were absolutely harmless.'

'It's to be hoped that they are,' Gelert observed. 'I suppose the air-holes are not big enough for them to squeeze through? I have heard that it is remarkable what a genius for escape even quite large reptiles have.'

'It is some time since they were fed,' Sir Rudri admitted. 'I particularly told the man that I did not want lethargic, distended serpents. I shall give them some milk later on. But I don't think they can get out through the air-holes, which are extremely small as you see. Perhaps, though . . .' he added. He raised his voice. 'Hi! Ivor! Kenneth! Stewart!'

The little boys affected not to hear him. They had returned from their explorations, and, scratched, grubby, very hot, and rather hungry, had been given a drink from Mrs Bradley's store and were now in pursuit of occupation. They conferred speedily as they walked.

'Shall we go, or not?'

'Might be grub.'

'Not yet. It's not twelve o'clock.'

'Another drink? I could do with another drink.'

'He wouldn't think of it,' said Ivor, who knew his father well. 'No, it's some rotten sweat. I vote we pretend not to hear.'

'Is it true he's got some snakes, do you think?' said Kenneth.

'As Highlanders, we can't have anything to do with snakes,' said Stewart.

'Snakes?' said Ivor. 'Who said he'd got any snakes?'

'You little devils,' said Armstrong, coming upon them from the direction of the road. 'Don't you hear Sir Rudri calling you?'

The little boys glowered at him, but he had pointed so dramatically with his arm swung over their heads towards Sir Rudri, and had blocked their way so determinedly with his large and powerful body, that they deemed it best to give in.

'Silly swine,' said Kenneth, when they had turned about and Armstrong had gone on his way. 'What's he want to interfere for?'

'Father's got it in for him for getting all blotto for the Mysteries, you ass.'

'All right, you ass, I know that.'

'Well, use your gump, man.'

'Oh dry up, man. Skin the wasp's toe-nail.'

Sir Rudri said, 'Was that Armstrong? If so, I want him here with his camera.'

'I'll get him, sir,' said Stewart. He ran off, regardless of the pitiless sun which was now beating down upon the stony valley with all its midday fierceness, and, miraculously dodging boulders, broken ruins, and outcroppings of the slaty-looking rock, soon caught up with his enemy.

'I say, Sir Rudri wants you.'

Armstrong turned with a snarl.

'I say, honestly he does. You've to go over there with your camera.'

Armstrong cursed, turned sharply, and walked towards the cars to get his paraphernalia. Stewart, glad to think that the three of them were avenged, walked beside him, chatting helpfully about tripods, hypo, dark-rooms, time exposures, ciné-cameras, and the possibility of faking a photograph of murder.

'It's a thing I should like to see done,' he concluded earnestly.

'So should I – but not a fake!' said Armstrong sourly. For so young a man he was singularly disagreeable, Mrs Bradley thought. She was seated in the foremost of the cars, and could hear his blasphemies clearly as he pulled out from the third car the things that he was in search of. She wondered what effect his language had on the gravely watching Stewart, but decided that to call attention to this point would probably do more harm to Stewart than good.

'Isn't he a *beastly* boy?' said Cathleen, climbing in beside her. 'I say, this leather's hot.'

'I don't like him at all,' said Mrs Bradley, watching him walk away.

'He quite spoils the party,' said Cathleen, with an involuntary shiver. 'I can't bear him.' She hesitated, and then added: 'Ian's here. He came as one of the drivers. I've had a row with him.'

'I recognized him,' Mrs Bradley responded. 'He drove the third car, with the snakes. What does Sir Rudri propose to do with the snakes? I thought they represented the god in his most insinuating form. I did not know that there had to be *real* snakes.'

'I expect he knows. How glad I am that I'm not going to sleep in the camp.'

'Are you not going to sleep in the camp, child? But, no. Of course you are not. You will spend the early hours of the darkness in making up the quarrel with Ian.'

'I don't know. He's frightfully touchy, and I said – well, rather a lot about his being idiot enough to come with us here like this.'

Mrs Bradley put her head out of the window in a manner reminiscent of an old and cunning tortoise putting out its head from its shell. She looked about her, but, except for the chauffeurs, two of whom were playing some gambling game in the only patch of shade near at hand, the third standing watching them, his cap pulled over his eyes and his hands in his breeches pockets (for his dress combined a dirty tennis shirt with the lower portion of a dilapidated suit of plus-fours and a chauffeur's cap) there was nobody anywhere within hearing.

'Ian!' she said with sharp clearness. The watcher swung round sharply, glanced about him, and then came over to the car.

'Madame?'

'Come off it, Ian,' said Cathleen. Ian scowled at her.

'There's a village somewhere about,' said Mrs Bradley conspiratorially. 'Where are you leaving the cars?'

'We're to drive them just off the road.'

'The village (probably lousy, of course) is down there, at the end of that valley. I know there are two shops, at one of which, if not also at the other, sometimes one can purchase

Turkish delight. I read about it in a book.[1] Sneak off, my children, sneak off. Mr Currie has announced his intention of sleeping in the museum, so that he will not notice his daughter's absence from the camp. But don't be late back in the morning.'

'What about the other drivers?' asked Cathleen.

'Don't tell me we have a friend at court,' said Ian. He was a sun-burned, black-haired boy, long-armed, short-legged and very strongly built. He looked pugnacious, Mrs Bradley thought.

'Of course we have,' said his wife, in the matter-of-fact tones of her race. 'Shall we go?'

'There's an unnecessary question,' replied Ian. 'Those lads —' – he indicated his fellows – 'do not speak English. And if they are any trouble I will be hitting them with my fist.'

Mrs Bradley smoothly emerged from the car, leaving the two of them together, and walked briskly, in spite of the heat, which was now intense, towards the photographer's party.

'After all,' Sir Rudri was saying as she came up to him, 'I am not sure that it was the most scientific course to follow. I am not at all sure that we shouldn't have done better to allow the god to speak for himself, as it were.'

'My sentiments entirely,' said Gelert. 'I see no object in producing the reptiles so that the god can claim the credit of manifesting himself through them. It's surely up to him to provide his own serpents.'

'Your tone is unnecessarily flippant,' said his father, 'but your point, in essence, is the same as my own. You and Armstrong had better carry them back to the car.'

1. *From Olympus to the Styx*, by F. L. and Prudence Lucas. Cassell, 1934.

'I think,' said Mrs Bradley, looking towards the part of the ruins in which the box of snakes had been placed, 'that the poor creatures should at all events be exercised.'

'If we make up our minds not to use them, then, they must at any rate be fed,' Sir Rudri observed. 'Are you afraid of snakes, Beatrice?'

'I am almost the incarnation of one,' Mrs Bradley replied. 'I am almost always considered to be definitely reptilian in type; sometimes saurian as well – at least, I don't know whether I mean that, but I am always one or the other.'

She was wondering how to warn Ian and Cathleen that the snakes were going to be brought back and put in the car. By this time, she reflected, they would be in the full throes of their lovers' quarrel, or else at the commencement of making it up. Neither condition was the state in which a third party ought to find them. 'I must beg to be allowed to look upon my relations,' she said firmly.

Sir Rudri, who was still in two minds about the snakes – for they had been expensive, and might, he still thought, jog the memory of whatever strange force had once held power in the valley – welcomed the idea of showing them off to someone who would regard them with a reasonable amount of interest free from fear, disgust, or untutored excitement, and willingly led the way to the heavy box.

'It looks more like a coffin than anything,' said Armstrong, who appeared to have recovered the major portion of his temper. He picked up various bits of his photographic paraphernalia, and Megan and Gelert followed their father. Sir Rudri knelt down and fitted the key. Megan retreated a step or two. Mrs Bradley stood beside Sir Rudri, who, with faint chirruping noises suggestive of the sounds made by those who call chickens to be fed, lifted the lid. The audience, craning forward – most of them from the safe distance of a yard or two – were able to get a good view of what lay within the long box. Half a dozen short, thick, English vipers, with broad, flat heads and dark diamond-shaped markings, were disclosed to the shocked gaze of those of the company who knew one kind of snake from another. Sir Rudri shut the lid hastily.

'Awkward,' said Mrs Bradley. 'Did you not inspect your purchases when you paid for them?'

'I bought four serpents,' said Sir Rudri, endeavouring to speak with studied calmness, 'of the kind that snake-charmers have. I bought them *from* a snake-charmer! I went across to Tangier for the purpose! I really cannot conceive —'

'Perhaps,' said Gelert from behind his father's shoulder, 'this change in the kind of snake is our first manifestation of the power of Aesculapius.'

'It's the second or third manifestation of damned meddling and stupid practical joking, that's what it is!' said Alexander Currie, who had come strolling up sneering, but who now seemed angry and afraid. 'And I'm going to find out who did it. These snakes are of no use! They're not the right kind at all! Besides, they are quite unpleasantly dangerous!'

'It is a good thing, then, that Aunt Beatrice wanted to see them,' Megan observed. 'But, father, are the vipers really dangerous?'

'They certainly are! I should not dream of touching them, nor of allowing others to do so,' Sir Rudri smoothly replied. Alexander looked furious.

'I have my evidence,' he said, turning suddenly on Sir

Rudri. 'No wonder I'm encouraged to sleep anywhere but in the camp with your other dupes!'

'My very dear fellow,' said Sir Rudri as though in great, though courteous, astonishment. 'What in the name of goodness are you suggesting?'

'Oh, nothing, nothing,' said Alexander Currie, glowering darkly. Sir Rudri's Viking moustache, which had begun to stick out straight, thought better of it, and subsided. 'However, there is no question now of using the serpents to-night,' Sir Rudri observed.

'No, indeed. We must trust only to the abilities of the god,' said Mrs Bradley, casting a shrewd eye upon the closed box, and taking Alexander Currie off with her so that he could not make his way to the cars, if such had been his intention. It would never do for him, of all people, to know that the gregarious Ian was once again of the party, she decided.

'The thing I can't understand,' said Dick to Gelert, as they also strolled off together, 'is how the vipers came to be in the box. The whole affair is rather mysterious, isn't it? I mean, it can't be a mistake. Would anybody mistake a viper for anything but what it is? I mean, they're such nasty, dangerous little brutes.'

'I know,' said Gelert. 'I rather bet that Armstrong knows something about it all, but I don't suppose he will tell us if he does. He doesn't get on with anybody except you.'

'Does he got on with me? I hadn't noticed.'

'Well, one doesn't notice the contrary, anyhow.'

'No, that's true,' said Megan, joining them. 'But Mr Currie gets on with Armstrong, too. They are united in scorn of father, I suppose.'

'Father's quite bats, Megan. Still, it makes a holiday, and, to tell the truth, I'm not at all sorry to be away from Athens for a bit.'

'Why, what have you been up to? Go away, Ronnie.' Dick meekly took himself off.

'Nothing. That is to say —' Gelert looked about him, but, by wandering over the ruins which were widely scattered and partook of the nature of the stony valley itself, he and his sister had left the others a good fifty yards away. 'I'm in rather a mess in Athens. I suppose you haven't twenty quid you could lend me?'

'Well, yes, I suppose I have. I've got most of my birthday money – it's lucky I had nothing but cash from England – but what do you want it for?'

'Well,' said Gelert, glancing round again, 'I believe that twenty quid would buy off the father. He's sticking out for thirty, but I believe, spot cash, he'd take twenty and be glad of it, and, after all, I've done nothing to be ashamed of. It's only that cad Armstrong, out for what he can get.'

'Good lord!' said Megan. 'Not *another* girl!'

Gelert's greyhound face looked thinner and sharper than usual. It also looked rather sulky.

'It's all a lot of rot,' he said. 'We got hung up for a boat, and stayed the night on Andres, and, of course, the old idiot of a father pretends to think the worst.'

'Did it come to that?' asked Megan with sisterly directness.

Gelert was already slightly flushed with the heat, so that she could not tell with any certainty whether he blushed. He looked sternly and nobly at her.

'Naturally not,' he replied.

'I see. You can have the money. Pay me back when you can.'

'Oh rather. Nice of you.' He dismissed the subject. 'What a tick that chap Dmitri is.'

'How especially?'

'Toadies to Armstrong, I think. I say, Megan, does Armstrong *know* anything?'

'Know anything?'

'About Cathleen and that chap what's-his-name?'

'Ian?'

'Yes.'

'I shouldn't think so, but he might. He *is* a blot on the expedition. Couldn't *you* have managed the photographs?'

'Father would drive me mad.'

'So he would me. I expect he drives Armstrong mad. Hullo, they're whistling us.'

Melancholy hooting from the cars – now vacated by Cathleen and the devoted, persistent Ian – announced that lunch was served. With the healthy instinct of youth, Gelert and Megan turned and walked smartly towards it.

At the meal, which was taken in the shade of large spiked umbrellas stuck upright in the ground wherever the subsoil was sufficiently yielding to allow of this being done, the chief topic of conversation among the young was the mysterious box containing, now, the vipers. The general view that the bite of these snakes was fatal was dismissed by Sir Rudri with good-humoured contempt.

'Nonsense!' he said, taking the word 'Rubbish!' out of Alexander Currie's mouth. 'The bite is painful and dangerous. It's not actually fatal.'

'What makes it dangerous, then, father?' Ivor suddenly inquired.

'Get on with your lunch,' said his father. 'I have arranged for us all to take a siesta in the museum this afternoon.'

'I shouldn't have thought there was room for all of us,' said Cathleen, surveying the lonely little shack. 'And suppose it has other visitors whilst we are there? Do we continue our siesta, or do we get up and make room?'

'It is unlikely that there will be visitors here this afternoon,' was Sir Rudri's unreasoned reply. Nevertheless, all hoped that he would be right.

When lunch was over, and all its picnic evidences had been deleted by a fatigue party consisting of Dick and the little boys, the company was assembled in age-groups and marched off by Sir Rudri to the museum for the promised siesta.

CHAPTER FIVE

'Then why are you crying?
There's a smell of onions.'

I

IT was, as Cathleen had observed, a very small museum, but its interior, although not particularly fresh, was a good deal cooler than the open air of the valley, and, after a cursory inspection of the exhibits and a more detailed study (insisted upon by Sir Rudri, who constituted himself lecturer) of the reconstruction plan of the temple whose ruins they had seen outside, Cathleen pillowed her head on the lean abdomen of Gelert when at last they all lay down, and Megan, to poor little Ronald Dick's excitement, laid her somewhat heavy head on his chest. The little boys lay on their backs, knees up, palms against the cool floor. Mrs Bradley, not an adept at daylight sleeping, sat with her back against a wall and wrote up her diary. Alexander Currie sat back to back with Sir Rudri, and the three chauffeurs, the two servants, and the custodian of the museum sat in a corner between marble fragments of the ruined temple and played a complicated gambling game with different-sized pieces of stone. Armstrong, who had brought his apparatus in with him, spent a short time in inspecting his camera, and then played cards with Dmitri and the two Greek chauffeurs, whom he beckoned away from their other game for the purpose.

Cramped and uncomfortable, for the most part, the company later got up, dusted itself, and went outside again. The day was still hot and the valley looked parched and arid. As though by common consent, nearly all of the pilgrims walked back across the intervening belt of land to the high bank near the theatre, climbed it, and sat down on the stone seats to converse and gaze over to the northerly mountain Titthius, or to look behind at the rising wall of Cynartium on whose lower slops the theatre in which they sat had been built.

Tea, consisting of honeycakes and water, was brought to them by Dmitri, who, whatever his shortcomings – none of which, in fact, so far, had manifested themselves to any inconvenient extent – at least possessed the gift of ingratiating cheerfulness. He bestowed food and drink and a gentle smile on everyone in turn, and shady-hatted, sun-spectacled, nose-blistered, the pilgrims received what he had to offer with careless thanks. A slight, unmistakeable feeling of depression seemed to have attacked the party, and it was with minds not very well attuned to the thought of staying up all night, as they knew they had to, that they talked in plaintive tones as they sat and ate.

'My bones *ache* from that beastly floor,' said Megan.

'What about us?' said Gelert. 'We had to be pillows as well.'

The little boys, who had made their own plans for the evening, were clambering about on the theatre and eating as they climbed. The heat did not appear to affect them, and they, alone of the company, had taken no ill effects from the hardness of the floor in the museum. At intervals they came to Dmitri for drinks of water which he, still smiling, served to them.

'Dmitri,' said Ivor, 'have you seen the vipers?'

Dmitri still smiled.

'The snakes,' said Stewart.

'The serpents,' said Kenneth.

'Serpents. Ah, yes.' Dmitri smiled more widely. 'I have not seen.'

The little boys nudged each other, and, as though some idea had communicated itself to each of them simultaneously, they got up and went towards the ruins. The remains of Turkish lime-kilns were still too obvious a feature of the landscape to go unremarked, but, even so, there were stone foundations everywhere – results of excavations in the sacred valley – to show where temple, stadion, and colonnades had been. Still visible were the ground-plans of the rooms for the pilgrim patients of Aesculapius, and reminders of the once populous shrine of healing.

Dusk fell. The modern pilgrim company were summoned to camp by three blasts on a whistle, and, shepherded by Dish and Dmitri – according to whether they preferred to sleep in the cars or the museum – went to their quarters to remain there until half an hour before midnight. The little boys were given no choice. Accompanied by Sir Rudri himself, Alexander Currie, Ronald Dick, and Armstrong, they were marched to the museum and bedded down on coats, rugs, and sacks.

Mrs Bradley, Megan, Cathleen, Gelert, Dish, and the three chauffeurs occupied the seats in the cars – Mrs Bradley, Megan, and Gelert in the first, Cathleen and Ian in the second, the other chauffeurs and Dish in the third. At about eleven o'clock Ian started his engine and drove away with his wife. His conduct – an interesting sidelight, this, Mrs Bradley thought, on the Greek character – appeared to afford neither amazement or amusement to the other chauffeurs.

Megan and Mrs. Bradley, peering out from the back seat of their car, watched the lovers go. Gelert was asleep in the driver's place, and the departing car did not wake him. Mrs Bradley lay back in her corner, closed her eyes, and immediately fell asleep. Megan tried to sleep, but could not. She stared out of the window at the darkness. She was glad that her brother, although asleep, was with her. The lonely road and the lonely valley, the vast, bare, empty theatre, the Hieron of Aesculapius, a place of mystery and faith to generations who had gone, impressed her with a growing sense of fear. She half longed for and half dreaded the signal which was to arouse the party and bring them to the temple precincts for Sir Rudri's second experiment.

She found herself thinking of the first, and, the trend of her thoughts veering insensibly from fear to self-congratulation, she felt surreptitiously for the bruises on knuckles and shin with which that night of the Eleusinian experiment had provided her. Her mood soon changed again, however. She was superstitious. She had been greatly impressed by Cathleen's revelation (as she considered it) of the death of one of the party. The thought of it made her uneasy. She began to wish herself safe at home in Athens. She was worried, too, about the changing over of the snakes.

After a time she gave up staring out of the window at the darkness. She turned herself in her seat, leaned back in the corner of the car, settled the air-cushion behind her head, tried to persuade herself that she was comfortable enough to go to sleep, closed her eyes, and, strangely enough, fell asleep in less than five minutes. But her dreams were twined with serpents, and the sound of Sir Rudri's whistle, which cut across her writhing dreams with the sudden shock of a sword-thrust, brought her terrified to wakefulness, her face sweaty, her hands clenched, her throat dry with fear.

'What's that?' she whispered hoarsely. Mrs Bradley's

voice reassured her. They woke Gelert, and the three of them got out of the car, and, guided by Mrs Bradley's electric torch, they picked their way carefully towards the meeting-place.

Sir Rudri did not count the company. He took it for granted that all those who desired to be present were with him. As this was, in fact, the case, there was no occasion for question or argument. His directions were clear and easy to follow. The company were to repair, in the smallest groups possible – ones, twos, or, in the case of the especially timid, threes – to the ruins of the Colonnades, lie down there, compose their minds, think upon any small ailments from which they might be suffering – he himself, he informed them, had a couple of very bad mosquito bites – and wait for what might happen.

'But don't we have to sacrifice to the god?' inquired Gelert. 'Surely he would not cure the patients for nothing?'

'That is one of the things we might be able to discover,' was Sir Rudri's inspired reply.

'Hippolytus, son of Theseus, dedicated twenty horses to Aesculapius,' Gelert remarked *sotto voce*, as he walked away from his father. Sir Rudri called him back.

'Don't forget to think about your symptoms,' he adjured him. Gelert snorted, and swung round on his heel. It annoyed him that his father should be so pleased with himself.

'Stay with me, Aunt Adela, I'm terrified,' said Megan, holding Mrs Bradley's arm.

'Very well. We will watch for the god together,' Mrs Bradley graciously replied. 'What ailments have you? *I* have an uneasy conscience. Will the god cure that?'

'The sexes should be separate,' Sir Rudri suddenly

boomed across the intervening space of darkness. 'That disposes of my desire that Mr Dick should bear us company,' said Mrs Bradley regretfully. 'Good night, Mr Dick. Have you ills to cure, by the way?'

'One,' replied Dick. He sounded as though he meant it. Gelert, in the darkness, laughed. Armstrong, who was carrying his camera, stumbled against a stone. They could hear him cursing.

'I wonder whether Mr Armstrong has ills,' Mrs Bradley observed in Megan's ear. Megan giggled, knowing what she knew, for it was difficult to imagine the robust and godlike young man seeking the sanctuary of Aesculapius of his own free will, in patient, unquestioning faith.

The company dispersed themselves about the valley. The ground was hard and stony, but the Colonnades had once been a long portico where the patients of the god and his priests had spent the night. Now only the ground-plan was left. A certain amount of laughing, some chaffing remarks, a quantity of stifled blasphemy and muttered objurgations – the result of the hard ground, the peculiar circumstances, a feeling of superstitious fear from which none of them, with the possible exceptions of Sir Rudri and Mrs Bradley, felt entirely free – died at last into vague fidgeting noises and occasional scrabblings and grunts. Then all was quiet. Before midnight, it seemed that everything must be in readiness for any visitation which might come. Whether the visitation was to be in dream form or whether something more tangible might be expected, had not been made clear.

Megan remained close beside Mrs Bradley. After about a quarter of an hour she whispered:

'If only we didn't know about the snakes!'

'They are safely locked away,' replied Mrs Bradley.

'Don't think about them. Think about home comforts, as I am doing.'

'I keep hearing queer noises,' Megan continued. 'That's what makes me think of snakes, I believe. Besides, I'm supposed to be concentrating on my ailments. I suffer from flatfoot. It would be nice – oh, listen! What's that?'

'I think the little boys may be up and doing,' was Mrs Bradley's sane and comforting reply. 'In fact, I think that there can be no doubt about it. Were they to come to the revels to-night, do you know?'

'I am sure father did not intend it. Do you really think it's the boys? Oh, that's all right, then. I shall put all the rest of the noises down to them.'

Reassured by this thought, she was silent again, and looked up at the stars in the wide sky, and removed various small uncomfortable stones from beneath her reclining body. It was cold. She shuddered, envying the relaxed stillness of Mrs Bradley's spare and stringy form.

At about half an hour after midnight Sir Rudri, heralded by a lantern, made a visit of inspection, going from pilgrim to pilgrim in quest of something. It seemed as though he wanted to be certain that they were all where he expected them to be, and that no one was playing truant. To each person he put the same question:

'Do you *feel* just as you did?'

Having received complaining or flippant replies, he followed up each inquiry with the plain statement: 'I shall not come near you again. We must let the Power work undisturbed if it will. Be sure to remember what you dream.'

Just as he left Megan and Mrs Bradley, there was a sound of scuffling, stumbling, and curses. Mrs Bradley switched on her torch, and the man Dmitri was disclosed in the grip of the man Dish.

'No you don't, my hearty,' Dish was saying. 'You let that reptile-box alone now, do you hear? That ain't nothing to do with you. I got to see that nobody but Sir Rudri comes anywheres near it.'

Mrs Bradley switched off her torch, and Sir Rudri, coming up to the disputants, gave tongue. He sounded very angry. A Welsh whine, absent for years, began to creep into his voice. A little later various sounds suggested that Dmitri had settled down and that Dish was returning to the car, his sleeping-place.

'A trustworthy man, that,' said Sir Rudri, as he went away. Megan fell asleep, in spite of her earlier fears and the chilly night, and even Mrs Bradley, who, apparently resting, had been alert at first for every sound, including that of the scaly rustling of mythical snakes, soon slept, and remained asleep until the pallor of dawn broke over the distant mountains.

2

Instead of going to the village to sleep, Ian and Cathleen took the lane-like, dusty road to Nauplia, sure of finding there a respectable inn. There were customers still with the landlord. All stared admiringly at Cathleen, and a room was immediately offered with a view seawards which, their host informed them, they would be able to enjoy in the morning. The furniture comprised a bed, a chamber-pot, and about a pint and a half of water in a kind of earthenware vase.

'Here we have,' said the host, indicating the niceties of his provision for their needs. They thanked him, and soon went to bed. The bed was comfortable enough and quite miraculously clean.

'I don't like it about those snakes,' said Cathleen.

'Oh, we have no time now to talk of snakes,' said Ian.

3

The little boys woke up when their elders left the museum, but made no sign that they had done so. With the mysterious powers of telepathy given to intelligent boyhood, each knew that the other two were awake, and knew, equally, that no movement could be made to put their midnight plans into practice until it was certain that Alexander Currie and the guardian of the museum had gone to sleep again. It was easy enough to tell when the guardian went to sleep, because his breathing altered and grew considerably more audible with the passing in him of conscious life; with Alexander Currie it was more difficult to be certain.

They gave him plenty of time. The door closed behind Sir Rudri, Ronald Dick, and Armstrong, and the little boys lay in the darkness, surrounded by bits of the temple of Aesculapius. Ivor, who had a wrist-watch with a luminous dial, propped himself on his elbow and studied the movements of its hands. For a quarter of an hour, which crept by more slowly than any other of their lives, the other two lay waiting for his signal. It came at last; like cats they crawled to the door. It was ajar – a fact of which Alexander Currie could not have been aware, for he had a horror amounting to mania of small apertures.

One by one, the little boys glided out. Their movements, lissom and fluid, would have done credit to Red Indians or to sinuous beasts of prey. Outside the museum they retained their stealthy method of making progress until they were over the dip between the stretch of ground on which the building stood and the stony valley about which, they knew, their slumbering elders were dispersed.

Their plans were nebulous, except for the fixed project of obtaining possession of the vipers. What they proposed to do with the vipers when they had them they were not yet clear. They halted on the edge of the sacred ground, closed in, and literally put their heads together.

'The thing is,' Ivor whispered, 'are they, or aren't they, where they were put this afternoon?'

'Trouble is, somebody may be sleeping in that part,' said Stewart – for the boys knew the plans of their elders, although the elders seldom knew the plans of the boys.

'I'd like to scare old Armstrong into a fit,' said Kenneth. 'He hoofed me this morning. I've got a bruise from it, too.'

'He's a stinker. I'd like to get one of the vipers to bite him,' said Ivor. 'But if that happened I dare say it would completely muck the holiday. There have been worse holidays than this one.'

'Well, what?' said Kenneth.

'Yes, what?' said Stewart. 'Personally, I vote for having a straightforward shot at sneaking the snakes. We've got to chance who's with them or whether they've been moved.'

'But what are we going to *do* with them, you ass?'

'Well, you ass, let's get them, and then we can see.'

It was not so easy to find their way by night as it had been by day. The ruins (which comprised not only those of the hostels, temple, and Tholos, but a stadion with the goal still clearly marked and with one or two stone seats quite well preserved) were widely-spread and scattered. The stony plain had seemed vast by day to the boys; at night, with not even an electric torch or a lantern to help them pick their way, it seemed a desolate wilderness spreading out for miles in every direction.

'I don't know where we are,' muttered Ivor at last. 'I thought we ought to have got to that funny old maze bit by now.'

'Down there is where we ought to release the snakes when we've got them,' Stewart observed. To the others this also seemed obvious. The foundations of the Tholos were serpentine, and with their sunk walls and straight sides would make an ideal snake-run, they decided. There was a surprising unanimity about their unspoken thoughts on the subject of the vipers, and all were clear that the snakes must not be wasted.

'We shall just have to keep on scouting round until we find it,' said Kenneth, giving Ivor a slight shove onwards.

'Pity we can't separate,' grunted Stewart. 'We'd stand more chance like that, but we couldn't signal each other because of making a row.'

'No, we must stick together,' Ivor agreed. 'I wonder whether any of them can spot us against the sky?'

'It isn't light enough,' said Kenneth. 'I vote we shut our eyes, count a hundred, and then open them. It will seem as light as day out here when we do that.'

This did not prove to be the case. Nevertheless their eyes did become accustomed to the darkness, and, stumbling a good deal but stoically making no sound, even when they fell over and sustained contusions and abrasions from the rocky ground or the ruins, they came with some suddenness upon their objective.

There was only one place from which the inside of the

maze-like foundations of the Tholos could be seen, and Ivor was the first to set foot across the ditch which surrounded the intriguing little place, and peer downwards into the blackness. He backed hastily, dragging the other two by the arm.

'There's somebody in there,' he said, at a distance away from the ruin.

'It's one of them,' said Stewart, who had the scientific mind and did not intend to be intimidated. 'They're all over the place, man, to-night. They're all in ones or twos, to make the experiment. You know what Sir Rudri said.'

'But you don't *need* to make any experiment. *It wasn't one of our lot that I saw!*'

There was a horribly suggestive, ghostly quality about these last words that made the other two catch up with him and quicken their pace. Even Stewart capitulated. Stumbling, tripping, bleeding, bruised, they got back to the museum without realizing that instinct alone had guided them. They sank down by its friendly wall, and huddled like frightened animals together. They listened, fearing pursuit from the supernatural elements of the valley; but no sounds, nor any indication of vengeance, could be heard.

'Golly!' said Ivor at last. He wiped blood and sweat from his face with the sleeve of his shirt. 'I don't want to go there again!'

'What was it?' Stewart inquired.

'I don't know. It was in white. I couldn't see any face. It was too dark.'

'I expect it was your father, togged up like a Greek, or something.'

'It wasn't. However much he was togged up I'd know my father, you ass.'

'All right, you ass. But I wish I'd had a squint at him, all the same.'

'I'm going back to have a squint,' said Kenneth.

'You can go by yourself,' said Ivor, who now, so resilient are the young, was beginning to feel a coward and a bit of a fool, and did not want the others to know his feelings. 'I was only pulling your beastly legs. There wasn't anything there.'

'We might as well go, all the same,' said Stewart, unimpressed by this declaration. 'There *was* something there, and it doesn't chase one, anyhow. I know the way this time.'

4

But for the fact that the snakes were securely locked in their box and were not to be used for experiment during the night, it is doubtful whether Ronald Dick would have taken part in the vigil. It is certain that he would not have consented to spend the dark hours alone. As it was, and even admitting that he would have complete immunity from the serpents, he was highly nervous as he settled himself as comfortably as he could in his ground-plan ruin, and, having been disturbed once by Sir Rudri on his tour of inspection and a second time by the capture of Dmitri by Dish, prepared to make some effort to go to sleep.

But his position was cramped, the earth seemed hard and yet damp, night noises of that inexplicable kind which are audible to nervous people only, but to whom they are terrifying, assaulted his senses and made him strain his ears for more sinister and more significant sounds. Besides this, the attacking swarms of myriad insects – ants, he decided – assisted in preventing him from sleeping.

Some time passed. He was on the point of getting up and

going to his neighbour, Gelert – from whom, incidentally, he had heard not the slightest sound – when he thought he saw a white figure emerge from what had appeared to be the unpopulated darkness of the centre of the valley and move towards the theatre.

Dick was nervous and imaginative, but even he was not prepared to attach a supernatural value to the apparition. His first thought, after a sharply audible intake of startled breath, was that the figure must be Armstrong. Why he fixed upon Armstrong, except that he received some impression of more than average height, he could not afterwards tell, for the figure could as easily have been that of Sir Rudri, who was also tall, or even of Gelert, although Gelert was more slender than the average. Deciding not to go to Gelert's quarters immediately, Dick remained where he was, uncomfortably alert and with his heart beating faster than usual. Thus, less than four minutes later, he was aware of the slight sounds made by the three boys, who, without knowing it, passed fairly close to where he lay. He recognized them, however, and was half in mind to order them back to the museum. If Sir Rudri knew that they were roaming about in the orbit of the experiment he might be very much annoyed, Dick thought. His second feeling, however – for he was a diffident youth with very little faith in himself – was that the boys might not obey his orders, and then he would be sorry he had given them, because there could be nothing more humiliating, he felt, than to give orders as though you were somebody in authority and have them disregarded or scorned, and, in any case, disobeyed. Before he could have a third thought, the boys were out of earshot and had been swallowed up in the night. He did not propose to chase them over the ruins, he told himself; that was Sir Rudri's job if they were endangering the success of the experiment.

After a minute or two he proceeded to put his first plan into practice, and walked across the intervening space between himself and Gelert. As he had half expected, Gelert was not there.

Dick, however, did not want to believe this at first. He called his name in a whisper, 'Gelert! Gelert!' No reply came. He searched, reaching forward with his hands; half dreading lest they should come into contact with something which was not Gelert. The night seemed darker here. He wished he had stayed where he was.

5

In the museum, uncomfortably accommodated at the base of a fragment of the temple, Alexander Currie remained awake and brooded upon the serpents. He could not decide whether what had happened was for the best or the worst. He had in his own mind no doubt that the exchange of reptiles had been made at the instigation of Sir Rudri himself, chiefly because there was no other key save the one in Sir Rudri's possession. He himself, he reflected, had been a fool to come, but the detailed account he had received of Sir Rudri's proposed expedition and its object had tempted him. He could not understand, however, why Rudri had invited him to make one of the party, unless there was something more behind the invitation than the mere desire for his company. This desire he did not believe Sir Rudri to possess, and the thought of the snakes worried him.

Rudri, he told himself, was not the man to forgive and

forget that Apollo business. He himself regretted now the Puckish impulse which had persuaded him to the forgery of the statue. He supposed that Rudri had introduced the serpents as a means of recharging the genius of the valley with something of its original power – a kind of dig in the ribs, as it were, for Aesculapius. Serpents had been the instruments of fertility and of healing. His own rude and unnecessary insistence upon the evidence of Pausanias, which included instances of cures by sacred dogs and sacred geese, he chuckled to remember. His chuckle was enough to disturb the sleep of the keeper of the museum, who turned over heavily and groaned.

Nevertheless, the incident of the exchange of serpents puzzled Alexander. He had had experience of quarrelling with Rudri before; yet, underneath the acrimony he had too often displayed during their almost lifelong acquaintanceship, he had had respect and affection for the other, and now was prepared to curse his own thoughtless joke since it had led to the dissolution of their friendship. Although Rudri himself was by far the most likely person to have exchanged the domesticated pets of the snake-charmer for the unpleasant English adders which could not be released for experimental purposes, something told Alexander that it was more than possible that Sir Rudri knew nothing whatever of the matter. In that case the thing degenerated into a practical joke – the second which had been played since the pilgrims had set out from Athens. He thought of the little boys, but dismissed the thought immediately. Ivor had not been in a position to obtain six English vipers, even if he had desired them, and he could not believe that Kenneth and Stewart could have brought so many in their luggage without his knowledge, nor that they could have got them through the Customs if they had. True, the baggage had been examined in the most cursory way when he had given Sir Rudri's address, for Sir Rudri was a friend of Government officials, but six vipers surely would have managed to draw attention to themselves. Still, the Greeks, he knew, were a casual, tolerant people. . . .

He shook his head. His thoughts then turned to Mrs Bradley, and also to his daughter Cathleen. He hoped that Cathleen and Gelert might make a match of it. If they did, he thought that Sir Rudri might bury the hatchet. As for Mrs Bradley, Alexander Currie on the whole approved of her, chiefly because she was a genius at managing the little boys, whose company he himself had dreaded.

At this point in his meditations he heard the three boys return from their quest of the box of serpents.

'Little imps of Satan,' said Alexander Currie to himself. He knew what they had been after, for although children terrified him, he himself retained many childlike qualities, and he knew that in the boys' place he would have possessed himself of the snakes or perished; and that would have held good even though he loathed and feared the dry, scaly creatures, and, in his present state of mind, would have died sooner than touch them.

A faint rustling from the keeper's end of the building made him break out into a sweat. For an instant he thought it showed that the adders, in their slothful way, were not unaware of his sleeping-quarters, and somehow had sought him out. Then he realized that it was only the custodian of the museum turning over, so he relaxed again, gave his hard pillow a pat, then listened to the boys, who were crouching outside the museum. It was so obvious that they had been in flight that Alexander was interested to know what it was that had frightened or pursued them. He remained in a listening attitude for nearly ten minutes, but could make nothing of their conversation.

'Afraid of ghosts,' he said to himself. 'Been poking about to get hold of those vipers, and got scared.' Then he raised himself again, and listened harder. Not very far away, he thought he could hear the baying of a dog. Hastily, with heart beating faster, he lay down, and stretched out large feet blistered from the walking he had done between Athens and Eleusis. The dog might belong to some shepherd or peasant; the whole of the cures were a lot of nonsense; but, on the other hand, the healing tongues of the sacred dogs were reputed to have had power. The baying ceased. Feeling foolish, he covered his feet again. After a time he slept.

6

Gelert was full of his troubles; not as full of them as he had been before his sister had agreed to lend him the money, but sufficiently full of them to feel restless, scornful, irritated, and ill-used. He had spotted Ian as one of the chauffeurs, and was surprised that Alexander Currie had not done so. Stewart and Kenneth, he supposed, had not been hoodwinked, but they were staunch kids, unlikely to give the new-married lovers away. They must be staunch, he reflected grimly, to put up with the kicks, sly, ugly punches, and minor persecutions dealt out to them by Armstrong. True, they annoyed him when they could, but his retaliatory methods, Gelert decided, needed editing. It occurred to him that this ridiculous vigil they were supposed to be keeping offered as good an opportunity as he would be likely to get for putting his point of view to the offending person.

Besides, they had another little argument to settle. . . .

He knew where Armstrong was, and had heard him fidgeting about. All was still from that direction now, however. Perhaps the fellow was asleep. He got up and walked over to see.

Armstrong was not asleep. He said, as Gelert approached:

'Oh, Lord! What now? For heaven's sake, don't alter the instructions again.'

'Shut up,' whispered Gelert, 'and accept a piece of advice.'

'Don't want it,' said Armstrong. 'What are you supposed to be doing? I thought you must be Sir Rudri.'

'Shut up, and listen. Keep your blasted boots to yourself when you've got 'em on. Get that? I won't have those kids kicked by you. If you want to kick anybody, kick me. I'll know what to do about it.'

'Will you?' said Armstrong, savagely. 'Here goes, then!' He switched on a torch and kicked Gelert savagely on the shin. Gelert grunted with astonishment and pain, and flung himself on Armstrong. In silence, except for heavy breathing and grunts, they gripped one another and wrestled backwards and forwards. Armstrong was heavier than Gelert, and, by daylight, would probably have got the better of him; but the ruins were treacherous. He stumbled and came down heavily, hitting his head. He lay so still that Gelert searched him for his torch which he had slipped back into his pocket, found it, switched it on, and was perturbed to see his adversary lying like one dead, a trickle of blood from his fair head creeping, black and thin, across the Grecian stones.

CHAPTER SIX

'After that you'll see snakes . . .'

I

WHEN dawn came the company were reassembled by Sir Rudri, who went to each dormitory and roused those pilgrims whom the dawn light had not waked.

Breakfast was taken in the cars because this meant the least porterage of food. Tea was made by Megan and Cathleen (heavy-eyed from an almost sleepless night at Nauplia) on oil-stoves. Bottles of grape-fruit and orange juice were opened for those who preferred them to the brew which the two girls were decanting from the teapots.

The little boys had recovered their spirits entirely, and, food in hand, chased about over the theatre and delivered themselves of vulgar rhymes from its stage. They came back occasionally for drinks or for more to eat.

Gelert, glum and (the others supposed) stricken in conscience because he had not made any attempt to get medical aid for the wounded Armstrong, but had sat beside him all night apparently without the slightest idea of whether he was alive or dead, ate nothing, drank two cups of tea, scowlingly refused a third, and, when the meal was over, accompanied Mrs Bradley, to whose professional care the injured young man had been committed by Sir Rudri, and asked her, as they walked towards the museum :

'I suppose it isn't serious?'

'No, it's not serious,' Mrs Bradley replied.

'I suppose you wonder why I didn't come for you when it happened?'

'I don't wonder, child. I know.'

'What?'

'You thought you had killed him.'

'I didn't know what to do,' said Gelert, miserably. 'I'm in trouble enough already. I didn't know what on earth I should do if I'd killed him.'

'What happened?'

Gelert told her.

'I see. And what was your real reason for picking a quarrel with him, child?'

'I told you. I didn't agree that he should act as he does towards my young brother and the other kids.'

Mrs Bradley nodded several times, not as though she accepted this pious statement, but as though she had come to some conclusion about it or him. Gelert glanced at her, but did not offer to add to what he had said.

They entered the museum, to which Armstrong had been taken. He was conscious but looked heavy-eyed and was pale. His head was bandaged.

'I can't be moved,' he said abruptly when he saw her. 'And I won't have the bandage off. It's stuck.'

Mrs Bradley grinned.

'You'll do nicely, child,' she said. She eyed the bandage, gave him a drink of water, asked him whether he felt sleepy, and, being told that he did not, went away, leaving Gelert with him.

'Sorry, you know,' said Gelert.

'Sorry be damned.'

'All right, then.' Gelert walked out and caught Mrs Bradley up before she got back to the cars.

'Gentlemanly apology not accepted,' he observed, falling into step beside her.

'Gelert,' said Mrs Bradley, slowing down her pace so that

they should take longer to get back to the rest of the party, 'has your father ever been kept under observation, do you know?'

'You don't mean he's bats?'

'In the strict sense of the word, no, child. But I feel he could bear watching.'

'So do I. I think he was watched last night.'

'By the boys?'

'The boys? No. By that fellow Dmitri. I don't like that lad.'

'The boys confided to me this morning that they had seen a ghost last night.'

'Where?'

'Among the ruins. To-night they propose to hunt it.'

'Are you suggesting we're going to put in another night at this place? I thought father intended pushing on to Mycenae.'

'He did, but —'

'Armstrong, of course. I suppose he can't be moved.'

'He could be moved. He's had a nasty crack on the head and he has a scalp wound, but he's not too bad to travel. It's a pity you worried yourself.' She smiled. Gelert kicked the stones.

'Well, well,' said Sir Rudri genially, as they came back to the circle, 'what of our crack-pated photographer?'

'Aunt Adela thinks he could travel if he liked,' said Gelert, before Mrs Bradley could reply.

'Nonsense,' said Sir Rudri briskly. 'I can't risk the poor lad's health. Nonsense, Beatrice! Nonsense!'

'Very well, child,' replied Mrs Bradley, grinning. 'I like this place very well. Who says Nauplia and a bathe?'

A shrill clamour broke out, and in less than two minutes

her car was packed. The three little boys were in it, and Megan, Gelert, and Dick. Mrs Bradley, motioning the chauffeur aside, got in and took the wheel. Gelert sat beside her. The others had managed to get themselves wedged into seats for four.

Sir Rudri, whose instinct was to protest against this sudden exodus of the major portion of the party, watched the car heading up the defile which led back to the main road for Nauplia. Soon the dust settled again, and, except for an eagle which hung high over the valley, and Cathleen Currie and her father, who were seated in the theatre taking their ease before the day grew too intensely hot, he found himself left alone. He glanced round as though in search of occupation, and then decided to walk to the museum. He examined the plans and the pictured reconstruction of the Tholos, and then went in to see Armstrong.

Outside, on the fifteenth tier of the theatre, Cathleen said to her father, 'Kenneth says that Ivor wouldn't admit that it was Sir Rudri.'

'But Kenneth didn't see the figure, you say?'

'No. They were afraid, and ran away. But Kenneth went back later and had a look. There was nothing to be seen at all. This morning, at dawn, he went again and took his magnifying-glass. He says they're Sir Rudri's tracks.'

'They mayn't have been made last night.'

'I know. That's what I said. Do you think there's something funny going on?"

'I don't know what to think. Kenneth's a good laddie. I'll give him – what's the drachma worth at present?'

'I don't know. A little less than a halfpenny, I believe. Father, I don't want to stay another night here. I'm afraid of the snakes. I know he means to use them in some way or another.'

'Oh no. He couldn't do that. They're poisonous snakes, do you see?'

'Yes, but – you know, father, something terrible is going to happen before we get back to Athens. I'm afraid. I'm horribly afraid. I'm more afraid than you think.'

'I can see you are afraid,' said Alexander. 'Cheer up, lassie! Nobody's dead yet, and it's not poor Rudri's serpents that will kill us.'

2

The bathing party returned in the late afternoon. They had lunched in Nauplia, and had had a pleasant time. The museum was again turned into a place of siesta, and after tea, when the sun began to abate his fiercest heat, the party broke up into twos and threes, and went exploring the valley and its environs.

Cathleen strolled off on her own, and met, by prearrangement, at the village of Lygouria, not more than four miles from the Hieron of Epidaurus, her husband, Ian. They sat down in a little shop there, and were given tar-flavoured wine. Then they went out to look at the well, and then walked back towards the theatre.

There were a few fields and vineyards round about the village, but soon the carriage road branched off. The bare, sad mountains closed round the valley in which the sanctuary lay; evening deepened, and the sun set. Where the road ran right, Ian and Cathleen stopped. He said:

'It's good night, I'm thinking, is it not?'

'Yes, it's good night, Ian.'

'Maybe I did wrong in marrying you so early in your life, and you with great beauty.'

'Whom would I marry, else? You're a great fool, my dear man.'

'Maybe I am.' He looked at her wistfully. They returned separately to the valley. By the time that Ian came lounging back to his car, Cathleen had taken Mrs Bradley to the top of the theatre for the view, and to ask to be allowed to spend the night with her and Megan for company. Ronald Dick, almost inarticulate with pleasure because he had had Megan as the sole companion of his walk, proposed himself, bluntly and blushingly, as the fourth member of their party.

'The sexes,' said Mrs Bradley, looking at him severely, 'must be separated. Those are Sir Rudri's instructions, dear child. Who am I to gainsay them?'

'I don't see that it matters. Nothing happened last night, and father's an old fathead,' said Megan decidedly. 'Why shouldn't Ronald stay with us if he wants to?' She patted him kindly on the back. 'You stay. If Aunt Adela doesn't like you, she can go off on her own, because three of us together will feel quite safe, I'm certain.'

'That's an ungrateful remark,' said Mrs. Bradley, 'and I think I shall take you at your word.'

'Please stay with us,' said Cathleen. 'Ronald knows about Ian,' she added. 'I told him. When father has done his rounds, Ian can come as well. The other drivers won't know, and, if they do, they can't speak English, so that it won't matter either way.'

'But Sir Rudri can speak Greek,' Mrs Bradley pointed out.

'*Father* can't,' said Cathleen. She smiled at Ronald Dick.

'We'd better have Gelert as well, and that will include us all.'

'What about Armstrong?' asked Dick.

'And there's Dmitri,' said Mrs Bradley.

'We can't have them,' said Megan. 'Besides, Dmitri sleeps in the car. He did last night. And Armstrong will sleep in the museum to-night, I suppose. How bad is he really, I wonder?'

'Why do you wonder that, child?'

'I think he's up to mischief.'

Mrs Bradley's black eyes lighted on those of the speaker. Megan's glance slid sideways, dislodging, as it were, Mrs Bradley's questioning gaze. Mrs Bradley raised her eyebrows and pursed her thin lips into a little beak.

'You interest me, child,' she said; but the remark was not interpreted by Megan as an invitation to disclose what she knew or suspected.

Dusk came, and the campers dispersed. Gradually, however, they mustered again, and before midnight everybody except Sir Rudri, Alexander Currie, Armstrong, Dmitri, Dish, and the chauffeurs, had gathered in Mrs Bradley's vicinity and were carrying on whispered conversations until, one by one, they dropped off to sleep. Cathleen and Ian slept side by side. Ronald Dick, rigid with nervous joy, lay between Megan and Mrs Bradley. His face was turned towards the object of his love. Daring above his wildest aspirations, he put his arm over her. Megan squeezed his thin arm with her heavier, stronger one, and heaved her large, Amazonian frame six inches nearer to his. Gelert lay alone, brooding upon his mis-spent life and wasted opportunities. At two o'clock in the morning, or thereabouts, a large snake glided among the sleepers, liked their warmth and quietness, and coiled itself neatly and unobtrusively between Mrs Bradley and Dick. Mrs Bradley, waking at dawn, put her hand on it. She was startled, but, as the snake did not attempt to move, she kept her hand where it was, and raised herself by imperceptible degrees, until she could get a good look at it. It was not a viper. So much she could see at a glance. It was a much longer snake, and was differently marked from the adders.

'Hail, Aesculapius,' said Mrs Bradley politely, thinking it best to be on the safe side in placating the deity which, so far as she knew, still ruled in the stony valley. Then she reached over for her leather suitcase (which she always kept by her at night because it contained, besides clothes, her case-book, note-books, and bed-books), tilted the contents neatly out and placed the empty case, with some care, over the coils of the reptile. Then she rested her head on the suitcase, having placed a roll of spare clothing under her neck, and settled herself as comfortably as she could to await the call to breakfast.

3

Alexander Currie expected to spend a disturbed and restless night. He was one of those people to whom the presence of others in a room is a direct source of irritation, and the presence in the museum that night not only of the little boys but of Armstrong, evoked in him a frenzied restlessness. If he had been a little child he would have kicked and screamed. Had he been an adolescent girl he would have had an attack of hysterics. Being himself, he merely champed, tossed, twisted, muttered, swore, sat up, lay down, and, finally, walked out, bedding and all, preferring to brave the serpents of Aesculapius rather than remain in the museum in the unseen but nerve-trying company of others.

He did not go far away, but lay down under some trees between the museum and the theatre, where he was soon asleep. The little boys, again full of plans, jabbed each other in the ribs and expressed, in pantomime, considerable joy at being relieved of his presence. As soon as they judged it was safe, they followed him out of doors, and, led by Kenneth (since Ivor on the preceding evening had failed so signally as leader), made their way directly to the maze-foundations of the Tholos in which Sir Rudri's son was supposed to have seen the mysterious figure of which this time they were in search.

Ivor, as a matter of fact, had stuck vigorously to his version that his apparent fright had been with intent to deceive the others; but neither Kenneth nor Stewart was prepared to accept this apostasy.

As they drew near their objective, Ivor began to hang back, but a vigorous kick from Stewart urged him onwards. Kenneth crept to the edge of the ruin, and peered over.

He backed away hastily.

'He's there,' he whispered. 'At least, I can see something white.'

'Let's have a look,' said Stewart. The white figure, dignified and stately, yet giving an impression of virility and power, advanced towards him. Scientific curiosity was one thing; a ghost was another. Again the boys fled; this time, in their panic-stricken haste, away from the camp, and so were not heard by the pilgrims.

They soon tripped over and fell flat – Kenneth first, then Ivor, and lastly Stewart, and got up sobered, bruised, in pain, and with the sudden panic gone. Slowly they limped to the museum. There was no moon, and from where they were the building did not show up against the sky. Suddenly, however, up it loomed. Again they crouched down in its shadow and took stock of themselves and were angry.

'You *are* silly cuckoos,' said Ivor. 'If you'd have let *me* lead again, I bet I wouldn't have scooted away like that! We nearly saw who it was, and then you two scooted off. I jolly well bet *I* wouldn't have scooted off. I —'

'You!' said Kenneth, and punched him in the chest. 'If you're so definitely marvellous you'd better go back by yourself. Go on! I dare you to go!'

'That isn't a fair dare,' said Stewart. 'But if you'll go, Ivor, *I* will."

'We'll all go, then,' said Kenneth. 'It can't be much. It hasn't chased us, anyway.'

'It might be Aesculapius,' said Ivor.

'He wouldn't hurt us,' said Stewart. 'Come on, Ivor. Are you on?'

'We're all on,' said Kenneth, unopposed. They followed his lead towards the ruins. This time there was nothing to be seen.

'That's twice we've been had,' said Ivor, unconfessedly, and secretly relieved. 'I shall mention it to father in the morning.'

'I still bet it *was* your father,' Stewart observed.

'What would he poke down holes for?'

'Exactly,' said Kenneth, hopefully. 'Perhaps he's on to something here – treasure or something – and doesn't intend that anyone else should know. Let's have another look to-morrow morning. I'm going back to bed.'

They crept back into the museum. The keeper was breathing heavily in his sleep. On Kenneth's bed a large snake lay asleep. Kenneth, however, did not see it until the morning, when Stewart, noticing it with its head next to Kenneth's, said softly:

'I say, you men, Aesculapius.'

Then, a sensible child, he crept to Kenneth, woke him, and drew him away from the snake. Kenneth, although horrified, remained outwardly calm, except that his face went brick-red.

'We ought to kill it,' he said. The boys held whispered counsel, Stewart championing the snake, the others agog for its destruction. The snake, apparently missing the warmth of Kenneth's body, woke up. It raised its head six inches on a thickish, mottled neck, and regarded them steadfastly. They stared back at it.

'It's no good running away,' said Stewart, with his usual gravity. Out of a deeply freckled face, his green eyes regarded the snake with an earnest interest which triumphed over vulgar fear. 'You know, I believe it's used to human beings. I vote we give it some milk and see how it responds.'

'It'll respond by sinking its fangs in you,' said Kenneth, 'but I'll go and scout for the milk if you like.'

Ivor, stoutly asserting that he was not afraid of the snake, went with him. Stewart was going to follow them, but, observing that the snake had lowered its head and showed every sign of desiring to resume its interrupted slumbers, he elected to remain where he was. He waited, quite still, for five minutes after the others had gone, not caring to move in case he disturbed the reptile. After that, however, he grew bolder and walked towards it with the intention of inspecting it more closely. The snake, with great sociability, watched him come. Then it seemed to stretch itself, and, moving with swift neatness, it shot across the floor and wrapped itself affectionately round his leg. Stewart was horribly scared, and yet, as he stood petrified, and the snake dropped its head to his sandalled feet and nestled its throat against his instep, it began to dawn on him that this could be no ordinary serpent, but must be one of the snake-charmer's pets which had disappeared from Sir Rudri's tin box to be replaced by the vipers.

The others came back with some goat's milk and Sir Rudri.

'Ah,' said Sir Rudri, 'this is very gratifying.'

'And what is this?' asked Mrs Bradley's voice from the doorway. Coiled round her skinny arm, its head on the palm of her hand and a slight grin (extraordinarily reminiscent of her own) upon its serene and Oriental features, was another snake. 'The third is with Gelert, who seems to boast a previous acquaintance with it, and the fourth —' She disappeared through the doorway, and walked quietly away to where Alexander Currie was sleeping, his head, like Jacob's, resting upon a stone pillow. The fourth snake, with a devotion worthy of Cleopatra's asp, was nestling warmly in his bosom. His left arm was thrown carelessly across its scaly coils. His breath and the breath of the morning blew, at different temperatures, but with equal gentleness, on its neck.

The wounded Armstrong, Mrs Bradley noticed, was nowhere to be seen, either inside or outside the museum. Tenderly the company woke all the snakes and fed them, innocent of the knowledge that the snake-charmer's stock-in-trade were, one and all, considerably more dangerous than the adders, being deadly poisonous reptiles with their poison glands intact. But ignorance was bliss, and it must be chronicled on behalf of the snakes, that they behaved like nursery pets throughout the meal.

4

It seemed to be a matter of tacit general agreement that Alexander Currie should not be informed that he had shared his self-chosen couch with a snake, however friendly and unassuming. Failing the tin box, the four snakes were put into the luggage holder in the back of the car driven by Ian, and the incident, although not forgotten, was soon obscured by the invasion of the valley by sightseers from a cruising liner which had called at Nauplia that morning.

Several dozen car-loads of well-dressed, imperious-voiced, ignorant, exclamatory tourists stood about the theatre, infested the museum, followed their voluble but imperfectly instructed guides about the ruins, put up sunshades, dabbed themselves with anti-fly lotions, sweated, squeaked, smoked, giggled, and at last went back to their ship.

Sir Rudri, literally dancing with fury, announced on their departure that they had destroyed every influence for good in the valley, and that 'things' would need to settle down again, perhaps for weeks, before it would be possible to continue the researches profitably.

Armstrong had been discovered under the trees not far from the theatre. He explained, in a dazed manner, that he must have walked in his sleep. The little boys, examining themselves and one another for bruises, discovered that they had none.

'And I came an absolute *mucker*,' said Kenneth, amazed.

No one had anything to show for the serious falls that they had had upon running away from the Tholos.

'If the tourists have prevented us from spending another night here, I'll drink their health,' said Gelert to Mrs Bradley, when the dust had settled on the roadside. Sir Rudri, still breathing out fire, and equipped now with sun-glasses and a pith helmet, was writing up his notes. He had not, he said, come to any conclusion about the serpents. He would record them as facts, and draw his deductions later.

Mrs Bradley confessed to a longing to get to Mycenae. The three chauffeurs were to continue in charge of the cars, and Cathleen, when she knew this, was caught between apprehension and delight.

'I still can't think why father doesn't recognize you,' she said several times to Ian.

'He is not expecting to see me. He thinks I am in Scotland,' Ian replied. 'Therefore it would be a queer thing if he did recognize me.'

So noon found the pilgrims back in Nauplia, and while their elders remained in the inn, in the shade and comparative coolness, the little boys, who had fraternized with the tourists, were taken off to the liner in a launch and were encouraged to explore from end to end of the ship, and from the sports deck to the engine room. The ship put off again at six, and at half past six the pilgrims took to the cars en route for Mycenae by way of the Argos-Corinth road.

It was a short journey. Argos was reached after seven miles of a north-westerly incline with the railway on the west of the road all the way along until, three-quarters of a mile from Argos, the road crossed the line. The little boys cheered the trains.

The chauffeurs did not take their vehicles through the

city, but skirted it, and the cars ran on across the thirsty plain, through fields of corn, tobacco, and fruit irrigated by well-water. Six miles farther on the travellers reached the village of Phychtia, the nearest village to the ruined citadel. The road reached the lowest level of the Argive plain, passed between plantations of cotton and tobacco, then a lesser road, branching eastward, brought the party, at the end of another mile and three-quarters, within sight of their objective.

The acropolis of the city of Agamemnon stood up boldly at the head of its savage glen. The Argive plain stretched southward, and the road was wild and deserted. Bare uplands, dead as the mountains of the moon, rose one to the northward and the other to the south of Mycenae, and at the end of an inclined path was the Lion Gate of the citadel. The path itself was bordered by walls of the huge grey stones.

'Golden Mycenae,' said Sir Rudri. In an exaggerated manner he kissed the Cyclopean masonry and saluted the lions which reared themselves on either side of a pillar over the gateway. He put his fingers in the door-sockets and stroked the sides of the archway as he passed underneath it. 'Golden Mycenae,' he repeated.

They followed him through the archway where great wooden doors had once hung, but which now was guarded by a short iron fence with a gate in it, and ascended a steep, rough path beside a broken wall. Stony, and bearing the plants of the wilderness, the ground sloped downwards away towards the road. The wall grew higher, the path even steeper as they walked, until, at a short distance, they came upon the grave circle with its surrounding narrow walk, bordered by upright slabs of stone, flat, wide, and placed neatly edge to edge. It was difficult to imagine that the stones had been placed so more than three thousand years earlier.

'Seventeen bodies were found here – eleven men and six women,' Sir Rudri observed to the little boys, who were desirous of exploring this promising site on their own account, but had been bidden by the leader of the party to walk beside him.

'Buried in that place?' asked Stewart, indicating the deep, stone-built pits of the grave-circle.

'Shaft graves. Agamemnon. Haven't you heard of the Trojan war?' said Alexander Currie.

'He came home from it safely, didn't he?' asked Kenneth, who knew how to annoy his father.

'Where was he murdered, sir?' asked Ivor, who also knew this game. Alexander glared at both of them, and caught up with Gelert, who had walked on ahead of his father, and now was standing gazing into the excavations as though in search of something.

'Why do they call it Golden Mycenae, sir?' asked Stewart, appealing innocently to Sir Rudri.

'Because it was a very important place at the time of the fall of Cnossus, in Crete, my boy, and because of all the gold which was used, and afterwards found, here.'

'Found?' The boys clustered about him. 'Do you mean that if we were to search we should find some gold, sir?'

'Well,' said Sir Rudri good-humouredly, 'you might. I shouldn't *think* there's anything left, but of course, one never quite knows.'

'I know what sort of things to look for,' said Ivor suddenly. 'I've seen the stuff in the Athens museum. Wedges and wedges and wedges, all in glass cases.'

'Now, now! You stay with me! We can't have you falling into the excavations,' said Sir Rudri, immediately nervous and filled with fussy anxiety. 'Beatrice, I don't think the boys should be encouraged to wander hereabouts on their own.'

'They shall wander with me, dear child,' replied Mrs Bradley soothingly. She was accepted, through no desire of her own, by all the party as the heaven-sent mentor, preceptor, and nigger-driver of the little boys, and nobody else attempted to cope with their high spirits, adventurousness, idiosyncrasies, or downright disobedience.

'Good egg,' said Kenneth. 'Bags we descend into Avernus.'

He walked down a broken piece of wall and gazed steadfastly into the depths. 'I bet I could jump that.'

He jumped, staggered, recovered himself, and walked at the bottom of the excavations. It was not intrinsically interesting down there, but he felt satisfied and at peace with himself for having expressed his desires in action – defiant action, for he raised a face of angel sweetness to encounter Sir Rudri's angry protests from the top.

'Bags I,' said Ivor. He followed Kenneth's lead, and, falling, cut both knees. Stewart walked over to one of the pits on the other side of the path, near the fortress wall. He gazed earnestly into it.

'Interesting place,' he said. 'When are we going to see the beehive tombs?'

'Now, I fancy,' Mrs Bradley replied. But Sir Rudri who, having called his tribe about him, was directing his steps towards the gate, hesitated, and then halted.

Kenneth and Ivor, tired of the shaft graves, climbed out

of them up a steep and stony incline, and joined Stewart and Mrs Bradley.

'What should you have done, inquired Ivor suddenly, 'if we had broken our legs?'

'Set them for you. It would have hurt you,' Mrs Bradley replied. The boys laughed happily, because they had not broken their legs. Sir Rudri said:

'Candles, candles?'

'Nonsense,' said Alexander Currie, who had scrambled to the top of the hill to get the view over the plain of Argos, and had been disappointed in it. 'We shall barely see the beehive tombs before dusk. The sun is beginning to set.'

Armstrong, who had taken the bandage off his head, but was wearing a large coloured handkerchief underneath his hat, produced half a dozen bits of candle from the pockets of his linen jacket and handed them to his employer.

'Ah, good,' said Sir Rudri, ignoring Alexander Currie, who continued to stand in the middle of the path and expostulate. 'You boys shall have your turn later. Stay where you are for the present.'

He turned and led the way to the almost invisible ruins of the palace above on the hill. The boys looked at Mrs Bradley. She shook her head.

'The postern stair. We can go down later. Let us forestall Sir Rudri at the Treasury of Atreus,' she said. The idea of being in the van of the sightseeing appealed to the three little boys. They followed her under the Lion Gateway, down the broad entrance, back to the road, and across it and up a bank on the farther side to the vaulted tomb, the haunt of innumerable bees.

A wide path, bordered by great walls, led up to the entrance of the tomb or treasury, and over its opening a lintel-stone of a hundred and thirteen tons was fitted upon the hewn-stone walls. The interior was pitch dark until Mrs Bradley switched on her electric torch, and by its light showed the boys the walls. Then they penetrated to a smaller, inner chamber where the blackness was thick and seemed to have weight and body. Ivor suddenly clasped Mrs Bradley's arm.

When they were back in the vaulted chamber they stamped upon the hard ground and the sound seemed to run in ever-lessening circles through the floor and round the whole foundation of the tomb.

'I like this place,' said Stewart, as they came out on to the entrance path. 'I hope we stay here a week.'

'I shouldn't think we'd stay here more than a night,' said Kenneth. 'The whole thing's a wash-out so far.'

'What do you mean?' said Ivor as, on impulse, they all walked back towards the tomb again, and stood in its entrance waiting for the others.

'Well,' said Kenneth kindly, 'it might have been all right if your father could have got away with the snakes, but everybody knows it was a plant.'

'Oh, was it? Well, then, what cured that beast Armstrong? Didn't he nearly die?'

'No. That was your brother's funk.'

'My brother isn't a funk!'

'Yes, he is,' said Mrs Bradley mildly. 'So should we all be if we thought we had killed a fellow-creature by accident at night, in a strange land, in a strange place, with neither witnesses nor apparent justification.'

The little boys accepted this judgement, which seemed to them reasonable, in silence, and were soon engaged in chasing one another along the entrance way, and over the rough ground which bordered the road.

Sir Rudri and the rest of the party, daubed with candle-grease, came on with the keeper who had unlocked the Treasury previously for Mrs Bradley and the boys. He liked the boys, and took them back into the tomb to show them, by the light of his lantern, the walls once studded with bronze rosettes, and to light for them again the inner chamber.

Armstrong did not go inside the Treasury. He lounged in the doorway, and when Cathleen, who soon grew oppressed by the darkness inside the vault, came out again and began to stroll back towards the cars, he followed her. He said :

'So you go off at nights with one of the drivers, do you?'

Cathleen swung round and looked at him. Not liking what she saw, she continued her walk. He lengthened his stride and caught up with her.

'Get away,' said Cathleen, reading his intention, which was to kiss her. Her voice, which she had raised, brought Ian leaping up the bank from the road where the cars were stationed.

'Mind away,' he said. He clumped Armstrong on the mouth, but not very hard, because he remembered that Armstrong had hurt his head. 'You must not annoy the ladies, sir,' he said.

Armstrong, whose front teeth had begun to bleed, dabbed at his mouth, and turned to walk back towards the tomb.

'If you please, I will escort you, madam,' Ian continued loudly.

'You men,' said Armstrong, shouting, 'are employed because you can't speak English. I shall get you dismissed, you half-breed lout, do you hear?'

Ian took no notice, and walked respectfully beside his wife.

'It would not do for that one to know who I am,' he said serenely.

'I love you,' said Cathleen. She spoke violently because she had never said those words before, and they sounded, in her ears, strange and immodest. 'He tried to kiss Megan the other day,' she added very quickly, to cover them up, 'but she slapped his face and stamped on his toe.'

'She's a fine, big girl,' said Ian with approval. 'I am for seeing the tomb of Clytemnestra, and the tomb of Aegisthus. They are just at the top of this road. Are you willing?'

'Wait for me,' said Mrs Bradley behind them. 'I, too, want to visit the tomb of Clytemnestra. Ian, go back to the car. Sir Rudri and Alexander Currie are immediately behind me.'

Ian grinned, saluted, and walked off.

'Armstrong is making himself a nuisance,' said Cathleen, as they stood before the smaller ruinous beehive tomb just beyond the Lion Gate.

'I guessed it. We ought to send him home. He is altogether out of his element, I think. I wonder what is Gelert's quarrel with him?'

'Do you not think it is true about the boys?'

'Oh, no,' replied Mrs Bradley. 'The boys are irritating to any right-minded young man. Gelert should be helping Armstrong to kick them, not trying to stop him.'

'I see. Do they irritate you?'

'No. I see them through a glass, darkly, because of my sex and my advanced years. The young men see them face to face, and exceptionally clearly at that. Gelert must long to correct all his own faults in Ivor, and, of course, Kenneth must be a very trying boy. He epitomizes boyhood. The other two are much more individual.'

'Is Mr Armstrong a very clever photographer?'

'I think there is no doubt of it.'

'Shall we have to take him to Ephesus? If so, I don't think I'll go. Ian won't be coming. His engagement with Sir Rudri terminates at Athens. I think I'll go back with him to Scotland, and write to father from the ship.'

'An excellent idea,' said Mrs Bradley, who realized that nothing would be gained at the moment by either party if Cathleen told her father to his face that she was married to Ian and intended to return to their native land with him.

'I suppose,' said Cathleen, 'you couldn't do anything for us?'

'Oh, yes. Of course. To begin with, I can get Ian a job when he's finished his college course. I suppose he is bound to do well?'

'I don't see how he can help it. He's very clever and works tremendously hard. But I didn't mean anything like that.' She looked distressed.

'I admire him, child, on both accounts,' said Mrs Bradley firmly, waving the protest aside. 'Do you wish to penetrate this tomb?'

'No. I know more about Clytemnestra without doing so. I wonder why I didn't like you at first?'

'These mutual antipathies are interesting,' Mrs Bradley replied with a gentle cackle. Cathleen looked startled. 'I – I hope we've *both* changed our minds,' she said hesitantly, with attractive simplicity.

'Oh, yes, I am sure we have, child.' They walked back to meet the rest of the party, which, headed, as usual, by Sir Rudri, and gambolled round by the three little boys, was coming to find them in order to make arrangements for the night.

'We're going to make Homeric sacrifice both at the palace and at the Treasury of Atreus,' Sir Rudri observed. 'The difficulty is the oxen. However, this good man' – he indicated the keeper of the keys – 'thinks he can prevail upon one of the peasants to let us have two goats. No doubt the result cannot be the same as with oxen, but with blood and entrails at our disposal, we surely should be able to evoke something.'

'Yes, a putrid stink,' said Kenneth, *sotto voce*, behind his father. Alexander Currie turned and smiled upon his son.

'I don't think goats are a good idea, father,' said Gelert. 'They have a definite connexion with the Black Art. I think we should pause and consider before committing ourselves to goats.'

He broke off and held a spirited conversation in modern Greek with the custodian.

'He says they are black goats,' he added, after he and the Greek had adjusted themselves to one another's system of pronunciation. 'To my mind to introduce black goats as an offering in a place like this is simply asking for trouble.'

CHAPTER SEVEN

'There are weighty, weighty doings afoot among the dead, and a great deal of party feeling.'

I

BEFORE the sunset had gone from the sky, Sir Rudri had made up his mind that cattle must be found for the sacrifice. The sleeping-bags were brought out of the cars, and preparations were made to camp by the roadside. Gelert and Dick went off in one of the cars, although not the one driven by Ian, and Dmitri, who had skill in driving oxen, went with them to manage the beasts.

Before Sir Rudri could get to sleep his servant Dish came and stood before him, and said:

'Sir, come to make a complaint.'

'What is it, Dish?'

The spectacle of his employer rearing up, caterpillar-like, in a sleeping-bag, had no effect upon Dish. He answered stolidly:

'Mr Armstrong took upon hisself to refer to me as a slow-moving swine, sir, as I was assisting of him to stow away his photography, so 'ead or no 'ead, sir, I took upon me to resent what he had to say.'

'Oh? And how did he – what did you do?'

'I dotted him one, sir, for luck.'

'But that,' said Sir Rudri mildly, 'was very wrong of you, Dish. Have you hurt him, do you think?'

'Yes, sir.'

'Oh – well, ask Mrs Bradley to have a look at him, then.'

So saying, he resumed a recumbent attitude, moved his head irritably as though he found the soil of Greece uncomfortable and blamed it for the fact, and then remained perfectly still. After about three minutes he observed, 'Do you think they'll be back with those oxen by daylight, Dish?'

Dish, however, did not answer. He was nearly fifty yards away, in earnest conversation with Mrs Bradley.

'Go away, Dish,' was her first response to the summons to attend to Armstrong.

'But, mam, Sir Rudri's orders to me was to fetch you.'

'What's the matter with Mr Armstrong, anyway?'

'I struck him, mam.'

'Good for you, Dish. Where?'

'On the sn — in the front of the head, mam.'

'Ah, yes. What for?'

'He called me a swine, mam.'

'Oh, did he? That wasn't kind.' She emerged from her sleeping-sack and put on the skirt she had discarded and her shoes. 'Lead on, Dish.'

Armstrong was somewhat bloody. Mrs Bradley looked at, without touching, his bleeding nose.

'What a nuisance you are, Mr Armstrong,' she said pleasantly. 'I wonder why you don't behave yourself better? I'm not interested in your wounds. From what I know already of your blood, I suppose it will clot quite nicely. You'd better go to sleep now, and wash off the mess in the morning.'

'I don't need to behave myself. I've got this whole joint cold,' said Armstrong, bubbling out the words and spitting and swearing.

Mrs Bradley went back thoughtful to her sleeping-bag, crawled into it, and very soon was asleep.

Morning came, but brought no sign of the oxen. Sir Rudri sweated as the day grew hotter, but not from the heat alone. Two or three times he climbed to the citadel to look over the

Argive plain in search of the sacrifice patiently plodding towards the altar which he had built at dawn near the grave-circle, and at intervals of fifteen minutes he sent the little boys up to look, and even lent them his field-glasses as a bribe. It made something for them to do, for the countryside was desolate, and even the postern stair, which the keeper good-naturedly lighted for them with candles – Armstrong having possession of all those belonging to the expedition – palled when they had been down it seventeen or eighteen times.

Megan and Cathleen spent the hours together, chatting, doing bits of needlework, reading a book aloud to each other by turns, and occasionally writing a two-handed letter to a mutual friend in England.

At times Sir Rudri would break off from his preoccupation with the plans for the sacrifice, and call upon Armstrong to take photographs. The Lion Gate, the entrance to the tomb, the grave-circle, the ruins of the citadel – what there were of them – and various other objects were carefully photographed, and Alexander Currie, bored, hot, and fly-eaten, could be heard, at intervals, demanding to know what point there was in photographing all that had ever been photographed before.

'You can buy it on a picture-postcard,' was his bitter and erroneous summing-up of the proceedings.

'Not these you won't be able to,' said Armstrong in a voice that was loud enough to carry to the ears of Alexander Currie, who turned to the young man, and said:

'I should be glad to know what you mean by that, my boy.'

'I dare say you would,' said Armstrong. 'But Sir Rudri would prefer that you didn't.'

Alexander Currie glowered at him, and then walked off. He sought Mrs Bradley and found her, in the full glare of the sun, dark glasses shielding her eyes, writing up her diary.

'Look here, what's going on, do you know?' he demanded.

'Yes, I think so, child.' She patted the bank whereon she sat. 'Sit down.'

'What, there? I'm nearly cooked to death as it is! For goodness' sake come into the shade and talk.'

'I like it here,' she answered, and directed her attention solely to her little note-book. Alexander unwillingly sat down.

'Now, what's all this?' he said. Mrs Bradley looked up at him. 'Try my sunshade,' she said. He opened it and sheltered under it gratefully.

'Well, to cut a long story short,' she began with great enjoyment, 'you shouldn't have upset poor Rudri.'

'I'm sorry about that.' He mopped his bald head, a gesture as much of remorse as of necessity.

'I think it turned his brain a bit, Mrs Bradley continued deliberately. 'He has schemed and planned to be even with you. He hasn't yet succeeded.'

'The snakes were obviously a plant.'

'Quite so. He knows you know that.'

'What about it, anyway?'

'That's all I know.' With an air of absorption very provoking to watch, she applied herself to her writing.

'How does Armstrong come into it?'

'I think he's going to fake some photographs, child.'

'Rudri wouldn't do that! He must be mad! He's got a freakish mind about all these things, but he's honest. I ought to know.'

'You ought,' said Mrs Bradley. Her tone was a rebuke. 'You traded on his honesty, didn't you, child?'

'It was only a joke,' said Alexander Currie.

'Very well. Now I'll tell you another joke, and mind you take it as well as you expected poor Rudri to take yours.'

'What are you talking about now?'

'Your daughter Cathleen.'

'Cathleen?'

'She is married to Ian MacNeill.' On the words, she took smelling-salts out of her pocket and held the unstoppered bottle underneath his nose. Alexander inhaled too deeply. His eyes filled. He choked, and then pushed the bottle away.

'That's enough! That's enough!' he said.

'Furthermore,' continued Mrs Bradley, 'it's just as well, perhaps. It has saved her two very unpleasant experiences out here, both of them on this trip.'

'But —'

Mrs Bradley waved his words away, and went on calmly but irresistibly:

'Both in connexion with this wretched boy Armstrong. The first Ian doesn't know about. It took place at Eleusis. The second he does know about. It took place here.'

'But —'

'Ian, like a good man and a husband, hit Armstrong. I think he will very soon give away the fact that he is Cathleen's husband' – she underlined the last word very slightly – 'and that is one of the reasons why I am telling you the news before Armstrong gets the opportunity to do so.'

'But —'

'Ian is a fine young man,' said Mrs Bradley firmly, 'and I shall get him a job with a commencing salary of three hundred and fifty a year. They will be making him a partner before he's thirty-five. A fine young man,' she repeated, taking off her sun-glasses and bending a hypnotic gaze upon Alexander's face. 'Don't you think so, dear child?'

'A MacNeill once beat me over a bargain,' Alexander muttered childishly.

'He must have been a very astute man,' said Mrs Bradley cordially. 'I shouldn't think there are many people who could possibly manage to do that.'

'You are right,' said Alexander, mollified. She nodded, her gaze now bright and bird-like. 'So now that we know you are prejudiced against poor Ian's name and not against himself, I think I had better call the young people here and you can give them a father's blessing. . . . Now don't be silly, child,' she added, as he began to fidget and mutter. 'What's done cannot be undone. They are married, and that's an end of it. You don't need to give your consent. It's been taken for granted. And,' she went on in gentler tones, with her skinny but compelling hand on his sleeve, 'I think poor Cathleen could bear to have you a little kind to her. You know, she's been living under very severe nervous strain for the past few months – clandestine meetings and scowled-upon correspondence with Ian MacNeill, a secret marriage – the sort of thing which you *must* know she would dislike – a breaking off of all true companionship with you. It has been the worst thing possible for her. Why, even I, with all that *I* know about such things' – she grinned disarmingly at him, as a cobra might possibly grin before it struck – 'disliked the poor child intensely when we met. Now, is that fair? Is it nice? Is it kind or fatherly? Do you want the poor girl to be haggard and old before her time? Do you want to wreck her beauty?'

'Oh, Lord!' said Alexander, now utterly reduced in spirit.

'Very well. Bring them along. I suppose I shall have to put up with it.'

'And mind you wish them happiness. You ought to be glad that you have such a sensible son-in-law,' said Mrs Bradley severely. Alexander looked at her, decided that she meant it, grinned, and wagged his bald head.

2

Gelert and Dick returned in the late afternoon without any cattle. Dmitri, they said, was in Corinth, doing what he could. Sir Rudri replied that in that case he would offer human sacrifice, and looked keenly at the three little boys. Kenneth and Stewart laughed, and, calling out, 'Here, I'll be it,' Kenneth advanced towards him. Sir Rudri waved him away.

'Not yet. Not yet,' he said. He had produced from his miscellaneous collection a broad-bladed, gleaming knife. The sun's rays falling on it turned it to a blinding sheet of flame. Ivor held his hand to his eyes, and, walking backwards and sideways, got close to Mrs Bradley and pulled her by the arm. She went away from the circle of listeners, and said :

'What is it, child?'

'Father,' said Ivor. 'I don't believe he's – I think he's – I mean, he isn't well.'

'I know. I expect it's the sun, child.'

'He means it about the human sacrifice, you know.'

'Yes, yes. But I think that Dmitri will come very soon with the oxen. Don't worry.'

But Dmitri did not turn up, and by sunset all was ready for the sacrifice. Dick and Gelert separately sought Mrs

Bradley, and commented on Sir Rudri's extraordinary manner, but nobody else seemed to notice that anything was amiss, and when all were assembled at the Lion Gate for the ceremony, and all the men had washed their hands in some of the precious bottled drinking water and had taken up handfuls of barley meal, Sir Rudri, putting out his hands, palms upwards, prayed to Apollo.

'One moment,' said Mrs Bradley, when he had finished praying. 'What about the billets of olive wood, child? We're not ready for the sacrifice yet.'

Sir Rudri opened his eyes and then blinked, like someone awakened from sleep.

'What did you say?' he asked.

'Billets of wood,' said Mrs Bradley, clearly, in a practical, pleasant voice. 'You've forgotten the olive wood, child. Don't you remember how, in the first book of the Iliad, when Odysseus takes back Chryseis to her father, the meat of the sacrifice was burnt on wood and over it the priest poured wine, whilst the young men beside him held their five-pronged forks? Where,' she continued, fixing him with bright black eyes, and speaking with greater sternness, 'are your billets of wood for the altar, your wine, and your five-pronged forks? Is this the manner in which you make sacrifice to the Far-Darter Apollo, you wretched, ignorant man?'

Sir Rudri, the Viking moustache having wilted with the heat of the day, looked perplexed, uncertain, and sad.

'It's true,' he said at last. 'Yet why do I think of the sacrifice of children? We don't need the pronged forks for children.'

'Children?' said Mrs Bradley. In the sunset light of the wild glen of the Atrides she stood before him like some ancient prophetess and waved her skinny arms and menaced him with her hideous, leering lips. Her black eyes, reddened, it seemed, by the last rays of the sun, the declining Apollo, held his, and he felt he could not take his gaze from hers. 'Children?' The word went echoing over the hill and against the thick walls, and shouted itself to silence over the plain. 'What of the young sons of Thyestes, who seduced the wife of Atreus? What of their spilt blood crying aloud for vengeance? What of the curse which descended to Agamemnon and to Orestes? Listen! Do you not hear?'

She pointed to the sculptured Lion Gate. Even the young men half-fearfully followed her thin yellow forefinger, as though they expected to see some manifestation of the ancient hatred there. But only a great bird, black against the light, perched there for half a moment before it gave a hoarse-throated, mournful cry, and flew off towards the other side of the road.

'It's gone to the tombs! It's gone to the tombs!' said Cathleen. Sir Rudri stood staring after it. Then he rubbed his arm across his eyes, turned with an apologetic smile, and said in his normal tones:

'My dear Beatrice, my dear Alexander, I beg your pardon. I've been losing my sense of proportion.'

'We mustn't, any of us, do that,' said Alexander Currie. 'Cathleen, my lass, go and bring me that scallywag husband of yours. Rudri, these two have got married without my leave or consent!'

After the diversion thus created, Mrs Bradley took Gelert aside.

'I should like to have your father under observation, dear child, but at present that is impossible in the sense I mean. He needs a rest.'

'He needs to get his own back on old Currie,' said Gelert.

'That would get rid of his troubles quicker than anything. Pity those serpents were a flop. The Eleusis do was good, and almost took us all in.'

'The second Iacchus, you mean?'

'Yes. Armstrong, of course. It's a nuisance about that blighter, but he had to be in on the ground-floor because of his looks, you know. I believe he's managed to get on father's nerves. The old boy was on the point of confiding in me this morning, and then Armstrong came up with some yap about the photographs. We'd just got as far as mentioning his name and that was all. I expect he heard us, and that's why he came and butted in.'

Mrs Bradley nodded.

'Perhaps Ephesus will solve all our difficulties,' she said.

'You won't let father go to Ephesus?'

'I don't see how I am to stand in his way, dear child.'

'But he's perfectly bats, you know. I mean, if you hadn't stepped in and fobbed him off just now, he'd have clawed one of those kids for a sacrifice. I was rolling up my sleeves to dot him one when you stepped in and declaimed your little piece. Congratulations, by the way. You ought to have been the original Pythoness of Delphi.'

'Perhaps I was,' said Mrs Bradley modestly. 'What do you think about Cathleen and Ian?'

'Same as I did before, worse luck. I say, can you think of anything I could do instead of going back to Athens just now? Megan subbed up the money, but I don't feel like meeting the people I know until the thing has blown over.'

'I think you had better go back. You have nothing to fear. Is there a baby, by the way?'

'Good Lord, no!' said Gelert aghast. 'It's only a species of breach of promise, or something. I wouldn't care, only that rotter Armstrong knows all about it. It happens to be his half-sister, do you see, and that's torn it, of course, completely. He's got me where he wants me, damn his eyes! He hasn't put the screw on yet, but he will. And then it won't be twenty or thirty quid!'

'I see,' said Mrs Bradley. She went back to the little boys and watched them wriggle into their sleeping-sacks. She placed her own sack near at hand, and sat on it. The party were spending the night in the entrance between the great walls which bordered the path that led to the Lion Gate. Night darkened the path over which, after Troy, Agamemnon's chariot had passed. The gateway, topped by its vast and weathered lintel, stood open now, bereft of its great wooden door, and with nothing to show that the great door had ever existed except for the pivot holes left in the stone to hang it by. Night hid the little iron gate which the keeper had had instructions to leave open, but, ghostly, and guarding still their tapering pillar, the stone lions, lighter in colour than the vast, surrounding walls, gazed outwards over the heads of the trysting pilgrims. Suddenly, on the walls that looked over the Argive plain, there appeared the tall figure of a woman. A garment like a great cloak was gathered about her, and she looked statuesque and brooding, more than life-size, silhouetted against the sky.

'Clytemnestra!' thought Mrs Bradley, holding her breath and not knowing that she did.

The woman stood there, motionless, for four or five minutes. Then she climbed down, and came out through the gate, and Mrs Bradley perceived that it was Megan.

3

A good deal later Mrs Bradley went to sleep. An hour after this, Dmitri returned to Mycenae. He was driving a slat-ribbed cow, and the first indication the camp received of his coming took the form of a bellow of protest from his charge, which then fell over Sir Rudri, who had elected to sleep with his sack across the centre of the path. Sir Rudri's exclamations of fear and annoyance helped to wake the rest of the pilgrims. Dmitri, without a word, tossed the end of the cord by which he had led the cow over a spike of the modern iron fence in which the little gate which led to the grave-circle was fixed, and lay down, with a low moan, in the fairway. Here he went to sleep. Mrs Bradley switched on her torch, went over to Dmitri and looked at him, and then went over to the cow, which could not lie down, even if it desired to do so, because the rope by which it was tethered was too short. It mooed reproachfully at her as she came up. She unhitched it and, calming it as well as she could with a Homeric quotation referring to ox-eyed Hera, the wife of Zeus, she took off her stockings, tied them together, and fastened the rope thus made to the end of the animal's tether. Then she hitched it on to the fence again. The cow, without ado, reclined on the stony ground, lifted its head and gazed at the thick, soft blackness of the crumbling, hilly bank on the right of the doorway, wedged itself firmly against the Cyclopean wall, and apparently followed the example of its erstwhile captor and guide. Satisfied that both man and beast were asleep, Mrs Bradley returned to her place, but scarcely had she settled herself when a large, dim shape, voiced like the leader of the party, sidled up and said, in a whisper which startled her :

'Beatrice, who went into the excavations just now?'

'Just now, Rudri, dear child?'

'Yes. Somebody slipped through the gateway just before the wretched animal nearly blew my hair off my head. I watched him go. That's why I didn't see the cow.'

'But you must have *heard* the cow,' Mrs. Bradley observed.

'Yes, yes! But I wasn't thinking of cows,' Sir Rudri testily replied. 'The thing is, what are they up to? What the *devil* are they up to?' he amended. 'It's very dangerous by night. They might fall into the deepest part of the excavations and kill themselves. Easily they might. I'd better go and see what is happening.'

But before he could do so there was a sudden scream, a torn-throated, masculine scream, of horrid surprise and terror.

'He's fallen in,' said Sir Rudri, not, Mrs Bradley thought, without satisfaction. She was on her feet and had tied up her shoes in a trice, and together they made for the gateway. The cow snorted suddenly as they passed her, but she did not attempt to rise. Mrs Bradley's torch was powerful. She had brought spare batteries with her, and had fitted one that evening. The bright light showed them the path. They ran, stumbling on the uneven, stony surface, and calling as they ran. No answer came from the shaft graves. Except for a wind which came at them with fury and then died down, there seemed nothing but lifelessness anywhere.

Mrs Bradley and Sir Rudri leaned over the stone-slabbed wall and shone the torch on to the blackness of the depths below them.

'I see him,' said Mrs Bradley. She gave the torch to Sir Rudri. 'Keep the light placed where it is.' She left him and groped her way down the easiest slope into the treasureless graves. She had a box of matches in her pocket. Sir Rudri, training the torch on to the bundle of grey below, could watch her progress and count the matches she used.

'Don't set the vegetation alight, if you come to any,' he cried.

By this time the cow, the scream, and the activities of Mrs Bradley and their leader had roused the camp. Guided by Gelert, who also had a torch, they came stumbling through the gateway and up the path. Gelert made his way down to Mrs Bradley, and held his torch whilst she knelt by the injured man. It was Ronald Dick.

'There's nothing broken. He's come round,' said Mrs. Bradley. 'Bruises and shock, and lucky for him it's no worse. Up you get, dear child. You must look where you're going next time.'

'I should think he walked in his sleep,' said Stewart to Ivor. 'He's been poking about in the grave-circle all day long.'

The little boys were preparing to descend into the pit when they were collared by Sir Rudri and by Megan, and were instructed to remain where they were. Armstrong improved the occasion by cuffing Stewart, who retaliated by swinging round and butting him in the belly. Ian, who had joined the party, took the clout that was meant for Stewart on a large forearm, and returned it with such interest that Armstrong, with a noise between a gasp and a gurgle, was jolted against the stone slab which bordered the path on which he stood. Collecting himself, he withdrew from the dangerous vicinity of Ian and the boys.

Between them, Gelert and Mrs Bradley got Ronald Dick to his feet and persuaded him that he was well enough to scramble out of the tomb. Sir Rudri, who was thoroughly exasperated by the whole occurrence, said shortly that he should be glad of an explanation in the morning. He then warned the party not to tread on the cow, and fell over her himself, she having elected to transfer herself to the blackness of the archway and lie down in the very centre of the path. The cow, with an inquisitional bellow, scrambled to her feet. Sir Rudri scrambled to his. It was Dish who came forward and moved the animal out of the narrow gateway.

The rest of the night was peaceful. Mrs Bradley woke, as she had intended to do, at dawn, and, treading carefully, passed the sleepers and the cow, went through the iron gateway under the arch, and explored the grave-circle, its surroundings, and the acropolis above. She looked abroad, over the misty and indeterminate landscape which soon the sun would reveal as the Argive plain. She looked to the shadowy mountains, dark purple, and massed like cloud, and, nearer, to the citadel of Larissa, and thought of the burning beacons, heralds of the fall of Troy. By night the place had seemed no wilder than and not as lonely as many English country districts she had stayed in. The great walls had been companionable; the cow a pantomime animal; the little adventure of Dick's tumbling into the pit an incident far removed from the terrors which lived in the plays of Aeschylus. But at dawn, and, even more, she knew, beneath the hot noonday sun, Mycenae came into her own. Her tragedy and her greatness loomed like battle on the landscape. The walls enclosed the dead, and the great excavations, where Schliemann had kissed the gold death-mask of Agamemnon, yawned like the graves that they were.

She stood there a long time, watching the day grow

brighter. There was a slight sound near her, and Dick came limping to join her. They stood, without speaking, ten minutes or so, and then at last he said :

'I've got the key of the treasury. Come with me to unlock it.'

'I should like to do that, child,' Mrs Bradley replied. Soberly, not speaking to one another, they walked to the iron gateway, passed underneath the lions' arch, followed the path to the road, and walked down it towards the tomb.

'Thank you for coming to my rescue last night,' said Dick.

'Who pushed you?' Mrs Bradley inquired in an artless, careless tone. She had seen the marks on the stony ground. He flushed.

'It was Armstrong, I think. I don't know where he could have come from. I am sure that nobody followed me through the gate.'

'What were you doing there, child, in the dead of the night?'

'I think I might be psychic. I wanted to see what would happen.'

'Did anything happen?'

'No. I was afraid.'

'To go up on to the acropolis?'

'Yes. So I stood there hesitating, just where the wall is broken away, and somebody came behind and shoved me. I cried out because I was startled.'

'Yes, I see. What makes you think it was Armstrong.'

'He's the only one who'd do a thing like that.'

'We don't know that, child, do we?'

'No. Will you unlock the entrance gate?' They had crossed the ditch and ascended the rough, steep bank. Soon they came upon the entrance to the beehive tomb. Mrs Bradley waved the key away, so he kept it, and unlocked the gate, and they walked towards the gaping mouth of the treasury.

'Do you mind waiting just a second until I whistle?' was the young man's strange request. He disappeared into the darkness of the massive conical structure, a shaft sunk into the hill and vaulted over by means of courses laid flat and their inner surface cut to the shape of the dome; and Mrs Bradley turned her back on the Treasury of Atreus and waited for him to emerge. He was less than a moment gone. It seemed to her that he reappeared directly with something cupped in his hands.

'Look,' he said. 'I want to show it to somebody. That's what I found.'

It was gold, earth-encrusted – a fattish, pale bit of metal, about seven inches by four, beaten out in designs of fish. 'What do you think of that?'

Mrs Bradley gazed at the wonder, and shook her head in congratulatory amazement.

'I don't believe it,' she said. 'Cretan origin, if it's genuine, but I don't, as I say, believe it.'

'That's what I feel about it, too. It's like the gold plate that they found here when they excavated the grave-circle. How do you think they missed it? And where can I keep it hidden until we get back to Athens? I don't want anyone else to see it until the museum gets it and puts it on show. Already, I rather fancy, somebody knows I've got it, and I found it only yesterday.'

'Presented by Mr Ronald Dick – I know,' said Mrs Bradley. She and Dick looked again at the beaten gold.

'I know some collectors who'd give a fortune for this,'

said Dick. 'I wish I knew where I could keep it. I wouldn't have some of these people see it for anything. Sir Rudri is horribly immoral – I remember him when we dug up a barrow in Devonshire, and I shall always believe that that statuette of his – the Roman one —'

'Came from Pompeii,' said Mrs Bradley. She considered him, her head on one side. 'And Alexander Currie played that nasty trick on Rudri, and Gelert is in need of money, and Ian can't afford his college fees, and Armstrong's capable of anything – even of impersonating a god and of pushing a mortal into a grave – yes, yes!' She then cackled harshly, but with sincere amusement.

'It's all very well,' said Dick. Mrs Bradley waved her claw.

'Take heart, dear child. I have a botanical case which should meet your purpose exactly. I will lend it you. But tell me why Armstrong should come behind you by night and push you into the excavations like that?'

Dick took off his glasses and wiped them.

'I think I annoy him,' he said. 'I believe I give him a slight feeling of inferiority.'

He was so obviously in earnest that Mrs Bradley, adjusting her expression to fit this fact, pursed her lips and nodded solemnly.

'I see, dear child,' she said. They returned to the base and she found the botanical case and gave it to him.

'I wish you'd take charge of it,' he said. 'I'm nervous about Armstrong. He might already know something. I wouldn't trust him. He was trying to search me, I'm sure, before he shoved me into these graves.'

'I must take care not to explore the grave-circle by night,' said Mrs Bradley, receiving back the case and its priceless contents. She put it in the bottom of her sleeping-sack. Armstrong and Dmitri, who had placed their sacks at the bend in the path where it led down on to the road which was not visible from the Lion Gate, came strolling up about a quarter of an hour later, and found her reading a volume of modern poetry.

'Breakfast?' said Armstrong. Dmitri bowed and smiled. Mrs Bradley patted the coat on which she had seated herself.

'Sit down, Mr Armstrong, and tell me all the gossip of the night.'

'What night?'

'Last night.'

'Was there any gossip?'

'Mr Dick fell into the excavations and nearly broke his neck.'

'Oh that!' said Armstrong. He laughed, lifting his flawless head to look up at the lions above the lintel. 'I know nothing about it. What was he doing there, anyway?'

'He was practising mediumship,' Mrs Bradley replied very solemnly.

'Oh? Raising spooks? I say, Dmitri —' He addressed the Greek youth lispingly. Dmitri nodded and smiled.

'I also,' he said, addressing himself to Mrs Bradley, 'I also am immoral with women.'

'I have no doubt of it,' replied Mrs Bradley, in the tones of congratulation he seemed to demand.

'The English,' said Dmitri, seating himself and clasping thin hands round his knees, 'are like the Greeks in all things, and I admire them. It is the English and the Germans, and, to some extent, the mobile French, who have made the Greeks what we are. I do not remember the Turks' – he spat conscientiously – 'not even in hatred nor in horror. We are cruel, too. Cruelty, it is of man. Also the politics. In England you are politics in mind, and affect not. In Greece, too, we read the newspapers always – all the time.'

'I have noticed it,' said Mrs Bradley, cordially.

'Of a quite. We, too, are the sport, but we love more seriously. The Stadion, good. We the patriotic. We imitate with respect the old Greeks. Do you like my country?'

'Yes, I like it. But it's time that something was done about the water-supply, don't you think?'

'But we make,' replied Dmitri, wounded. 'There is good water in Athens now. We show to improvement.'

'Good, good,' replied Mrs Bradley. Her voice, which she had purposely pitched louder, stirred the sleepers near at hand. First one dark cocoon, then another, moved, expanded, and reared up. Soon the company was out of its sleeping-sacks, clamouring to Dish for food.

After breakfast Dick sought her out and asked to be given his Mycenean gold.

'Hardly fair to thrust the responsibility on you,' he said with a laugh.

'I should give it to Megan to mind,' said Mrs Bradley.

CHAPTER EIGHT

'And, who pray, may they be?
The Initiated.
Yes, by Zeus, and I'm the ass who celebrates the mysteries.
But I'm not going to endure this much longer.'

I

PUBLIC opinion being against the sacrifice of the cow, who proved to be disconcertingly friendly and of almost maudlin sociability, Sir Rudri reverted to his first idea of the goats.

'It is unnecessary,' said Mrs Bradley composedly. 'You should make some clay cows and some statuettes of Hera, Rudri, dear child. So much nicer and so much less messy than the sacrifice of animals,' she added coaxingly. Sir Rudri pondered.

'We haven't any clay,' he pointed out.

'Well, where did the original clay come from, dear child? It wasn't, surely, looted from Crete.'

'*We'll* scout for some clay,' said Ivor, hopefully. The little boys, glad of occupation, scampered away. The sun was not yet hot enough to be enervating.

'Terra-cotta,' said Gelert, who had returned to the languid manner which had been evident in him at first. 'And the springs are bound to be dry, I would say, at this time of year.'

'Never mind! Never mind!' said Alexander Currie. 'It's something for those laddies to do. Leave them be.' He broke off, noticing Ronald Dick. 'Ah, how are the bruises this morning? You ought to have warned us you walked in your sleep, you know.'

Dick flushed. He was tired of reciting his réason for having gone through to the excavations. It had been received sympathetically by Cathleen, amusedly by everybody else, including Megan. He was feeling very unhappy. Sir Rudri also seemed miserable. He gazed feelingly at the cow, now referred to by everyone as Io in memory of the priestess of Hera of that name who was transformed into a cow, and then gazed anxiously at the heights whereon the citadel stood, as though seeking counsel and instruction from those who no longer could give it. Mrs Bradley watched him carefully. There was no doubt that his mind was precariously balanced between pseudo-scholarly enthusiasm and some more obvious form of insanity. Sometimes he seemed to incline the one way, sometimes the other, but always it seemed to her, an unprejudiced observer, that he dipped deeper each time towards madness and that the vessel of his mind found greater difficulty now in righting itself than it had done before they left Athens. She had not liked the Iacchus business at Eleusis; still less had she liked the serpent business at Epidaurus; and least of all did she like this preoccupation with the idea of bloody sacrifice at Mycenae.

The legends of the Atridae hung brooding over the heavy, broken walls, about the Lion Gate, and round the unguarded graves. The dark passion of Clytemnestra, the anguish of young Orestes, made heavy the lowering atmosphere, soaked beyond bearing already, with the heat of dead air before a storm.

Sir Rudri was not her only source of anxiety. The little boys, bored, and tired that morning for the first time since the pilgrims had left Athens, had been by turns listless and tiresome. Alerander Currie had been severely attacked by flies, and one of the bites showed signs of turning septic. He announced that the quality of the food had had an adverse effect upon the quality of his blood. He said this peevishly.

Armstrong, too, was a perpetual menace to the general good-temper and forbearance, and Gelert had given up any attempt at cheerfulness, and all the morning had seemed determined to irritate his father and Alexander Currie, to upset Megan, and to pick another quarrel with Armstrong. He also asked why on earth they were all still hanging about. This from a young man who wished to remain away from Athens as long as he possibly could, seemed to Mrs Bradley unreasonable.

As she was indulging in this contemplative review of the party, the manservant Dish came up to speak to her.

'Mam,' he began without preamble. 'I should wish to explain once more that I can't go on no longer with that there Mr Armstrong. I can't put up with his insolence no longer, and it isn't right I should try.'

'Very well, Dish,' replied Mrs Bradley, willing to placate somebody, if it would ease the general tension. 'What's the matter this time?'

'Finding is keeping,' Dish informed her mysteriously. 'And what I finds is my own business, so long as it don't belong to one of the party. And it's no odds to no one if I don't choose to say what I found, nor to put it on public show. But Mr Armstrong, he's on at me all the time, to know what I picked up, and to let him see it, and photograph it, and let him make me an offer for it, and show it to Mr Currie, what, he says, collects old things. And I ain't going to do it. I don't want to, and if he goes on poking his nose in my business I want to know where I stands. That's what, mam, with all respects and begging your pardon.'

'What did you find?' asked Mrs Bradley, deducing that the man was willing to give her this information although he had refused it to Armstrong. 'Don't tell me *you've* discovered a museum specimen, Dish?'

Dish looked about him. Mrs Bradley rose. Armstrong, who did not seem to notice the intense, oppressive heat of the midday sun, was playing clock-golf with stones and a crook-handled walking-stick, and doing it very well. Megan was with him. In a minute they went out of sight, in search of the 'ball' which Armstrong had lofted neatly across a little dry watercourse. Dick, who was loitering behind them, still limping slightly from his fall, looked after them, then, turning his head and seeing the other two, Dish and Mrs Bradley, he shrugged his shoulders and strolled away with a dragging movement of his injured foot, until he, too, was out of sight.

'Mr Dick has found something, too,' said Mrs Bradley.

'Gold?'

'Yes, I think it's gold, Dish.'

'Two of us found something gold? Hardly makes sense, mam, does it, when you think how them graves must have been worked over, like.'

'I *said* I didn't believe it,' said Mrs Bradley equably.

'Isn't it gold, then, mam?'

'I've no doubt about its being gold, Dish, but I think it's modern gold. I shouldn't trouble about presenting it to a museum. Sell it for the price it will bring you when you get back to England.'

'I don't understand you, mam. Who'd leave modern gold about in a place like this, do you think?'

'That, Dish, is a question which I don't propose to answer. Are you fond of Sir Rudri, Dish?'

'He's been a very generous employer, mam. And Lady Hopkinson, she's done me proud. I'd do a lot for her.'

'Good. Well, my advice is, keep the gold if you want to, and keep your mouth shut. That's what Mr Dick is going to do.'

She walked away briskly, regardless of the sunshine as a lizard, and caught up Dick, who was walking towards Charváti.

'Child,' she said, 'I've a disappointment for you. You are not the only person in this assembly to find gold objects in the excavations, I hear.'

'More gold? Impossible!' said Dick.

'I am glad you think that,' said Mrs Bradley dryly. 'I don't know what Dish has found,' she added, after she had repeated her conversation with the man, 'but, as you say, it is —' – she did not repeat 'impossible', a word not at home in her vocabulary, but substituted 'most unlikely'.

'Sir Rudri!' said Dick, alighting on the name like an eagle pouncing on a rabbit. Mrs Bradley nodded.

'I shall be very glad to get him back to Athens,' she remarked. 'By the way, child, I've stolen his sacrificial knife. I thought it wise to do so.'

'He has never got over that trick that Mr Currie played on him,' said Dick. 'I do think that was too bad. People ought not to make other people look fools.' He jerked his head to indicate the direction from which they had come. 'Did you see that blonde beast with Megan – with Miss Hopkinson?' he asked, leaping, with the sureness of a chamois, on to the crag of his troubles.

'I did,' said Mrs Bradley, noting the connexion between this question and the general statement that people ought not to make other people look fools. 'Don't worry, child. We're all a little bored and hot and fractious to-day, I think, Megan as well as the rest. She doesn't like Armstrong at all.

She's probably working up to have a scene with you. It ought to stand you in good stead, child. Exercise your talent in such matters, and make sure that you end up with a delightful reconciliation, complete with proposal of marriage.'

'But I don't stand a chance if that – if Armstrong is going to compete,' wailed poor little Dick, from the depths of a cowardly nature. 'He's so awfully good-looking, and he's – I mean, I've seen him with girls – and, of course, he's as thick as thieves with Sir Rudri nowadays.' He dropped his voice, his troubles forgotten for the moment. 'You can understand, from what we all know of the nonsense about the second Iacchus, and the fiasco of the snakes at Epidaurus, that Armstrong has only to supply the proofs of all that spoofing to Mr Currie to make Sir Rudri look a bigger fool than ever. The trouble is, he can do it. He gets photographs of everything that happens. Of course, he's wizard with a camera. Sir Rudri thinks he's only taken the official photographs – if you can call them that – to prove the Iacchus business and the snakes of Aesculapius – the phenomena, as Sir Rudri called them in my hearing the other day – are genuine. But Armstrong took other photographs – he told me so – and has only got to demonstrate what beastly fakes the others are to show Sir Rudri up. I can't bear him to have Megan! Even if I don't get her – and I shan't – I know I shan't – I've never yet had anything I wanted – I'd do anything to prevent his having her.'

'There's not the slighest chance of his marrying Megan. You wait until we get to Athens – or even to Corinth – I'm going to telegraph to Marie Hopkinson,' said Mrs Bradley, cheerfully. 'Come, child. Let us return. Lunch must be on the table.

'Lunch! The table!' said Dick, with a hollow groan.

Like the other young men he was by this time suffering from shortage of food. Mrs Bradley sighed and shook her head. She herself, if it was necessary, could exist upon an amount of food which would cause a sparrow to look round for more, but her heart bled for the young and the hungry.

'We could take one of the cars into Nauplia for a meal,' she suggested, but Dick shook his head, determined to spite his stomach as Megan had broken his heart.

Suddenly he said:

'You knew that bit of gold? It's gone. I'm sure he's got it. I can't make a fuss out here, but I'm going to as soon as we get back.'

'Are you sure it's gone? I wish you had left it with me.'

'I took it out of your case and buried it. It's been dug up again, but nothing's been said.'

'Armstrong?'

'It must be. Although, Sir Rudri – I wouldn't trust him, either, over a find like that.'

2

'I can't see why on earth we're to spend another night here,' Megan said. 'It's quite ridiculous, father.'

'But nothing has happened here yet. That damned fool Dick upset the auguries by falling into that hole last night and scaring the cow,' said Sir Rudri. Dick went white and stood up.

'You'd better take that back, sir, if you please. I didn't fall – I was pushed.'

A simultaneous shriek of laughter broke from the three little boys. Dick glared at them as though he could have strangled them, and walked away from the company up to the citadel in the heights. Here he sat down and suddenly burst into tears. The heat, the terrible feeling of oppression due to the approaching storm, his disappointment over the gold he had found, his distress about Megan and Armstrong, combined to unman him completely. Suddenly there was a scurrying sound. Cathleen plumped down beside him and put her arm on his.

'Oh, Ronald!' she said. 'I *am* sorry. Sir Rudri must be mad. And Megan's acting the fool! Don't take any notice. She'll get over it. She can't like Armstrong, really.'

'Sir Rudri *is* mad,' Mrs Bradley was saying at the same time to Alexander Currie, as they sat in the shade of a Cyclopean wall after lunch. 'Has he tried to persuade you to hunt in the excavations?'

'Now that you mention it,' Alexander answered, 'I did receive some impression that he held the opinion that there were treasures still to be found here. I said it was impossible, and that, anyway, it was much too hot to dig.'

'You've got to be a good man over all this,' said Mrs Bradley. She patted him encouragingly on the shoulder. Alexander bore this patiently.

'He can't go to Ephesus,' he said. 'He isn't fit.'

'Ephesus!' said Mrs Bradley. 'I hope my responsibility will end at Athens, child.'

'He's determined to go to Ephesus. I expect we shall have to give in. It wouldn't do to thwart him. By the way, did you ever hear what became of all those vipers?'

'They are still in the locked tin box. The children feed them under my supervision. Sir Rudri, I think, has forgotten all about them.'

'And the snakes that became so much attached to us?'

'They are still in the sanctuary, child. The warden

offered no objection. The last of them that I saw was when he was feeding them with goats' milk out of an earthenware saucer. It made a charming scene,' she continued, visualizing it again, 'and was completely in keeping, let us hope, with the spirit of the history of the valley.'

'Well, what are we going to do about him?' Alexander inquired.

'I'm going to put him right. I don't think it's anything more than a —'

'Don't be technical. I don't understand the jargon. Good luck to your efforts, anyway. Poor Rudri! If I had thought he would take it so badly or remember it against me so long, I'd never have played the trick on him that I did. They're queer people, the Welsh.'

'So are the Scots,' said Mrs Bradley tartly. Alexander looked at her and grinned. 'How's that bite of yours getting on?' she inquired, abruptly changing the subject. She unfastened her portable medicine chest and treated the inflamed and swollen leg. 'I should not walk about, child. If that gets any worse, one of the chauffeurs must drive you into Corinth.'

'What I want is whisky,' said Alexander Currie simply.

'A good idea,' replied she, putting away her lint and bottles neatly. 'We will give the job to Gelert. He needs a little change.' She hailed him. He was seated in the shadow of another bit of the wall, and came over to her when she called.

'I can't think why those cruise tourists haven't shown up here yet,' he remarked as he came within distance for conversation.

'They were before us,' Mrs Bradley answered. 'They

came straight away here on the afternoon of the day they came upon us in the morning at Epidaurus.'

'Thank God. Then we shan't be seeing them again.' He seated himself on about three inches of Mrs Bradley's coat, which was spread on the ground, and looked interestedly at the grave-circle. 'Is it true that some of the party have been making finds here?' he asked. Mrs Bradley grinned.

'It was quite like a treasure hunt,' she remarked. Gelert, who was intelligent, lifted his eyebrows.

'Father again?' he inquired. 'Good Lord! The man ought to be put in a home! He must be absolutely cracked.'

'So much so,' said Mrs Bradley lucidly,' that whilst you go off in one of the cars and find whisky, and, if you like, some Fortnum and Mason food, I shall conduct your father to Epidaurus, and Aesculapius there will work a miraculous cure.' Contrary to the expectation of Gelert, who was in the habit of making little bets with himself as to the kinds of things she would laugh at, on this occasion she did not so much as smile.

'I wish he would cure my leg,' said Alexander Currie.

'Let us give him the chance. I may need your help with Sir Rudri,' Mrs Bradley replied immediately.

No help, however, was needed. By three in the afternoon, Sir Rudri, having been shown Alexander's inflamed and swollen leg, remarked that it was a judgement on Alexander, that he had heard of legs being amputated for less, and that some people's blood was continually out of order because they were accustomed to eat and drink to excess. Eventually, having talked himself into a good temper, he proposed that the party should return to Epidaurus for a cure.

'Not the whole party,' Mrs Bradley put in. 'Just Alexander Currie, you, and myself.'

'And who is to manage Armstrong?' demanded Sir Rudri, staring at both of them from underneath beetling brows. 'Gelert's gone hopping off in one of the cars on some tom-fool errand of his own, and young Dick's worse than useless.'

'He doesn't *sound* exactly insane, you know, does he?' said Alexander Currie, when Sir Rudri had gone off to order Armstrong to accompany them to Epidaurus.

'No. But I didn't want Armstrong with us, child. Never mind. Perhaps we can lock him in the museum when we get there.'

But this idea was never put into practice. Alexander Currie's leg was so seriously inflamed that at six o'clock that evening Ian, Cathleen, Mrs Bradley, and Alexander himself were driving towards Corinth as rapidly as Ian's imperfect knowledge of the road would allow. Fortunately it was not very far. It was an interesting drive. At the apex of the Argive Plain the road ran for three miles through a defile not more, in places, than eighteen feet wide. On either side of the road the great walls of the mountains Hagios Elias and Zara towered two thousand feet above the travellers.

At Corinth, Doctor Emil St Pierre, whom Mrs Bradley had known for thirty years, took Alexander and Alexander's leg into his expert care, and the other three went to stay at a hotel. In the morning they inquired after the leg, and Mrs Bradley inspected it. The inflammation was subsiding, and the swelling had disappeared.

'It is necessary that he should rest his leg a little,' the doctor announced. 'He shall join you in Athens in a day or two.'

The others obtained a supply of bread, some cheeses,

honey, grapes, and bottles of wine, and returned to Mycenae to provide the rest of the party with more palatable food than that which they had recently enjoyed.

Sir Rudri appeared to be his usual self. The little boys, however, were disconsolate, although they attacked the new bread, the honey, the cheese, and the grapes with the hearty enthusiasm for which Mrs Bradley had hoped.

'Somebody's pinched the cow,' said Kenneth later.

'Most regrettable,' said Armstrong, throwing back his head in silent laughter, a disconcerting habit he had formed since the second day of the expedition, Mrs Bradley's casebook informed her.

'Mr Armstrong,' said Mrs Bradley, 'where's the cow?'

'How do I know?' said Armstrong. He was sitting next to Megan, and occasionally their fingers intertwined. There had been no storm. A high wind had blown it away. The air, although hot, was not oppressive. The spirits of the company gradually began to improve.

'Bags I we trail the cow,' suggested Ivor. The other little boys agreed. Having found her hoof-prints on a sandy patch, they trailed her over the hillside and on to the road, and up the farther bank. In a quarter of an hour they were back at the base. Kenneth looked mysterious and excited. Ivor looked pale and as though he were going to be sick. Stewart said solemnly :

'We've found the cow, what's left of her.'

Mrs Bradley thought of the sacrificial knife, but it was still among her belongings, locked up in her twenty-inch despatch-case. She went with the boys to the cow. Io's throat had been cut according to Homeric tradition, and with the still sticky pool of her coagulated blood some hundreds of flies were engrossed. A vulture, perched on her head, was so gorged that it did not make any attempt to fly. Her entrails, frankly displayed in the shape of a Greek letter A, were stinking to heaven in the sunshine, and were covered with every carnivorous insect known to Greek entomology.

Mrs Bradley inspected the relics of Io with scientific detachment, and slowly shook her head.

'A for Acrisius, A for Atreus, A for Agamemnon, A for Aegisthus, A for Alexander, A for Armstrong, A for ass,' she observed, when they all had removed themselves from Io's unpleasant vicinity. 'Now I wonder which was intended, and by whom?' No answer seemed forthcoming to these questions. Sir Rudri and Dick, escorted separately to the spot, pronounced themselves mystified, shocked, disgusted, and unwilling to believe that one of the party had killed the cow for amusement. Armstrong insisted upon photographing the remains as a preliminary to burying them, but it was Megan who borrowed Mrs Bradley's parasol and a spanner out of the car and proceeded to inter the entrails. Cathleen had refused to inspect them, and nobody – for Dish refused his services, and Dmitri turned green at the smell – offered to assist the resolute girl in her labours.

Armstrong came back with his camera over his shoulder, and smacked the palms of his hands together, looking rather pleased with himself. Mrs Bradley gave Megan some wine for which she thanked her. But, raising the cup in the air, she poured the wine in a great splash on to the dusty ground. Mrs Bradley raised her eyebrows, but poured her some more. This time she drank. A little later she wandered away and found Armstrong asleep in the shade, his god's face pillowed on his arm. Megan seated herself beside him, and with the parasol, which she retained by inadvertence, she began to trace on the earth. When Mrs Bradley came that way a little later, she found both Armstrong and Megan asleep, with the bitterly brooding Dick watching jealously from the shadow of the wall. A peacock – unmistakable outline – emblem of Hera, the patroness of Io – was drawn in the dust in the curve made between Armstrong's head and his knees.

Mrs Bradley climbed to the citadel in the fierce afternoon glare, and looked across the Argive Plain to where the hill of Larissa, marking the site of Argos, stood high above the rest of the landscape, demonstrating its medieval fort. Of ancient Argos there was nothing to be seen. She could not see, either, the busy modern town.

She contemplated the acropolis of Mycenae on which she stood. Even the ruins of the sixth-century temple, built on ruins a thousand years older than itself, had been almost obliterated by time and destructive mankind. She murmured as she gazed, the lament of Alpheus:

> 'The goatherds pointed at thee. And I heard an old man say,
> "The giant-builded-city, the golden — here it lay." '

After this she went down to referee a game of noughts and crosses over which Ivor and Kenneth were quarrelling shrilly as they scrawled, like ancient Euclid, lines and circles, nothing but lines and circles, in the dust.

Stewart squatted beside her. After a bit he said:

'It was Armstrong, wasn't it?'

'I think it must have been, child,' Mrs Bradley responded.

'Why did he do it, do you think?'

'I expect it was a combination of greed and sadism, child. The two sometimes go hand in hand.'

Stewart detached the one he could understand.

'He *is* greedy. He always stuffs food in his mouth when there's plenty, and lots of it drops on the floor.'

'Always?'

'Oh yes,' broke in Ivor, looking up. 'He did it several times at home, and mother won't have him to dinner any more, he's so messy.'

'Filthy of him to be messy with poor old Io, though,' remarked Stewart. Ivor looked at Mrs Bradley expectantly.

'But it was Sir Rudri himself who wanted to kill the cow,' Kenneth pointed out as he took advantage of Ivor's momentary distraction to fill up two or three squares with some hurried noughts.

'Hey, rub those out!' yelled Ivor, returning to things of importance. 'You filthy cheat and cad! It wasn't your turn!'

'Don't be an ass, man. It was!'

'It wasn't, I tell you!' He rose to his feet and scuffled his sandalled feet all over the noughts and crosses. 'I shan't play any more games. You're just a low, double-crossing swindler, you beastly ass!'

'Oh, am I?' said Kenneth, hitting him in the face. 'Take that, you lousy little cissy!'

The next minute they were hard at it, Stewart and Mrs. Bradley moving back a little out of the rising dust.

'Ivor can win if he keeps his head,' said Stewart. 'He's a better boxer than Kenneth. Feet! Feet!' he added, as a coach instructing Rugby football forwards. 'This is a very poor show. They can both do better than this,' he added confidentially.

'And what about you?' Mrs Bradley politely inquired.

'I'm training to be a professional,' Stewart replied. 'At least, that's one of my ideas. Oh, step in and finish him off, you silly clown!' he shrieked in exasperation as Ivor, lunging, missed Kenneth by several inches and, losing his balance, blundered on after the blow. Mrs Bradley, at this point, walked in and firmly separated the combatants, holding the shirt of each in a muscular grip of which neither had believed her capable, but saying nothing for fear of imbibing the dust which hung like gun-smoke over the whole arena.

'Now let's sit down and finish the grapes,' she said, when the dust had died and the panting breath of the fighters had changed to more normal respiration. So they sought a patch of shade – not an easy thing to find at that time in the afternoon – and all sat amicably together, the erstwhile enemies engaged in a spirited contest to see who could spit the pips farthest. Stewart, however, with tongue thrust cannily against the pip in his mouth, his lips pursed solemnly, could spit much farther than either. Armstrong and Megan, having finished their afternoon siesta, came by and found the competition nearing its close because almost all the grapes had disappeared.

'Dirty little beasts,' he said reprovingly. Mrs Bradley looked at him and cackled.

CHAPTER NINE

'I think so, too. In that case we had best keep quiet till we know for certain.'

I

THE story of the cow had shocked Sir Rudri. At tea he announced his intention of proceeding at once to Corinth.

'Shan't we spend another night here, father?' asked Ivor.

'No. I want to be far enough from here before the sun sets,' Sir Rudri answered. He seemed eaten up with nervousness, a trait which his family (except his wife) deemed to have no place in his character. He glanced about him most of the time, and once he held up his hand and commanded them all to be silent.

All thought they would be glad to leave the place of the Atrides, but when it came to the point of going to the cars the general feeling was voiced by Gelert, who had returned, without whisky, some hour and a half earlier. He said, looking back at the Lion Gate:

'Half a minute. I want to have one more look at the Treasury of Atreus before we really go.'

He went, and the others went with him. They stood in the entrance to the tomb, gazing at the blackness within. They did not go inside. One by one they turned and walked back to the cars. Gelert and Armstrong were the last to leave. When it was certain that the others had all gone, Armstrong said to Gelert, as he opened his smaller camera-case and took out a flattish piece of beaten gold carrying a design of fish:

'Give me your opinion on this thing, Hopkinson, would you?'

Gelert took the rough-edged rectangle of gold. Then he

took a small lens from his pocket. After scrutinizing closely the bit of metal he handed it back and said :

'Genuine, I should imagine.'

Armstrong put it away with the greatest care, and with hands which trembled a little.

'You can call it O.K. about that little affair in Athens, then, if it's genuine,' he said.

'It's genuine enough,' said Gelert.

'I shall have to get somebody at the museum to vet it, I suppose,' said Armstrong in tones which he tried to make careless. Gelert nodded.

'Yes, I suppose so, he said. 'Where did you find it?'

'On the acropolis. I – I dreamt where it would be, and there it was.'

'You dreamt it?'

'Yes,' said Armstrong in a voice which seemed to Gelert to be unnecessarily defiant. He did not press the question. He had heard that some people had psychic gifts of this nature, and he prided himself on his ability to believe such things. Together they walked after the others, and took the last two places in the cars. In Sir Rudri's car this time were Ian, who was driving, Cathleen, Megan, and Ivor. Megan beckoned Armstrong into the vacant seat. In the second car came Dick and Dmitri, and in the third Mrs Bradley, Kenneth, Stewart, and Dish, who sat beside the driver. Gelert climbed in beside Stewart.

The party had dinner in Corinth, and then drove on to Athens. After Corinth Mrs Bradley's car took the lead, because the driver knew the road and Ian did not, and Sir Rudri's car brought up the rear.

Eighteen miles out of Corinth the cars crossed the Great Pass at two thousand four hundred feet, and thirty miles on reached Megara. From here the road ran between sea and mountains and then over fertile land through olive groves, cornfields, and vineyards. It was dark by the time they reached Megara. The road ran due east, and nineteen miles from Athens it skirted foothills near the sea. The hills were low and wooded – chiefly with pines. They could see them, dark branches and trunks which melted into the general darkness and were lost.

The country became more open. Then they reached Eleusis with its factory chimneys, and from there, so familiar was the road, it seemed no time before they reached Athens. Sir Rudri, very cheerful, helped the girls out of his car. Gelert handed out Mrs Bradley. The drivers went off with the cars. Armstrong and Dmitri went with them, but Dick, who was saying a shamefaced, heartsick good night to Megan, was seized upon by Sir Rudri and almost dragged into the house.

Marie Hopkinson was at home. Her daughter Olwen had been delivered of a fine boy and both were doing well. Marie had been back in Athens two days. She took Sir Rudri straight up to their room and pushed him into a chair.

'You go to bed. You'd better see the doctor to-morrow. You look a wreck,' she said. Sir Rudri shook his head. He looked haggard and tired out. All his enthusiasm had gone. His moustache drooped dolefully. 'I'm all right, Mollie,' he said. 'I want to come down to dinner.'

'Come on, then, my poor old man. I've been thinking about you all the time. Have they all been behaving very badly?' She held him by the arm affectionately as he rose to his feet.

'No,' he said. 'No. They've all been very good.' He tried to smile. 'The fact is, I believe the expedition was doomed from the beginning. I ought not to have taken Armstrong.'

'I knew there was something! I never liked that boy! What's he been up to? Shall you take him to Ephesus, or aren't you going on to Ephesus?'

'Oh yes, I shall go to Ephesus. The fact is, Mollie, I don't know what to do about Armstrong. I'm afraid I shall have to take him, whether I want to or not. He's – you see, he intends to come. I never thought the day would come when I'd let myself be worsted by a – by a – really, I don't know what to call him – I don't know what he is.'

'I think,' said Marie Hopkinson, filled with so much misgiving that she felt she wanted to postpone an evil hour, 'you'd better tell me about it after dinner. We'd better go down, if you're coming. How long are you staying in Athens?'

'It depends. A week perhaps. It depends upon Beatrice really. I must have her with me. Have you any idea of the date she intends to go home?'

'She's got a conference in Bucarest just after Christmas. She won't go home before that.'

'That's good. I need her pretty badly.' He put his arms about Marie Hopkinson, and, although he was a tall man, taller by three or four inches than his wife, it would have looked to an observer as though he was leaning his weight upon her, handing over the burden of his body as well as the burden of his mind.

'Cheer up, Rudri, my poor darling. I dare say nothing is really as bad as you think it is, you know. How has Alexander behaved?'

'I thought he might be difficult at first. But really he's been pretty good, Mollie. He's been better than I would have expected. I told you, though, didn't I, that Alexander has poisoned his leg. A mosquito bite, he thinks. We've had to leave him in Corinth. And Cathleen Currie has sprung a husband on us. Did you notice him?'

Marie Hopkinson had wondered who the quiet, dark, bow-legged, long-armed man could be.

Dinner was a great success. The various high spots of the pilgrimage were discussed, mostly with laughter. In the middle of the meal Kenneth remembered the vipers. Mrs Bradley went out with him to feed them. The key of the box was returned to Sir Rudri afterwards, and they all went out to stroll in the streets of the city except for the little boys, who went to bed, and Sir Rudri, who was left at home in charge of them.

Good-naturedly – for fear of the future had begun to give him a strange, pathetic patience with the present, whatever it held – he read them the first three chapters of a detective story which Mrs Bradley had lent him for the purpose, whilst the owner of the book, walking beside his wife towards the temple of Olympian Zeus, described the tour from an angle different from the one which had orientated the conversation at dinner.

'But, my dear, he must be crazy!' Marie Hopkinson exclaimed. 'Whatever can we do? Do you really suppose that Armstrong has got these idiotic photographs? You see, it wouldn't matter so much if poor Rudri hadn't been shown up so very cruelly over that business of Alexander Currie and the Apollo. But, coming on top of that, those ridiculous photographs will ruin him! Why ever did he play into Armstrong's hands like that! Oh, Beatrice, think of something! Can we get hold of the plates or negatives, or whatever the beastly things are? Oh, why on earth isn't Dish an ex-burglar instead of an ex-sailor! It would be so much more useful.'

'The thing is,' said Mrs Bradley, 'to persuade Rudri to have no truck with blackmail. Persuade him to defy the young man to publish the photographs. Then let him try to pass off the thing as a joke. It's the only way out of the mess that I can see.'

'A joke?' said Marie Hopkinson, very thoughtfully. 'Do you think it could be done? It's a pity we don't know exactly what the photographs are like. Besides, he couldn't have photographed Iacchus. He *was* Iacchus, wasn't he, didn't you say? Rudri picked him because he was like a Greek god! He is, in more ways than one!'

'As flies to wanton boys, we to the gods,' said Mrs Bradley, nodding. 'As for his mania, I really think fear has cured it. And Alexander Currie, after I had pointed out Rudri's state of mind, has behaved remarkably well.'

'He *used* to be a nice man. Rudri was very fond of him at one time. Do you really think that people would believe it was a joke, though, Beatrice? Wouldn't they be certain to think the worst?'

'What do you call the worst, dear child? Let me know.'

'That the photographs weren't taken merely to hoodwink Alexander Currie, but to hoodwink the scientific world.'

Marie Hopkinson had never been a fool, Mrs Bradley sagely reflected.

CHAPTER TEN

'Then, when I tried to get the money out of him, he gave me a nasty look. and kept bellowing.'

I

THE next morning Gelert was up as soon as it was light, and did not appear at the family breakfast-table. He walked to Hermes Street, and then turned off until he came to a shop which sold tobacco. At that time of day it was not open, neither was it broadcasting its collection of gramophone records, as it did, once it opened, for most of the remainder of the day. Gelert could, and did, curse the gramophone. It was because it had been rendering an excerpt from *Don Giovanni* one morning as he passed by, that he had stopped to listen. Listening, and casting eyes upon the daughter of the house, he had embroiled himself in a Don Giovanni adventure from which, it appeared, there was no escape, except by paying away money.

He pushed open the unlocked door and entered the shop. Except for a smell of garlic which indicated a family at breakfast, the place bore little evidence of the presence of human beings. The garlic, however, was sufficient indication, and Gelert raised his voice and shouted for the proprietor.

'Here I am, Aristides,' he said. 'How much was it we agreed on?'

The Greek spread his hands and shrugged.

'Did we say thirty pounds?'

'Twenty. I won't pay more.'

'But my daughter is compromised! No true Greek will marry her. She is yours.'

'The hell she is,' said Gelert, with considerable annoyance. 'Very well, I'll marry her and desert her. I'm going back to England after Christmas.'

'Too bad, too bad,' said Aristides gently and sadly. 'How much do you offer? Wait. Let me work that in drachmas. Ah yes. I will consider it. Twenty pounds. Give me the money, if you please, and I will count it.'

'I can't give it you now, you chump. I've got to cash my sister's cheque.'

'Oh, you have not the money?'

'Not on me, no. And, in any case, you'll have to sign a denial of the story that we stayed – were stranded that night. Here it is. I'm not taking chances. You sign along here, look, and I'll bring you the money this evening, as soon as I've cashed the cheque.'

'I do not wait. I do not sign anything,' said Aristides simply and plainly, 'until I see your twenty pounds on the counter before my enravished eyes.'

'You needn't think I'll cheat you, you rat,' said Gelert, his thin face flushing, and his knuckles white on his thin, hard, trembling hands.

'Ah no, no. You would not cheat me. I shall see to that,' said Aristides, smiling pleasantly. 'Give me the money now. I know you have it. It is nonsense, this talk about a cheque. Why did you come, unless you have the money? I shall not believe you would have come.'

Gelert put his left hand in his pocket.

'And Mr Armstrong, my relative by marriage, he will support my case,' Aristides calmly cautioned him. 'You were better to give me the money and close my mouth.'

'But I've no guarantee it *would* close your mouth! That's the point. You don't seem to grasp it.'

'There is that,' Aristides regretfully agreed, 'but I ought

not to have to wait for my money until to-night. I will not sign any papers. You must trust to my honour. You see?'

The conversation had been carried on, slowly and constrainedly by Gelert and with good-tempered fluency by Aristides, in modern Greek. Their cat-like spittings and elegant lispings brought the daughter into the shop. She uttered a shrill squeal at the sight of Gelert, and, darting at him, smacked his face very hard. She was followed into the shop by a man whom Gelert did not know, but who turned out to be her husband. Gelert stroked an inflamed cheek tenderly. 'You will be had up for your daughter's behaviour to me, Aristides,' he said indignantly. 'I'm not going to put up with that. I shall go to the police and complain.'

'The police!' yelled the newcomer violently. 'What do we care for the police. They know nothing, they see nothing, and what they do know and see they do not understand. We have not good police in Athens. We have not a good government, not good newspapers, not good anything in Athens.'

'The government is all right,' said Gelert, reasonably willing to change the subject. 'It's a better government than most of you Greeks deserve.'

'You mock me,' said the man. 'It is like this.' He seated himself. Aristides sat down too. He looked at Gelert in friendly fashion and called to his daughter to bring them something to drink. Then they began to argue, good temperedly at first, but then, in the case of the Greeks, more and more savagely. Gelert, amused, remained on the side of Aristides. Suddenly the son-in-law was seized with violent fury. He crouched like a cat and approached Gelert. 'Do you make good your remarks? I do not use my knife on my friends, but you are different!'

Gelert, stepping aside as the young Greek rushed at him knife in hand, hit him under the chin. The knife flew wide. Both dashed for it. Gelert was horribly frightened now at the turn the quarrel had taken. Getting first to the knife, he picked it up and drove at the other man's breast. Aristides, crying out in horror, his daughter, screaming with terror, leapt to the wounded man's assistance. Gelert turned and bolted, running up the street with loping strides, his head strained forward, his lean frame stretched in flight. He looked more like a greyhound than ever.

'There's blood on your shirt, dear child,' said Mrs Bradley, meeting him as he came galloping into the house. He stopped short, touched the blood-splashes and then laughed shakily. His body was soaked in sweat. It streamed down his face. His palms were wet with it.

'I was arguing about the government,' he said. 'One doesn't argue – with Greeks – about the government.'

Mrs Bradley gazed after him thoughtfully. It would take a good deal, next time, she decided, to break his heart. No more tobacconists' daughters would manage it, at any rate.

CHAPTER ELEVEN

'I understand. Poor little devil! Now what can have been wrong with the omens when I started?'

I

DICK and Megan climbed the Areopagus and looked over the cleft of the Eumenides down to the temple of Theseus. To their left, blue mountains rose behind brown ones, the sky was almost cloudless, and the air, although it was hot, was so clear that they felt energized, not enervated, by it. Dick, breathing deeply, was suddenly emboldened to say:

'Will you – I suppose you wouldn't marry me, Megan?'

'Well – not yet,' she replied. He nodded, took off his sun-glasses, blinked, put them back, and said:

'That means, at any rate, that you might.'

'I expect I shall,' said Megan. 'But I don't want to marry until I'm three or four years older. I haven't had much chance yet to see what I think about life, and —'

'You've had nearly twenty years.'

'Ah yes. But I want to do heaps more things before I marry, Ronald. You do appeal to me, but I think it's only to my motherly side. I might be a really passionate person, you see, and it might not be at all convenient for me to dis-cover that after we were married. Because passion, in such a case, wouldn't have any connexion with you, I expect. I should probably find myself in love with somebody else, and that would be rather a mess.'

'Yes. You'd leave me, in that case, wouldn't you?'

'Oh, of course. It wouldn't be right to stay. And then, you see, if we had a child, or children, I should have to take them with me, and the other man mightn't like that very much.'

'And I should be lonely. I should want them myself. They would be all I should have to remind me of you, you see, Megan.'

'You're sweet,' said Megan. She kissed him. She was three inches taller than he was, and very much bigger and heavier. She liked it, and kissed him again. Then she pushed him away and wiped her mouth with her hand.

'You're rather nice,' she said. 'I expect I'll have you. But, Ronald, you're to say if you change your mind.'

'No, I shan't change, Megan, ever. I know that for certain. I love you.'

'All right, then.'

They scrambled down the slope, and, by the time they had arrived in Hermes Street again on their way back to the house, Megan had shelved the question of their marriage and was detailing her opinion of all the people who had gone on the pilgrimage with them.

'But you never really cared for Armstrong, did you?' Dick asked, a little timidly, after she had catalogued what seemed to her to be Armstrong's sins and virtues.

'You silly! But he makes a lot of nasty, insulting remarks about all the other people, and that's amusing sometimes. For a big boy – he is a good size, isn't he? – he's really terribly spiteful.'

'He's half – he's only half English,' Dick remarked.

'And I'm not English at all. Oh yes, of course I am! Mother is. At least, I think she is. But what I really want to know is what Armstrong is playing at over father.'

'Your father? But he employs Armstrong.'

'Oh yes, I know. But, sad to tell, father is completely off his onion. Oh, I don't mean that he ought to be in an asylum, or anything like that; he isn't silly or dangerous.

But he's perfectly cracked, all the same. I think Aunt Adela ought to put him under some sort of treatment, but I suppose it's very difficult if he doesn't realize for himself that he is bats. I mean, it's only the willing patients that these psychology people seem to do anything with, and father can't show willing if he doesn't know he needs treatment. I'd drop the hint to mother, but she'd be so terribly worried about his going off to Ephesus if I did.'

Dick nodded.

'You mean Iacchus, and the snakes, and hiding that bit of gold plate where Dish could find it,' he said. 'I should think that's only eccentricity, you know. I don't see that you could class it as anything more. I mean, if he really were strange, as you say, it would have come out in you, or Gelert, or Ivor, wouldn't it? I don't mean —'

Megan giggled.

'Thank you for your kind certificate of sanity,' she said. 'But, not to deceive you, my dearie (if we *are* going to get married some day), I wouldn't be so certain about Gelert. He can be a queer fish when he likes. There's this – what shall I call it? – penchant of his for girls. I *know* it will get him into trouble one of these days before we leave Athens. There's a tobacconist's daughter or something at this very minute. I thought boys got over tobacconists' daughters whilst they were still at college, but apparently I'm wrong, because Gelert hasn't.'

'He hasn't been swine enough to tell *you* all about her?'

'Well, not exactly. But he thought twenty pounds of my money might be enough to buy him his freedom, and I wasn't going to part with my twenty quid unless I knew what it was going to be spent on.'

'But I call that damnable to borrow money from his sister for such a purpose!'

'Oh, Ronald darling, don't be a fool! Boys always have borrowed money from their sisters for such a purpose, and jolly glad the sisters are, too, usually. What on earth could we do with a Greek tobacconist's daughter in the family? Heaven knows I'm the matiest thing on earth, but I couldn't stomach – is that the right word? – it is? – I couldn't stomach any such thing as that.'

'But why didn't he borrow off me? Or even off Armstrong or MacNeill?'

'He wouldn't want you to know because you'd disapprove. Gelert's funny like that. Everybody *must* approve. He patronizes you a little bit, doesn't he? And Ian, poor lamb, hasn't a bean until some relative dies or he gets a job or something. As for Armstrong, between you and me, my dearie, the less that lad knows about our family failings, the better. He's got father on the end of a string already, as I think I mentioned before.'

'Those beastly photographs?'

'Those beastly photographs. By the way, I mean to have a look at those. It's no good asking him to let us see them, because, of course, we *shall* see them – the official ones. He's working on them now. And if we then say: "Yes, but show us the others. Show us the faked Iacchus; show us the flashlight of somebody changing the snakes; show us the snapshot of father flourishing the carving-knife over the young son of Alexander Currie; show us all the other photographs you think you'll be making capital out of later on!" What's he going to say?'

'That he doesn't know what on earth we're talking about. The same as he said to me when I asked him if he'd got my

Mycenean gold. Oh, Megan, I feel terribly disappointed over that.'

'Yes, rather,' said Megan perfunctorily. 'What worries *me,*' she added, halting him by a shop and gazing closely at the goods – 'all right, don't look round. A most fearful woman that I loathe the sight of is just passing, and I don't want her to know I've seen her, or else she'll send me home with a general invitation for us all to go and visit her, and nobody will want to, and I do think we might be allowed *five* minutes' peace and quiet in Athens before we go to Ephesus.'

'You were going to tell me what particularly worries you.'

'Oh yes. Well, *you* may think it is a mad idea of mine, but just before we started out for Eleusis – or was it the next day? – oh well, round about the beginning of the whole do – Cathleen gave me the impression that something very beastly was going to happen.'

'What was that?'

'Well, she's got second sight a bit – or thinks she has – and she seemed quite clear that one of the party was going to die before we'd finished our trek.'

'But nobody has.'

'Not yet. There's still the journey to Ephesus, though. And, you see —' She pulled him away from the shop, and they continued their journey homewards – 'it's all right now. That odious creature's gone. She's got Turkish blood. It's the nicest part of her. Yes, well, I often think that father is the suicide type. That's all.'

'I shouldn't have thought that,' said Dick.

'Ah, but then, you don't know him as we do.'

'I've worked with him, you know, for three years now. I –

as a matter of fact, and not because he's your father, or anything silly like that – I like him very much.'

'But he doesn't *know* much,' said Megan. 'He's rather an old fraud, archaeologically, isn't he?'

'Well, not as much as you might think. It's true he isn't *sound* on some points, but he has the vision, the enthusiasm, and, of course, the imagination.'

'I should think he had the imagination all right,' said Megan, with a grin. They gained the house, and sat down in the little portico. Dish came out with a tray.

'Good for you, Dish,' said Megan. 'Dish, are you looking forward to Ephesus next week?'

'I am not proceeding to Ephesus, Miss Megan.'

'Too bad. Why not?'

'I was asked my opinion as to the necessity and advisability, miss, and my notion was it was my place better to stay here, where I might be able to do a bit of good.'

'Don't you like picnicking, Dish?'

'Not so's you'd notice, no, miss.'

'Look here, Dish. Suppose I suggest you alter your mind, and come?'

'Very good, miss. But it would be contrary to my notion of what's for the best.'

'You're dashed mysterious. What's the matter with you?'

'Mr Armstrong, miss. I was brought up violent, and the old Adam dies hard. I have been within a – what shall I say, miss? – of dotting Mr Armstrong a couple already, and he knows it, and eggs me on.'

'Yes, he is annoying. Mr Dick thinks so, too, don't you, Ronald dearie? But, Dish, I'm sure my father didn't take kindly to your idea of leaving him in the lurch like this.'

'I haven't broken it yet to Sir Rudri, like, miss. I had it out with —'

'Mother? And what did she say?'

'Said she'd never liked him herself, miss.'

'No, she never has. I respect mother's judgement of young men. That's why *you'll* have to pass the censor, Ronald, before our engagement can be announced. Did you realize that, my lad?'

Dish left them, and, almost as soon as he had gone, Gelert came in and sat down in the nearest chair.

'Washed your shirt?' asked his sister unsympathetically. 'I hear Aunt Adela had the deuce of a job working the authorities to get them to turn a blind eye on your deed of violence. In England you'd have got about fifteen years for stabbing a man like that, you nasty, messy, weak-minded, puling, yes-man.'

'Shut up,' said Gelert. He got up.

'Where are you going?' asked Megan.

'To the museum, of course.'

'I wonder you have the neck. Go with him, Ronald, and keep an eye on him. He can't be trusted. He bites.'

Having delivered herself of these sisterly comments on the ending of her brother's seventh love-affair, she herself rose, and went out. Gelert gazed after her, then looked across at Dick.

'Have you two fixed it up, then?'

'Not quite, actually,' said Dick. 'May I really come with you to the museum?'

'I suppose so, if you want to.'

'Well, I wanted to go to the museum. I say, Gelert, have you, by any chance, seen any of Armstrong's photographs?'

'They're not printed yet.'

'Will he show them to you?'

'Not the ones you mean.'

'Gelert, is his game – blackmail?'

'Oh yes, I expect so. Father's asked for it, anyhow. By the way, I'm not going to Ephesus.'

'Not going? Oh yes, you must.'

'No, I needn't. I can't go anywhere else with Armstrong. That idiot I stabbed yesterday – I suppose you thought I was mad?'

'No, I could quite understand. All these Greeks carry knives. I've seen them fighting in low restaurants.'

'Didn't know you haunted low restaurants.'

'Well, one ought to see the life of the city, don't you think?'

'I shouldn't have thought you felt like that. Well, anyway, when I went for that silly beast I was really going for Armstrong.'

'Yes, I know. I have felt like that about people. I remember chopping a little tree down once, when I was eight or so. It was really an aunt of mine.'

'Good Lord! George Washington in person!'

"Yes, and no.' He smiled. 'I've told a good many lies, if that's what you mean.' He stood up. 'Let's go, then, shall we? You know,' he added suddenly, 'the trouble about Armstrong's photographs, as I see it, is not that people will think the stunts were faked – as we, of course, know they were – but that they were real – that we actually did get the real Iacchus to come to us at Eleusis, and that Aesculapius really did send the serpents to heal the sick at Epidaurus.'

'What about Mycenae? Nothing happened there. Father had given up faking. All he did there was to hide that bit of gold – the bit Dish found. I hope *your* stuff turns up. You think Armstrong's got it, don't you? So do I. In fact, he showed it me – I suppose it was your bit – and asked me whether it was genuine. Why don't you stand up to the blighter and get it back?'

Dick nodded, and then said:

'Yes, but what about those boys and that beastly knife? And what about the cow? It struck me that there was something fearfully sinister, somewhere, about the poor old cow.'

'Just Armstrong's silly, filthy cruelty.'

'Ah, but don't you see, Gelert, that it couldn't have been he who killed the cow?'

'How do you make that out?'

'I don't know. It stands to reason.' He looked helpless, and then added, 'I just feel it. It doesn't make sense. He doesn't know anything about that sort of thing. The cow had been properly killed – ritually killed, I mean. And it couldn't have been the people who went to Corinth. And Sir Rudri *didn't* go. . . .'

CHAPTER TWELVE

'These are my friends and I'll not judge them. For I have no mind to quarrel with either; one I think clever, and the other gives me joy.'

I

'BUT if you're not coming to Ephesus, I don't think I'll go, either,' Cathleen said. 'But why can't you come?'

'Because I'll wring Armstrong's neck if I do come,' Ian replied. Mrs Bradley, from her seat in the long, shady portico, clicked her tongue and observed :

'I wonder whether all the rest of his acquaintances dislike the young man as much as we do?'

'Oh, he's very thick with Greeks,' said Gelert, turning the leaves of a book in which he was not interested. 'Dick and I, with Megan, went round the town a bit in the late afternoon, after tea, and I saw him in a café. He didn't see us – at least, I don't fancy he did – doesn't matter, anyway – but he seemed to be the life and soul of the party which, I imagine, he was treating to drinks. By the way, look at what I bought.'

He displayed it – a crudely coloured picture of the Acropolis by moonlight – a hideous distortion of the truth.

'It's a beauty,' said Megan, with enthusiasm. She and Gelert collected such monstrosities. He tossed it over.

'Here you are! It's yours. I've got that delightful study of the Theseon, and the no less adorable set of morning, noon, and night on the royal palace.'

'Oh, Gelert! You angel!' said his sister, seizing the daub gladly and rushing away with it to add it to her collection.

'I owe her something. She lent me twenty quid,' said Gelert, in languid apology for his generosity; the picture, Mrs Bradley surmised, was even more horrible, and, in consequence, of more value to them, than the majority of those they had acquired. 'Then when fatuous fatheads at home start raving about Greece, we're going to dig out the whole lot, and rhapsodize over them,' he added. 'We collect *objets d'art,* too. I think Dick must have been bitten with the mania. Give you three guesses what we saw – and he bought – to-day in the bazaar.'

'An ostrich-egg left by the Turks.'

'No. We've got one of those. I think I'll give it him. Go on. Have another shot.'

'Carved elephant-tusks?'

'I say! Are you a thought-reader? But, of course, you are! That's your profession, isn't it? Anyhow, you're so close that I think I'll give it you. A pair of ibex horns.'

'But how Homeric,' said Mrs Bradley, delighted.

'By J – Zeus! So it is! I never thought of that! You know, the expedition must have occasioned acute suffering to Dick. He's really keen; and I expect he thinks the whole thing has been a burlesque. I shouldn't be surprised if he turned down the Ephesus journey.'

'I should,' said Megan, who had returned.

'Oh? Don't tell me he has —'

'Yes, I do tell you. He has.'

'And – er – if it's not in bad taste to ask – just to allay a brother's natural anxiety about your future —'

'You weren't so chirpy the day you stabbed the tobacconist's son-in-law in the gizzard, you meat-fed lamb!' said Megan, with some austerity. 'But, to set your mind at rest, and so that you can get over all the hooting before you see Ronald – and don't you dare to laugh about it and upset him, because he's easily upset and I won't have it – yes, I am, and we jolly well are!'

She looked defiant. Gelert rose and planted an untidy kiss on her left cheek. Megan turned and hugged him.

'I'll give you your twenty quid back for a wedding present,' he said, seizing her arms and taking them forcibly from his neck. He shoved her into a chair. He was stronger than he looked, Mrs Bradley was interested to notice. It was a phenomenon she had observed before in slight and languid young men. 'But I thought you'd fallen for Armstrong's pagan charms,' he added, grinning broadly.

Cathleen turned to Ian.

'An evening walk, Ian, around the city?'

'Not for me,' said Ian. They both got up and went out.

'I suppose we might as well all go to bed,' said Gelert, correctly foreseeing the goal of the married lovers. 'It isn't hot now.'

'We ought to wait up for Ronald, I suppose,' said Megan, slowly.

'Nonsense,' said Alexander Currie, now happily recovered from the mosquitoes. He came in and seated himself. '*I* will wait up for Ronald Dick. Where are the laddies?'

'They've been in bed ages, I should hope.'

'I doubt whether they have,' said Marie Hopkinson, coming in with Sir Rudri. 'Let's all go and see.' So, leaving Gelert, after all, to wait up for Ronald Dick, they all trooped in to say good night to the little boys, who were all in Ivor's room rehearsing the modern Greek vulgarisms which they had spent the past two days in acquiring. The night closed in on pleasant domesticity.

Dick came in at twelve. He had been to the play, but had come out before the end.

'What was it?' Gelert inquired. 'The usual Romeo and Juliet?'

'No,' Dick answered, winding a strip of ox-hide, about fifty inches of it, round his hand, and smiling at the recollection, 'it was *Lady Windermere's Fan.* I would have stayed to the end, but the man next me was sick, and it rather put me off, so I came away. Besides, I didn't really want him to know that I had spotted him.'

'Who was it, then?'

'The excellent Dish.'

'Dish? Sick?'

'Horribly.'

'I bet he would be, if he was sick at all. He's a very thorough fellow.'

'It was most unpleasant,' said Dick. 'He came in halfway through, making rather a disturbance and talking, I think, in Hindustani.'

'Pidgin-English, more likely,' said Gelert. 'His ship was in Chinese waters at one time, I believe. The China Station, don't they call it, or something?'

'Well, I wish they'd taught him out there how to hold his drinks.'

'Oh Lor! Has he reached home yet? Mother will have a fit. She thinks Dish quite incorruptible.'

'Well, so he is, I expect, under ordinary circumstances. I expect he's just celebrating the tour. Is he coming to Ephesus, do you know?'

'Are you coming to Ephesus, then?'

'Of course.'

'I thought you were doubtful about it this morning. I am. Frightfully doubtful. I'm tired of the crack-brained affair.'

'Oh, this morning? Yes, that was a long time ago.'

'By the way,' said Gelert, getting up and patting Dick on

the shoulder, 'awfully glad about you and Megan, and so forth.'

'Megan and I?' said Dick. 'But nothing is settled, you know. By the way, I asked Armstrong again for the Mycenaean gold.'

'What happened?'

He aimed a kick at me, and swore. I dodged the kick, and called him a blasted jackdaw, and threatened him with the police. He only laughed. He said if I went to the police I should never marry Megan. He would take care of that.'

CHAPTER THIRTEEN

'Small beer, all of it.'

DISH had left the house at six because it was his evening out. He went, as usual, to Phaleron, with his telescope, to look at the ships in the bay. There was nothing very interesting to see. Ever since they had been in Athens he had looked for warships, but, except on one occasion, he had not seen any that enthralled him. However, he still made the port his first objective, and spent about an hour focusing the ships in the harbour. To the smell of the sewage he was utterly impervious, and, if asked, would probably have admitted that he thought it was the ozone.

His next proceeding – also a matter of habit – was to charter a small boat and have himself rowed towards Salamis and back by a couple of sweating Greeks. After this his programme varied. Sometimes he would go to the pictures, and would sit, silent and non-critical, while an English film of, possibly, the year 1920, with German captions, would be shown. Then he would come out, buy himself a drink and a packet of Greek cigarettes, and listen to a loud-speaker rendering dance music. Then he would buy himself a beer at one more café, and so home.

On this particular evening, however, after the boat-trip, he went to the café first, and there saw Armstrong in the company of two young women. He ordered his drink, and asked for his cigarettes, and then Armstrong saw him. He lounged over to him and said :

'Oh, Dish, just trot back to the house and fetch me my small camera, the one I use for snaps. My friends here want me to take their photographs.'

Dish stared solemnly into his glass and took no notice.

'Cut off, Dish,' said Armstrong. 'Don't sit there like an owl.'

Dish said:

'It's my afternoon off. I don't go back to the house for nobody, without it might be my employer, and then as a favour.'

With that, he picked up his glass. The girls giggled, and Armstrong, flushing angrily, said suddenly:

'*I* shall be your employer soon, you obstinate old fool, and you'll soon find yourself without an employer after that!'

Then he shoved the glass which Dish had raised to his mouth, and splashed the drink in all directions, mostly over Dish.

The ex-A.B. put down the half-empty glass and wiped his face. Then he spat on his hands. Then he hit Armstrong in the belly. When Armstrong got up – and it took him some time to do that – he hit him on the nose and among the teeth. Then he slogged him in the ribs. Then, with his great, horned palm, he struck him across the face. To conclude he put his hand across Armstrong's nostrils and literally pushed him over. Then he sat down and began to drink again, waiting for Armstrong to get up. The girls, who had giggled at first, and then grown frightened, hustled their escort out of the café along the crowded street. Dish sat still, his eyes glinting as they had not glinted for years. He became aware that he had a thirst on him that seemed to call for more beer.

At last, when he had drunk rather more than he needed, he patronized the theatre at which Dick was watching *Lady Windermere's Fan*, was sick, and, later, went on to another café to replace the beer that he had lost. At half-past one that morning he was informing a group of total strangers that she was the honey-honey-suckle, and that he was the bee. He returned to the house an hour later, apparently sober. Dick was waiting up, and let him in.

CHAPTER FOURTEEN

'Boy, boy!'

'WHAT I still want to know,' said Stewart, playing jazz rhythms on the woodwork of the portico, 'is what that white figure was.'

'What white figure, child?' Mrs Bradley inquired, without interest. She was counting the rows on a sea-green jumper she was knitting, and did not want to lose the mathematical sequence of the pattern.

'The white figure – *horribly* mysterious – I keep on thinking about it, and wishing we'd had the – wishing we'd thought of investigating it.'

'What are you talking about?' She had finished her count and had made a little prick with her knitting-needle on the book from which she was following the directions. Perceiving that the little boy desired to hold a serious conversation with her, she laid down her work, folded her yellow hands, fixed her black eyes upon his face, and nodded.

'That's better. Thank you,' said Stewart. His face was now such a mass of freckles that they had merged, giving him the effect of being both tanned and dirty. He was dressed in a bathing-costume and a pair of cotton trousers, from which his feet hung down and looked, even in sandals, small. His face, as usual, was grave; his green eyes lighted it. He was, Mrs Bradley decided, of all the very nice small boys she knew, the most solemn and the most attractive. 'Don't you *know* about the white figure?' he demanded.

'What white figure, child?'

'At Epidaurus. We saw it twice. Both nights.'

'Where?'

'In that little maze-thing.'

'The foundations of the Tholos? At what time?'

'I don't know *very* exactly. It was absolutely in the night. We went exploring. Well,' he amended, 'we were going to see if we could bag the snakes – for a rag, you know. And that was how it was.'

'Sir Rudri,' said Mrs Bradley.

'Yes – I know it ought to have been.' He sounded so doubtful that Mrs Bradley said :

'Very well, we'll ask him.'

'He might be shirty.'

'No, he won't be, child. Stewart, how many photographs did Mr Armstrong take?'

'We've got a record of that! We've got records of everything. We all kept our eyes skinned, and Ivor put it down, and we all initialed it. It just made something to do,' he added artlessly.

'I wish you'd get those records. I'd like to see them. I suppose you didn't record any flash-light photographs, did you?'

'Well, the one of Iacchus. Sir Rudri took that himself. I don't know of any others. I'll go and get the book now.'

The record, kept in a twopenny note-book and transcribed into Stewart's diary, was interesting. Mrs Bradley asked whether she might take a copy of it. Permission was granted. Stewart dictated, and she wrote, in her unreadable, medico-legal calligraphy :

'Before we started. Group in the porch. Plate.

'At the convent of Daphni. Mr Currie taking off his boots. Sir Rudri cursing Dmitri. Us eating. Snaps.

'On arrival at Eleusis. The wagon and oxen and everybody looking cooked. Plate.

'The ruins and all that. Plate.

'Sir Rudri crawling about doing measurements and cursing. Snap.

'The Statue of Iacchus. Sir Rudri's one that he brought on afterwards. Plate.

'The second statue. Flash-light.

'The place where the statue had stood up high, the second statue, the flash-light one. Plate. He spent a long time over this one and nobody was near except us, and he did not spot us.

'At Nauplia. A few snaps, especially of Sir Rudri when he was cursing or looked blotto or anything. A snap of the ship we came in.

'At Epidaurus. The snake-box. He took it out with the help of Dmitri, when Sir Rudri wasn't there. Plate.

'The vipers when the snake-box was first opened. Snap.

'Sir Rudri and Mr Currie having a row. Snap.

'The ruins, in lots of bits, according to what they were supposed to be. Plates.

'The theatre, different views. Plates.

'The museum. Plate.

'The snakes, when Sir Rudri cleared everybody off, only we snooped. Ciné-camera. They were shied out of their box and did not snake about much

'The other snakes. Everybody went for walks, and Sir Rudri and Armstrong and Dmitri watched us all go, only we saw we were watched go, so we snaked back. The other snakes were taken out of the car Armstrong and Dmitri came in, only they were in a suitcase which just looked ordinary. Snap.

'The snakes being put in the museum in a glass case which had been covered up with a piece of dark stuff, when the keeper was asleep. Snap. We shouldn't think it came out. It was a bit dark in the museum.

'The snakes asleep with the people they were put with. Plates.

'At Mycenae. The grave-circle. The tomb of Agamemnon from outside. The Lion Gate. The ruins at the top. Plates.

'Sir Rudri wanting us to be a human sacrifice, but nobody thinks he meant it, it was merely sucks. Snap.

'The poor old cow. Snap.

'R. Dick and Megan. Ian and Cathleen. All looking a bit soft. Snaps.

'Mr Currie looking at his bites. Snaps.

'Us talking to Mrs Bradley. Snap.

'R. Dick with a little fork and trowel in the grave-circle. Plate.

'R. Dick with ditto up at the top. Plate.

'Where they found the red bath of Agamemnon. Plate.

'Where the men's hall used to be, called the Megaron. Plate.

'That ass Gelert coming back without any whisky. Snap. But the light was bad.

'The cow's beastly innards. Plate.

'R. Dick cutting skin off the cow. Snap. He cut ever such a long thin bit, and wound it round his hand.

'Mrs Bradley and R. Dick walking away from us towards the Tomb of Agamemnon. Ciné-camera. Also of R. Dick and Gelert.

'Dish quietly cutting off a piece of meat from the cow and making a little fire and toasting the piece of meat and wolfing it nearly raw and it must have been smoky, but he wolfed it. Ciné-camera.

'Mr Currie tipping up his pocket flask to get the last drop because of his bites. Snap.'

'That's all we *saw*,' said Stewart modestly. 'Of course, he may have taken some that we didn't spot him taking.'

Mrs Bradley closed her note-book with a sigh of joy.

'I envy you,' she said. 'I can't tell you anything about the white figure now, but I will give the subject some thought.'

'I didn't think you'd know,' said Stewart wistfully. 'But it's jolly interesting, isn't it?'

'So interesting,' said Mrs Bradley, 'that, together with the list of Mr Armstrong's activities which you have been so obliging as to give me, it is worth – what do you children like to do?'

'Have a boat out,' said Stewart, without a pause.

'Then have a boat out, child.'

'Coo, no, I say, that's *frightfully* decent of you!'

He ran off, clutching the money. Mrs Bradley gazed after him indulgently, and then went to find Sir Rudri. When she had found him, she asked for Armstrong's address.

Armstrong lived in a house at the foot of Lycabettos, curiously enough (Mrs Bradley found herself thinking) with his mother. She had not conceived of a domesticated, filial Armstrong. The woman was probably sixty, but must have been beautiful. It was from her, Mrs Bradley supposed, that Armstrong had his good looks, and yet the young man and the woman were not alike.

Armstrong regarded Mrs Bradley with the expression of glowering dislike which he bestowed indiscriminately upon all the members of the party. He was looking extremely battered, the reason for staying indoors, Mrs Bradley supposed.

'Yes?' he said brusquely, when the visitor was in and was

seated. His mother spoke quietly and rapidly in Greek. He nodded gloomily.

'I suppose *you* haven't done any harm,' he said.

'No. Not yet,' said Mrs Bradley. She produced her note-book. 'I understand that you have some photographs for sale.'

'What made you think that?'

'I have a list here of the photographs, including snap-shots and the records you made on your ciné-camera, connected with, and explanatory of, Sir Rudri Hopkinson's tour.'

'Oh?'

'Yes. How much do you want for the set?'

'If you've come from Sir Rudri you can tell him to go to hell!' He glowered, and then added, almost spitting with rage, 'And you can tell him to take that fellow Dish along with him. I'll be even with that swine before he goes!'

'But you want to make money, don't you?' asked Mrs Bradley. 'I thought that that was the point. Or isn't black-mail your object?'

'I've got him cold, and I'm sticking to those photographs, don't worry,' said Armstrong, twitching his chair round and refusing to meet her eye.

'I shouldn't worry,' said Mrs Bradley gently. She got up to go. 'A thousand pounds wouldn't tempt you?'

'Of your money, no. Of his, perhaps it would. I know he couldn't afford a thousand pounds. That's what I'd like. To bleed him. But not all at once." He nodded.

'It would be my money, child.'

'That'll be all, then, thank you.'

'I see. I thought Gelert – yes, I see.'

'Wait a bit,' said Armstrong. He conferred so rapidly

with his mother that Mrs Bradley, whose modern Greek would have been better had she had no knowledge of ancient Greek, could not follow the trend of the discourse. He turned to her abruptly at the end.

'My mother would like your thousand pounds, but I haven't made up my mind. She wants to go to America. I've got one or two of the negatives still to finish. I'll think things over while I'm doing them. I'll let you know by the time you come back from Ephesus.'

'We leave for Ephesus in three days' time. I don't know how long we shall be there.'

'Perhaps I'll let you know before you go, then, and, again, perhaps I won't. I've been asked to tea some day by dear little Megan.' He smirked. 'I might let you know then. Are you coming back to Athens afterwards?'

'Yes, I shall come back here and remain some months, I expect.'

'O.K., then.' He rose and showed her out. Mrs Bradley walked back to the Place de la Constitution very thoughtfully. She tackled Sir Rudri immediately upon her return to the house.

'Has Armstrong a grudge against you, child?' she asked. Sir Rudri looked troubled, not indignant. His moustache, which had gone to Set Fair during his stay at his own home after the vicissitudes of travel, drooped again, and looked discouraged.

'Whatever made you think that?'

'I'm trying to buy up his photographs,' said Mrs Bradley.

'I'll buy them from you.' The moustache cheered up again. 'How much?'

'I'm not prepared to sell them, dear child. I'm buying them because I'd like to have them, and because I feel rather sorry for the quite detestable young man. His mother has a desire to go to America.'

'He's taking her, do you mean?'

'Well, we'll hope so, for your sake. He didn't say that, quite.'

'How old is Armstrong, Rudri?'

'He'd be thirty-two or three, I should imagine. Beatrice, I've been a damned fool. That young devil could ruin me to-morrow if he liked to publish those photographs. I meant to score off Alexander Currie. Upon my honour, that was all. I never thought of Armstrong trying to turn round on me like this. I could never stay in Athens. I should have to resign from my Societies. I – Beatrice, I *have* been a fool!'

'Oh, Rudri, my poor dear child, don't be so morbid. By the way, we haven't had our little session to-day.'

'Do you think we need to, now that I've come to my senses?'

'Just as you like, child. Didn't you dream last night?'

'Oh yes. About clear blue water.'

'Elementary, my dear Watson,' said Mrs Bradley briskly. She seated herself beside him, 'Go on. Let us exorcize the devil. You'll be all the better, then, when we go to Ephesus.'

'I shall have to take Armstrong to Ephesus, Beatrice. He'll want to do the photographs again, and I don't see how I'm to get out of taking him with me if he's made up his mind to come.'

'I think you are ill-advised to give in to him so completely. Leave the young man behind, and take another photographer. Couldn't Ronald Dick take photographs? Feeling as you do, the less you have to meet Armstrong, the better, I should say. It can't be pleasant for you. Besides, I gathered that he didn't expect to be asked.'

'I suppose Dick could take the photographs,' Sir Rudri said, the worried frown deepening between his eyes. 'Armstrong is waiting, though, I expect, to see whether Megan is going. She *did* say something about staying here with Molly. The whole business is terribly involved.' He looked resigned and martyred. Mrs Bradley clicked her tongue. Resignation, whether Christian or otherwise, irritated her beyond measure. She repudiated the whole theory of martyrdom, regarding its victims as invariably obstinate and more often than not ill-informed. She considered that they were lacking in essential balance and judgement.

She wondered whether the woman she had seen really was Armstrong's mother; she was older, certainly, than he was, but her appearance of age was partly due to worry. Mrs Bradley wondered whether she was ill-treated.

Turning these things over in her mind, she left Sir Rudri, and came out into the garden. Tea was set out in the portico and Megan was counting the number of cups. As Mrs Bradley came up the two wooden steps she called to the servant:

'Two more, please. You'll be in to tea, will you, Aunt Adela?'

'No, child. I've promised to have tea with the wives of the scientists from Czechoslovakia in the gardens of the Academy. I told your mother at lunch that I did not expect to be in until dinner to-night.'

'Oh, blow! I was depending on you to entertain the company. We're having a last rally before we go off to Ephesus. Dinner's at ten. Don't be late!'

She smiled – a big, fair-skinned girl, tall as an Amazon, strong-limbed, determined and proud. It struck Mrs Bradley, not for the first time, how like her mother she was, and how unlike. She waved as Mrs Bradley went into the house, and Mrs Bradley waved back before she went up to her room.

The little semi-official party in the Academy garden was pleasant but not exciting. Conversation was easy, because the scientists and their wives spoke both French and German, but it was with a feeling of relaxation and pleasure that Mrs Bradley sat in her taxi and resigned herself to a breakneck dash through the streets to Sir Rudri Hopkinson's home.

She was met at the door by Marie Hopkinson. The lady of the house was in a flushed and dishevelled condition. She was wearing evening dress, but her hair was in disarray, and she was still in bedroom slippers.

'My dear Beatrice!' she said, clasping hold of Mrs Bradley's arm. 'I am ever so glad you've come! My dear! What *do* you think! The drains! My dear! They've gone *wrong*! We shall have to turn out of the house for *at least* two days. I'm taking you off at once to dine at the Grande Bretagne. The others have all gone on.'

'You haven't changed your shoes, and your hair wants doing,' said Mrs Bradley, unperturbed. Delicately, whilst her hostess was concluding an interrupted toilet, she sniffed the air, and then, a little less delicately, sniffed again.

'One thing, there's no smell,' she said, as Marie Hopkinson rejoined her.

'Isn't it fortunate,' her hostess absently remarked. 'We'd better go out through this way. The whole of the portico's *up*.'

'Up?'

'The drains are underneath it.'

Dinner at the Hotel Grande Bretagne was a great success. Megan and Gelert were in almost hysterical high spirits. The little boys, who had spent the afternoon in a boat, again paid for by Mrs Bradley, and had not been in to tea, were interested to hear about the drains.

'Dish positively *shoved* us round to the other door,' said Ivor. 'But nothing smelt more than usual. I took a good sniff to see.'

'Of course not, dear. It's the dryness,' his mother remarked. She refused three courses of the dinner, complaining that the smell had got into her inside.

'But you just now said —' remarked Ivor. His elder brother kicked him under the table.

'I packed all the servants off except Dish. He's coming round here with the odds and ends I collected up for the night,' Marie Hopkinson continued. 'The servants are terrified of typhoid fever. They all cleared off at once, as soon as I'd finished talking to the man. They all live in Athens, that's one comfort, so that I can get them all back when I want them. The job may take only one day, but you know what Greek workmen are!'

Mrs Bradley said she did not. By noon on the second day, a message from Dish informed the party that everything was ship-shape and that 'the sanitary had passed the job as O.K.'

Beyond the fact that all the woodwork of the portico appeared to have received a good cleaning – Mrs Bradley saw in this the hand of Dish – there was nothing at all to indicate a domestic crisis of magnitude.

'So now,' said Marie Hopkinson, having narrowly inspected the now reconditioned portico, 'you can all go to Ephesus in peace.'

CHAPTER FIFTEEN

Ee-aw!'

I

THE ship ran between the southernmost end of Euboea and the north of Andros, and set her course to bring her north of Chios to take the long sweep into the Gulf of Smyrna.

A sea-voyage, however short, again made a welcome change, and while the little boys explored the ship and familiarized themselves with the appearance, name, characteristics, and disposition of every member of the crew, their immediate elders – Gelert, Cathleen, Ian, and Ronald Dick, played deck games, lounged, read, smoked, betted, and, some aloud, some privately, thanked providence that Armstrong had neglected, at the last, to come to the embarkation stage and proceed with the party to Ephesus. That Megan had elected to remain in Athens to keep her mother company was news not as rapturously received.

Sir Rudri, torn between relief and anxiety when Armstrong did not appear, discussed the situation in all its aspects with Mrs Bradley as they stood at the rail and watched the distant mountains. She comforted him, for his fear that Armstrong would be making mischief whilst they were away was greater than the relief he felt at being without the young man's company.

'I suppose I ought to have gone to his home,' he said, 'and notified him again about the date. But what with the upset about the drains – I suppose, by the way, that they've all been properly re-laid? I shouldn't like Molly and Megan to be exposed to any risk – and my natural reluctance to open the subject of the photographs, I procrastinated until it was too late.'

'I expect it is all for the best,' remarked Cathleen, who overheard him. 'All I hope is that he won't pester Megan whilst we're away.'

'She has her mother with her,' Ian pointed out.

'I hope she won't feel lonely without us all,' said poor Dick wistfully.

'Cheer up, Romeo,' said Gelert, whose troubles appeared to be over for the time. He smacked him between the shoulders, took his arm, and led him down to the saloon.

The older members of the party read, knitted – Alexander Currie had a sock, Mrs Bradley her apparently perennial jumper – played cards, gossipped, threw darts, discussed Saint Paul – to Sir Rudri's obvious dissatisfaction, his desire and intention being to keep the issue strictly to a consideration of the worship of Artemis at the sixth- and fourth-century temples at Ephesus – and told fortunes.

The miniature cruise was pleasant. The sea was calm, the islands, like banks of the green morning, rose high out of the sea as the ship approached where they lay, and dropped astern in faint and lovely haze as the ship passed gently onwards. Their mountains were old and like dreams, and produced in Cathleen and Ian the same romantic nostalgia. They spent all of the second morning leaning over the rail and gazing at the islands, rising in greenness, declining in purple and grey, fading in faint blue far away, beautiful as a former life remembered in this life, or the recollection of an old story told once, and ever afterwards groped for in the golden clouds of the mind.

Smyrna had a mountain-encircled harbour, and the ship could not get to the foreshore, but landed the party in a boat. A main road leading to the station and served by modern vehicles of transport led along by the sea, and when all the baggage was landed – a part of the work which Sir Rudri left to Gelert and Dick whilst he and Alexander Currie commandeered a couple of Turks and questioned them regarding the way to the railway station – the party hired cars, and were soon set down outside an extraordinarily impressive station through which ran trains which were comparable with those on English railways.

After the easy, self-indulgent, West-Irish ways of the Greeks, it was bracing and delightful, for a change, to come upon the efficiency and activity of the Turks. Two porters and the station-master came up and explained in English, French, and German, when the train for Selçuk would come in, how many train would come first, where they would go, and what was the advantage of travelling by rail in Asia Minor. Everywhere, in a strange, phonetic language invented, legalized, and enforced by Kemal Ataturk, were words which all the travellers could pick out and understand, and of which the examples greeted with the greatest enthusiasm by the party were those spelt 'Vagonli Kook'. They were pointed out first by Dick, and were cheered to the echo. The vault of the station rang triumphantly with the sounds of the travellers' voices chanting the magic words which signify home from home, an oasis in the desert of foreign incomprehensibility, a shepherd of English sheep in an unfamiliar fold.

The train came in at the time appointed for its arrival. More beer was taken aboard when it was known that the travellers were British. Alexander Currie, however, who believed that a combination of hops and malt had been the ruin of a nation's teeth, clung tenaciously to his pocket flask, which he had managed to get refilled at the hotel in Athens.

The train moved off after a Turkish official had inspected the party, had seen that they were seated and that the windows were closed. It passed through the town and, from the windows, mountains could be seen, a low range between the railway and the sea, and a high one farther inland. The line ran almost due south, and was soon passing through miles upon miles of beautiful fen-land, the haunt of numberless birds, and covered with acres of water-lilies.

After about forty miles of smooth journeying, the train stopped at the little station of Selçuk, and the party trooped on to the platform. The way out led through the garden of an inn, and soon Sir Rudri, gesticulating to shy villagers to get out of the narrow road, was pushing the party on to the local motor-bus, which had been chartered for the purpose, and pointing out the Roman aqueduct and the storks' nests on the roofs of the villagers' houses. A group of solemn children stood and stared, ready to take instant flight, a little girl scowled and spat, some women turned away their faces, and a young woman carrying a tiny baby made a sign to avert the evil eye and hurried away with the child, the Turkish driver, in European clothes, climbed aboard, the railway porter, assisted by Gelert and Dick, shoved all the luggage on to the vehicle, and then, when all was in readiness, off went the bus with the gait of a camel and at the pace of an express train.

The vehicle had a roof, but no sides. Travelling in it was both exhilarating and highly dangerous. The seats were four-inch boards placed from side to side of the vehicle so that the passengers, in rows of three, faced the way that the bus was going. Here and there an upright of wood, which also supported the roof, provided a welcome means of holding on to the conveyance.

The driver, talking rapidly to himself in Turkish, changed gear; the speed of the bus changed from fifty-five to sixty-five miles an hour; the road narrowed into a homely, dusty lane, and the party hurtled towards Ephesus.

In about three minutes the bus pulled up, the party assisted one another out over the side, and Sir Rudri, warning them all to keep close together because the neighbourhood was the haunt of the wild boar, led the way across vegetation which tore their legs in a thousand tiny lacerations, every one of which bled in the most unsightly manner, to a large, unpleasant-looking pond.

'Mosquitoes!' said Alexander Currie. He turned in his tracks and made back at full speed for the bus.

'The site of the temple of Artemis,' said Sir Rudri, gazing at the mere, in which a broken column or two gave some sort of support to his otherwise incredible statement. 'A great deal of the stone has gone to build that place up there.'

On the hillock on the other side of the lake was a fort, or a mosque – it was not easy, observing its ruinous condition, to say which. All stared obediently at it, except for the little boys, who conceived an ambition to paddle.

'Leeches,' said Mrs Bradley, who had not the slightest idea whether the site of the temple was the abode of leeches or not, but who knew that those creatures are dreaded by most of the young. The boys put on their socks and sandals again, and decided to play at trying to push one another into the water.

'Now for Ephesus,' said Sir Rudri.

Cathleen, who had been glancing round very anxiously for the wild boars, led the way back to the bus. The party assisted one another in scrambling aboard. The bus careered on towards the sea, but suddenly swung left through a gap, and then drew up.

'Here we are,' said Sir Rudri, his face alight with enthusiasm, sweat gathered beadily on either side of his nose, and the Viking moustache at its most optimistic angle. 'We have here —' he consulted a small map.

'I say, Dick,' said Gelert, as the party climbed over the sides of the bus and Dick was paying the driver, 'what on earth made father bring the vipers?'

'The vipers?' said Dick. 'Oh, the vipers!' He lugged the box on to the ground, then thrust it back on to the bus. 'I don't see why we should sweat to carry the baggage any farther than we need. Those sleeping-sacks alone weigh a ton. Leave the lot of them together, and the rest of the stuff, and let's see how far the bus can drive towards the ruins. We're to sleep in the theatre, I believe.'

The driver, nothing loth, started up his engine again, and, the two young men coming loping behind like lurchers behind a country cart, drove carefully past the Gymnasium of Vedius, and came to a bumping halt at the ruined Stadium.

Dick tipped the driver and wiped his own face. 'Get Ian to come along and give a hand,' he said. Whilst Gelert was gone he lugged out the sleeping-sacks with the help of the grunting driver, who proved to be an able and obliging assistant, and by the time Ian, bandy-legged and powerful, came trundling along with Gelert, the sacks were laid out on the ground, each discreetly but plainly labelled with the name of its owner. Most of the sacks were bulging with parts of the portable camping outfit, which was larger and more varied than Gelert thought necessary.

'This one – it's mine, I think – yes, it is – has got all the stuff for the photographs bundled into it,' said Dick. 'I think all the pots and kettles and things are in yours and Ian's, Gelert. The kids have got all the spare socks and vests in theirs. I should think that everything could remain here for the present, though, it's not in the way. Perhaps, after all, that hilly bit above the Greek market-place would be the best site for the camp, but Sir Rudri suggested the theatre because there we could get under cover in the stage passages.'

'Better, perhaps, to leave all the stuff stacked here,' Gelert agreed. 'I don't see why each person shouldn't take his own sack and camp out where he likes, though. Bags I the top of the theatre. I'm not going to be cooped up in a passage.'

The last port of call on Sir Rudri's extraordinary tour was certainly the largest, the most interesting, and the most romantic. Even Epidaurus, for all its upland beauty and the glory of its almost perfect theatre, could not compare – at any rate, in the eyes of the little boys – with a district which was in many ways so like an English landscape as to banish all sense of strangeness, all feeling of not being at home. There was nothing remote or fearful, nothing awe-inspiring or uncomfortable about Ephesus. Before them, as they gathered about the baggage near the Stadium, stretched a winding, inviting path which soon branched off to give a wide view of the ruins. The ruins themselves were not desolate. It was rather as though some experimental building had been abandoned before completion. There was nothing sad about Ephesus. The uncovered, excavated part of the Sacred Way, the exciting and inviting little path which led up to the back-stage passages of the theatre, the theatre itself, weed-grown, ruinous, and delightfully sunny and friendly, the royal road, the Roman arcadiane, leading from the harbour to the city, the stepped library of Celsus and his solid, inviolate tomb, combined to enravish the party, particularly Cathleen, Ian, and the utterly contented little boys.

'Now this I *call* a holiday place,' said Kenneth. 'I say!' He paused and looked round, but his elders, deep in learned discussion, were, if not out of earshot, at least completely oblivious of what he was saying. 'I say, you men, let's give the jolly old vipers a little run.'

'We'd never catch them again,' objected Ivor, visualizing his father's wrath if the vipers were lost or anybody got bitten. 'They're off like a streak of lightning.'

'Oh, rot,' said Kenneth. 'I bet you they're the slowest snakes on earth. I bet you if we had a race with them – I say!' he added, his face lighting up with the joy of a new idea. 'Let's just have three of them out and have a race with them. I say! Do let's do that. I say! I think that would be too beastly good for words. I *say*!'

'Oh, stow it,' said Ivor brusquely. 'To begin with, we'd never know them apart, and you'd be sure to swear yours was the winner, whether it was or not, just because we couldn't tell from the markings. It'd be like it was with the golf balls that time, just because yours was needled and mine was needled, and I jolly well *know* I threw mine ever so much farther than you did, and just because, when we found it, it was needled —'

'Oh, dry up,' said Stewart. 'I'll tell you what we'll do. We'll just go and take a snoop at the old vipers, and see if they look as if they thought they *wanted* a run. If they seem sleepy and fed up with being shut up in their tin, we can let them out for a bit, but if they seem as though they are going to scoot about and bite people, we won't.'

This eminently reasonable programme was accepted by the others without argument, and the boys trotted back to where the baggage had been left. There Kenneth turned on Stewart.

'You ass! We haven't got the key. We can't open the box they're in.'

Stewart replied:

'Yes we can, you ass. I spotted long ago that the lock was broken. It broke when the beastly box fell off the train. I spotted it when the Turkish porter lifted it. I say, I'd like to have seen his face if he'd dropped it and all the beastly snakes had fallen all over him.'

The other little boys agreed that this would have been an agreeable spectacle. Kenneth knelt down and gingerly lifted the lid. The vipers, with lidless eyes, took no notice whatever of the sudden inrush of light and the golden air. Nevertheless, the little boys hesitated, and it was in agreement with the general feeling, although this remained unspoken, that Kenneth gently closed the lid and stood up, brushing the palms of his hands together as though he had actually touched the scaly creatures.

Later on the boys took another look at the seemingly comatose creatures. But the broad flat heads scarcely moved, the short, thick snakes remained stolid. They had dark diamond-shaped markings on their brownish backs. Two were lighter in colour than the others, and one was cream and black instead of two shades of brown. But, unprovoked, they remained disappointingly languid. The boys studied them closely, kneeling on the ground and breathing with heavy interest on to the backs of the reptiles. Kenneth even prodded one of them gently with his finger before the lid was closed down again and the boys had taken a second farewell of what they now regarded as their pets.

2

Sir Rudri's instructions with regard to the sleeping arrangements were to be followed on the second and not on the first night of the stay in Ephesus. On the first night, members of the party were to sleep in any part of the ruins that pleased them.

'My chief idea is that for the next twenty-four hours or so we all familiarize ourselves with the lie of the land,' he said. He issued numbered plans of the excavated parts of the city – plans which even the little boys could understand – and the company spent a zestful couple of hours in the late afternoon exploring every yard of the site and commenting upon their findings.

Mrs Bradley, having familiarized herself with the plan, set up a small camp stool in the arcadiane, and read and knitted whilst Sir Rudri, Dick, Alexander, and Gelert discussed the Austrian excavations and agreed it was a pity that the Austrians had not explored the Hellenistic and Ionian cities.

'Of course, the site of the temple is the all-important place for my investigations and experiments,' Sir Rudri concluded, looking hopefully at Alexander Currie. But Alexander Currie, shying like a badly startled horse, pronounced a malediction in the pond in which the broken columns, half-pathetic remnants of glory, witnessed to the temple never to be restored.

'Mosquitoes!' he said, dancing about to emphasize his

point. 'The place is a hot-bed of mosquitoes: If you go there, you go without *me*!'

'Well, well, never mind that now,' said Sir Rudri soothingly. It was amazing, Mrs Bradley thought, how much better he seemed since the short stay at his home in Athens. The party joined together to eat their second meal and, for fear of wild boars – referred to in accents of horror by Cathleen – it was arranged that the young men should act in turn as watchmen over the camp. Cathleen said that she wanted to sleep in the village; that there was an inn there; that they had walked through part of its yard when they came from the station platform on to the road. With difficulty she was persuaded to remain with the rest of the party.

'But, look here,' said Ian, 'you'll not be wanting, all of you, to sleep in the same place, most likely. As to the boars, I think there is little to fear. Do you all go where you will. Cathleen will be safe with me. We can sleep in the passage of the theatre. That will be almost the same as being inside a house.'

It was arranged that the little boys and Mrs Bradley would also sleep under cover. The others dispersed themselves as they would, all of them in or very near the theatre passages. Each one was within shouting distance of the others.

This last fact was discovered in dramatic and terrifying fashion at about one o'clock in the morning. The inside of the passage was almost as black, and almost as oppressive to the spirits, as the interior of a tomb. The masonry, which was very heavy, was arched overhead, and the whole passage was a vaulted tunnel with openings at either end. These were doorways to the theatral area for which it formed the back of the staging. Mrs Bradley could sense the discomfort of the others, and although the little boys were soon asleep, she was not surprised to hear Ian fidgeting and grunting, and, later, Cathleen muttering in her sleep. After those two were at rest, Ivor woke up, crawled out of his sack, and crept along to her side.

'I don't like it here,' he said. 'Is everything all right?'

'Yes, quite all right, dear child,' Mrs Bradley murmured comfortingly.

'But people have been killed in this place, haven't they, by the Romans?'

'No, not in this place, child. This was not an arena for beasts.'

'Oh, but I thought —'

The child did not tell her what he thought, for suddenly a most unearthly babbling and screaming broke out at the opposite end of the passage. Ivor; reverting to his babyhood in immediate reaction to the sounds, flung himself into Mrs Bradley's arms, clasping her with agonized fear, shaking, trembling, and sweating like a frightened animal.

Cathleen's voice cried, 'Ian!'

Sir Rudri shouted, 'What's that?'

Alexander Currie swore loudly and fiercely at the noise, and, not succeeding in divesting himself entirely of his sleeping-sack, crawled with it cumbering his legs, bumped his head hard against the wall in the dark, swore again, and, reaching out, clutched Stewart and Kenneth who, flattened against the wall, were prepared to sell their lives dearly.

Gelert said, 'Stand still, you devil, until I get at you!' His voice was hysterical.

'I don't think we're behaving very well,' said Mrs Bradley

suddenly, loudly and cheerfully. 'Ronald Dick, where are you?'

'I say! I'm terribly sorry! I'm afraid I must have shouted in my sleep. I woke myself, I expect. I think I had a nightmare or something,' said Dick's voice out of the darkness.

'Well, don't have it again,' said Alexander Currie crossly. 'Never heard such an unearthly screeching in my life. You couldn't have made more noise if you had been murdered.'

He sat down and, after some difficulty, shed the sack. Then he rearranged himself in it and in about two minutes was asleep.

'I – I think I'll get up and walk about outside,' said Dick, still very apologetically.

'Best thing. Best thing. Shake off the dream completely. Don't make a noise coming back,' said Sir Rudri, not at all cordially.

'Perhaps,' said Dick, with diffidence, 'I'd better not come back. I might disturb you again. Look here, I'll take my sack and sleep outside.'

All right, my boy. Good night.' Sir Rudri also composed himself for sleep.

'I vote we go with old Ronald and explore by night,' said Kenneth, who had soon got over his fright.

'Oh, rot,' said Ivor, who was still exceedingly nervous, although he had now returned to his place. Stewart's reply was to grope his way back to his sack and crawl inside it, and the intrepid proposer of the jaunt was left to go alone or to remain where he was. He found his sack and snuggled into it.

Mrs Bradley lay awake for half an hour, but nothing further disturbed the peace of the night. Next morning at breakfast (a curious meal at which there was nothing to drink but beer and goats' milk, liquids combined in one mug with some success by Kenneth, who pronounced the mixture palatable and betted that it was beneficial to health, 'beer being best and a food' as he happily expressed it), Dick was encouraged to recount the dream which had so much upset the whole party.

'Oh, I don't know,' he said nervously. 'I believe I was dreaming about poor Io at Mycenae. At least, I think I was dreaming that *my* entrails were spread all over Piccadilly Circus, only I was Io and the Circus was, somehow, in Athens. You know the kind of thing.'

They all said they did.

'I don't call that much to yell the whole place down for,' said Ivor, disparagingly. He had watched Mrs Bradley furtively all the time since the party had gathered for breakfast. Mrs Bradley now caught his eye and made a little, friendly grimace at him to indicate that she understood that no reference was to be made to his atavistic lapse of the night before. Comforted, Ivor grinned, and took a long gulp of the extraordinary liquor which Kenneth had poured into his mug before he began on the biscuits, cheese, and tinned tongue, the principal items of the meal.

Breakfast over, Mrs Bradley strolled off by herself without conscious aim, and found herself back at the entrance to the excavations. She took the road back to Selçuk, intending to spend the morning visiting the remains of the cathedral of St John and the ruined mosque of Isa Bey II. When she came opposite the site of the temple, however, she could not forbear taking the turning, walking twenty yards or so off the road, and crossing the field of spiky, lacerating vegetation to gaze at the flooded foundations. Two women, one of them holding a tiny baby, stood there like gipsies, and watched her, curiosity struggling with apprehension. The one with the baby took care to keep the child's face turned away.

Mrs Bradley walked on towards the water. It was of considerable extent, for the estimated base of the temple occupied eighty thousand square feet, and she stood there for some time, considering the pond and mentally placing on the site an imposing reconstruction she had seen of the sixth-century Ionic temple. Suddenly her attention was caught by a sight at once familiar and extraordinary. This was the bloated, dark-marked, floating, headless body of a snake. Vastly intrigued, she descried another, and yet another, whilst a fourth was harboured in a weed-grown little inlet farther along the bank. There had been six of the vipers originally – for she had no doubt whatever that these were not snakes indigenous to Asia Minor, but must have formed Sir Rudri's still mysterious collection of English adders – and she spent an interesting twenty minutes, while the sun grew hotter and flies began to hum, in locating the bodies of the other two. She found them – one tossed in a small, low-growing shrub; the other in the weeds that bordered the eastern end of the pond. She retrieved the bodies with the help of her parasol, and examined them. Where the heads were she did not know, and she felt that this did not particularly matter.

She looked around. The woman and the baby had disappeared. Nothing living was near her, so far as she could tell, except the flies. She arranged the dead serpents on the ground and gazed at them in tranquil contemplation. Then she poked them among some bushes, walked briskly back to camp, and, without a word to anybody, began an unobtrusive search for the tin box in which they had travelled.

It interested her to discover that she could not immediately find it.

'Somebody wanted the tin so badly that he was prepared to kill the adders to get it,' she said to herself. 'Now, what did he want it for, I wonder?'

Possibly (she privately considered) because of Cathleen's vague fears that one of the party would die before the expedition was concluded, the tin box had always reminded her of a coffin. It was fantastic to think that one of the party should require a coffin, and yet – her musings were interrupted by the little boys, who had trailed her very skilfully and silently whilst she had made her search for the missing box. They now showed themselves, popping up suddenly on the steps of the library of Celsus and hailing her as she emerged from the subterranean chamber in which his marble sarcophagus still lay.

'I say, what are you snooping round for?' asked Kenneth. 'You're not exploring the ruins, or anything, are you? We've trailed you from the Sacred Way fountain and all round the back of the theatre.'

'No, child,' replied Mrs Bradley. She looked at them earnestly, and then made up her mind. 'You are not to breathe a word to anybody else, but I'm very anxious to find Sir Rudri's snake-box. It was brought here – I don't know why' – this, she realized, was a small mystery in itself which the elucidation of the slightly greater mystery of the disappearance of the box might possibly help to solve – 'but it has disappeared. Nobody has told me it has gone. But it has. If anybody mentions it to you, do not tell them that I am looking for it.'

'You want us to help you look?' said Kenneth. 'Good.

That'll be something pretty decent to do. We'll comb the place for it. Thanks awfully for the tip.'

'And mum's the word,' said Stewart.

'You bet mum's the word,' said Ivor. Bending low, they sneaked away.

Mrs Bradley quietly and methodically continued her own search. She also looked out for any indications which might show that the box had been buried. She and the boys spent an interesting, grubby kind of morning, but by lunch-time the box had not been found.

Early in the afternoon, while siesta was being taken under the shade of the arches in the theatre where the sleeping-sacks were still laid, Stewart crawled up to Mrs Bradley, put his lips to her ear and whispered :

'Did you know there's blood on one of the sacks?'

'Whose, dear child?'

'I don't know. Somebody has gone all round and cut off the name-tabs for a joke. It's the one in my place, but I don't really think it's mine. I suppose it was *meant* for a joke.'

'No, not for a joke,' thought Mrs Bradley intrigued. Aloud she said :

'Show me, when the others have gone.'

There was no doubt about the blood. She gave Stewart her own sack and retained the blood-stained one. She had no means of telling whether the stains were human blood or not, but in the light of what had happened to the vipers, she thought the child's discovery was interesting.

During the afternoon the search for the box was abandoned by Mrs Bradley but prosecuted by the little boys, who appeared to find the quest compensation for the heat. By night, however, there was still no trace of the box. Mrs

Bradley, having waylaid the leader of the expedition, encouraged him to sit beside her on the steps of the library of Celsus, and then questioned him concerning the vipers.

'What made you bring them, dear child?'

'I didn't bring them. There must be some mistake.'

'Who might have thought they were needed?'

'I really can't imagine. Not Dick or Gelert. They would have known that I shouldn't require them at Ephesus.'

'What *do* you require at Ephesus?'

'Nothing. I am merely experimenting. I thought perhaps we could try the Attis blood-bath.'

'As part of the worship of Artemis?'

'Well, she was worshipped after the same manner here, at times, because of the influence of Asiatic religions upon the colonists.'

'I see. And where do we get the blood, dear child?'

'Well, of course, there must be a victim – or the priests – we could gash ourselves with knives – do you like that idea?'

'It is admirable,' said Mrs Bradley. She looked at him sharply.

'Then we might try the mere offerings of nature and so forth,' Sir Rudri continued, indicating a very small fig-tree which grew near to where they were sitting.

'But you'd rather be thoroughly wicked. I think I understand.' She cackled, an eerie sound in the sunny, silent ruins. Sir Rudri shuddered.

'What is your opinion of the story of Iphigenia?' he inquired.

'I have no opinion about it,' she replied.

'You do not recollect the story, perhaps?'

'I recollect it, child.'

'Well?'

'Listen, Rudri. There is no need to sacrifice Megan. I am sure we can buy the photographs. Besides, I expect Armstrong's married already. Has he asked you to let him marry Megan?'

'You mean Iphigenia, Beatrice. No, he has not. I expect, though, that he will.'

'Then you will be able to refuse.'

'I can't face the publication of those photographs.'

'Nobody wants you to do so. Take heart. We shall buy them all back.'

'You mean you would lend me the money? It's very good of you, Beatrice.' He became slightly maudlin. His eyes filled with tears. 'If it all comes out I shall kill myself, you know. And then it will be good to know that Molly has a kind friend.'

Mrs Bradley cackled, and poked him very painfully in the ribs.

'I wish I knew why you have brought the vipers,' she said.

'But I *haven't* brought the beastly things, I tell you!' Sir Rudri yelled loudly and crossly. All trace of any emotion except exasperation, she was relieved to notice, had disappeared from his voice and countenance.

'That box you keep them in has always reminded me of a coffin,' she continued pleasantly. 'It *is* like a coffin, child, isn't it? Had you ever thought of that before? Yes, I can see you have.' She peered at him with interest.

'Oh, bother the beastly box,' said Sir Rudri flatly. 'I didn't come here to talk about corpses and coffins.'

Mrs Bradley thought of Cathleen's prophecy. Coffins and corpses suggested that the prophecy must have come true. Without another word she got up. She no longer wanted the little boys to discover the box which once had housed the adders. If it now housed what she supposed it did, it would not be a thing for children to see.

'I wish,' said Sir Rudri peevishly, as though she were still beside him, 'the man with the dogs would come.'

CHAPTER SIXTEEN

'You know, whenever I go to the theatre and see any of those clever turns I go away feeling more than a year older.'

I

LATE that night, as though the granting of the wish had been delayed by the agency of an unseen, unsympathetic power, the baying of hounds could be heard.

Mrs Bradley sat up and listened. The sounds approached the theatre, apparently along the Sacred Way. She heard Sir Rudri get up. She heard the voice of Alexander Currie. Then she heard Gelert call out:

'That chap with the dogs is here, father. What shall we do?'

The whole party groped its way out to see the dogs. Black as the hounds of hell in the light of the moon, the dogs were held in leash by a short squat man whose whip cracked, flicking a thin lash up against the moonlight. It was apparent that everyone but Mrs. Bradley and the little boys had been notified of the coming of the dogs. There was haggling, the clinking of coins, mutterings, grunts, and then the man went away towards the harbour, and the party gathered round the animals, which the man had tied to a tree.

'What are they for?' asked Kenneth, holding on to Mrs Bradley's sleeve.

'They have to be crowned, dear child.'

'Why do they?'

'I don't know. It's part of the worship of one of the goddesses Artemis.'

'I thought there was only one.'

'Did you?' said Mrs Bradley absently. She was watching

whilst Sir Rudri lighted a torch of the kind he had used at Eleusis and held it above his head to look at the dogs.

They were shaggy, snarling creatures, half-wild and wholly savage. Mrs Bradley, accustomed to the sheepdogs of Greece, kept her distance and retained firm hold of Kenneth who showed signs of wishing to pat the animals. Sir Rudri, still holding the torch up, appeared undecided as to the next move. The dogs strained and leapt. Their howls of anguish and fury – anguish because their only friend (as far as they knew) had deserted them, and fury because they did not care for the smell of their new owners – rent the night and echoed round the ancient city. It was obvious that those present would be risking their lives if they made any attempt to free the dogs, and the circle gradually moved away from the frenzied animals, and discussed in low tones the inadvisability of attempting to hold a religious ceremony in which the dogs took part.

'We ought to feed them, though. We must be humane,' said Dick. He disappeared into the darkness and came back later with meat.

'I went into Selçuk for it this afternoon,' he explained. 'I think it might be mule. It's rather "off", but I don't suppose it will harm the dogs. They are probably bred and born scavengers.'

He fed the dogs with the meat, and for a short while all other sounds were subordinated to the unpleasing evidence that the faithful creatures were gulping the chunks of mule and almost choking themselves to death in the attempt to secure it all before it was taken away.

Whilst they ate, Dick advanced and, taking advantage, riskily, of their preoccupation with the nauseous food, he patted them gently on the shoulders. The dogs growled, choked and swallowed, gulped, wolfed, growled, and dribbled. It was an interesting but not a pleasant scene.

'I believe,' said Dick, when the animals had eaten all that they could, 'that we might venture to crown them now.' Again he advanced. This time the quietened creatures showed evidence of pleasure at his approach. They fawned on him, licking his hand. The rest of the party made friends with them.

'No, no,' said Sir Rudri violently. 'I am not in favour of crowning them. I am not convinced that the Greeks of Ephesus ever crowned their dogs at the feast of Artemis. The time of year is wrong, too. I think we had much better leave the animals tied up. The man will come and fetch them in the morning. It was just an idea of mine, but I regret the impulse now. Leave them be. Much better. Let us go to bed.'

The dogs, slobbering and moaning, lay down and composed themselves for slumber.

'Besides,' Sir Rudri added, 'we haven't any crowns.'

'We ought to crown them with serpents,' Mrs Bradley suggested. 'Would they belong to Hecate if they were crowned with serpents?'

'None of that nonsense about the hanging woman! I don't want her brought into it,' said Sir Rudri peevishly.

'The hanging woman?' said Ivor. His voice held a note of fear. Now that the night had returned and brought back its terrors, he was nervous again, and afraid of the dark. Mrs Bradley looked on him compassionately. She was greatly in sympathy with children who feared the dark, knowing the years of torment through which such children go.

'A rather interesting story. Don't you know it?' she said. 'The woman hanged herself, and then was dressed by the goddess in her own clothes and called Hecate. Since then Artemis has often been identified with Hecate, and the one was worshipped as the other.'

This straightforward version of the story comforted Ivor. Soon after they had returned to the shelter of the passage of the theatre, he was asleep. It was Stewart who lay and fidgeted. Suddenly he whispered.

'I've been thinking. I know where it is.'

'Where, child?'

'On the hillside above the theatre. We've only looked among the ruins so far.'

'It couldn't be taken up high. It must be on level ground somewhere.'

'It isn't very heavy, you know.'

'We'll explore in the morning, dear child.'

In the morning the boys led the way. They climbed to the top of the theatre so that from where they stood the excavated city and the marshes by the old harbour formed a clear picture almost like the view from an aeroplane.

'Now, then,' said Stewart, shading his eyes as he looked about him, 'let's use our brains.' His face lighted suddenly. 'And the dogs!'

'One point,' said Mrs Bradley. 'The box would be so heavy that it couldn't be carried far away. Let us go back to where all the baggage was first set down. I don't think we had better untie the dogs. I fear they might eat us, dear child.'

They went back towards the stadium.

'There ought to be clues and things,' suggested Kenneth. He looked at the area of cultivated land. 'Footprints and motor-car tyres, and all that sort of thing. But there's nothing except the places where that chap picking beans is treading.'

The Turkish husbandman, seeing them, waved a greeting.

'We ought to have the dogs – well, *one* dog, anyway,' said Stewart, looking appealingly at Mrs Bradley. She followed him back to where the dogs were tied up. The animals leapt the full length of their chains and fell back, choking.

'Poor dogs. They ought to have a run. Stand by! I'm going to unchain them,' said Ivor, anxious to prove that, although he was afraid of the dark, he was not afraid of anything else, not even of Turkish dogs. The dogs stood still to be loosed. Then they bounded away towards the harbour.

'Oh, dash!' said Ivor, gazing after them. 'They might have waited and let us go with them, I think.'

'Want any help?' inquired Gelert, suddenly coming up.

'Yes, child, please,' Mrs Bradley replied, as though she had not detected the ill-humoured irony in his tone. 'Go with the little boys after those dogs, if you will. Take a walking-stick with you. You may need it.'

Gelert lounged off along the Arcadiane, carefully picking a track. As soon as he and the boys were out of sight, Mrs Bradley made for the stadium again and persuaded the Turkish peasant to scratch over the surface of the ground. He did as she asked him, and then pointed to a group of his plants, spoke eloquently but unintelligibly, and suddenly pulled them up.

Mrs Bradley walked on to his land and, bending down, helped him to dig. She knew now what he had meant. The wilted plants proved it. They had been pulled up and then replanted on top of the box.

She rewarded the husbandman, carried away her treasure trove, and, away from all observation, opened the lid, for the lock had been broken off and the lid lifted easily. Inside the box was the putrefying head of Armstrong. She pushed the box in among some bushes, wrapped up the head in a large coloured handkerchief which she had been wearing as a turban, and walked out on to the road which led to Selçuk. She had noticed the hole of some animal – possibly a fox, she thought – as she had come along the road from the site of the temple. She unrolled the head from the handkerchief and, having examined it carefully through a powerful magnifying glass, she placed it in the mouth of the hole and pushed it in with her parasol as far as ever she could. Then she walked on to the flooded site with her handkerchief and rinsed it in the water. Whilst it was drying in the sun she took out her notebook and began to make indecipherable hieroglyphics after the name Armstrong. Her mind worked rapidly. She had come immediately to the conclusion that the death of Armstrong had better be a secret for the present. She wondered whether it could still be a secret in Athens. What had his mother done, she wondered, when he did not return to his home. She wondered whether Marie Hopkinson or Megan knew of his disappearance.

She speculated also as to the whereabouts of the rest of the body. Her first theory had been that the whole carcass would be found in the snake-box, but now she felt sure that the body must still be in Greece. It would have been safer, from the murderer's point of view, to have brought it to Selçuk and disposed of it in the neighbourhood of Ephesus, but the transport of a dead body is always a problem, she reflected. The head had been brought in the blood-stained sleeping-sack, of course, and another home had been found for it when the sacks were needed for the night.

She wondered when the vipers had been killed. To go to the trouble and possible danger of killing them when it would have been easier and simpler and far less likely to lead to his own apprehension merely to set them free in the marshy, sunny country round about the ancient harbour, argued a mental attitude in their murderer which might give a strong hint of his identity, she thought. This gave rise to a further question in her mind. She wondered whether there was any connexion between the slaughter of Io, the cow, and the beheading of the serpents. Her thoughts turned from that speculation to a consideration of Alexander Currie. Would a man who had been prepared (in the phraseology of the little boys) to stick a penknife in the bum of Iacchus, kill a cow and some snakes? She did not think so. In the case of the statue, Alexander's ill-considered action was the result of a belief that the statue was no statue but a man; he had proposed to put this belief to a simple test. The death of the cow, Io, came under a very different category of actions. To begin with, it was not a hasty action at all. It had been carefully planned and artistically executed. The killing might have been to test a belief, but, if so, the belief must have been one different in kind from the simple conclusion arrived at by Alexander Currie. It might have been a religious belief, a scientific belief, a sadistic impulse rooted in heaven-knew-what kind of belief, it might even, she thought with a shudder, have been a belief that the death and evisceration of the cow was a joke.

The death of the snakes did not seem to her to typify a mind in the least like Alexander Currie's, nor the mind which had conceived the death of the cow. Whoever had killed the snakes must have been conscious of his social obligations to the party. The snakes had been killed by someone who did not want the members of the party to be bitten by the snakes. Instead of merely freeing them, he had destroyed them. He must, she reflected, have been horribly nervous about snakes.

She nodded her head, retrieved her handkerchief from the bushes, put away her notebook, and walked slowly and very thoughtfully back to the camp. She knew who had killed the snakes.

The little boys and Gelert had rounded up the dogs, which had proved less difficult to recapture than the party had any right to expect. They had been fed again, and were now the faithful followers of the camp. In their present verminous condition, their attentions were embarrassing, however, and their friendliness not altogether an asset.

'There's no doubt,' said Sir Rudri, regarding the dogs with a certain amount of favour, 'that the people of Britain have a remarkable faculty for the handling and taming of animals.'

Mrs Bradley, observing both dogs and human beings with detached amiability, said that she did not doubt it.

'Except for snakes,' she added.

'Snakes! Ugh!' said Alexander Currie.

'Yes. Snakes,' said Sir Rudri thoughtfully. 'I'd still like to know who changed my snakes at Epidaurus.'

Except for Gelert, the party, who had made up their minds long ago that he had changed the snakes himself, gaped at this statement, and then ignored it.

'Did you find the box?' asked Stewart. 'If not I vote we look for it again this afternoon. It makes something quite decent to do. I've got another idea. I believe it must be somewhere fairly obvious.'

He proved this with striking success immediately after lunch, and the little boys brought the empty box in triumph to Mrs Bradley, who was sitting resting in the shade.

She accepted it with thanks, and complimented them upon finding it.

'It's pretty nifty,' said Kenneth, taking a resolute sniff at its interior. 'Stinks as though something pretty foul had gone pretty bad in it.'

Mrs Bradley considered this to be so exact and acute a rendering of the actual facts of the case that she gave the little boys money to go with Ian and Cathleen next morning by train to Smyrna from Selçuk, to buy figs and Turkish delight and anything else they liked.

'We have to be whipped for Artemis Orthia first,' said Kenneth cheerfully. Noticing that the prospect did not appear to daunt them, Mrs Bradley inquired as to the nature of the proceedings.

'Oh, I don't know exactly, but I believe it's only going to be a sort of token whipping,' explained Kenneth. 'Anyway, if we don't make any row, we're to have ten shillings each from Sir Rudri Hopkinson, and my father will give me five shillings more, I should think.'

'Stewart thinks we should stick out for a pound,' said Ivor. 'What do you think, Aunt Adela?'

'Who's going to do the whipping, though?' Kenneth cannily inquired. 'We don't want to jolly well annoy whoever it is.'

'But why worship Artemis Orthia in Ephesus?' Mrs Bradley pertinently inquired of Sir Rudri, a little later.

'I know, I know.' He looked worried. 'It was Armstrong's

idea. It seemed quite a good idea at the time. His theory was that we should worship the goddess in all the ways in which she had ever been accustomed to be worshipped – the Spartan, the purely Attic, the Ephesian, as such – and so on.'

'I wonder what you mean by the purely Attic, and by the Ephesian, as such,' Mrs Bradley innocently inquired.

Sir Rudri scowled at her. Alexander Currie laughed.

'At any rate,' said Mrs Bradley calmly, 'the boys will not be whipped for Artemis Orthia or anybody else.'

'But why not?'

'Because such whipping of boys was always done by a priestess of the goddess, and in Sparta. Sparta isn't Ephesus and you haven't a priestess.'

'We were depending upon you, of course.'

'Nonsense!' said Alexander Currie. Mrs Bradley beamed upon him. 'She isn't —'

'She certainly isn't,' she agreed wholeheartedly.

'Isn't what? A virgin? Oh, I see,' said Sir Rudri. He seemed staggered by the thought that his careful composition of the party had now gone completely astray.

'A pity that Megan isn't here,' he said with a sigh. 'She would have been the person, without a doubt.'

'Well, it's your own fault that she isn't,' said Mrs Bradley decidedly.

'No, no, Beatrice. It had nothing to do with me. Megan herself elected to stay with her mother.'

'I see,' said Mrs Bradley.

'We could get a Turkish girl,' suggested Sir Rudri suddenly. 'She needn't hit them too hard. And then, of course, there were the eunuch priests of Artemis here in Ephesus.'

'I thought the idea was to kill them,' argued Alexander

Currie, who had a father's rational objection to the flogging of his son by anybody – man or woman, whether eunuch or virgin.

'Nonsense!' said Sir Rudri, stealing Jove's thunder thoughtlessly. Alexander Currie glowered at him, his bald head throwing a golden gleam in the rays of the afternoon sun. Mrs Bradley put up her parasol and held it over him.

'My son is not to be beaten, anyway,' he said, concisely, savagely, and finally.

'Very well! Very well! Two will be plenty, I suppose,' Sir Rudri testily agreed.

'Nor Stewart Paterson, either. I'm responsible for him to his mother,' Alexander continued triumphantly. 'And as for your own wee laddie, I wonder you'll look him in the face to think of beating him all for nothing. If lads are bad,' Alexander continued, becoming excited, 'that is one thing. But to beat an innocent lad in the wrong portion of the empire of the Ancient Greeks, to worship a goddess, who, ten to one, is not the goddess you're thinking she is, but another, is no more than the foolishness of a silly, cracked old gomeril.'

'I'm not a silly, cracked old gomeril,' Sir Rudri shouted, the Viking moustache rising grandly to the fray. 'It's you, afraid of a few, small, harmless snakes and a statue on a rock and suchlike small, childish things, that have been the trouble all along in this party. Wouldn't I have crowned the poor dogs, isn't it, but for you and your foolish complainings? What, indeed, are we here for, if not for experiment upon the dogs and the boys, and why have I spent all my money, that is all I am asking, indeed?'

'Hold your whisht, you wee Welshman,' said Alexander Currie composedly, eyeing the Viking moustache with a militant eye.

Mrs Bradley planted herself between them.

'My dear Rudri! My dear Alexander!' she said, in shocked, amazed accents, whilst her black eyes gleamed with amusement. 'Please, please! At any rate, wait until it is cooler.'

She took Alexander's arm, and led him into the shade. Alexander wiped his brow, sighed, and began to chuckle.

'Child,' said Mrs Bradley, 'it is time that Rudri went back to Athens, and everybody with him. There is nothing to gain by staying here any longer.'

'He is wishful to conduct two or three experiments on the site of the temple,' said Alexander Currie. 'Poor Rudri! Maybe I should not have called him a Welshman.'

'Well, not a wee Welshman,' Mrs Bradley agreed. She half-wondered whether to take Alexander into her confidence, but decided to continue her investigations alone for a time, and see where they led. She was not afraid that the head would turn up to complicate matters again. There were jackals in the neighbourhood, and she thought that the head, if found, would be unrecognizable.

She spent the rest of the day in a thorough exploration of the ruins, and made a plan of them for herself, having found Sir Rudri's handy but inaccurate. It was easy enough to do this. The road from Selçuk came in by the north-east corner, and the gymnasium of Vedius lay almost due south of it. She made the gymnasium her starting-point, paced her distances southward past the stadium to the theatre, and westward up the Arcadiane to the Harbour Gateway, and then added the rest of the ruins to the plan. She was less concerned with the plotting of the ruins, however, than with the problem of Armstrong's death. Apart from the general dislike in which he had been held by the party, she could not think of anybody who ardently desired his demise. Even Sir Rudri, so far as she knew, had nothing to fear from the young man except the publication of the photographs, and even that contingency had seemed remote after Mrs Bradley's offer of a thousand pounds had not been repudiated by the photographer.

He had quarrelled with Gelert, of course. He had not been friendly with anybody in the party. Ian was resolute enough to have killed him; so, in his queer, unassertive way, was Dick. Alexander Currie was quick-tempered and bold enough. Megan was stout-hearted and callous enough, Cathleen was superstitious enough, and Dish had sufficient natural dignity. Dish, of course, had hated Armstrong. She considered Dish, screwing up her eyes in the brilliant light of the sun.

She went to the hole into which she had thrust the head, and groped for it. Flies flew off it in clouds. She unfolded the camp stool she was carrying, sat down, put the head in front of her on the dry ground, and considered it carefully from all angles. Olfactorily it was disgusting, but the most careful examination of it failed to give any clue to the way in which its owner had met his death. After a lengthy scrutiny of the decomposing, unlovely object, she concluded that her first opinion had been justified. The wound, the poison – whatever it was that had caused the death of Armstrong – was still the secret of his body. The head, once beautiful, now one of the most repulsive objects imaginable, could tell her nothing at all beyond the fact that Armstrong was dead. Whoever had hacked it off had done so, Mrs Bradley concluded, without skill, but boldly, in a couple of strokes. So much, and nothing more, was evident.

She picked up the head and poked it back into the hole,

washed her hands in the murky, stagnant water of the flooded site of the temple, dried them on a handkerchief, and walked back to the ruins to tea.

Alexander Currie and Sir Rudri had made up their quarrel, it seemed. The little boys, however, looked disconsolate, although they ate with their usual heartiness. Mrs Bradley, watching them, concluded that the prospect of a beating and ten shillings had appealed to them very greatly, and that her and Alexander's humanitarian interference on their behalf did not appeal to them at all. Even Ivor, the nervous and imaginative, muttered, as he walked away, kicking stones :

'Fat lot of use our going to Smyrna now.'

Alexander Currie overheard the remark, and, so pleased was he at having defeated Sir Rudri that he called the boys aside and gave them their money. Mrs Bradley could hear the joyous :

'Thank you very *much*, sir,' of Stewart, and the mumbling accents of Ivor. It was Kenneth, however, who came running back to her.

'I say,' he said, 'do *you* like Turkish delight?' Mrs Bradley thought this very nice of him, and said so, handsomely.

'Oh well,' said Kenneth, flushing brick-red with embarrassment, 'after all, if it weren't for you, we shouldn't jolly well be *going* to Smyrna, should we?'

2

The party went to bed early, for at half past ten they were going to the flooded site of the temple of Artemis so that Sir Rudri could conduct his last series of experiments.

Nobody went to sleep. The reeds on the edge of the sea-marshes whispered, and little winds moaned round the otherwise silent stones of the ancient, deserted city. Cathleen, who, with Ian and Ronald Dick, had been more interested in the village of Selçuk with its people, its station inn, its little café and its storks' nests on the house-tops, was restless. After lying beside Ian for half an hour, she got up, and groped her way to Mrs Bradley.

'You know what I said about somebody being killed before we finished our wanderings?' she said.

'Yes, child, I remember.'

'Well, I feel – I feel it's happened.'

Few attributes of the human mind held any astonishment for Mrs Bradley. She said :

'That's very strange, but, if I were you, I'd think no more about it. Ian, at any rate, is well, and so are your father and your little brother.'

'Yes, yes, I know. But something has happened. I feel it. Tell me what it is, and who it is! I *know* that something has happened!'

'Hush, child. You'll disturb the little boys. They ought to get some sleep. There's this silly business to-night, and tomorrow they're going out for the day, and that will be very tiring. Go back to Ian, now, and lie down, and don't fret. There's nothing to fret about. You mustn't be foolish and imagine things.'

'But I'm not! I'm not!' said Cathleen, wildly. 'And it may be Megan! I love her dearly. I can't bear to think she may be dead!'

'Why should she be dead?' asked Mrs Bradley reasonably. 'It's the hot weather here, and the unhealthy situation of the ruins that have made you nervous and tired. Be a good girl, now. Go along back to Ian.'

She went with the girl, shining her small torch on to the ground to light the way. Like corpses waiting to be interred, or shapeless bundles of merchandise awaiting shipment, the pilgrims lay huddled in their sleeping-sacks, this time outside the theatre, along the Sacred Way. The white stone glimmered in the starlight. Later the moon would rise, the new moon for which Sir Rudri had waited before carrying out his latest experiments.

Ian was sitting up, waiting for Cathleen to come back. He said, when Mrs Bradley had settled Cathleen into her sleeping-bag again :

'I am wishing to go for a walk in the city before the moon is up and we have to go to the temple.'

'Very well, child. I will get my sack and sit on it, and talk to Cathleen. We're far enough away from the others here not to disturb them,' Mrs Bradley replied. He nodded, grunted, and soon his squat, bow-legged figure was lost to sight. He had passed along towards the theatre, to take the ghost-road of the Arcadiane out towards the ancient port. He went slowly, picking his way, until he came to the Harbour Gateway. From here he crossed to his right, to the ruins of the harbour baths and the gymnasium. Ephesus, never quite silent, always exciting and lovable, was fascinating, mysterious, and full of ghosts by night. He was imaginative, and the city was one he had always longed to see. He halted, listening for the steps of the long-dead Romans, those most persistent ghosts who haunt Timgad equally with Pompeii, and march up a street where no street can be seen, and change guard on walls which are no longer there. But no ghosts seemed to haunt Ephesus; or, if they did, Ian knew nothing about them.

So absorbed, so interested was he, however, that the moon

rose and still he did not return. He went north-east to the double church of the Virgin, then slowly made his way round the fortifications and at last went back to the camp. The Sacred Way was deserted. The pilgrims had all gone on to the site of the temple of Artemis.

It occurred to Ian that he must have been a very long time gone. He began to run, but the going was treacherous, so he dropped to a walk, crossed the back of the staging of the theatre, and soon was on the rough but less treacherous little path which wound back beside the theatre gymnasium and the Roman market-place. It skirted the hills, and led on to the Selçuk road by way of the stadium and the gymnasium of Vedius.

Once on the narrow, dusty road which ran between arable fields, Ian again commenced to run. He ran well, with bounding strides which yet seemed effortless and tireless. He enjoyed himself, and the distance, rather less than a mile, was nothing to a man accustomed to cross-country running. Well inside five minutes he had slowed to a walk to be sure he did not miss the opening which led from the road to the pond.

CHAPTER SEVENTEEN

'Well, there's one which starts from rope and bench. You hang yourself.'

I

IAN had been gone about three-quarters of an hour when Sir Rudri gave the signal for the party to move on towards the flooded site of the temple. The new moon, thin, and as yellow as a golden sickle, gave little light, but filled the night, nevertheless, with the virgin beauty of her presence. Kenneth surreptitiously turned his money, after he had bowed to her three times.

'What are you doing, you silly ass?' asked Ivor. But when he was answered, he followed Kenneth's example. Stewart seemed wrapped in thought, and said nothing. He looked at the moon, and then at the dark, low-growing bushes, and then down at the stone as white as marble – marble it probably was – and at the broken columns by the wayside, all blue-white in the glimmering night as they walked. He said at last, dreamily, without a glance at the others, who were stumbling along behind Sir Rudri and Gelert in the van :

'I wish we could think of a jolly good rag, don't you?'

But none volunteered a suggestion. By the open Roman market, its ground-plan sketchily visible, the dark bushes almost encroaching even upon the excavations, past broken buildings and all the deserted glory of the vast, once-marvellous city, the little band of pilgrims, treading the way St Paul had trod, and where, before him, the Greeks had gone, and, before them, Pelasgian men of whom no record remains, went forward towards the north-west gate of the city and so out on to the road. On the road they walked briskly, guided by torches carried by Gelert and Dick. Sir Rudri carried his sacrificial knife, an implement which had been regarded dubiously by everyone when he had produced it first at Mycenae, and which now was looked upon askance by all the serious-minded members of the party and also by Mrs Bradley.

'He has to cut himself, if he thinks he's the priest,' said Ivor importantly to Kenneth.

'I'm glad my father's not cracked,' said Kenneth pointedly. Ivor giggled, unaffected by the slur thus cast upon his father. Kenneth giggled, too, and gave him a shove. The dusty little road led on towards Selçuk, that huddle of sleeping roofs and sleeping birds. The way seemed long. The little boys flagged and were silent. They had run about all day, and were tired and in need of sleep.

'I'm just as glad they're not going to have us as Artemis Orthia victims,' said Stewart precisely.

'Hear, hear!' said Kenneth, yawning.

'Oh, I don't know,' said Ivor, belatedly loyal to his father. 'After all, if it's part of it, it's part. It's rotten to want to back out.'

'Who's backing out?' said Kenneth. Again they proceeded in silence.

'Do you remember that lousy sort of loft they wanted us to sleep in at that first place? What was it called?' said Kenneth, after they had gone about two hundred yards without speaking.

'Rather! Eleusis,' responded Stewart, wishing that he did not feel so sleepy, and that his legs were not so heavy.

'That was a funny sort of night, that night those asses planted that statue on the rock in that little opening. I wonder what the idea was?' Kenneth resumed.

'Joke,' said Ivor, who wanted to change the subject. He

was all the time glancing nervously right and left at the fields on either hand which bordered the road. 'Let's catch up Aunt Adela,' he suggested. So they trotted, weary-legged, and caught up Mrs Bradley, and walked on either side of her; then Cathleen joined their party, and walked along next to Ivor.

At last they reached the turning to the flooded site of the temple – the short and narrow opening between fields. The torches blackened the bushes and flung into sudden, witch-like silhouette a tree or two. The spiny vegetation again made innumerable tiny cuts on the boys' legs and tore the women's stockings. Gelert, also in shorts and bare-legged, cursed the prickles audibly, but his father bade him to be silent, since the mysteries were about to begin.

The torches were stamped out, and the party disposed themselves in a semi-circle, facing west, for they circumnavigated the pond until they were gazing at what would have been the long side of the temple. There was profound, unearthly silence. Then Sir Rudri poured wine for an oblation, scattered corn, beans, olives, grapes, pomegranates, and flowers, and prayed aloud, with splendid effect, in Greek, addressing Artemis first as a fertility goddess, on the 'marking backwards' principle, as Alexander muttered, grinning, to Mrs Bradley.

The sickle moon rode the high sky, the stagnant water which covered and marked the foundations of the temple smelt slightly unpleasant – or perhaps that was imagined by the worshippers – a night-bird flew from a bush with a suddenness which made most of the party start and touch the next person for reassurance, and a distinct 'plop' in the water, inexplicable in the circumstances, since it was not supposed by any of the party that there were fish swimming over the ruins of the temple where Croesus once had worshipped, were the only evidences that the goddess herself was present.

After ten minutes of this, Sir Rudri gave it up.

'Not to the Greeks. Not to the Greeks,' he said gravely, causing Alexander to snort with sardonic amusement. 'Disperse a little, please. Men and boys, I want you to retire on to, or near, the road. Leave what would have been the precincts of the temple. Women, please remain. We are now going to worship the goddess as huntress and maiden.'

The male element, as Megan would have called it, shuffled away, and Sir Rudri raised his arms, and began to pray. There was silence when he had finished. Cathleen was holding Mrs Bradley's arm in a tight and terrified clutch. It hurt, but Mrs Bradley made no move to free herself from the vice-like, long, thin fingers.

Sir Rudri then tip-toed away, and left the two of them there together by the water. A breeze rustled dryly in the tangled vegetation low-growing on the fringe of the flood, and then died down, and everything was still.

'I can't bear it!' Cathleen whispered in sudden agony. But scarcely had she said the words when down the road came the sound of running feet.

'All right! All right! It's Ian,' said Mrs Bradley, gripping the girl with the arm she had managed to free. They stood still, listening, and in a moment the sound of the footsteps ceased, and they heard Sir Rudri's disappointed tones.

'Oh, it's you, Ian, is it? I'm afraid you've ruined the atmosphere, my boy.'

The men and boys, at Sir Rudri's suggestion, came back to the temple precincts, and everybody moved about a bit, and Cathleen was asked by Gelert whether she had been scared. She admitted to having been panic-stricken when she heard the footsteps on the road.

'I thought,' said Dick, speaking suddenly out of the darkness, on her right, 'that we really were going to get something. I don't think I'm psychic, either, but the atmosphere seemed to change in the most remarkable way. I feel that we almost stepped over.'

'Stepped over what?' asked Kenneth. The little boys, however, were keeping very close together, Mrs Bradley noticed.

'Fourth dimension stuff,' said Gelert, answering for Dick. 'It *was* a bit odd. I noticed something myself. Of course, I'll tell you what. This is father's *chef-d'œuvre*. He really believes in this one. He was pretty serious about Eleusis, not serious at all about Epidaurus, a bit superstitious, but nothing more about Mycenae – it broods, that place, don't you think? – but here he feels altogether different. Artemis was worshipped hereabouts, in various guises, well into Christian times. The Greeks first, then the Romans, and afterwards the early Christians worshipped her. You remember legend tells us that Ephesus was the last home of the Virgin Mary.'

These trite remarks were soon interrupted by the leader of the expedition.

'We're ready to try again now,' he said. 'Will you please go back as you were at the beginning. We shall try, this time, the worship of the Attic Artemis, goddess of the moon, of women in labour, goddess of hunting and of maidens, goddess of Corinthian, Athenian —' His voice died away. The worshippers, feeling slightly self-conscious after the anticlimax of Ian's arrival, moved unwillingly to the edge of the pond in twos and threes, and placed themselves in a semicircle again.

Sir Rudri himself did not join them for a moment or two. When he appeared, it was seen that he had lighted a great torch, of the kind they had used at Eleusis. He handed it to Dick, who seemed somewhat surprised at the gift, and went back into the darkness. He reappeared again with offerings, which he proceeded to distribute among the worshippers, retaining for himself the head of a lamb.

'Where on earth did he get that from?' Gelert inquired of Ian in a whisper which could not be heard by anyone else. Ian shrugged and noiselessly laughed. Sir Rudri moved forward to the very fringe of the pond. Then, with a gesture, he cast the head of the lamb upon the water, and said in Greek, as it splashed and immediately sank :

'Be this offering brought to the altar of Artemis, goddess of the moon and of maidens; and do thou, the true, the beautiful and the free, the protector of youth, the friend of women in labour, whose bow we see bent in heaven, accept our gifts and look upon us with favour.'

He paused, as though to draw breath; then, raising his arms, palms upwards again, he cried loudly :

'O thou who carriest the bow of the hunter, who art the grave and most fair sister of Phoebus Apollo; thou, who with divine light shinest upon us now; come, manifest thyself to these thy worshippers, that we, dedicating to thee our diverse gifts, may know that thou art favouring unto us and wilt bring us without undue hardship or the travail of dark night, to the conclusion of our journeying.'

Before its ending, Mrs Bradley had given up following the prayer, for in the distance she could hear again the sound of running footsteps. As, this time, Ian was with the party, she could not think who was coming. The prayer ended. In the silence that followed, the sound of the footsteps, which were now appreciably nearer, was audible to them all. The party closed in on one another.

'Make way!' cried Sir Rudri suddenly. He waved the torch so that the flames leaped and sparks flew up in clouds. The worshippers, with strained faces, moved out of the orbit of the flaring, smoking torch, unwillingly, and keeping close together. In a moment, into the circle of ruddy, fitful light which rudely eclipsed the gentle light of the crescent moon, there ran a girl. She was tall and fair. Her head was adorned with a Phrygian head-dress such as the Artemis in Athenian sculpture wears; she had on the big cloak, the short tunic, and the buskins of the goddess. She stepped into, and out of, the torchlight, flung up her arms, one heavenwards, the other across her eyes as though in grief. They all saw her clearly. The next instant she was gone, and Sir Rudri had flung the great torch sizzling into the water.

Cathleen, on Ian's shoulder, was sobbing with fear. The three little boys were huddled against Gelert's long legs, and he was tightly grasping, without his own knowledge, Kenneth's thick red hair. Dick, after his first gasp of horror, had held Mrs Bradley's hand and had muttered, 'Not Artemis! Iphigenia! Iphigenia! Iphigenia!' Alexander Currie was swearing softly and fearfully. Then he glanced up at the moon and, with quick and jerky movements, like those of a man who is acting under compulsion and in defiance of his sense of the ridiculous, he bowed three times and solemnly crossed his fingers.

'Reactions of an avowed agnostic,' said Mrs Bradley, with a heartening chuckle.

'Now!' said Sir Rudri in the trembling tones of great triumph following greater strain. 'Now will you all believe?' He had lighted another torch, and was holding it on high, his left arm was stretched out, palm upwards, to the heavens. Everyone stood still except Mrs Bradley. Releasing her hand from Dick's grasp, she waited a minute, and then, unobtrusive as a shadow, she began to walk back away from the light of the torch, which was smoking and flaring wildly, a brown column of reddish, rough, crude brightness, yellow flame, dense, dark, cloudy vapour, and falling and flying sparks, and edged her way on to the road. There, concluding that the party had now had all the entertainment out of the worship of Artemis which they were likely to enjoy that night, she turned and made at a brisk pace for the ruined city and her bed.

2

Whilst Sir Rudri was still standing in a rapt and prayerful attitude, nobody else liked to move, so they all stood about, recovering themselves and restoring to the place from which the vision of Artemis, capped and buskined, had caused them to fall for the moment, their critical and sceptical gifts.

'Hefty wench,' said Gelert, aside, to Ian. Ian, who had managed to reassure Cathleen and now had his arm about her – a gesture more possessive than protective – grinned and replied:

'Strange things are seen on this tour. A god in Eleusis, a goddess in Ephesus – it is too much to swallow. The dose should be smaller, I am thinking.'

'But how did he work it?' asked Gelert. 'No Turkish girl, surely, would do a job like that and pull it off. The hussy was most convincing. Except that she was a trifle buxom, she was the spit and image of a bit of sculpture – know it? – in the British Museum.'

'I'll not have seen it, but, man, if Artemis came, she wouldn't look like Artemis! Isn't that what you're saying the now?'

'Yes, I am. What's the game, I wonder?' He crossed over to where Dick, small, and pathetically lost, was standing alone. 'What do you make of it?' he asked. Dick shook his head.

'You don't think it could have been a genuine manifestation then?' he said.

'Genuine jiggery-pokery, very likely. Too strapping a wench for a ghost. To tell you the truth, if I didn't know she was stuck in Athens with my mother, I'd have said it was my sister Megan. It was just her height and build.'

'Cathleen was saying it was Megan, but she thought maybe it was Megan's spirit she was seeing. Cathleen has said all along that someone would die on the tour. She thought it was a sign of Megan's death.'

'Nasty thought!' said Gelert, with a smile which went slightly awry. 'Oh, I think we shall find her all right when we get back to Athens, you know.'

The conversation was interrupted by Sir Rudri.

'We ought to sit down and wait for the moon to set,' he observed belligerently, for the tone of the comments had reached him although he had not caught the words in which the comments were expressed. 'However, the ground is quite unsuitable for sitting, therefore I propose that we all walk quietly back to the great theatre, employing ourselves with our thoughts about the goddess and the wonderful manifestation we have all seen.'

At this, convinced that what they had seen was Megan Hopkinson, the devil entered into Kenneth.

'What have we all seen?' he whispered loudly to Stewart.

'*I* don't know,' replied Stewart, who knew this game. 'Ivor, what have we seen?' All the little boys, frightened by the sudden arrival of the buskined goddess upon first seeing it, had made up their minds by this time that all they had seen was Ivor's sister Megan.

'Oh, the old moon and things,' said Ivor, playing up. All the same, he glanced fearfully over his shoulder, superstitious to the last.

'What's that? What's that?' said Sir Rudri.

'Kenneth was asking what we're supposed to have seen, sir, and I said I was afraid I couldn't tell him,' Stewart replied.

'You don't mean to say —' Sir Rudri sounded quite staggered. 'Alexander! Alexander! What do you make of this?'

'Make of what?' asked Alexander Currie, whose awe had now changed to a great determination to minimize the effect on the party of the sudden vision of the goddess. 'What was there to make of anything? Mass hallucination, that's all.'

Neither he nor Sir Rudri could see the other in the darkness.

'But these boys, these children say that they did not see the projection of the goddess!'

'Well, a good thing, too.'

'What goddess?' asked Kenneth, whose plastic mind, having recovered from the advent of the goddess, was now ready to receive the amusement due to it. He drew confidingly near and switched on a little electric torch the better to contemplate Sir Rudri's surprise and interest.

'Surely,' said Sir Rudri, leading the way back to the road, 'you saw what came running into the torchlight?'

'Oh, the *deer*!' said Kenneth.

'I *think* I caught sight of its antlers, now I come to remember,' said Stewart slowly. 'I thought at the time it was one of the wild pigs they hunt round here.'

'Do you know,' said Sir Rudri, taken somewhat out of his depth, 'this, to me, is one of the most extraordinarily interesting things that has happened yet.'

He sounded, not interested, but puzzled.

'I suppose they were paying no attention,' said Alexander Currie.

'Not paying any attention!' said Stewart, as one calling heaven to witness that he was being wronged. Sir Rudri put his hand on the thin shoulder of his younger son who was walking silently beside him.

'What did *you* see, Ivor?' he inquired. Ivor answered slowly and unwillingly.

'Someone exactly like Megan. I thought it *was* Megan dressed up.'

'Now that's what *I* call interesting,' said Alexander Currie in tones of peculiar malice. Sir Rudri refused to pursue the subject, however.

'She certainly was rather heavily built for a goddess,' said Kenneth sweetly. 'I didn't know you meant Megan when you asked us.'

'And she smelt a bit sweaty,' said Stewart. Sir Rudri suddenly turned on them in a fury.

'Get on back to the camp,' he said, 'as quickly as ever you can go! Go on! Get along with you! Get along! You're missing your sleep! Ought to have been asleep some hours ago, some hours!'

'Nonsense,' said Alexander Currie. Gelert, Cathleen, and Ian were ahead of the larger party, but their voices could be heard down the road. The litle boys hastened forward, deeming it the best policy, now that they had recovered their spirits and had their fun, to get out of Sir Rudri's way, lest in his mind was still the idea of worshipping Artemis Orthia. 'And we don't want a *real* tanning,' Kenneth said softly to Stewart. Ivor said nothing. He was wondering what his sister was doing, and whether she had run all the way to the station, and whether, before she left Selçuk, she had noticed the storks' nests on the tops of the little houses. He had been horribly frightened when the goddess first ran into the glare of his father's torch, but that feeling had almost gone. The theatrical nature of his sister's appearance appealed to him. He visualized it again as he walked along.

At the turning off the road which led to the ruined city, the rest of the party had halted. It was the first time that any of them had approached the ancient city by night from the dusty little road, and the thought of re-entering the dark passages of the theatre at that hour of the night filled even Gelert and Ian with superstitious discomfort. Very slowly, and keeping close up together, the group stumbled and lost their way, found the rough, winding path again, tripped, started back at the sight of the looming bushes, and drew sharp and nervous breath at the sound of the wind in the reeds of the silted, marshy harbour. At last they gained the theatre and negotiated the steep, very narrow little path which led up to it.

'Which reminds me,' said Alexander Currie, groping his way with the aid of the spotlight from the boys' electric torch, 'where's Mrs Bradley?'

'Here, child, nearly asleep. What a time you've taken to get back,' said a beautiful, deep, soft voice from the depths of the back of the staging.

'Golly!' said Kenneth. 'She came back here alone!' It

was, at any rate, as sincere a compliment as had ever been paid to Mrs Bradley's courage. She cackled in acknowledgement of the tribute.

'And where's Dick?' asked Ian suddenly.

'He was with us as we came along the road. He must have lost the path when we went in single file, and we didn't notice,' said Gelert, hoping that no one would think it his duty to go and rescue the missing wanderer.

'I'm not sleepy. I shall be glad, in fact, of a chance to think things over,' Sir Rudri observed very readily. 'I'll go and see whether I can find him.'

They heard him leave the theatre. He did not return, and, one by one, Cathleen last because she still felt uneasy, the party dropped off to sleep. At dawn he had not returned, and neither had Dick, and Gelert, who woke very early, not knowing that his father and Dick were not there, disengaged himself from his sleeping-sack, and stole out alone to walk in the early morning coolness.

The ruins, eerie by night and informed with the strange power which seeps into such places in the darkness, were colder and more desolate in the dawn. The broken columns along the Sacred Way, its paving stones with the vegetation pushing up like rough hair between them, the banks, earth-covered, rising on either side and overgrown with bushes among which the loose stone even now asserted its greyish presence, the deserted nature of the place which man had abandoned, combined to make the picture of a city conquered by time and not by force of arms. Gelert wandered along the road which led to the harbour gateway, turned off it, climbed a bank, looked back towards the theatre, wandered back again, away from the sea marshes, and went to the library of Celsus, where he climbed the steps, and put his hand in the niche which once held a statue of Minerva. Then he went round, idly, touching the recesses in the walls where the book rolls of the consul Aquila once had had a home. The place was double-walled against damp. Between the walls was a passage leading to the sarcophagus of Celsus, the father of Aquila. Gelert stopped at the mouth of the passage. There were spots of fresh blood on the ground. Supposing that a jackal or a fox must have hunted in the ruins and found prey, he passed on down the narrow passage towards the sarcophagus. The passage made a turn at the end, and there was the solid imposing tomb, looking as though it had recently been placed in position. Face downwards at the end of the passage was the body of a man. It was naked to the waist, and was otherwise clad in the respectable twentieth-century trousers of Sir Rudri Hopkinson.

Gelert knelt beside his father and tried to turn him over. The passage was not wide enough for this, but he was able to feel that the body was still warm. He thought it better not to attempt to drag him out of the passage, so he raced back to the theatre at risk of tripping and breaking his neck on uneven stones and half-hidden, broken columns and holes in the ground, and encountered Mrs Bradley coming away from the Hellenistic Agora.

'Well met, child,' she said.

'Well met, indeed!' said Gelert. 'Have you a flask? Something's happened to my father.'

'Mr Currie has a flask.'

'I'll get him. Do go along and see what you can do. Library of Celsus. Over there.'

'I know.' She hastened off. She saw the bloodspots sooner than Gelert had done. They came from the Sacred Way, and led her into the passage to the sarcophagus.

The passage was so narrow that it was impossible to do very much. Soon Gelert, Ian, and Alexander Currie came along, and with much difficulty and with great care Sir Rudri was carried back to the library steps, and laid in what might have been the main hall of the building, where Mrs Bradley examined him.

His breast was covered with deep, wet, blackish gashes, some of them still oozing blood. Some of the blood had matted with the hairs on his breast. The highest wound was on the left shoulder, the lowest on the left side of the ribs a little higher than the level of the navel.

'This is a mess,' said Gelert, who was trembling. Mrs Bradley, kneeling beside the unconscious man, worked busily.

'Bandages, Ian,' she said, without looking up. 'You know where I keep them. And tell Cathleen to keep the children away for a bit.'

'Is he going to – will he live?' asked Gelert.

'Good gracious, yes, child. These are only cuts. I should think he became a little too enthusiastic over last night's experiments, and has gashed himself, as the priests of Diana sometimes did. Wounds of this kind are often inflicted by the subject upon himself in moods of religious ecstasy.'

She saw Sir Rudri carried back to the theatre and laid on his sack. When he was conscious again, in spite of the anxiety of the others, she left him, and walked back quickly to the Sacred Way. At the fountain the blood was splashed heavily on the stones. She followed the trail of it, lost it on the plants, found it again – she scarcely needed its guidance, for the track of it followed the Sacred Way back towards the site of the temple.

She emerged on to the road. Dark and sinister, clotting

the thick dust, the bloodstains, larger and more numerous, led her by the way she had come on the previous night. On the ground by the pond there was more blood. There seemed no doubt of what had happened. Suddenly her eye was caught by another object. Behind some bushes there grew a thin-trunked tree. Almost bending it double, something was hanging on this tree.

Mrs Bradley, moving with great celerity, shot round the bushes, regardless of wild pig or anything else which might be lurking in them, and took a knife from her pocket.

Hanging by the neck from the treetop, its heels just reaching the ground and the tree bent over in an arch, was a figure dressed as they had seen the Artemis dressed the night before. Phrygian cap, great cloak, short tunic, buskins and all, the costume hung all of a heap on the hanging figure, which appeared to have shrunk to almost half its previous size.

Disregarding everything else, however, Mrs Bradley cut the goddess down. The tree flew up with a force which, had she not cut, with a single slash, every strand of the cords, would have jerked the hanging figure into the pond. Birds flew screaming from every part of the landscape. There was a heavy crashing of a startled animal in the thickets. A black goat, strayed from its owner, gave a long cry of terror before it fled for safety.

Mrs Bradley knelt by the figure she had cut down. The Phrygian cap had come off. The cloak gaped open. The short tunic displayed a thin, hard, hairy leg instead of the girlish thigh of the virgin Artemis. Pitiably grotesque in the panoply of the goddess of hunting and of maidens, Ronald Dick lay on the ground before her.

'Dear me!' said Mrs Bradley, setting to work on him. 'Hecate in person!'

'The hanging woman!' said Sir Rudri feebly, when he heard the dramatic news. He and Dick, both laid out in the shade by zealous nurses and attended with every care by the little boys, had become the heroes of the expedition. Kenneth, particularly, entranced by the thought that both of them had been set upon by members of a secret society for the preservation of Asia Minor from archaeologists, could not sufficiently volunteer his services on their behalf, and the other little boys were scarcely less pestilentially helpful and concerned.

'For God's sake go away and play at something, or eat something, or something,' said Gelert at last, entirely exasperated by their solicitous anxiety over the patients' condition. 'Anybody would think you were a lot of young vultures waiting for both of them to peg out.'

As the little boys did devoutly hope that Dick at least would expire of the effects of partial strangulation, this shot of Gelert's was so near the mark that they complied with his request to remove themselves from the vicinity of the theatre.

'I suppose we shall go home now,' Stewart remarked dejectedly to Mrs Bradley when she met him practising shooting in the Arcadiane.

'Where did you get the bow and arrows from, child?' she inquired, not immediately answering the question.

'Me?' said Stewart. He looked at the little light bow and the feathered arrows guiltily. 'I – I sort of found them, you know.'

Mrs Bradley took the bow and one of the arrows from him. She tested the string, glanced keenly over the arrow with her bright, black eyes, and then, fitting the arrow to the string, she shot at a little fig-tree. The arrow struck the tree, but fell away. She went over and picked it up. She examined its tip and then inspected the tree-trunk.

'Hardly a lethal weapon,' she observed. 'Where are the others, Stewart?'

'Looking to see what else the goddess dropped when she hopped it away from the temple last night in the dark.'

'Ah, yes, of course. And did she drop anything else?'

'I shouldn't think she had anything else to drop. But where do you think Dick got her clothes?'

'I imagine she gave them to him, but he may have stolen them from her.'

'Where?'

'At Selçuk, child, before the train went back to Izmir this morning, I imagine.'

'Lumme, then it *was* Megan!'

'Well, I expect it was.'

'Who put her up to it? Sir Rudri?'

'I don't know, child. I expect so.'

'To give sucks to Mr Currie, that would be. He hates Mr Currie like poison.'

'Nonsense, child.'

'It isn't,' said Stewart sturdily. 'May I have my bow and arrow, please?'

'Certainly.' She handed them over and walked back the way she had come. Dick was so far recovered that he was sitting up on his sack playing patience with two packs of cards which nobody in the company knew he possessed. He swept the cards together when Mrs Bradley seated herself beside him.

'Well, child,' she said. 'How are you now, I wonder?'

'Oh, better, thanks,' stammered Dick. He seemed embarrassed, and took off his glasses and rubbed them on a silk handkerchief.

'Did you wound Sir Rudri last night or early this morning?'

'No – no, I didn't. I – if you really want to know —'

'You went to see Megan at Selçuk before she returned to Smyrna. Yes, I knew that.' She nodded. Dick looked surprised.

'*You* knew it was Megan?'

'Yes, child. Did you know of the plot to deceive us all into thinking that we were favoured by a manifestation of the goddess?'

'I told him afterwards that I thought it extremely idiotic.'

'And he replied —?'

'He went for me, of course, and knocked me unconscious. When I came to I was tied up to that beastly tree with just my feet trailing the ground.'

'Very fortunate for you. Sir Rudri must be a strangely merciful man.'

'He's a monomaniac. That's what he is, you know.'

'A deceptive one,' said Mrs Bradley, as though she were thinking aloud, as perhaps she was. She looked at Dick. 'Did she give you the bow and arrows as well as the clothes?'

'I didn't know there *was* a bow and arrow.'

'Oh, Artemis *must* have had a bow and arrow, surely?'

'Must she? Oh, goddess of hunting. Yes, I see. What did she do with them, then?'

She dropped them, and Stewart found them. I myself found rather a curious thing here the other day, you know.'

'Did you? What was that? A skull, by any chance?'

'It was. How did you know?'

'I didn't. I thought that a skull would seem to you a strange thing to pick up among the ruins, but, really, of course, it is not, when one comes to think.'

'No. Not when one comes to think,' Mrs Bradley absently agreed. 'Tell me, child, does your head ache?'

'No, not now. I feel wonderfully better.'

'Do you think Sir Rudri remembers what he did?'

'Most unlikely, I should say. I've worked with him now for a long time in Athens, you know, and he really is the most unaccountable man.'

'The whole expedition has been a little odd, don't you think, child?'

'Knowing Sir Rudri, no, I don't think it has. Of course, it was odd of Cathleen and Ian to marry, but that was not the fault of the expedition, since it appears that they were married before it commenced.'

'Yes. What did you think of the happenings at Eleusis, child?'

'That they were not more strange than the happenings at Epidaurus and Mycenae. Sir Rudri is a very unaccountable man.'

'Yes, you said so before, and I am sure you must be right. Do you really think Sir Rudri intended to kill you?'

'I don't think he thought about that. He wanted to finish the deception in style. He had produced for us Artemis in person; he then conceived the idea of presenting Hecate as well, in the guise of the hanging woman dressed in the garments of the goddess.'

'But in the legend, surely, the woman hanged herself first, and was *then* clothed by Artemis.'

'I believe that is so. Possibly he would get muddled.'

'Unlikely, child, believe me.'

'In any case, it doesn't matter, does it? You cut me down, and for that I am very grateful.'

He looked at the scattered cards. Mrs Bradley took the hint. She rose, shook out her skirt, and went across to her other patient, who was lying full length, quite still.

'Don't brood, child,' said Mrs Bradley, squatting like a toad beside him. 'Tell me what you've been up to.'

'You said I was to keep quiet and not to exert myself, Beatrice.'

'Yes, but that was several hours ago. How do the wounds feel now?'

'A bit stiff and very sore. Two of them throb rather badly.'

'Serve you right. You shouldn't take your silly games so seriously. I wonder when Megan will get a ship back to Athens?'

'This evening. I mean, there *is* a ship that leaves Izmir this evening. What's Megan got to do with it?'

'Don't be childish, dear child. Everybody knows that Megan was the goddess Artemis, just as everybody knows that at Eleusis Armstrong was the god Iaccus, and at Epidaurus – who *was* it at Epidaurus, Rudri? The white figure in the Tholos two nights running?'

'A white figure in the Tholos?' For a minute she thought he was going to have a seizure. He struggled to a sitting position, appeared to claw at the air, grew purplish-red in the face, and puffy under the eyes, opened those eyes until they looked like those of a cod on a slab, and gave vent to several snorting sounds of mingled grief and fear.

'And I never saw him! I never saw him!' he said. Mrs Bradley reached for his pulse. She received the impression that the grief and the fear were genuine.

'Tell me about it later on,' she said, in her deep and soothing tones. 'Rudri, did you know that Armstrong was dead?'

'Armstrong dead?' The news, instead of being a further shock, appeared to afford Sir Rudri some considerable relief. 'I thought perhaps he might be about now. I've been looking forward to the news, I might tell you, Beatrice. It makes a lot of difference to me to know that the fellow is dead.'

'But, Rudri, he was murdered!'

'Murdered. That's what I mean.'

Mrs Bradley regarded him with serene interest for a minute or two. Then she gave him two little pellets to swallow, and a glass of the bottled water to drink with them.

'I think,' she said deliberately, 'that I'll leave you now, and walk into Selçuk to get some bottled beer. The walk will do me good, and the beer will be nice for lunch.'

Sir Rudri grunted in acquiescence, or what she took to be such. She got up, dusted her skirt, and went to find Ian and Cathleen.

'I want you both to go back with Megan to Athens,' she said. 'As soon as Sir Rudri and Ronald Dick feel well enough to travel we shall all come, but I want some people there to tell Marie Hopkinson that her husband will have to be kept under observation for a time.'

'I thought soon after we began the tour that he wasn't quite right in the head, maybe. We should never have come here,' said Ian. 'There's no doubt he inflicted the wounds on himself, I am thinking.'

'You are thinking correctly, child. Be off with you both. You have to get a train for Izmir to catch the boat that goes back to Athens to-night. Manage as best you can. Good-bye. Good luck.'

Ian shook his head when she had left them.

'That's a strange chiel,' he said. 'What would you suppose her to be meaning?'

'She wants us out of the way. Lady Hopkinson knows that Sir Rudri's almost crazy. She told me so, long enough ago. Ian, where is Armstrong? Why didn't he come to Ephesus with the rest? Surely he was wanted to take the photographs?'

Ian looked uncomfortable. He stared miserably away across the desolate, hilly countryside and said:

'Do you not ken that Armstrong's dead, my lass?'

CHAPTER EIGHTEEN

'Yes. And nobody in the world shall dissuade me from going an finding him.

'What? From going down to the depths of Hades?

'Good Lord, yes, and further down still if there is anything further down.'

I

ATHENS looked much as usual, Mrs Bradley decided. The invalids had so far recovered as to be able to travel by the morning of the third day, and Marie Hopkinson, forewarned by Ian and Cathleen, was ready to receive the whole party. Dick excused himself on the plea of extreme fatigue, and went to bed immediately after dinner. He and Alexander Currie, Ian and Cathleen, Stewart and Kenneth were to remain under the roof of the Hopkinsons. When Dick, still suffering from the effects of the hanging – about which he had not been questioned – had gone to his room, Sir Rudri, a trifle stiff still, but with all the gashes healing very nicely, took Alexander off to his study for the remainder of the evening, whilst Gelert, Megan, Ian, and Cathleen went to the cinema and took the three little boys.

Mrs Bradley, left alone with her hostess, sat knitting an orange jumper. Marie Hopkinson pretended to be busy with letters to catch the morning mail. Actually she sat and fidgeted, and watched her visitor. After ten minutes or so, she said:

'Beatrice, tell me what's happened. Of course I know about poor little Dick and his attempted suicide, and of course I know all about Rudri. But *why* should Dick think of suicide? He's nothing to blame himself for! And how on earth did he manage to hang himself up like that?'

'Those are the questions. How do you know he has attempted suicide, Marie?'

'You don't mean – it couldn't be an accident?'

Instead of answering the question, Mrs Bradley inquired, 'Is there any news about Armstrong? Did he say why he didn't turn up?'

'Of course, you don't know that. My dear, his poor mother came here. She seemed in the most dreadful way. She felt, she said, that something must have happened to him. She asked me whether I would advise her to go to the police. Of course the police here, Beatrice, are really very good. I think you would be surprised. *Quite* on English lines, and no lethal weapons of any kind – so unlike the decidedly over-decorated men one sees in most foreign capitals. I told her to do as she pleased. I suggested trying all his usual haunts. She told me she did not know them. He seems to have been a dreadful boy – quite dreadful. It all came out in the end. She wanted to be allowed to assume his death. He was insured. She herself had insured his life with an American company, and they are perfectly anxious to give her the money. They want to advertise their scheme, you see, and all these Greeks seem to live for ever, so there isn't much rush to take out policies, apparently, and the company thought if only they could pay up over Armstrong that this woman could be – oh, I don't know – photographed, and perhaps filmed for the local newsreels, and all that kind of thing. You know what Americans are – they're so terribly keen and unprincipled.'

'Unprincipled?'

'Well, of course, they don't want to find out that Armstrong is still alive. They want to presume him dead, the same as she does. I know it sounds quite wrong, but she wants to get away from him and go to America on the money.'

'But he *is* dead,' said Mrs Bradley calmly. 'I just wondered what you knew about it, Marie.'

'I don't know anything. Why should I? What makes you think that he's dead?'

'I've seen his head in Ephesus,' Mrs Bradley replied concisely.

'You've seen — *What* did you say?'

Mrs Bradley repeated what she had said, and Marie Hopkinson stared at her with dilated eyes, white-faced and horror-stricken.

'Beatrice, you can't mean that! My poor Rudri! We – I can't understand it. He went away feeling so much better about those awful photographs. We'd quite agreed to sell my diamonds. It would have brought in enough, yes, more than enough to buy the things from that wretched, blackmailing boy.'

'I see,' said Mrs Bradley. She meditated. 'What makes you think that Rudri committed the murder?'

'Beatrice, don't call it that.'

'Even if Rudri didn't do it?'

'But Rudri – you know, he's terribly violent when once he takes to action. He's so enthusiastic, that's the trouble.'

In spite of the serious occasion, Mrs Bradley cackled.

'Rudri isn't the person who committed this murder, Marie, my dear, so don't suggest it,' she said.

'I'm not so sure,' said Marie Hopkinson. 'I like to look facts in the face. And, after all, it isn't as though it were England.'

'How do you mean, dear child?'

'The publicity – so horrid over there. And then, over

here, they are certain not to be *too* unpleasant about it. The English School would be sorry to lose Rudri's services, in spite of his mad ideas. And the Greeks – the officials here and even the Government – he gets on very well with all of them.'

The *naïveté* of this point of view intrigued Mrs Bradley, not as much as it would have done in a stranger, for she had known Marie Hopkinson since their schooldays, but sufficiently to afford her entertainment. She replied very gravely, however:

'Now, Marie, listen to me. You must not try to make me believe that Rudri killed this young man. I don't think it likely. And don't, for goodness' sake, broadcast such an opinion, even if you hold it. I am perfectly certain that Rudri is not the guilty person. What's more, I expect I can prove it.'

'Poor Rudri!' said his wife inconsequently. 'I wish, all the same, you'd speak to him when he comes down.'

'I intend to,' said Mrs Bradley. She spoke to him at the first opportunity. Sir Rudri, as brown as an Indian and now looking extremely well, drew forward a chair and offered her a cigar. Mrs Bradley waved the cigar away, but seated herself in the chair.

'A pity we cannot get a view of the Acropolis from here,' she remarked. 'Well, child, what conclusion have you come to? Was the expedition all that you expected it to be?'

Sir Rudri picked up a pen, tried the nib on his thumbnail, put the pen down, and turned round to look at her.

'Am I really mad, Beatrice?' he asked.

'No, child. Not in the least.'

'You're going on with the treatment, though, aren't you?'

'As you like, child. Just as you like.'

'There's one thing I want to ask you. For God's sake tell me the truth. Marie's been hinting at fearful things in connexion with that young Armstrong. Is it likely, Beatrice, that I could kill a man and not remember anything about it?'

'Not only is it unlikely, it is impossible,' said Mrs Bradley firmly.

'Oh? Well, what *about* Armstrong? You remember he didn't turn up to go aboard ship?'

'What *about* Armstrong? How do you mean, child?'

'Armstrong is dead. Did I kill him?'

'Did anybody kill him?'

'Well —'

'And how do you know he is dead?'

'Well, Marie seems terribly upset – she blurted out various things – and there are rumours – an insurance company – apparently he's missing from his home. Isn't that the expression?'

'Look here, Rudri,' said Mrs Bradley, fixing her bright black eyes on his dreamy ones, 'what are you trying to tell me?'

'Nothing. I merely thought that the boy might be dead. Why should he disappear if he *weren't* dead? Tell me that. He had everything to gain by sticking closely to all that blackmail stuff. Why, woman alive, my poor Molly had arranged to sell her diamonds!'

'To buy the set of photographs?'

'To buy the set of photographs, and to make him hold his tongue about the Iacchus, you know.'

'I see,' said Mrs Bradley, lowering her eyes and looking

pensive. 'Rudri, just what was in those photographs to make them so terribly incriminating?'

'Nothing. But I couldn't look a fool.'

'No. But you didn't tell me at Ephesus that Marie was going to sell her diamonds.'

'I hadn't agreed that she should.'

'Were there any photographs that I didn't know about?'

'I – I don't know what you knew.'

'Where are the photographs now?'

'Armstrong had them at his home. I presume they're still there.'

'What?' Haven't you applied for them there? Haven't you offered his mother money for them since you've been home?'

'Well, no, of course not. Molly's diamonds we'd thought of, as I said. But that was before I realized Armstrong was dead. I haven't had another chance since. I thought I would go there to-morrow.'

'I see. Who was supposed to take the photographs at Ephesus?'

'Dick was supposed to. He didn't take any, though.'

'Why didn't he?'

'We forgot the flashlight apparatus.'

'What about daylight photographs?'

'We didn't want any. I only wanted to photograph any phenomena.'

'And there weren't any? What about Artemis?'

'There weren't any during the hours of daylight.'

'And yet you had the hall at Eleusis photographed, and the sanctuary and other parts at Epidaurus, and all kinds of photographs were taken at Mycenae. Why was not Ephesus photographed?'

'I thought we might get more than we bargained for at Ephesus.'

'Well, child, as a matter of fact, we did.'

'I don't know what you mean.'

'Armstrong's head turned up in the baggage at Ephesus. I believe it had been wrapped in one of the sleeping-bags.'

'What? Why on earth —?' Why wasn't I notified of that?' His surprise and horror were genuine, Mrs Bradley decided, and his last question certainly was characteristic.

'Because it was removed to the snake-box so that the sacks could be used. The person in charge of the head made the mistake of not keeping the blood-stained sack for himself, however. Rather careless, I thought. Obviously the error of inexperience. The head is now in a hole behind some bushes near the site of the flooded temple.'

'But, Beatrice, that's blasphemous, surely?'

'What is?' asked Mrs Bradley, watching him very keenly.

'Why – why —' He rose, and walked up and down. 'Don't you realize – that head, the head of that – no, I won't call him what I could – Beatrice, we must go back to Ephesus and take it away at once. It's horrible to think of it there, in that sacred place.'

'The jackals are certain to have removed it. Be calm, dear child. You do yourself no good by these frenzies. That's better. Sit down and rest.'

'Sit down and rest,' said Sir Rudri. Like the majority of nervous people, he found the last word hypnotic. He repeated it, slowly and sadly. Tears came into his eyes. In less than five minutes he was in a self-induced sleep. Mrs Bradley looked longingly at him. In that condition he would answer truthfully any questions she might put to him. True to her principles – since the questions she would have to put to him would have nothing whatever to do with his cure – she tip-toed out of the room, and closed the door so quietly behind her that the tranced man did not stir.

2

The first move, obviously, was to interview Armstrong's mother. The second, Mrs Bradley decided, would be to arrange another talk with Sir Rudri and one with Ronald Dick. She wanted to hear what account each could give of the injuries he had received at Ephesus. Her own theory, like that of Marie Hopkinson, was that in both cases the injuries must have been self-inflicted. She connected Dick's queer adventure with the appearance of Megan in Artemis. Sir Rudri, she thought, had been experimenting with a form of Attis-worship. The cult of Attis, in some form of its manifestations, was not unlike the orgies connected with the worship of the Asiatic Artemis, she believed.

Mrs Armstrong was at home. She was cooking. She gave Mrs Bradley some of the food. Although it consisted of lamb, vine-leaves, a clove of garlic, and had been prepared with olive-oil, Mrs Bradley enjoyed the meal. When it was over the woman said :

'You came to ask about my son?'

'Yes. Where is he?'

'I think that he is dead.'

'That is for the insurance company. I do not come from them.'

'Still I think that he is dead.'

'That is your true opinion?'

'I think – I think so.'

'Who killed him, Mrs Armstrong?'

'I cannot tell.'

'Had he enemies?'

The woman shrugged and half-smiled.

'He had plenty of enemies. He was a very bad man. Even I, his mother, was his enemy.'

'Are you his mother?'

'No. But he said I was to say so.'

'Are you his wife?'

'We were married ten years ago. I was then beautiful. Now – he has made me old.'

'I thought you were not his mother.'

'I am old enough to be so. I am fifty-two years old. He married me in payment of a debt. I mean that the debt was owed by him to my brother. I was a widow since I was twenty-nine. My brother was tired of keeping me. He gave me in marriage to Armstrong to clear the debt which Armstrong owed to him. It is I that have paid the debt.'

'And now you have killed your husband. Is that what you mean?'

'No, no,' said the woman with another pitiful smile. 'It would be against my religion, and my religion is all the comfort I have had since I have been a wife for the second time. They that killed Armstrong had good reasons; many reasons.'

'They?'

'Do not ask me. You are good, but I shall lie, for the sake of those to whom I am beholden.'

She rose and began to clear away the dishes.

'Tell me one thing. Did you see him die?'

The table was clear and the woman was going out of the room as Mrs Bradley asked the question, but, half-turning, she raised her fine brows, and hesitated, and then nodded:

'I saw him die. I am glad.'

'Which day would that have been?'

The woman looked at her, and again gave a little smile before she spread out her large-palmed hands to soften the refusal.

'I do not tell you that.'

'Why not?'

'You are clever. You would know too much if you knew that. You might find out who had killed him. I am to keep their secret. I lied just now. I did not see him die.'

'Very well. I thank you for your hospitality,' said Mrs Bradley, not attempting to argue with the woman. She went to Dick's room as soon as she got back to Marie Hopkinson's house. Dick was reclining on the bed, but he was dressed in shirt and shorts. His eyes were dark-circled, and his neck still showed signs of the rope, but he put down his book and smiled politely when, in answer to his invitation, she opened the door, and went in.

'Doctor?' he asked. She cackled.

'Mother-confessor, dear child.'

'I was so upset about Megan. That business —' he spoke jerkily – 'that Artemis get-up – it seemed a kind of sacrilege. I couldn't bear it. And then she said she wouldn't marry me after all. That was when I caught her up at Selçuk. Of course, I knew it was Megan. I never stop thinking about her, and so, of course, I recognized her at once. Her father had asked her to do it. Cranky fellow. I shan't work with him any more. Nothing but lies, deception, and play-acting all the time. Megan's known all about it from the beginning. It was she who suggested Armstrong for the Iacchus.'

'So you came back to Ephesus and hanged yourself. Was that it?'

'Yes, it was. But it didn't come off. The tree was too young. It bent, and my feet were all the time on the ground and taking my weight. I had all the discomfort without the triumph of dying. I always manage to make a fool of myself.'

He grimaced. Mrs Bradley wagged her head and cackled.

'And now Megan has changed her mind again, and will marry you after all.'

'How do you know? Did she tell you?'

'No. I went by your general demeanour. By the way, what happened to the gold you found at Mycenae?'

Dick flushed.

'Armstrong took it away from me. That's what he was after – you know – that night at Mycenae when we struggled, and he pushed me into the excavations and hurt me. He couldn't get it from me then, because I'd hidden it in the beehive tomb, you remember. He knew it was valuable stuff, and not just one of the fakes.'

'Dear me,' said Mrs Bradley. 'And the ibex horns you purchased? Were they a fake, or real?'

Dick looked startled and nonplussed. Then he said hastily:

'Oh, real enough. Why should they be a fake? They had nothing to do with Sir Rudri.'

'Nothing at all, dear child?'

'Nothing. Some time or another,' said Dick, 'I wish you'd let me talk to you about the events of the tour. There are heaps of things that want explaining, you know.'

'I know. Child, *who* was the white figure seen in the Tholos?'

'In the Tholos? At Epidaurus?'

'Where else?'

'As you say, I'm stupid. I can't tell you. *I* want to know about the snakes.'

'I want to know about Io.'

'Io?'

'The cow.'

'Oh – Armstrong, I suppose, filthy creature.'

'Armstrong?'

'Yes.'

'You know he's dead, child, don't you?'

'Armstrong dead? Good Lord! Oh, well, then, Sir Rudri gets the photographs back, I suppose?'

'Surprise not genuine, and he knows I'm not deceived,' thought Mrs Bradley. 'And neither was Marie Hopkinson surprised. Oh dear!' Aloud she said:

'He's got them back, child, yes. I got them for him this evening. He doesn't know he's got them. I haven't handed them over to him yet.'

'Where did you get them from – his home?'

'Yes. From Mrs Armstrong.'

'What – the poor old mother?'

'No. The poor old wife.'

'So *that* was it,' said Dick. 'I'm glad to know. I thought she wasn't his mother. She never seemed – the relationship wasn't like that.'

'Ronald,' said Mrs Bradley, 'what made you go on the expedition with Sir Rudri? You, an archaeologist?'

Dick blushed.

'I know,' he said. 'But, really, the temptation was too great. I've – of course, it was Megan. As soon as I knew there was the slightest chance that she might go, I told Sir Rudri I'd go with him. He wanted me: You see, I suppose I lent colour to the proceedings.'

'And suppose that Megan had not been going after all?'

'After I'd promised to go, do you mean? Oh, I expect I'd have gone. I'd said I would, and I wanted to go to Mycenae again, you know.'

'Why to Mycenae?'

'Oh – Homer. And Schliemann. I've more admiration for Schliemann than for anybody else I know.'

'The inspired Schliemann.'

'The inspired Schliemann.' He nodded, looking out between the shutters into the street below. After a pause he said, 'I say, you don't know how I could get back my piece of Mycenaean gold? I want to present it to the museum.'

'Yes, child. I know how you can get it back. You'll get it for a wedding present.' She looked at him expectantly, but Dick licked his lips and asked her:

'What else do you know, I wonder?'

'I know that Armstrong is dead.'

'That's what you said before. What killed him? How did he die? I didn't think people so objectionable died off so quickly and conveniently.' He tried to smile, but could not.

'They don't die off like that in the ordinary way,' said Mrs Bradley. 'I fancy he was murdered. We took his head to Ephesus in our luggage.'

'Really? How did you find that out? Are you pulling my leg, by any chance?' His face, by this time, was ghastly.

'No, child, you know I'm not. One of the sleeping-sacks showed bloody traces, and the head was in the snake-box. Didn't you know?'

'In the snake-box? Heavens alive! Where, then, were the snakes?'

'In the floods, child. All decapitated, just like Armstrong.'

'Just like —' He shot off the bed. 'Excuse me!' He rushed

away. Mrs Bradley sat down and looked closely at a five-inch statuette, a replica of the Winged Victory.

'Better?' she asked when, white-faced, he returned.

'Thank you.' He settled down on the bed and rested his head on the pillows. 'I'm not very fit yet, I'm afraid.'

'Horrid to be sick,' said Mrs Bradley. 'Yes,' she went on, with scarcely a pause, 'all the snakes had their heads cut off. I didn't find the heads. I didn't look for them. One arrived at their existence by a process of mingled memory and deduction.' She cackled heartlessly.

'Yes, you *are* pulling my leg,' said Dick, with the air of one who had formed an important opinion. 'Go away and pull somebody else's for a change. I'm tired. I want some sleep.'

'Very well, child.' Mrs Bradley rose. 'And you really think you're going to marry Megan?'

Dick looked at her. His face began to work. Mrs Bradley watched him, not cruelly, but with interest.

'Don't cry. I'm not going to stop you from marrying her,' she said with a curious smile.

3

'You're determined to find out about Armstrong, I suppose?' said Marie Hopkinson. She was looking at the whole collection of photographs and had been listening to Mrs Bradley's detailed descriptions of the tour.

Mrs Bradley nodded.

'That is why I've been boring you like this for the past two hours and a half. A shape is gradually emerging,' she said with a terrifying smile.

Marie Hopkinson shuddered.

'A *shape*? What on earth do you mean?'

'That I begin to see the light. Well, no, I can't say I *begin* to see the light, but more and more light floods upon me, like the rising of the sun upon a mountain. Talking of mountains, my dear Marie, it is amazing, is it not, that the scenery of Greece really is as romantic, as improbable, as convincing, as fascinating, and as familiar as people would have one believe.'

'Improbable? Convincing?' said Marie Hopkinson. 'Beatrice, are you *sure* it wasn't Rudri?'

'Quite sure, dear child. I want to see the ibex horns Dick bought.'

'But we *did* see them,' said her hostess, looking at her wild-eyed. 'He *showed* us them. We all saw them – or weren't you there?'

'Yes, I was there. I want to see them again.'

'But why? You don't mean there's *blood* on them, or something?'

Mrs Bradley cackled.

'No, I don't think there's blood on them. I'm sure there isn't, in fact. I just want to see them, that's all.'

'Well, ask him for them. He must have got them somewhere.'

'I did ask him. He doesn't seem keen to show them. I wish *you'd* ask him for them.'

'Pretending I don't know they've been refused to you?'

'Exactly, child. But the way, did you know that Dick and Megan are engaged?'

'Yes, I know. They told me. He seems delighted about it. But, Beatrice, they can't be engaged if poor Ronald murdered Armstrong.'

'I don't see any connexion,' said Mrs Bradley. 'In any

case, I thought you plumped for Rudri. But we don't know that poor Ronald did murder Armstrong, do we? Any more than we know that Rudri did.'

'That's what we've *got* to know, though. I mean, it's got to be one of them. It was you who suggested Ronald by talking about those horns. Anyway, we must *know*.'

'Yes, we had better know. Then the whole thing will be over and done with, won't it?'

'But no, of course it won't. What about justice and things? Although, mind you, Beatrice, justice is quite a different thing out here from what it is at home, and it's as well not to get yourself mixed up in it!'

Mrs Bradley cackled.

'What is justice?' she said.

'Oh, don't let's begin a *political* argument. I want my tea,' said Marie Hopkinson. Mrs Bradley now recognized this as her hostess's favourite way of changing the subject.

'And I,' said she, sticking closely to her point, 'want to see those ibex horns, and then I want to go to Eleusis.'

'Eleusis? What on earth for?'

'Knowledge. Comfort. All that the Mystae ever went there for.'

'But you can't go alone, Beatrice, can you?'

'I could, but I think I'll take Ian and little Stewart. Ian can drive the car, and Stewart can put me right in my facts and check my memory for me.'

'You're really going to – investigate, do they call it?'

'Yes, I believe they do.'

'The thing I can't understand,' said Marie Hopkinson, 'is why they haven't discovered the *body* before this! You'd think, in a place like Athens —'

'The body of Armstrong lies at Ephesus, I think. Didn't *you* think the snake-box was like a coffin, Marie?'

'But the weight?'

'The box was handled chiefly by railway porters, stevedores, and stewards – people who wouldn't know what it was supposed to weigh.'

'But I always thought – one reads these horrid stories of corpses left in luggage, and someone's suspicions always seem to be aroused.'

'Ah, that's at Charing Cross,' said Mrs Bradley. 'Ephesus isn't a bit like Charing Cross, in spite of all that poets try to tell us. I didn't find the body there, although I looked for it. I found the head, as I told you. It really was all that mattered.'

Marie Hopkinson looked at Mrs Bradley. They had known one another for more than thirty years. Her face was grave and reproachful as she said:

'And to think you used to be such a *nice* girl, Beatrice.'

Mrs Bradley screamed with delighted laughter.

'I'll go to Ronald Dick, and get those horns from him. I'll tell him it looks suspicious,' she added, 'if he keeps them to himself after I've asked to see them. Poor boy! He always listens so respectfully to everything I tell him. I suppose I have your permission, Marie, to inform him that I am investigating the death of Armstrong in case suspicion should later fall on Rudri?'

Marie Hopkinson did not make any reply. She rang the bell, unnecessarily loudly, for tea.

'In the portico, madam?' asked the maid, in her delicate, lisping English.

'Of course not! You know we don't have it in the portico at this time of year!' snapped Marie Hopkinson.

'Pardon, madam.' The black-haired girl went out. Marie, with a return of her usual manner, said despairingly:

'That was the second of Gelert's broken hearts!' Scarcely had she spoken when Gelert himself came in. Mrs Bradley took advantage of his entrance to slip quietly away to speak to Ronald Dick. Dick, who was even more haggard than she had seen him on her previous visit, looked at her guiltily when she demanded the horns, and mumbled something about his lodgings and the museum. Mrs Bradley looked at him reproachfully, and went back to Marie and Gelert.

'But what would the museum want them for?' Marie Hopkinson demanded, with what Mrs Bradley interpreted as a warning glance at Gelert. Mrs Bradley's reply took her and her son off their guard.

'Have you heard of the ibex horns that made the back-bent bow of Odysseus, children?' she said.

Marie recovered first.

'Oh, all that mythology,' she said. 'Poor Ronald. He is *so* enthusiastic.'

Next morning Mrs Bradley was driven by Ian towards the plain of Eleusis. Beside her sat Megan. The seat next to Ian was occupied by the politely smiling Dmitri. Ian drove fast. They had set out from Athens at dawn. By the time the sun had risen they were running beside the bay on a road bordered right by the mountains, left by the sparkling sea. The air was still cool. There was nobody about. Ian stopped the car at the entrance to the ruins. Dmitri remained in his seat. The others got out, and walked up to the Hall of the Mysteries.

CHAPTER NINETEEN

'Yes, and all that garlic.

I

'BUT I don't know what we've come for,' Megan said. 'Armstrong wasn't killed here. I don't see what Eleusis has to do with it.'

No secret had been made of the object of this second expedition. Even Dmitri had been told why they had come, and his collaboration had been asked for. He had volunteered two statements as they had come along the road in the car.

'This Armstrong,' he said in English, 'he is one bad man. I do not know what is the trouble he should be dead.'

Mrs Bradley explained that they did not want the wrong person blamed for the death. Dmitri had grunted and then had followed the grunt with his polite, incredulous smile.

'You are with amusement,' he said, staring straight ahead through the windscreen.

'I think we ought to begin at the beginning,' said Mrs Bradley to Megan, as they stood in the ruined Hall and looked south to the island of Salamis and its mountains and then north-west to the rest of the excavations. 'Now, child, let us go back to the night on which all the interesting events took place. First of all, the coming of Ian.'

'He was at Daphni with us.'

'So he was. We established that before. Then he came on here, and first met Cathleen – where?'

'I don't know exactly, Aunt Adela.'

'He was not on the mysterious ship, that's certain.'

'That was a plant of father's – to pretend that the second Iacchus – Armstrong really, you know – was on board the ship, when really, of course, there was no one on board except the sailors.'

'Dressed like ancient Greeks.'

'Yes. He's potty, of course. They had to wave a lantern to shine on one of them dressed like Iacchus as soon as they got father's signal.'

'You knew about this from the beginning?'

'I helped him plan it all out. I'd do anything to score off Mr Currie. He behaved disgustingly to father.'

'Yes. I see.'

'My job was to convince all the others that we really had seen something supernatural. It made me rather windy, I might tell you.'

'How was that?'

'I don't care to muck about with such things. Suppose something *really* supernatural had turned up, as it did at Epidaurus. I should have screamed myself silly.'

'Let's leave Epidaurus out of it for the present, child. You sent Stewart with me to the acropolis.' She pointed a yellow finger.

'To make certain that some unbiased person saw the second Iacchus.'

'But I wasn't unbiased, child. I was convinced that you and Sir Rudri were up to mischief.' She cackled. 'I've met fathers and daughters before.'

'Well, you'd have had to say what you saw,' said Megan stoutly.

'Yes, I see. Then, a little later, Cathleen disappeared. She went to meet Ian, I presume.'

'Well, yes, but the chump got lost. Places *do* look different in the dark. And Armstrong, the second Iacchus, grabbed hold of her, the beastly idiot, and she was scared stiff, and I hit him pretty hard, and told him to get back to his place on the acropolis, or else he'd lose his job.'

'So that's how you bruised your knuckles.'

'Yes. And that's how he bruised his shins. But that wasn't the only time that night. He must have gone off his head. Ian hooted like an owl, and Cath went off to find him and hooted back – I'm surprised she went; it was rather plucky of her, really – and young Ivor trailed her part of the way, and then the fun began.'

'All that chasing about,' said Mrs Bradley. 'First Ian and then Armstrong running like hounds before the Mystae —'

Megan giggled.

'It *was* a bit silly,' she said. 'But you and Stewart – Armstrong *must* have been mad. I'm glad young Stewart got him on the thigh with his catty. But I don't think Armstrong could help it where girls were concerned. He even tried it on me, and I'm definitely not his type. He was just made like that.'

Mrs Bradley concurred in this charitable view by solemnly wagging her head.

'And then Ian. Poor kid! She *did* have a night,' said Megan reminiscently. 'Of course, she ran into Armstrong again instead of Ian, who was waiting where they'd arranged, not far from the site of the temple of Artemis. Queer how Artemis keeps cropping up in this do! Of course, I didn't know then that Cath and Ian were married.'

'And now, what happened at Ephesus?' They seated themselves on one of the tiers of stone seats. Megan looked away across the water.

'I really did stay in Athens. I mean, I wasn't smuggled on board your ship, or anything. I simply followed up later, with the Artemis clothing, and did what we had arranged.'

'You and Sir Rudri again?'

'Yes. It went very well – or rather, it would have done if poor little Ronnie hadn't recognized me. I suppose you spotted me, too?'

'I did, child. Dick, then, followed you back to Selçuk?'

'I should think he did, the lunatic. I had an awful job. He came to the inn where I was staying – you know the one that looks like a deserted manor house, with that big, empty garden and the railings through which all the little Turkish children come and stare? – and kicked up a frightful fuss. He cried, and hung on my arms, and said he would never leave me, and a lot of rot like that – as though I should let him, anyway! And in the end I said that if he really wanted to show that he loved me a little he could take the clothes I'd been wearing back to Ephesus and throw them away on a hillside, or do anything else he liked with them, but not trouble to try and hide them because he wasn't good at hiding things. So off the poor idiot went. I nearly had a fit when I heard he'd been trying to hang himself.'

'Why do you think he did that? Did you quarrel before you parted?'

'Oh – I don't know – he's touchy. I shall have to get him out of it when we're married.'

'You do intend to marry him, then child?'

'Of course.' She looked surprised.

'I see,' said Mrs Bradley equably. 'Who changed over the snakes at Epidaurus?'

'Armstrong, the lunatic! Thought it would be a joke. I got that out of him while we were at Mycenae.'

'But how did he get possession of the adders?'

'Thereby hangs a tale. Mr Currie brought them out with him, in his luggage.'

'Six vipers?'

'Six vipers. He's frightfully childish, you know.'

'But I thought he dreaded snakes.'

'Oh yes, he does. But he seems to have thought it would be a rag. . . .'

'You're not telling me the truth,' said Mrs Bradley. 'Are you sure it wasn't Ian who brought the snakes?'

'How do you know Ian brought them?'

'I don't know it, child. I'm asking for information, so don't tell any more lies. Why should Ian bring six vipers to Greece?'

'He thought they would eat the frogs and things in his garden. You see, he isn't going back to the University. He's got a job out here.'

'Who with?'

'The company that makes the French wines.'

'I must ask him about the vipers,' said Mrs Bradley. 'Who cut their heads off at Ephesus?'

'I haven't the least idea, unless it was Dick. He always thought they were dangerous, that I *do* know.'

'Why did Gelert quarrel with Armstrong?'

'All about a girl. Gelert always says it was Armstrong's half-sister, and that caused the trouble, but I don't know whether that's true. I think it was just a case of a girl they both wanted. Or perhaps Gelert found out about Armstrong and Cathleen, and the way he behaved here that night. Gelert was rather keen on Cathleen until Ian turned up, you know.'

Mrs Bradley sighed. Without another word she got up and walked down to the car. Dmitri politely saluted her. She asked him about the vipers.

'Now that Mr Armstrong fortunately is dead, I tell what I know,' Dmitri replied obligingly. He got out of the car, came round, and stood beside her, checking off the points on his fingers.

'The snakes, they are six. Sir Rudri he has your snakes. The six, they are English, very slow and rather not pretty. The four, they are to belong to the snakeman of Morocco. I am to believe that Mr Currie has brought the six snakes. He has the mind. Exchange of snakes, he says, are as good as to cultivate.'

'But I *know* that Mr Currie couldn't have brought the vipers!' said Mrs Bradley firmly. 'Why do you tell me lies?'

'Then it is the man of this car, yes,' said Dmitri, politely changing his statement to please her. 'Which you like. The snakes come from England, yes, no?'

'Oh dear, oh dear!' said Mrs Bradley. Megan, who had followed the conversation, giggled again.

'What *is* the mystery about the vipers?' Mrs Bradley inquired. 'Why are you and Dmitri determined to invent an explanation of their presence in Sir Rudri's box at Epidaurus?'

Megan grinned.

'Better take it we really don't know, but won't confess that we don't,' she responded flippantly. 'If you *really* want to know,' she added, meeting Mrs Bradley's basilisk eye, 'Gelert and I saw them for sale in the market, and I bought them, thinking I saw my way to a rag. I pinched the key of the snake-box – it's easy to pick father's pocket – he keeps his keys in his coat, and takes his coat off and leaves it about, you know – and we put the snake-charmer's snakes in that round thing – the Tholos – and I went to feed them in the evening. Now, honestly, that is the truth. I had to tell Dmitri and swear him to secrecy, that's all.'

'So you were the white figure, were you?'

'I wore a white frock, I believe – yes, now I remember, I did, and because of the beastly midges just at sunset, I muffled my head in a shantung jacket I've got. I expect you've seen it on me.'

'Did you see the little boys peep over the top at you, Megan?'

'No, I certainly didn't. I shouldn't have minded if I had. These kids are sports. They wouldn't have let on. Later on I told father, and we put the snakes in a case in the museum. It was his idea to strew them about among the pilgrims.'

'So you didn't go there at night, but only at sunset?'

'Yes, just at sunset. Does it matter?'

'Only that you slept in the car beside me on the first night at Epidaurus. Do you remember?'

'Ah, yes, until we had to go to the sanctuary with father.'

'Yes, but, child, you could have fed the serpents then, if you'd been very quick —'

'I could have done, but the fact remains that I didn't.'

'I knew you didn't. You couldn't have been the white figure that the children said they saw.'

'Pulling our legs, or else the moonlight, or something,' said Megan, who seemed anxious to change the subject. Mrs Bradley let her have her way. They got into the car, and drove back to Athens to arrive in time for a second breakfast at nine.

2

At ten Mrs Bradley popped Stewart and Cathleen into the car, and, with Ian driving again, set out for Mycenae by way of Megara and Corinth.

Ian, knowing, this time, a little about the road, made what speed he could – good time to Corinth, where they lunched, and slower progress to Mycenae by way of the pass through the mountains.

The wild glen, grandly forlorn, impressed the travellers no less than it had done the first time they had seen it. The car drew up not far from the Lion Gate, and Mrs Bradley got out, requesting the others not to accompany her, and not to go too far away from the car.

She walked through the gate to the grave-circle, and studied again the scene of Ronald Dick's accident. She examined it closely, and then climbed up on the wall and looked out over the plain. She could see the hill of Larissa, where Argos stands to the southward, and the cup of the mountains round about lonely Mycenae. She descended from her vantage-point on the Cyclopean masonry of the wall, and went to the spot where the entrails of Io the cow had been spread out to form the letter A.

She looked round about her at the great walls. The huge blocks of stone had been laid cunningly to withstand all enemies, time among the rest. The place was so wild and desolate that it seemed to her a more fitting place than either Athens or Ephesus for the slaying of the young man Armstrong.

'Slaying.' She repeated the word once or twice. 'Slaying.' She noticed with amusement, her tongue's apparent aversion to calling the man's death murder. She seated herself in the car, but did not give Ian the signal to drive on. He was going to start up the engine, but she shook her head, still brooding. Whatever the secret of Armstrong's slaying, she felt that the key to it lay in this lonely glen.

'Justice,' she said to Ian. 'What is justice, dear child?'

'I don't know,' he said. 'I have no experience of justice. I'm thinking nobody has.'

He smiled. His dark blue eyes were merry, friendly, and sincere. He looked into her brilliant black ones as if he would read her thoughts. His smile faded. He knit his black brows.

'What is it?' he said. 'Are you not satisfied? Why are you not content to let the whole matter rest?' He stopped. Then he added gently:

'I would have killed him myself, if I'd thought he was worth it, do you see.'

'I know you would. It is just that I want to know. Psychologically I know, but I want material proof. Put it down to inordinate curiosity, child.'

'I think the thing is better left alone,' said Ian doggedly.

'Why didn't you and Cathleen stay in Athens instead of coming to Ephesus with the rest of us?' asked Mrs Bradley suddenly.

'I was wanting very badly to see Ephesus.'

'But at one point you said that you would not go to Ephesus because you wouldn't go anywhere else with Armstrong. That means you knew he was dead when you changed your mind.'

'Maybe. Maybe not.' He gazed serenely ahead of him, down the road. 'Are you wishful I should be driving you on to Nauplia?'

'No. We had better go back by the way we came. It was Armstrong, of course, who pushed Ronald Dick down that slope? Dick told me so, and I am inclined to believe him. Do you know anything about it?'

'They were fighting,' said Ian simply. 'So Dick was telling me later.'

'Was Armstrong trying to get the gold Dick found?'

'Gold is always leading to trouble,' said Ian gently.

'Mrs Bradley, please,' said Stewart, 'why have we come here to-day?'

'I don't know, child. It doesn't seem to help. And yet —' She looked back at the mighty, massive walls.

'Is Armstrong really dead?' asked Stewart presently.

'Yes, I'm afraid he is.'

'Hu – bally well – ray!' said Stewart, with considerable emphasis. Mrs Bradley gazed at him benignly before she told Ian to drive on.

3

Dish was counting the silver. He looked up, then got up, as Mrs Bradley entered. He seemed a little confused.

'Making sure that no souvenirs have been removed by the visitors, Dish?' she asked, with a cackle, glancing keenly and appreciatively at him.

'Mam,' said Dish, with dignity, 'you never know, in these days, what is what, nor even who is who, so, after a big dinner, like the one we had yesterday to all the archaeologists and such, I generally makes my tally. Not as we can ask for anything back, but just to add a few more words to a chapter.'

'Really?' said Mrs Bradley. She seated herself. 'Do you speak metaphorically, Dish?'

'Not altogether taking your meaning, mam, I couldn't say, I'm sure. But I'm writing a book, and it helps to get a few sidelights. I'm calling it *Red Light to Port*, mam, that being a title as all can understand, and yet, if you take me, it's wheels within wheels, like everything up to date, too.'

'I think it an excellent title. I hope you haven't laid yourself open to being misunderstood, Dish, in the book.'

'Mr Gelert's going to edit it when it's done, and guarantee the camouflage, mam, you see.'

'I see. Dish, did you kill Mr Armstrong?'

'Funny you should ask me that,' said Dish. 'If I'd had an Army training, instead of the Navy, mam, I dare say I should have done – often.'

'But you didn't.'

'But I didn't, except as a kind of what-do-you-call-it, mam.'

'As an accessory before the fact? You mean, you made the bow? You wouldn't know at that time, I take it, that the bow was a lethal weapon?'

Dish blushed.

'A little job after my own heart, mam. Course, I didn't know what was the little idea. But bless your heart, mam! Lethal weapon? That bow, by the time I'd done with it, would have killed an elephant, easy. It wanted a good pull, mind you! Even doing it the way Mr Dick showed me when I'd finished making it. Not as *he* could do much with it – a little whipper-snapper like him.'

'Dish,' said Mrs Bradley suddenly, 'were *you* the white figure in the Tholos at Epidaurus?'

'The how-much, mam?'

'The maze-thing. Those circular foundations.'

'Oh no, mam, that wouldn't be me. Sir Rudri's first orders, mam, it was me as had to e – merge from them ruins when he said, and be flashlight photographed by that there Armstrong, mam, but it never come off, though, because Miss Megan kept them snakes in there. It *was* me, though, as handed round them snakes. Ah well, it's no good going on against Mr Armstrong. He's dead now, come what may.'

'What about his poor old mother, Dish?'

'Collecting up the insurance money as fast as the company'll pay it out to her, mam, and off to Philadelphia in the morning.'

'Yes, I believe that's true.' She pondered awhile, and then asked:

'Dish, you didn't come to Ephesus because you didn't want to make one of a party which included Mr Armstrong. Is that so?'

'Just about, mam.'

'How did Armstrong's body get to Ephesus?'

'Not knowing, mam, I can't say.'

'Can't?'

'Can't, mam. And I don't mean won't. I didn't know it went to Ephesus. Pardon me, mam – it's only curiosity, like – but was it took, or did it, so to speak, walk, mam?'

'It was taken, Dish.'

'Then Mr Armstrong was done in here, in Athens?'

'I'm trying to establish the spot. There was very little difficulty in establishing the approximate date.'

'You being a doctor, like? Begging your pardon, mam, but why not leave well alone?'

'Because – this for your private ear, Dish – it wouldn't be well if the police here got hold of the facts. The more I know, the more I can hide. You see before you, Dish, your fellow-conspirator – the accessory after the fact.'

'Right, mam. How do we go?'

'Honest fellow!' thought Mrs Bradley. 'He has been about his unlawful occasions before now, I'll be bound.' Aloud she said:

'Dish, I want that bow.'

'My belief. he's broke it up.'

'Put it together again. I'll get you the bits. I want an exact reconstruction.'

'With guarantee it'll never be used in evidence, mam?'

'Exactly, Dish. See to it, will you?'

'Very good, mam.' He saluted as he let her out into the passage.

4

The bow was a marvel of craftsmanship. Holding it in her hands, Mrs Bradley was amazed at the cleverness shown in its making. The ibex horns were joined, Homeric fashion, with a binding of wood, horn, and sinew. The weight required to bend it was greater than she herself possessed, but Dish, who was heavy and muscular, could manage it, shown the right way to set about the business. He gave it back, shaking his head.

'Said he wanted it for the museum, I thought,' he said.

'I dare say he did, at first,' said Mrs Bradley. Taking the bow in her hand, she went to Dick again. He was up, and was working at a writing table. He turned his head over his shoulder, and then got up and came over to her.

'What's that?' he said. He took the bow in his hands.

'The back-bent bow of Odysseus,' Mrs Bradley replied. 'Why did you take it to pieces instead of presenting it to the museum, my child? It's a fine bit of work. Dish did it for you, I know, but I suppose you gave him the instructions.'

'Dish doesn't read Homer,' said Dick, blinking with great rapidity behind his thick-lensed glasses.

'How far will it carry? Do you know?'

'I haven't tried. It's beyond – I just mean, I haven't tried. Quite a good way, I should think. I wouldn't risk – well, anyhow, quite a good way. Dish made a good job, didn't he?'

'A very good job. He has managed to repeat it for me. How far away was Armstrong when you shot him?'

'How far —' He swallowed, and then squared his shoulders. 'Excuse me,' he said. He took a small comb from his pocket and solemnly combed his hair. 'About twenty yards, I should think. The arrow entered his throat. That's why I cut off his head.'

'Did you mean to kill him, or was it an accident, child?'

'It wasn't an accident, no. You see, he was annoying Sir Rudri, and that upset Gelert and Megan, and, later on, I knew it would upset Lady Hopkinson, too, and she has been very kind to me. Then there was the question of Megan's attachment to him. That I found I couldn't bear. Then there was the man himself – so vile, so vicious, so cruel – it seemed, as I *had* the bow – the suitors, you know – there was classic justification —'

'Quite, quite,' said Mrs Bradley, fascinated by this recital of the facts. 'Where was he when you killed him?'

'In the stadion.'

'In the stadion, child?'

'Yes. It is rather a good place, really, for anything of the kind. The bow made very little noise, and, unless you get tourists and people, the place is often deserted. You've only to pick your time.'

'But the custodian in costume at the gate?'

'He didn't seem to notice. I think some American girls were taking his photograph. Armstrong was showing off. He climbed into the arena and I was up on one of the marble seats – you know how hideous the whole place is, although built with the best of intentions and very patriotically and all that – and I just took a pull, and down he went, gulping a bit, and the arrow sticking out of his throat. Of course, on that dry, parched ground, the blood hardly showed at all. I went to some men outside (when I'd pulled out the arrow and put it on one of the seats), and said that my friend had had an accident. They were awfully good, and came up and lifted him up – I was wearing a dark-coloured scarf – dark-blue, I think it was – a silk thing – to keep the sun from the back of my neck – and I'd taken it off and wound it round his throat – and we got him into a taxi and down to Piraeus. After that it was easy. We rowed him out to the ship on which we were going to Ephesus, tumbled him on to my bunk – the others went back with the boat – I tipped the man on watch and told him Armstrong was drunk – these Greeks will believe anything so long as they're not asked to take any trouble, or plan ahead or do anything really constructive – and then I bundled him into one of the sleeping-sacks, and kept him in the hold.

'After that I dropped the body overboard half-way between here and Chios, having previously cut off the head. Some blood was on the sleeping-sack, and the head was beginning to – I thought I ought to bury the head when I could. Then —'

'I know all about the snake-box,' said Mrs Bradley. 'Did you also decapitate the vipers?'

Dick began to look rather sick.

'I didn't like doing that, but I wanted the box for the head, and it seemed rather mean to let loose those poisonous things where kids were going about without socks on, and so forth,' he said.

'I see,' said Mrs Bradley. 'Are you prepared to give me your statement in writing?'

'I thought you'd been taking it down.'

She showed him her note-book. Her system of shorthand was indecipherable by anybody but herself. He adjusted his glasses, took the book in his hand, and studied the tiny signs. He handed the note-book back, and shook his head.

'I should not understand that unless I worked on it for a year.'

Mrs Bradley cackled.

'If I wrote out your statement in longhand, would you sign it?' she asked.

'I thought it was only the police who had the right to require one to sign a statement of that nature.'

'Are you prepared to tell your story to the police?'

'No, I don't think I am.'

'Perhaps that is just as well,' said Mrs Bradley.

'You don't intend to use my statement, then? – Unless somebody else is involved, of course. I should quite understand about that.'

'How much do you weigh?' asked Mrs Bradley. Before he could answer, she had gone.

'I hope you haven't been worrying that poor boy,' said Marie Hopkinson, when Mrs Bradley rejoined her. 'He's feeling very lonely without Megan. She's gone to stay with Olwen and her husband for a week, to see the baby, and make herself useful and generally to oblige. Beatrice, I'm grateful about Rudri. He really seems better already. You're quite sure, aren't you – oh well, I'm sure myself now. I *know* he didn't do it.'

'In any case, Ronald Dick has confessed,' said Mrs Bradley calmly.

'Dick?'

'You may well look amazed,' said Mrs Bradley, with a brisk, incongruous cheerfulness.

CHAPTER TWENTY

'Verdict, please!'

1

'HE might be speaking the truth,' said Gelert, frowning.

'Read this,' said Mrs Bradley. 'Don't speak until you have finished, and then tell me your conclusion.'

He took the sheets of paper she laid before him. They were typewritten, he was glad to notice, for he had had experience before of trying to read her handwriting. He laid them down, put on his pince-nez, crossed his legs, and took them up again. Mrs Bradley watched him settle down. Then she took up her book and forgot all about him for a bit.

The first sheet was a list of the members of the expedition, notes on the time of starting, and the route it had been proposed to follow. The second sheet was a map, very neat and clear, with times and halts marked on it as well as the places visited. The third sheet and the remainder of the sheaf ran as follows:

1. *Alexander Currie.* Could have used the bow with which I think the murder was committed. Had no motive, so far as I can discover. The method would not suit him.
2. *Cathleen Currie.* Could not have used the bow. No motive, particularly as the murder took place after she was under the protection of Ian. The method might have suited her temperament. This applies to all the women, as it precluded any necessity for actually grappling with the victim.
3. *Dish.* Could have used the bow. Not the method I should imagine he would choose. Admits to having made the

bow. Admits to a hatred of Armstrong so strong that he preferred not to accompany the party to Ephesus when he thought that Armstrong was to be a member. I am not inclined to suspect him. He is no fool, and, if he had committed the murder, would have realized that to remain in Athens, where the murder had been committed, might lay him open to suspicion. Besides, if Dish had committed the murder, he would have had to conceal the head. The head went to Ephesus and there was concealed by somebody in Sir Rudri's snake-box. This person must have been the murderer or a confederate. It is not easy to see who, of the party, would have acted as the confederate of Dish. On the other hand, Dish was fond of having a boat out at Phaleron or Piraeus, and could perhaps have rid himself of the body. He might also have smuggled himself on board with the head, followed the party from Izmir to Selçuk, and hidden the head himself, returning to Athens later. *Memo.* I must find out what he did with his time whilst the party was at Ephesus. Marie Hopkinson ought to be able to help me.

4. *Dmitri.* This man could not have used the bow. He seemed friendly with Armstrong whilst we were on tour, more so than some of the party deemed desirable. Their view was possibly the product of insular prejudice and snobbery. He is capable, perhaps, of a cowardly attack on an unsuspecting person, but I think Armstrong would have been keenly alive to danger from a man. A woman might have been able to hoodwink him. I know of no motive for murder in Dmitri's case.
5. *Gelert Hopkinson.* Could have used the bow. Had quarrelled with the dead man, on one occasion so violently that he presumed he had killed him, and waited until

morning to have the death investigated. Made no secret of his feelings. Was doubly capable of murder. Stabbed the son-in-law of a Greek shopkeeper whose daughter he had seduced. Is highly strung and nervous, suggestible, quick-tempered, volatile, passionate, and conceited. A likely suspect.

6. *Ian MacNeill.* Could have used the bow. What is more, could have hit the mark he aimed at, if I am a judge of character and ability. I do not suspect him of the murder. His only motive would have been the attempted seduction of his wife by Armstrong at Eleusis, before the company (Armstrong included) were aware that Cathleen was married to Ian. Armstrong twice waylaid the girl at night, but she was not harmed, because Megan reached her. Ian confesses that he would have killed Armstrong had it been worth doing. I believe this statement.
7. *Ivor Hopkinson.* A boy of twelve. Could not have used the bow. Disliked Armstrong. Highly strung and nervous.
8. *Kenneth Currie.* A boy of twelve. Could not have used the bow. Bold and predatory. Not the type even to commit acts of criminal violence. An extravert. Healthily mischievous. Strong and big for his age.
9. *Megan Hopkinson.* Could have used the bow. Could and did mislead Armstrong into believing that she was fond of him. Has the character and temperament for the deed. Knew that Armstrong was a menace to her father. This motive might have been, in her, a powerful one. Some daughters are particularly strongly attached to their fathers, especially 'only' daughters. Megan would count as such, now that her sister is married, and has a child.
10. *Ronald Dick.* Could not have used the bow. This man is small and delicate. He has the character and tempera-

ment for murder. He is shy, self-conscious, conceited, and suffers from an almost unmanageable inferiority complex. His motive would be a powerful one – jealousy of one whom he believed to be a rival in love. He has confessed to the murder, but the confession is not altogether in accordance with my deductions. 'This road is wrong; it is not like my map!'

11. *Sir Rudri Hopkinson.* Could have used the bow. Is mentally unbalanced. Is capable of murder, or anything else that the spirit moved him to attempt. Amoral and imaginative. Insensitive, except to ridicule. An ideal criminal. Practises deception. Has no conscience, even in connexion with archaeology, the thing he loves best in the world, not excepting his wife, of whom he is certainly fond. Was being blackmailed by the dead man. Probably had been asked to consent to a 'marriage' – the dead man already had a wife living, but Rudri did not know that – between his daughter and Armstrong. Lovable, like many graceless people.

12. *Stewart Paterson.* A boy of eleven. Could not use the bow. Incapable of murder. Too much character. Would find another way out. Intellectually above average. Good-tempered and courageous.

Gelert laid down the last sheet, and took off his pince-nez. 'Rubbed it into me, haven't you?' he said, rather ruefully.

'A characteristic first comment,' said Mrs Bradley, putting aside her book. Gelert flushed and grinned.

'I can't quite see the arrangement —'

'Alphabetical order of Christian names, except for Dish. I don't know his.'

'Oh yes. I understand. So you suspect my father, me, Dick, and Megan, do you?'

'Before I answer that question, a big task remains to be accomplished, child, I think. I'm assuming that the death of Armstrong was caused by an arrow. If it was caused by some other means I should have to revise my conclusions a little, perhaps.'

'Not much, though, I'll bet,' said Gelert, looking at her shrewdly. 'It isn't any good, I suppose, to tell you I didn't do it?'

'Not the least good, dear child. About as much good, in fact, as Mr Dick's telling me that he did do it.'

'I observe you say he couldn't have used the bow.'

Mrs Bradley shrugged.

'I can't prove that,' she said, 'but Dish and I have carefully compared our opinions, and in every case but one they tallied.

'Whose was the one?'

Mrs Bradley smoothed the sleeve of her golden jumper.

'Dish did not think that *you* could bend the bow,' she answered smoothly.

'Good old Dish,' said Gelert, not over-enthusiastically. He took off his shantung jacket when she had gone, flexed his biceps, and regarded them critically but with favour.

2

'Marie,' said Mrs Bradley, 'what did Megan do with her time here before she came to Ephesus and acted Artemis so nicely?'

'She was here such a very short time,' said Marie Hopkinson. 'Let me see. . . .'

'The thing I want to know is how long she spent in the house – actually within the four walls.'

'All the time except for a walk we took each day.'

'She was with you all the time, then?'

'Yes, all the time. You frighten me, Beatrice. Why are you asking me all this? You don't think Megan killed Armstrong?'

'Don't I?' said Mrs Bradley.

'Oh well, if she did,' said Megan's mother with spirit, 'it was no more than the horrible boy deserved. I never liked him. I shouldn't think anyone did. He was a positive Dionysus!'

'What happened at night? Who went to bed first – you or Megan?'

'We slept in adjoining rooms. You had better come up and see them. We went up together and talked as we prepared for bed.'

'What about after you'd got into bed?'

'You know, Beatrice, these questions aren't the least use! If I thought you suspected Megan – and, of course, I can see you do – I should just lie and lie. You wouldn't be able to believe a word I said.'

'I could pick out the lies,' said Mrs Bradley urbanely. 'You see, Armstrong was killed before the expedition went to Ephesus.'

'Oh, when he disappeared. Yes, of course, we all know that. But, at any rate, I'm not going to answer your questions. This I will say, however, and it's the truth, so far as I know. Megan could not have left her room at night without waking me. I've been a light sleeper ever since Ivor was born. The slightest sound wakes me.'

'Why have you sent Megan over to her sister? Did you want to get her out of the way?'

'Beatrice, don't be horrid! I told you why she had gone. She'll be back next week, in any case.'

'Very well, child. The difficulty was to get the body on the ship, you know. I don't believe it was done.'

'Who said it was done?'

'Ronald Dick. Do you think I should go to the stadion to look for bloodstains?'

'Bloodstains?'

'That's where Dick said he shot the young man. He shot him with the back-bent bow of Odysseus.'

'Ridiculous!'

'Yes, I know. But, if not the stadion, where?'

'I expect there are heaps of places. Athens isn't like London.'

'Not in the least like London,' Mrs Bradley agreed.

'And what's more,' Marie Hopkinson continued, 'one doesn't feel the same here about these things – murder, and being suspected of it, and regarding it as something belonging to the Sunday papers, and so on. One remembers all the old stories – one sees things as Homer saw them, and as Aeschylus and Euripides and darling Aristophanes saw them – and they seem – death seems – trivial compared with – I don't know how to put it – great things looming, and slaves' lives meaning nothing, and fate hovering – great wings, great mountains, great, clean, sweeping skies.'

Mrs Bradley broke into involuntary, unseemly laughter, but, waving her hand, her hostess continued, less vaguely, 'You remember the view from the Palamidi at Nauplia, Beatrice, don't you?'

'I do. But there are things I remember more clearly,' Mrs

Bradley replied. 'Are you trying to tell me that *you* killed Armstrong, Marie?'

'No. But, if I were, I should feel quite safe. You see, Beatrice, you wouldn't go to the police or anything sordid, I know. We have known each other far too long and too intimately. I could trust you where *I* was concerned. I'm not so sure about the others. Leave the whole thing alone. No one regrets that the wretched boy was killed. He was cruel and *horribly* immoral —'

Mrs Bradley laughed again.

'Show me his body, Marie, and let's be done with it,' she said.

'But I thought it was in the sea! Didn't Dish say he threw it into the sea?'

'Dish?' said Mrs Bradley, taking her up so suddenly that Marie Hopkinson, seeing the blunder she had made, clapped her hand to her mouth, and moaned.

'I *knew* their names were too much alike! I'd made up my mind to call him Ronald,' she said. 'Dish, Dick! Dish, Dick! Oh dear! I've done it now!'

3

Dish was stolid.

'I had my orders, mam.' He led her out to the portico. Mrs Bradley looked intently at all the woodwork until she found what she wanted, a hole filled in with putty.

'What was it, Dish? A meat-skewer?'

'No, mam. It looked to me more like a good, thick piece of very hard wood as had been sharpened to a seven-inch point and put in the fire a bit to make it harder. Anyway, there he was, took a fair treat through the throat, and pinned up tight against the woodwork. Done from a distance the length of this little balcony; not a yard over fifteen, as you can measure. He's dead when I finds him, of course, but whether instantaneous I couldn't say. Anyway, I takes him by the shoulders and wrenches hard, and away he comes, the arrow still stuck through his neck, and I takes him round the back and lays him down, and puts my foot on his chest and jerks out the arrow, and then I hacks off his head, as per instructions, right through the place the arrow went in, not to leave no trace. Then I wraps the head in vine-leaves and lays it in a basket to give to Mr Dick when he leaves for Ephesus.'

'So you didn't go to Ephesus because you had to dispose of the body.'

'That's right, mam. I had my orders. It laid in the shed till you'd gone.'

'And you took the body to sea and threw it in?'

'That's right, mam.'

'I don't see how you got it down to Phaleron from here.'

'Easy as kissing your hand. You remember the bullock-wagon, mam? The one that went with us to Eleusis?'

'In that? But what about getting the corpse to the boat?'

'That was the trickiest bit. L'odass, I thinks, so I puts it on me shoulder like a butcher carrying mutton, and walks to me little boat that I has every time I has my off-day – and *this* was my usual off-day – we see to that between us – and them Greeks, didn't they sweat! And they rows the boat out towards Salamis, and when we gets far enough out, as I thinks, I upsets the whole bloomin' outfit, and in we all goes, me and the corpse and all. Them Greeks can't swim, so all they thinks about is getting drownded and that. We clings to the boat for a bit, and then some chaps comes along and picks us up.'

'But cannot you swim?' asked Mrs Bradley.

'Well, I *can*, mam, in a manner of speaking, but judged it better not. By the time we got ourself rescued them Greeks were so full of water and the fear of never seeing their homes again, that the bundle I came aboard with didn't get mentioned. And when, later on (not to seem suspicious, if anybody remembered it afterwards), I said, surprised-like, "Oh, cripes, I forgot me laundry!" there was only a bit of a laugh, as you might say, and there the matter rested, and likely to, so far as I can see. These Greeks don't trouble about nothing what don't concern 'em. Easy -natured, that's them.'

'I see,' said Mrs Bradley. 'And Mr Dick took the head with him to Ephesus. Did Mr Dick kill Mr Armstrong, Dish?'

'Not knowing, mam, can't say. My orders came, as usual, from Lady Hopkinson. "Dish," she says, in a bit of a flivver, of course, "Dish," she says, "a most awkward thing has happened. We were playing with Mr Dick's bow, and Mr Armstrong is shot. He's killed, in fact. Instantaneous killed," she says. "Do what you can," she says. "We don't want every English idiot in Athens hearing all about it."

'So I goes and has a decko, and there he is. It must have been a quick job. A lovely shot, mam, too, whoever done it. But, naturally, being a lady, the missus don't think about that.

' "It's dreadful," she says. "I don't know what to do. It looks bad, very bad," she says. "I don't want to tell the police."

' "No need, mam," I says, "so far as I see," I says. "Why

not get rid of him, mam? Nobody won't cry over him, nor wish him back. I'll go round to his home," I says, "and break the news, if you gives me instructions so to do!"

' "It's so dreadful," she says. "I don't know what to do."

'Well, we talks it over, and then I gets my orders. As described. I also advised her ladyship, mam, to confide herself in you. "She'll help us out," I says (with all respect to you, mam), but the missus she thought better not.'

'But the blood from the wound?' said Mrs Bradley, inspecting the woodwork again.

'There wasn't very much, mam. I hosed it down and holystoned it over. Good bit of wood, mam, that. It was hacking off the head, but I done that on about twenty sheets of Sir Rudri's blottin' paper, mam.'

'But all this, Dish, was horribly illegal.'

'In England, mam, I don't say. I wouldn't try it on with Scotland Yard. But things seem different out here.'

'I really don't see why.'

'No, mam. It isn't easy to explain.'

He stood respectfully at ease, gazing modestly into the distance, northwards towards Delphi, with its mountain hollows and its green and purple heights; behind it the snowy slopes of divine Parnassus, the Phaedriadae, the shining peaks that overlook Apollo's ancient sanctuary.

4

The suspects, obviously, if Dish were telling the truth, were the members of the family of Hopkinson. For nobody else, Mrs Bradley decided, would Dish have taken the risks he appeared to have taken to rid the house of the body. Possibly all of them were in it. She ought to be able to work out a little more closely, she thought, the day and hour of the killing, and find out who was in the house at the time of the death. She wondered what she herself had been doing when it happened – if it really had happened in the portico.

She turned over the leaves of her diary until she came to the days they had spent in Athens before going off to Ephesus, and doing so, came upon an entry which made her blink. She re-read it.

Thursday. Dinner at the Hotel Grande Bretagne, where we also spent the night. The drains were being attended to at the house.
Friday. Still at the hotel. No news about the drains.
Saturday. Returned to the house for lunch, the drains having been passed by the sanitary authority.

Mrs Bradley read it again very carefully. There could be no doubt about it. The drains had never been touched. It was on the Thursday, after tea, whilst she had been disporting herself with the Czecho-Slovakian professors and their wives, that Armstrong had been lured to the house and deliberately murdered. The death had been planned then; it had not been accidental. She had known that all along.

She went to Marie Hopkinson again.

'Who were in to tea on the Thursday before we went to Ephesus?' she asked.

'Tea? Why, weren't you there?' Her large, untidy hostess frowned in recollection.

'I went out to tea. Don't you remember the day the drains were done?'

'I remember, yes, of course I remember. It wasn't the drains, though, Beatrice. It was the body.'

'So I imagined. Dish has told me nearly everything.'

'I shan't add anything to what he had to tell you. I don't think it's fair to you to burden you with the knowledge. I mean that, Beatrice. I'd love to confide in you really.'

'I see. It was one of the family, of course?'

'Yes. It was one of the family. You had better take it for granted that I did it. I'm capable of it, my dear.'

'Yes, but not of premeditating it. This death was planned. It would be too much to expect of Providence that anyone as bitterly disliked as Armstrong should conveniently be killed by accident. And I do know it wasn't Rudri.'

'Yes, so you said before. But how do you know?'

'I have had him under psycho-analytic treatment. If he had committed murder, or even killed by accident, I should have had to know it. He couldn't have kept it hidden. That isn't proof positive from a legal point of view, but you can take it that it's the truth.'

'I see,' said Marie Hopkinson.

'That leaves us Gelert and Megan,' Mrs Bradley continued briskly.

'Gelert and Megan, yes. Beatrice, do give it up and try to forget all about it. Gelert will be in America this time next year. That's not a new idea, mind. He's had it planned out since the spring. As for Megan – well, she'll be going back to England if she marries Ronald Dick. He's been given an appointment in Manchester. And it's better for everyone – I'm sure of it – if we keep the whole thing inside the family. Both of the children are fond of their father – at least —'

'At least, Gelert isn't,' said Mrs Bradley calmly. 'You didn't see the entrails of poor Io, Marie, did you, spread out like the letter A?'

'I am glad to say I did not. Who was Io, anyway?'

'Io was the cow; an engaging, lovable animal.' She pondered. 'I believe, you know, Marie, that Io was the match that set light to the train of gunpowder.'

'Armstrong killed this cow, did he?'

'I think he tortured it. Then I think it was killed by someone who knew the Homeric ritual, and its entrails (always inspected, even into Roman times, by augurs anxious to know the will of the gods) were laid out in the initial letter of the name of the man to be murdered. Several of us were absent from the camp the night that the cow was killed, so all this is only surmise.'

'I don't want to hear about the cow. It's nasty,' said Marie Hopkinson.

'Well, so is murder,' said Mrs Bradley reasonably. Having made this concession to popular prejudice, she resumed briskly.

'Of course it was Megan who killed Armstrong. She invited him to tea that day, didn't she? They played with the bow after tea, and then she made her opportunity. She must be a good shot, Marie. Does Dish know that Megan did it?'

'He may have guessed. I haven't told him. What a mercy it is that I know you well enough to be sure this won't go any farther! Of course it was horribly wrong of Megan, but, really, it saves so much trouble! But what about Dish? Does it matter whether he knows?'

'I think he would like to congratulate Megan. He thought it a very fine shot. It was Ronald Dick who took the head to Ephesus. It was because *he* did so that I could deduce the weapon. Psychologically he was the only person who would have seen it his social duty to kill the adders at Ephesus before he used their box. Then Megan gave him away, without intending to do so. She told him not to try to hide the Artemis clothing *as he was not good at hiding things!* "Things" obviously meant the head. A consideration of Dick as the accessory after the fact gave me the ibex horns, which he had purchased in Athens. The horns gave me the bow. Dick as accessory, the bow as lethal weapon, the Homeric ritual connected with the death of Io, all gave me Megan as the murderer.'

'But why couldn't Dick be the murderer? He knows all about the Homeric ritual, too.'

'Dick could not bend the bow,' said Mrs Bradley.

5

Mrs Bradley wrote up her case-book. She wrote quickly and without hesitation. Motive was clear; the character of the criminal was in accordance with the deed; the evidence all hung together. 'And yet,' she said to herself, 'in the back of my mind I know there's a clue that I haven't put down. I wonder what it can be?'

But she did not stop writing. Her pen flew over the paper, making the neat, indecipherable hieroglyphics which proved the case against Megan Hopkinson.

'Passionately loyal to her father, and could not stomach the thought that he might be under Armstrong's thumb.

'Of determined and ruthless character. Her own mother called her "utterly crude and heartless".

'Had the strength to use the bow of ibex horns. Incidentally, had I not foreseen the bow as soon as I heard of the ibex horns, I wonder how long it would have taken me to solve the problem of the weapon which apparently left no traces?

'Megan was superstitious; confessed on several occasions

that she did not like "mucking about" as her father was doing, but thought something unforeseen and harmful might come of it. She sacrificed the cow, the animal sacred to Hera, and, to underline her resolve, drew Hera's peacock beside Armstrong in the dust as he slept at Mycenae.

'She was acting in self-defence as far as she knew. She had heard (probably from Armstrong himself) that a marriage was to be arranged between them as a means of getting Sir Rudri out of his difficulties. Neither she nor Sir Rudri knew that Armstrong was already married.

'Gelert, too, was involved with Armstrong to a certain extent. A girl of this age would probably visualize herself as the family saviour. A pity the men of the family hadn't more courage.

'Dick, of course, confessed to the deed because he knew Megan had done it. It was interesting to note that although he had not decapitated Armstrong, his fears for the safety of the party had caused him to decapitate the vipers. The recollection of the deed made him sick, whereas all my references to the decapitation of the corpse (which Dish, not he, had accomplished) made little or no impression upon his sensibilities.

'I wonder how she had planned to commit the murder? She wouldn't have known about the bow until after we got back to Athens, whereas she made the vow before Hera at Mycenae.'

Mycenae! The clue came suddenly, illuminating everything. That dark glen, with its dreadful tradition of bloodshed, that was the factor which, all the way through, had been eluding her. Had the party not gone to Mycenae, she wondered whether the murder would ever have been committed. She laid down her pen, closed her eyes, and moved her lips as though she prayed.

She remembered the fall of night on foothills below the mountains, and the rock-built citadel built at the apex of the plain. She saw a tall girl, heavily cloaked in the darkness, standing on top of a massive gateway wall; standing and staring over a winding road and seawards over a plain as old as history. It was Megan Hopkinson, having a last look round as the night gathered in on the Lion Gate and over the Argive Plain.

But was it not also Clytemnestra, commanding the way to Mycenae; watching to see the beacon flares that told of the fall of Troy; listening to hear the chariot wheels coming crisp on the sandy roadway; plotting the death of the king of men coming home from a ten-years' war?

Outside the window an owl flew across the moon. Impressed, again, by this sign that the goddess Athena still guided and guarded the city, Mrs Bradley recited a prayer from the Greek Anthology before getting into her bed, and, as she put out the light, she followed it up with the only requiem that Armstrong seemed likely to receive:

'Weep not for him who departs from life, for after death there is no other accident.'

Then she composed herself for sleep. But her thoughts were still upon Megan Hopkinson, and it did not surprise her in the morning to find, when she stripped her bed, the piece of Mycenean gold come flickering out from underneath her pillow.

She turned it over in her yellow hands. She supposed she held the motive for the murder. She meditated, holding it, then said:

'Megan! Where are you? Come here!'

The tall girl came in from the little balcony.

'Don't complicate the issue, child,' Mrs Bradley continued, matter-of-factly. 'Nothing would be gained by anyone if you killed yourself. When did you get home?'

'I didn't go,' said Megan. Mrs Bradley nodded. 'I wasn't running away. Nobody need think that.' She came up to Mrs Bradley and received the gold from her thin and yellow claw. 'Ronald wanted it. That beast had taken it. I got it back,' she said. Mrs Bradley nodded approval of this calm recital of the facts.

'And what now, child?' she said.

Megan did not attempt to reply. She said:

'You remember you asked me about a white figure that the boys said they saw at Epidaurus?'

'Aesculapius, god of healing, child; the one positive result of all Sir Rudri's experiments.'

'And father didn't see him! There's death in that . . . after all he tried to do.'

Mrs Bradley nodded very slowly.

'Not death, but only a summing-up of life, child.'